Copyright © 2022 by Maddison Cole

All rights reserved. No part of this publication may be reproduced, stored or transmitted in any form or by any means, electronic, mechanical, photocopying, recording, scanning, or otherwise without written permission from the publisher. It is illegal to copy this book, post it to a website, or distribute it by any other means without permission.

This novel is entirely a work of fiction. The names, characters and incidents portrayed in it are the work of the author's imagination. Any resemblance to actual persons, living or dead, events or localities is entirely coincidental.

Maddison Cole asserts the moral right to be identified as the author of this work.

Maddison Cole has no responsibility for the persistence or accuracy of URLs for external or third-party Internet Websites referred to in this publication and does not guarantee that any content on such Websites is, or will remain, accurate or appropriate.

Designations used by companies to distinguish their products are often claimed as trademarks. All brand names and product names used in this book and on its cover are trade names, service marks, trademarks and registered trademarks of their respective owners. The publishers and the book are not associated with any product or vendor mentioned in this book. None of the companies referenced within the book have endorsed the book.

First Edition.

Ebook ISBN: B0B5FYNR6V

Paperback ISBN: 9798837189630

Editing: Mom Loves Books Editing and Proofreading

Cover Design: Jessica Mohring at Raven Ink Covers

Formatting: Emma Luna at Moonlight Author Services

AUTHOR NOTE

The writing in this book is the Queen's English, but please don't hold the fact I'm a Brit against me! I can't help it, but I have worked hard to make sure you understand what I am talking about. If anything confuses you, give me a shout!

TRIGGER WARNING

The 'I Love Candy series' features a feisty female lead and her broody harem. Candy is spontaneous, impulsive and reckless, which makes this book inappropriate for under 18's. She gives as good as she gets, causing chaos and usually leaves you wondering who is bullying who! Expect excessive amounts of steam, violence and cursing throughout. This series is a RH trilogy with a HEA… eventually. Speaking of…that time has finally arrived. Hope you love Candy's ending!

DEDICATION

*For all those times you're drowning in the dark and life sends you a light.
Amy Hughes became my light during this book, and if it weren't for her,
there wouldn't be a finished product to read.
Amy, I am beyond grateful for your love and support, and so are all of the
avid Candy fans. I hope I've done you justice.
This one is for you, love.*

I LOVE CANDY BOOK THREE

Friggin' Candy

MADDISON COLE

PROLOGUE

"This is ridiculous," I grumble, tipping the handlebar of my Harley Davidson. I don't care what orders we were given, I can't sit here and wait for a second longer. "I'm just going to go in there and get her." Throwing my leg over the bike, a sudden burst of shattering glass has me ducking for cover, losing the grip on my pistol in the process. Shards scatter overhead, slicing the custom paintwork. Noting the heavy fall of metal grinding against the ground, I peer over just in time to see Candy at the wheel of a beat-up Chevrolet that's missing all of its doors. The rusted shell propels forward, leaving a trail of sparks in its wake where the chassis is grinding across the concrete.

"Move it!" Ace orders me, speeding past on his own bike to take chase. Spade is next with the blonde Brit piggybacking on his Ducati. In no time, I'm tugging back my throttle to close the distance between us. My tie whips wildly, barely clinging onto the collar of my suit's shirt. The car up ahead swerves, navigating the rounded dock not so carefully. Wooden slats cause my wheels to judder as I press on, refusing to be deterred from my prize.

The beginning drops of rain smatter over my visor, but I refuse to remove my helmet, even if I could while hitting 90mph on the uneven slats. Too many turns have already nearly proven to be my last as I battle with the others for my spot up front, my tire grip being the only reason I haven't skidded off the dock completely. There's no chance of me hanging back in this chase for gloating rights when it's my future wife sitting in the driver's seat. As the sun dips below the horizon on what should have been the happiest day of my life, the darkness of night shrouds our chase further along the curved pier without a finish line in sight.

A muffled shout draws my attention to the brightened headlights coming in from behind - a Mercedes that must have snuck out of the warehouse entrance instead of using Candy's preferred method of flying out of the window. Gunshots ring out, causing my men to slow as one sails past me. I swerve my bike sideways just in time, pushing my foot down on the ground to shove myself upright once more. The Ducati veers into view, a concerned pair of blue eyes checking me over through his own hindered visor. After another bullet rips through the space between us, I scowl and signal for Spade to throw me the crowbar he's gripping.

"Go get Candy!" I shout, pointing forward with the object and hoping to hell he can hear me. Tugging on his accelerator, Spade veers off with his rear companion giving me a solid thumbs up. Dropping back, I lay low over my Harley to draw level with the Mercedes that is taking up most of the dock. I spare no time in slamming the crowbar into the window once, then twice, to shatter the glass completely. Forcing all my weight behind the next blow, I feel the reverberation of the metal through my arm as it hits home in the driver's neck. His body slackens, losing his grip on the wheel so that I'm forced to brake hard to remain on the road.

My tires wobble violently. Just before I'm tossed off the seat completely, an arm reaches out to steady me. I pat my savior on the shoulder before Ace and I have to veer around the car in front as it diverts off the edge of the dock with a gigantic splash. As a unit, we speed forward to catch up with Spade, who is currently trying to get around the driver's side of Candy's vehicle. She isn't allowing him to, with her erratic swerving, but as she shifts aside, I take my chance on a skinny pathway between her and the edge of the dock. My men take the other side, not needing my instruction. All four of us are acting on the instinct to protect what's ours.

"Candy!" I shout, hoping she can hear me through my helmet and the hardening rain. Any other words disappear from my tongue as my pink-haired woman spins her head my way, revealing the streams of tears leaking down her cheeks.

"He's dead!" She says, my eyes doing most of the hearing. Fighting to keep my wheels straight on the slip of wooden slats ahead, I shake my head in disagreement. "I can't live without him." If only she could see the mirrored tears welling up in my eyes. I wish I could tell her she was wrong, but I already knew that fact in the pit of my stomach. Still, I'm chasing her in the hopes she'll see there's a reason to continue on. The Monarchs are more than just five men; we have a queen now, one we'll all lay down our lives for. If only she could hear me, I'd reassure Candy that I'll spend every waking moment ensuring *her* life is worth living above all others.

Skidding aside, the Chevrolet knocks my bike sideways and I'm tumbling. Falling overboard, the icy waters drag me into their depths, soaking through my suit in an instant. Fighting to shove my helmet off, I breach the water and gulp in a breath of air as the bike's overhead race past. It's no use. She's given up, and she's not going to stop. Not for me, not for them. Even before my vantage point from under the dock gives me a panoramic view of the car speeding directly off the end, I know Candy is lost to us. Not that my body will accept the fact as my heart jumps into my throat, and before I know it, my arms are already pumping through the water in a bid to get to her before it's too late.

FIVE WEEKS EARLIER…

Wind in my hair. Arms swaying back and forth. Tunes blaring from the Lamborghini's sound system. A gorgeous blond behind the wheel. It's times like these, I wonder why I trapped myself in the Monarch's clutches in the first place. But then memories come flooding back, and I have to turn up the volume louder just to drown them out. Not going there, not today.

A firm hand slides over my thigh, brushing the frayed hem of the mini denim hot pants. I smirk as Jasper's fingers shift closer to the center stitching, noting the glowing tan clinging to my skin. For the most part, it's been a blissful few weeks. Even though reality is looming on the fringes of my mind, ready to come crashing down, I'm hanging onto it for just a little bit longer.

"You're freakishly quiet, love," Jasper remarks, lowering the music. His green eyes slide my way, and I reach out to brush my thumb over his scar. From the corner of his eye to the crease line by his mouth, all that's left is a slightly raised, pink line. When his gaze lingers on me rather than watching the road, I drop my hand and sigh.

"Was there a question in there?"

"Not at all," Jasper forces a smirk. "I was enjoying the silence until I remembered you cook up your best murder plots when you're quiet." Gripping his chin, I twist his head forwards to escape his knowing stare. Today would also be an ironic day to die when I'm supposed to be on my way to 'securing my future' or whatever the dull woman on my new burner phone tried to pitch me. I tuned out in favor of watching Angus and Hamish try to land acrobatic flips off the hotel bed and splatting into heaps of jelly on the floor.

"In my defense," I respond, realizing Jasper was making a dig about my murder plots, "I've only tried to kill that one bitch at the gas station since our road trip began. Someone had to teach her a lesson in keeping backward opinions to herself." Angus grunts his agreement in my head, backing me up as usual.

"She merely stated sparking a joint so close to a gas pump wasn't the best idea," Jasper drawls, taking that slut's side once again.

"Yeah, well, I don't need that kind of negativity in my life. I'd just scored a thick bud of weed for a bargain price in the out-of-order toilets, so Debbie Downer should have kept her opinions to herself. I would have succeeded in silencing her for good if you hadn't jumped in the way." I pin Jasper with a hard stare which he accepts graciously.

"And served a nice life sentence for it too. There were cameras all over that place."

"They'd have to catch me first," I grumble, sliding down in my seat. Chuckling sounds from my left, laced with the faint hint of worry Jasper struggles to hide well enough. It's been there for a while, more so as our summer vacation stretches on. No matter what we do, from cliff jumping to getting ourselves into a car chase with whoever we can piss off enough to participate, the carefree vibe just isn't there anymore. It's not Jasper that's changed, but I feel that strange distance between us I don't understand. We're fucking regularly; that should be enough. Or at least it used to be.

Exiting the freeway, a windy road takes us back into civilization. Rustic, brick buildings converted into rows of fancy offices along a main high street. For every open glass front and tailored receptionist at the ready, a coffee shop has been squeezed into the gaps in-between buildings. Businesswomen wearing way too many clothes retreat with their paper-bag lunches, sharing fake smiles to by-passers through sheens of lip gloss. The sight of a Lamborghini rolling through town has more than a few tripping over their own heels, gawking at the hunk behind the wheel.

"Where the fuck are all the men?" I ask, craning my neck in search of a hint of testosterone. No one said anything about visiting a fucking feminist cult. "Seriously, this must be the home of the world's biggest battery landfill."

A redhead in a pantsuit meanders over a crossing up ahead, catching Jasper's eye when he slows to a stop before her. She pretends to drop the purse in her hand, making a show of folding in half with her ass in the air. I dive over to grab Jasper's knee, shoving his leg down to stamp on the accelerator before he can stop himself. The Lambo jolts forward, just inches from hitting Miss Flexible, who screams and makes a run for it. Once she's cleared the road, Jasper pulls into a communal parking lot, gliding straight into a disabled space and twisting to look at me.

"We don't have to do this today." He smooths his hand up and down my thigh, his eyes too watchful.

"You say that every day," I roll my eyes. "Let's just get it the fuck over with so I can sleep tonight." Escaping the vehicle, Jasper doesn't get the chance to comment further. I wish I was exaggerating about the figures that have haunted my nightmares. They bind me with cable ties and ignore my screams. Lock me in my room and walk the fuck away. Usually, with betrayal burning in my throat, I throw my imagined self out the window and don't look back.

When I was a kid, I would spend whole weeks in bed at a time, preferring to stay in my dreams rather than to face reality outside. Not now though. Now, as much as waking up sweating and screaming has been one hell of a bonding experience with Jasper, all I wish for is my easy life back. The life where being let down was a daily occurrence, and emotions couldn't touch me.

"One of these days, you'll wake up and be that girl again," Angus tries to perk me up from the back seat of the Lambo. He and Hamish have utterly destroyed the leather with their goo-cum to the point that I won't sit back there. I give Angus a weak smile over my shoulder as I walk away, leaving him and his oddly comforting advice behind. *I wish it were that simple.*

Striding away in diamante high-tops, a floral vest billows around my midsection until Jasper's thickly-corded arm winds around my back. I melt into his side rather than keep up the pretense I have my shit together. The weight on my shoulders is too heavy to carry alone these days, and the more Jasper offers to share the load, the easier it's becoming to let him do just that. Especially as the 'Millerson and Co' lawyer's firm sign looms overhead, all pairs of eyes beyond the glass wall duck downwards, avoiding mine as if to say, 'please don't come in here.' Well, too bad bitches because I was invited.

Slinking away from Jasper's hold, I shove the door open when the prissy receptionist doesn't do it for us. The cool wash of air conditioning kisses my skin, as does an overpowering scent of floral air freshener. Perching one ass cheek on the reception desk, I state my name loudly enough for a porky man to poke his head out of a side room. I can see the dollar signs alight in his eyes from here. Wiping a handkerchief over his brow, he stuffs it in his slack's pocket to approach. I scrunch my nose up at his clammy, outstretched hand and walk past him in the direction he came from.

"Miss. Crystal," Porky addresses me, closing the door after Jasper has entered. I drop into the leather chair behind the desk, lifting the name plague that claims him as Thomas Anderson, Trust and Estate Administration Lawyer. "It's a pleasure to finally me-"

"Are you a Norman?" I ask, flicking the name plaque down. I'm met with a blank stare, his forehead starting to sweat again. My own eyebrows hitch when he doesn't have an answer to give. "Just out of curiosity. You're the first man...ish I've seen around town. Are you one of those Normans, and all the women out in that office are your wives?"

"You mean Mormons, love," Jasper pitches in, closing the blind between us and those peering through a dividing panel. I click my tongue, popping a finger gun his way with a wink. Jasper gets me. Porky, on the other hand, does not. He licks his lips excessively, ducking his gaze in favor of straightening his once-white shirt and pulling up his crinkled slacks by the brown leather belt hanging too low on his expanded waist.

"If this isn't a *Mormon* community," I wonder out loud, "it must be some kind of incestual refuge. You know, like your mom is also your sister and cousin twice-removed. Must make buying birthday cards tricky," I nod to Angus beneath the desk. The sweaty man stutters while Jasper just chuckles, striding around the cluttered room.

For a lawyer, Porky sure has a strange obsession with owl ornaments. Hundreds of beady black eyes stare at me from various shelves and cabinets, watching my every movement. Some are pure porcelain, whereas others are either extremely well decorated or have been stuffed. Maybe I've got this all wrong; the only 'chicks' this guy is scoring are hiding their feathery butts in hollow tree trunks.

"You're beautiful when your mind drifts to that dark place no one should know about," Jasper smirks, lifting my chin to settle on his emerald green eyes. I jerk out of his grip, thinking that absolutely everyone should know about the dark thoughts that churn in my brain. In fact, I've spent most of my life making sure of it. Stroking his fingers along my arm, Jasper gently draws me to my feet and guides me to a boring seat around the other side of the desk made from felt cut-offs. Before I can moan about the itchy material, Jasper lowers into the next chair, lifting my legs onto his lap and stroking in large circles across my thighs.

"Moving on," Porky clears his throat uncomfortably and takes his place behind the desk to shuffle some papers. Wet patches are appearing under both his arms and smattering the cotton across his chest. Dude either has a serious perspiration issue or is extremely nervous. Definitely a mother-sister-second cousin fucker in my books. A dotted tie hangs over the shirt buttons, barely containing his gut and wobbles with each sharp movement. "Miss. Crystal, we called you here today to sign the official release papers to your father's inheritance."

It's my turn to withdraw my legs from Jasper's grasp and sit uncomfortably. I've seen the papers Jasper showed me. I've heard the jargon they told me on the phone, but it's still hard to think of Big Cheese as my father. The man hated me. I was a burden to him, and if it hadn't been for the bail money I owed him, he'd have tossed me aside years ago. Then there's the hit he set to have me killed. Although if I were my daughter, I'd probably have had me assassinated before I could walk. It must have been clear that early on, I would only serve as a nuisance to the entire world.

"Before we start, I would like to extend my deepest sympathies for your father's passing. He was a charming man whenever he would visit. The entire firm was shocked and saddened by the news of his passing. I hope the police are able to provide you with information on the burglary soon so you may have some closure." I keep Porky's muddy brown eyes firmly locked with mine, even when I notice Jasper's face slide my way.

It's since come to my attention that Malik took it upon himself to send a cleanup crew into Cheese's mansion after his shooting to sweep the place clean of prints before a not-so-casual passerby reported the incident. She provided a detailed description of the man she supposedly saw fleeing the scene, and it's not a coincidence his apparent appearance in no way resembled any of the Monarchs. Sliding my hand onto Jasper's thigh, I squeeze him tight as a warning to keep his cool. An action Porky mistakes for an act of comfort if his small smile is to be trusted.

"Well, down to business. We at Millerson and Co. have the

privilege of handling Mr. Leicester's estate. It is my understanding all of his assets have remained inside the mansion, being cared for by..." he fumbles through his papers, "a Ms. Tanya Nicholls. His bookkeeper," Porky nods, seeming pleased. I snort, relaxing back in my chair. A rumble leaves Jasper's chest that's both humored and protective, his fingers linking with mine. "Once you leave here today, however, the estate will be solely in your name, and Ms. Nicholls will have to leave the property with immediate effect. We can organize for an agent to see that she has vacated before you return."

"Fuck no," I laugh. "I'm dragging that bitch out by her hair and setting alight to all her shit." Angus and Hamish high-five across my diamante high-tops, muttering about all the ways we can get our payback on Tanya just for being a prissy, self-entitled bitch.

"An agent would be good," Jasper agrees with Porky out of nowhere, and I scowl at him. I thought he would have been right by my side, nailing Tanya's coffin closed while she's kicking and screaming inside. We could have tossed her off a cliff and placed bets on if she died of fright or water inhalation first. Alas, it seems that'll have to remain a pretty fantasy in my head.

"Perhaps we should get on with signing the papers?" Porky suggests, swallowing thickly thanks to the stale atmosphere Jasper has caused. The next thing I know, sheets of tiny text are being thrust forward for me to pretend to read. I withdraw my hand from Jasper's to accept Porky's pen and scribble my name awkwardly at the bottom of each page. With each one, the scrawling adapts and changes until I'm happy with the natural flourish of my hand. A signature isn't something I've particularly needed before, yet here I am with my own autograph worthy of a Disneyworld employee. In the 'C' of each Candy, a mini penis pokes his rounded head up and smiles out from the paper, much to Porky's disapproval. This only makes me draw the peen bigger with weightier balls.

"Anddddd last one," the lawyer opposite sighs in relief. Whether from the joy of closing what must have been a documented headache or just the exasperation of being in my company, I can't be sure. I'm used to the latter. Hovering over the final dotted line, I pause and tap the pen against my chin.

"Riddle me this," I state. A collective sigh rings outs, some urgency I can't understand closing in on the owl-infested room. "Why would my so-called father choose some small-time lawyer in the middle of butt-fuck nowhere to handle his assets? Surely Cheese could have used the biggest and best firms in the city if he'd wished." If even possible, Porky turns paler among the flushed tint of his cheeks and clammy forehead. Reaching out, he sharply retracts the papers and pen from my hand. Sprawling the pages across the table, he then copies my made-up signature with frightening accuracy onto the final page, giving me all the answers I need. This pig-face is just as crooked as Cheese was.

"And that's everything. Congratulations Miss. Crystal, you're now the legal owner of the entire Leicester estate and fortune. Your inheritance will be wired to the account details provided. It was a pleasure doing business with you." I cringe at the mention of the bank account Jasper forced me to open. All these digits flying through the air, only to ever appear on screens is foreign to me, but apparently, it wasn't safe carrying $25 million on my person. Fuck that. I'm the safest person I know. Porky is out the door before we can stand, leaving it wide open for us to see ourselves out. The women in the main office sink behind their computers, avoiding our gaze as we step back into the balmy afternoon. What a strange place.

"Where to now, love?" Jasper asks his hand on the small of my back once more. I spin, shoving him into the office's glass front.

"Go fuck a moldy dildo," I sneer. His chuckle follows me back in the direction of the Lambo, as does a low muttering about there never being a dull day with me. At some point, I should probably cut Jasper some slack since being in my company 24/7 is a feat in itself. But not today. Not when we're in disagreement about how to fix the infestation problem in a mansion I don't even want.

"Ya sure this has no'ting ta do with Tanya being ya laddy's ex?"

Hamish points out, and I round on him sitting on top of a public trash can.

"She's not his ex!" I shout, catching the eye of a woman leaving the back of a café with a garbage bag in hand. She quickly retreats into the store, branding the same logo as her polo top, double-locking the door once she's safely inside. Squeezing either side of my head between my palms, arms wind around my middle, and a head rests on my shoulder.

"Damn straight, she's not if I'm following correctly," Jasper says softly. "Tanya was a convenience to get what I wanted before I realized what I really wanted was you." The tension drains from me on a harsh exhale and I sag into Jasper's hard chest. This shit is too heavy for a calm afternoon. Or anytime really. "Let's get out of here. Find somewhere to stay tonight."

"Soon," I nod. "There's something I need to do first. Meet you back at the car?" Jasper kisses my cheek, and the first smile since rolling into this inbred town crosses my lips. I jerk my head to Angus and Hamish, too once they pop out from behind the trash can, wanting full privacy for once. Pulling the burner phone out of my hot pants pocket, I tap in the only number I know by heart and press the device to my ear. I either hate myself, or I'm feeling especially brave in light of today's activities. Brave enough not to hang up before a feminine voice answers.

"Okay, I'm ready," I say evenly.

"Ready for what?" My Mom's voice hesitates, cracking slightly on the other end.

"To hear about why you never told me Robert Leicester was my father." Utter silence echoes through the line. Not even the radio that was playing in the background can be heard, and for a moment, I think she's hung up on me.

"Candy, listen to me. There's so much you don't know, but I can't do this on the phone," Mom's voice whispers. I frown now, not expecting this reaction. Suddenly, I wish I hadn't sent the gummies away so someone could tell me what to say.

"Fine," I roll my eyes at the drama of it all. "I'll come to the club."

"No!" Mom shouts before she catches herself. "I mean, that's not a good idea. The club has been under tight surveillance since you disappeared." A prickle runs down the length of my spine; at the same time a black Mercedes drives by, the sharp-eyed man behind the wheel taking a leisurely look in my direction. His sharp shave and buzzcut scream military, even though he's done his best to dress down in a hoodie. He continues on, and I turn to face the closest brick wall, shuffling through my thoughts. What does Mom mean – disappeared? I never check in with her during my ventures and could easily be presumed dead at any time. Yet she's never held a note of fear in her tone like the one present right now.

"Mom, what's going on? I've just been-"

"Don't tell me where you are, just keep running and don't look back." The line goes dead for real this time, leaving me staring at the reddish brick in front of my face. My eyes become unfocused, the red shifting before me as I fall into the clutches of a memory I'd forgotten.

Blood. Blood coating my hands. A sight that's not unfamiliar to me, but the hazy image of my Mom lying on the floor is. I can't even remember when this is, yet a slender figure hidden beneath a hood whips the knife out of my Mom's gut and shoves me as she runs past. The rest is a mix of out-of-order events. My Mom's well-choreographed routine, spinning around a pole center stage, to her longing glances at the same spot from behind the bar.

"Why did Shelia stop stripping?" Angus asks, making me jolt back to see the brick wall before me. He climbs me like a tree, popping up on my shoulder. "She always loved losing herself to the music. Performing was her art form."

"I don't know Angus," I admit, turning away from the building and stepping out on the road. I'm so lost in my thoughts I don't spot the car speeding toward me until it skids to a stop just inches from my legs. A familiar redhead in a pantsuit smirks at me from behind the wheel of her BMW, mouthing 'payback' through the windscreen. Bad move, Angus and I agree. Still clutching the phone tightly in my hand, I round to her open window and smash my fist into her cosmetically-appeasing face. The phone adds that extra punch for her trying to get the better of me, and after pocketing it, I grab her fancy pantsuit and hoist her straight out of the car. I've seen limbs flail like a demented octopus before and it never fails to tickle me.

"Let's see if your father-brother-second-cousin-in-law will want you now!" I scream, throwing my fist into her face one more time, and she's lights out. Wow, what a sap. Not so-caring citizens have frozen on the sidewalk, no one coming to her aid. I lurch forward, enjoying the symphony of screams that ricochet around the buildings. Serves them right for leaving one of their own to my mercy. Planting one diamante high-top in front of the other, I stride through the center of the parting crowd, holding my head high.

Consider this a warning to the world. I'm one big ball of erratic emotion I don't fully understand. Fending for myself was a life skill I prided myself on, yet it hasn't come as easy since I left the Devil's Bedpost. And until I master feeling like my soul has been ripped out without the chance of redemption, the general public should stay the fuck out of my way. Out of control Candy is a dangerous Candy.

The ring of an old-fashioned landline continues to fill the entire lower level of the mansion with its irritating chime. That's the third time today as if the insistent voicemails flashing on the mounted display weren't enough.

"You gonna get that?" Nick drawls on his way through the kitchen. He picks up an apple, tossing it in the air a few times before Gabriel enters, catching the flying fruit mid-air. Smirking, he takes a large bite and drops into a seat opposite me at the breakfast bar. It's safe to say, the three of us residing under the same roof was never part of the plan. Even with the mansion's generous square footage and sprawling land allowing us to go days without even seeing each other, just knowing they're still close by is grating on me. Not once have I let my appearance as the Mistress of this house falter though. My brunette hair is artfully curled, my robe perfectly pressed.

"No need," I answer Nick when he hovers by the counter. "The attorney will just leave another generic message about our time here coming to an end. It's a different call I'm waiting on." Glancing at the cell phone before me on the walnut surface, I drum my nails impatiently. My brother, Riley, always said I didn't play well with others when we were children, and the trait hasn't changed after all this time. In fact, being the only remaining member of our family tree suits me just fine.

Just then, my screen lights, sending vibrations through the tabletop. I snatch the device, striding through the mansion and slipping out of the rear patio doors. Securing the doors closed, I then answer the call I've been on for waiting weeks.

"Tell me you have good news," I order harshly. My fingernails dig into my palm, my teeth grinding together.

"You were right," a gruff voice replies. "Leicester was smart enough to use a different lawyer than the one listed on the documents you gave me. I was able to track down the attorney's office through a handful of café receipts stuffed in the bottom of his briefcase." A low breath leaves me. Finally, some good news.

"Tell me where," I demand, my hand on the patio door in anticipation of a quick dash to change ahead of whatever road trip I'm about to take.

"About that," he interjects, and my gut flips. "Your girl's already been here. Just left, in fact, most likely already named as the Leicester Heiress." Bile fills the back of my mouth, my grip on the cell phone turning white.

"Where is she?" I seethe, my jaw so tight I barely manage to get the words out. I've relived the night we skidded into the driveway in the stolen taxi over and over in my mind, still unsure how Jasper had packed, picked up Candy, and left before we were able to catch them. I was right on her tail, ready to reap my revenge on them both, yet they got away unscathed. Not to mention with the contents of the damaged safe I found in Candy's attic hideaway.

The P.I relays an address through the speaker with the warning that the pair have already jumped into the Lambo and moved on. Hearing this, I snap a short order to follow wherever they go and end the call. Anger courses through my veins, quickening my breathing until I'm panting. Overhead, the sun has begun to sink towards the horizon, filling the sky with a dusky red that matches my mood perfectly. Another day is setting on my time in the mansion, and for the first time, my confidence wavers. But it can't. I've come too far and fought for too long to lose now.

Time's like this call for a demonstration of power, and I know exactly where to get it. Stomping back into the kitchen barefoot, I catch Gabriel's eye and jerk my head to the closed door across the room. A malicious smile warms his usually stoic face, breaking free of the façade Malik has trained him to embody.

Thanks to their need to obey commands, I couldn't really have asked for better accomplices, especially when they were manufactured trial runs for handling the real Monarchs. Learning how they tick and how they'd react was integral in my master plan, even if Malik proved harder to predict as of late. Where Candy was involved, his moods grew more impulsive by the day, but he came through in the end. His skewered version of protection sent Candy running, straight in the direction I needed her.

Gabriel hops up from his seat, clicking his fingers for Nick to follow suit. Producing a key from a chain around his neck, he unlocks the door while Nick retrieves the bag stashed behind a loose panel in the wall. Chains can be heard rattling from the base of the darkened stairwell as Gabriel holds the door open for me to enter. Right behind, Nick heaves the bag onto his shoulder before flicking on the light switch. Fluorescent bulbs flicker to life, drawing pained hisses towards the staircase I descend slowly.

"Oh sweet Mary on a bicycle," Cherry scoffs upon seeing me. Her filthy hair covers most of her bruised face, the red curtain splitting just enough for her to peer out. "I know you're desperate to be just like Candy, but this is getting ridiculous." From her place chained to the concrete wall, she cackles as if the roles were reversed. I scowl, standing tall in a silky kimono with my black lingerie visible underneath.

Sure, I'd raided Candy's old wardrobe before the night she escaped me, figuring if I was about to become the heiress of the

Leicester fortune, I might as well look the part. The heiress part might be out now, but there's still the matter of money and revenge. Not that taking my brother from me was much of a loss, just another strike on the tally. My real vendetta is the years I spent at Leicester's side, doing everything he asked while he fretted over Candy's life choices. I'll be doing her a favor, reuniting the pair in death and finally, everything she never cared for will be mine. The men, the attention, the money. I've put in the hard work. I deserve the reward, damn it.

The chains clink again, this time from the taxi driver I haven't bothered to learn the name of. He pulls himself out of the curled position on the floor, easing his back flat against the wall by Cherry's feet. I don't know what all his grunts and hisses are for; he's barely received half the beating Cherry has, and she's still standing. Nick takes a few stale cereal bars from the bag and tosses them his way while Gabriel takes Cherry for her scheduled toilet break. She kicks and struggles with the same amount of vigor as when we first dumped her down here.

Freeing her from the wall, Gabriel keeps her arms tightly bound behind her back, leaving her mouth free to spit in my direction. I pay her no mind. She's served her purpose. Gabriel, however, has Malik's trait for swift and harsh punishment. Yanking her aside, Gabriel clubs Cherry over the head with a baton he keeps at his waist. Standard protocol from the Devil's Bedpost security training. Cherry's legs give out, and he shoves her back against the wall.

"Take the other one instead," he orders Nick. "We're going to learn a few lessons in manners first, aren't we Cherry?" She hardly replies before Gabriel rams her head against the wall and secures the manacle at her neck to the chain she was so recently freed from.

"Feels like you could use a few lessons yourself there Gabe," Cherry chokes out a laugh. "Needing to hinder your opponent doesn't make you a winner, just a pussy." She chuckles again as he levels a blow to her stomach, adding a pained chortle to her laughter. I have to acknowledge her spunk at times like this, although I keep my face impassive. Nick moves past with the taxi driver, who grabs at my kimono with his grubby hands.

"Please," he snivels. "Let me go. I won't tell anyone where I've been. Just let me go home to my cats." I shove him off me, ignoring the gentle way Nick whispers to him as they ascend the stairs. Unlike his teammate, Nick isn't cut out for the dirty work. He was drawn in by the money, unaware of the hard labor it would entail. Although in my defense, my plan ended the night I found Jasper's room empty and the safe cracked open. Since then, I've been winging it.

"Still haven't found her then?" Cherry breaks through my thoughts. Her grin is back in place, tugging at a split lip. The matching blood smear coats Gabriel's knuckles, and as much as an anti-chauvinistic asshole riles me, I ignore it in favor of slapping the smile from her face myself. My longest nail snaps on impact and I curse. Fucking karma. Rearing her face back to me, Cherry's brown eyes blaze with fury. "When will you figure out that nothing you do will affect her? She's untouchable."

"But you're not," I smirk. Cherry's face suddenly sinks, and that's when I know my words have got to her more than any of Gabriel's efforts. "Never mind the fate you dealt Jack, there's a little boy out there enjoying the perks of private education thanks to me." I brush my knuckles over Cherry's cheek and she bucks me away, all traces of humor gone. Rule number one, don't hire anyone until you have leverage. Leicester taught me that. For Cherry, it's a seven-year-old called Zak who thinks his mom is traveling the world, snapping photos for magazines, and sending the money back to the auntie raising him.

"Leave my son out of this," Cherry jerks against the manacle holding her neck in place. I could almost pity her. As if being allured away by the promise of a huge pay-off wasn't enough, she had to go and fall for her mark. Trying to escape me was her downfall, and ultimately it was Jack that paid the price.

"That decision is on you," I drawl, picking at my now broken nail. "The fact the Monarchs haven't stormed this place means they're too pre-occupied picking out flower wreaths, and the lack of Candy returning for my head means she is still unaware of their predicament. That gives us a small window to turn the tide and for you to redeem yourself." Cherry grunts in the back of her throat as if she really has any other choice. Either she works for me, or she'll be buried under the garage, never to be found. Looking to the top of the stairs, I briefly wonder where Nick has gotten to before returning my attention to Cherry.

"So, what's it going to be?" I smirk, toying with my prisoner. Her red hair flicks limply at her shoulders as she refuses to meet my eye.

"I'll play your game, then I'm out."

"You're out when I say you're out," I growl, sounding every bit like the mentor I devoted my entire adult life to. Leicester meant more to me than he ever did to Candy, even if he refused to acknowledge it.

"Or when Candy is parading up the street with your head on a spike," Cherry pipes up, her cocky smile returning. Gabriel catches my curious gaze flicking to the top of the stairs again, and offers to go check. Placing his baton into my hand, I feel its heavyweight before sparking the electrical taser at the end.

"I'd be very careful who you root for," I warn Cherry, taking a step closer. "Especially when I'm the one here holding the taser, and Candy is out there, ready to exact her own revenge when she finds out what happened to Jack. There's no winning side for you, only the lesser of two evils."

I jerk forward, stopping just short of tasing Cherry's exposed stomach. Her shocked scream is music to my ears and as I retreat, my own evil laughter vibrates through the cellar. Cherry can go without her toilet break for today in the hopes that she's more accommodating to whatever plan I come up with tomorrow. The satisfied grin on my face lasts all the way to the top of the stairs, where I find the front door wide open and Gabriel standing with a murderous look on his face.

"Nick and the driver are gone," he growls through the lobby. I grip the sides of my head, accidentally sparking the taser into my own temple. Just fucking perfect. My rattled brain stutters through the motions as I lock the cellar door, trying to extract a slither of dignity. This is fine. Just another issue that'll come between me and my self-procured happily ever after.

R eluctantly, I pull into the parking lot of the sleaziest bar I've ever seen. Candy keeps clicking her fingers and pointing at an open space between two beaten-up Volkswagens.

"Are you sure you don't want to talk about what's upsetting you, love?" I try one last time. Candy flips me off and I sigh, expecting nothing less. If I've learnt anything these past few weeks, it's not to argue. Even if I know I'm right, just give in and follow Candy's lead. The last thing I want to do when she's burying any emotion that's not anger is to rile her up even more.

Easing into the space, I raise the convertible roof before hopping out to rifle through the trunk. Grabbing a cover that I grabbed in the previous town, I make sure every inch of the Lambo is hidden from sight before jogging around potholes to catch up with Candy in the entrance. A busted door hanging off its hinges permits us entry. The pungent stench of alcohol and piss smacking me in the face.

"It's perfect," Candy beams. I've easily grown accustomed to the 5* hotels and spas we've been staying in, yet it never fails to surprise me how Candy feels more comfortable in rundown shitholes like this. I hope it's because it reminds her of comforting times rather than being where she thinks she belongs. I draw her another step inside, telling myself Candy's happiness makes this place just about bearable.

Dozens of heads revealing glazed, bloodshot eyes swing our way, leering at Candy. A growl sounds in my chest, silenced by the retro jukebox spewing a crackled tune from the sixties. I've never considered myself a snob, but one look at the bar spread out before me, and all I can think is it has nothing on the Devil's Bedpost. The single bartender was visible, drying a glass with a dirty rag. The motion causes his heavily tattooed arms to wiggle on either side of the ripped sleeves that used to be attached to his vest. From the bald head to the thick beard, I can only imagine this is 'Sticky Ricky,' as the sign hanging over the doorway outside would suggest.

Putting her fingers in her mouth, Candy whistles for anyone nearby to buy her a drink, and it dawns on me she'll never change. More importantly, I never want her to. She's a product of her own making, which makes her the most authentic person walking this planet. No bullshit, no fakery. And in turn, it dawns on me, that I should be the man she was first drawn to. Not someone who lets his worries hinder her, but the bad boy she craves.

Only a few feet into the room, a drunk stumbles into me, slurring an apology. Plucking the beer out of his hand, I shove him aside and plant my boot in his ass to send him toppling over. Then I make a beeline for the jukebox I'm not sure will have anything from this century, tipping the contents of the beer in my mouth without the bottle touching my lips. A few quarters and a kick start later, Kylie Minogue thunders from the machine's speakers and draws my girl directly to me, just as spontaneously planned.

With a shot in each hand, Candy makes her way over, shaking her chest and rolling her hips in a cute little number. The woman at Macy's called it a denim playsuit, which Candy has left the front unbuttoned to reveal a hot pink lace bra and her toned stomach. The lower half hugs her ass tightly with a lollipop motif embroidered on each back pocket. The only reason it appealed to Candy in the first place and is now wholly appealing to me too. Pressing her chest into my body, she tips the glass into my mouth, and I accept the harsh, burning liquid without so much as a whimper.

"I fucking hate tequila." I grimace inwardly.

"I know," she winks. Downing her own shot, Candy turns to push her ass into my crotch, and the bitter taste in my mouth is a distant memory. Every eye in the bar is still turned our way, just as enamored with this spunky beaut as I am. Her pink hair licks at my neck, clinging to me like Medusa's fuchsia snakes and I push my face further into her neck. Raising her arms into the air, Candy sways side to side, radiating a level of confidence I can't understand. Whether I was clinging to her waist or not, she'd still be right here, living a life free from restraint and prejudice. I wish I could say the same.

"I'm so in lo-" I start until Candy's body stiffens beneath my touch. Her back straightens and her head tilts, leading me to follow her eye line over her shoulder. A slender figure slinks into the shadows by the restrooms, disappearing before I can get a good enough look. There was something oddly familiar about the shape and size, but I can't quite put my finger on it. "What is it, love?"

"Hmm?" Candy twists her head, the tightness in her eyebrows easing as she smiles. "Nothing, I think. Ooh, I love this song!" She twists in my hold before I'd even noticed the track has changed. Gangsta's Paradise now fills the darkened area where an unused dancefloor sits. Candy grabs my right hand, tightening her arm around the back of my waist. Taking the lead, she twirls us into the center of the dancefloor, kicking up the thick layer of dust that has settled there. The glint in her eyes, though, couldn't be brighter. The tunes continue to play, and for this moment, among a crowd of strangers, the world is ours.

"You gonna stare at me all night, or are you actually going to kiss me?" Candy asks, then lunges at me without waiting for a response. My reply coats my tongue as it greedily dives into her mouth, tangling with hers in a dance we've become well accustomed to. She takes everything I have, stripping me bare, yet I keep coming back for more. Gripping Candy's hips, I chase her kiss, hanging on to the insatiable taste of bubble gum and tequila until we're both panting.

"Any more of that, and I'll have to fuck you right here on this dusty floor while these dirty hobo's jerk off over the show we give them," I threaten. Candy rolls her hips, grinding against my stiff cock with a malicious laugh.

"Sounds like my kind of Saturday night," she breathes huskily into my ear. I groan into her neck, stealing myself as the song ends and Candy twists out of my bruising grip. A chill washes over my front in response to her missing body heat and like a magnet, I'm drawn behind her all the way to a heightened table with six empty stools. Enough for each of the Monarchs, I muse internally and then frown at myself. Where the fuck did that come from?

A tray of drinks is slid onto the table by a bartender who tells us each one is courtesy of the various men lining the bar. I use the word bar loosely, grimacing at the scratched wooden surface with multiple chips missing. Currently, that surface is being used as a resting point for all the men sitting backward on their stools to watch Candy with nauseating looks of hunger. Not seeming to notice, Candy is on her third drink already, knocking each glass back and not caring for what the various colored liquid might actually hold. My guess would be roofies, and I promise myself to not let her out of my sight for a single second tonight.

"Those were some sweet moves," a graveled voice says. I can smell the insipid stench of alcohol and smoke before turning to eye the only man brave enough to venture over to our table. He jeers at me, showing the few teeth he has left, which are stained yellow. Candy doesn't pay him any attention, seeming to have a conversation with the empty stools on either side of her, so he turns his attention to me.

"I'll give you a pack of Jolly Ranchers for a night with your girl," a potbellied man with too much body-hair states boldly. Although, I wouldn't have known about the hair if his soiled, once-white tee wasn't struggling to cover his midsection. Coming close enough to toss a lime green box onto the table, his overriding stench finally chokes me out before I can voice my objection. Candy's attention has been captured by now, and she leans over the table, silencing my protests.

"Oooh, they're the sour ones. Can't argue with that." She shrugs, sliding the box towards me. Hopping down from her stool, she pauses long enough to place a kiss on my cheek and then gives the Grease Ball a once-over with her eyes. "He won't last long, swing back around to pick me up at ten? Make sure to save me one," she taps the box with her nail. I lash out, grabbing her wrist with more force than I intented.

"I'm not trading you for a pack of Jolly Ranchers," I grit out.

"But..." Candy looks from the Grease Ball to me, confusion claiming her features. "They're the sour ones."

"I don't give a fuck if they're flaked with real gold. What part of being my girl aren't you getting?" I didn't mean to condescend her, but someone decided to switch off the jukebox at that precise moment, and my voice spreads throughout the bar. I watch the gate close over Candy's emotions, locking her skewered sense of rationality firmly away. Yeah, I'm in for some trouble.

"The bit where you seem to think you own me," Candy growls, her face contorting with rage. Trying to twist her arm free to no avail, she settles for slapping me across the face with her free hand. A weak attempt, yet it rocks through the center of my chest. Fuck. Laying claim to Candy is never the right way to go about any situation, but still, my hand remains clasped around her wrist and refuses to let go.

"At some point, love, you're going to have to admit a small part of you belongs to me. I think I deserve that much, don't you?" Her chocolate brown eyes narrow, indicating her disagreement. Her actions when we're alone say different, but if she refuses to acknowledge her feelings for me, do we even have a future worth fighting for? Regardless, she's not leaving this club with anyone other than me.

Stepping down from my stool, I transfer Candy's wrist into my weaker hand and drag her behind me unwillingly. She doesn't stop bucking against me, but my focus shifts to the Grease Ball now in front. To his credit, he meets my eye and refuses to back down.

"I'm going to give you one chance to move along," I warn him. "There are only certain men I'm willing to share my girl with, and even they are on my shit list right now. Step away before I shove your face so far up your ass, you could bite your bunions off." There's a pause in the struggling from behind me, my words striking a cord not even Candy wants to envision. Then, she doubles her efforts to be freed. Shoving me into the Grease Ball, I release her wrist and yell out in disgust as his BO touches me.

Suddenly, bodies dive in from all sides. Hands drag me down, words are spat at my face. I fight against the crushing weights, each piling on top of the last, pinning me to the ground. My chest threatens to crack inwards, my lungs screaming for air as I'm lost to the bundle. And the worst part is, that Candy is nowhere to be seen.

Using my elbows, I land blow after blow into various temples around me, manufacturing enough of a gap to start army crawling out of. Gripping the foot rung of the stool, I use it to drag myself partially to my knees and then lift the stool clean off the floor. Swinging wide, I catch an oncoming drunk, knocking him aside, and that's when I catch a glimpse of fuchsia. Not that she's running, but standing over me with her prized, pink bat from the car. How did she make it to the Lambo and back in such a short amount of time?

A hand grabs my ankle, attempting to yank me back into the man pile that are now all fighting each other for no reason. Candy raises her bat, slamming it into the side of the man gripping onto me and audibly cracking at least two of his ribs.

"He's mine," Candy growls venomously. A relieved smile takes root on my face, my eyes crinkling in the corners as I peer up at her. "To deal with." Relieved smile gone.

The next time she raises her bat, it crashes down into my gut. Fuck this shit. Coughing, I sweep my leg out and bring her down to my level, aka the floor. Pulling the bat from her grip, we struggle in a mess of limbs for control. We've done this many times in the bedroom, and just like now, Candy only plays to win. Her knee crushes my balls, her hand closes around my throat and still, I hold the bat out of her reach. As she stretches for it, I take a brief moment to enjoy the feel of her breasts in my face and then flip us over. The Grease Ball pops out of nowhere, trying to pry me from Candy's hips. One blow of the bat in his non-existent crotch deals with him and I toss the weapon away. Far away.

"Remember what you asked me that night at the mansion?" I ask, catching Candy's fist as it flies towards my face. She bucks beneath me until I snatch her other hand and pin them both above her head. Lowering my mouth to hover over hers, I stare directly into her eyes and block out the chaos happening all around. "You asked if I would believe in you and stay by your side. Well, I'm asking you here and now if that still applies and if you'll return the favor. I've been with you, caring for you this whole time. If you turn on me, you've got no one left."

I watch conflicting thoughts pass behind her brown eyes, my heart jack-knifing in my chest. Using this tactic, especially when Candy's so raw, is a risk but one that pays off as she goes limp and ducks her head onto my shoulder. I feel her sigh in the depths of my soul, resonating with the woman who just wants a place to belong. Somewhere she can finally stop running from and someone to be right there with her. Glasses smash, Rednecks bellow. Yet, among the anarchy reigning down, this moment is as real as it gets.

"Come on, love. Let's find somewhere to stay tonight and get this party back on track." Planting a quick kiss on her mouth, I rise and pull Candy up to her feet beside me. The fight is still in full swing, with half the bar's punters laying limp on the ground and the other half battling to be at the top of the rummage pile.

Stepping over bodies to retrieve Candy's bat, I slide my arm around her waist and lead her away from the carnage.

"Hey, can I ask you something?" I mumble, pausing by the Lambo. Candy steps into my body, drawing a rumble from where her chest is pushed against mine. Her glistening brown eyes widen, her pink lips close enough for her raspberry gum to wash over my senses. Every time she looks at me so openly, I hesitate, not wanting to say the wrong thing. Can't come on too hard, but can't pretend I don't give a shit either. The wrath has disappeared from her features, for now, yet I hold her with the tentative grip of a ticking time bomb. "You…wouldn't trade me for a stick of gum, right?"

"Depends on what flavor it is," Candy simply shrugs, removing herself from my hold and leaving me standing in the parking lot. She's joking, I tell myself. She has to be.

CANDY

The green light flashes beneath Jasper's key card, presenting us with the suite he chose. I have to admit; maybe he does have better taste than I give him credit for. All paid for on my bank card, which the receptionist seemed rather alarmed Jasper has ownership over, but what the fuck would I do with it? Drug dealers don't take AMEX. Holding the door open for me, a glint sparks in Jasper's eye and I already know what he's thinking. It's the same with each hotel room, sauna, private charter hire, and rock concert bathroom stall. So many new surfaces to christen.

"Why don't you hit the shower, Stud?" I smack his ass, diverting into the kitchen area. "I'll work out the music system. No doubt, it's gonna get loud." Pressing a kiss to my lips, Jasper places our bag on the bed and heads off to do as he's told. Kicking my shoes off, I flop back on the mattress, testing out its buoyancy. Just like the rest of the room, the lavish satin covers are nothing less than luxury. Heavy, cream blinds cover the entire floor-to-ceiling window looking down on the thirty-seven floors below. Spotlights frame the room, lighting the areas above a vanity desk and wardrobe while leaving the rest of the space in the dimness. Stretched out, my eyelids flutter, and the grips of a blissful nap pull me into its alluring clutches.

My body shifts. The playsuit clinging onto my shoulders rolls down the length of my arms, sliding under my ass. Pulled free from my legs, a hand claims each of my ankles, spreading me wide. Lips carve a pattern from calf to thigh, then repeats on the other side. A hot mouth covers the lace thong that matches the bra I long to be freed from. A talented tongue slides up the outside of the rough material, adding twice the sensation of being dragged over my clit.

Cracking an eye, I smile lazily at Jasper's gorgeous gem-like eyes staring up at me. Water droplets glisten across his broad back, the thickly-corded traps in his shoulders doing something fluttery inside my channel. Gloriously naked, With a mischievous smile carved into his face, his tongue artfully slips beneath the panty-line to tease my slit. I groan lightly, rolling my head to the side. What a way to wake up.

Rolling the thong down to my ankles, Jasper uses the strappy material to lift my legs upright and sinks his teeth into my ass, just centimeters from my puckered hole. My hiss swiftly turns into a giggle, loving that this Adonis doesn't hold back. Let his teeth imprint a scar, to let the world know I gave myself up to his mercy. Releasing my legs, Jasper props them over his shoulders and shoves his face back into my pussy. No holding back this time. Jasper devours me like an ice cream sundae, lapping up every drop of cream on offer.

Arching my back, my fingers fly into Jasper's blonde locks, tugging and pulling in all directions. His tongue enters and exits me, lolling up to circle my clit and back again in a well-choreographed dance. The tightness of his lips locking around the sensitive bud coincides with Jasper plunging two of his fingers straight inside me. I gasp, savoring the little suckling, plucking at my nipple and rolling it between my fingers. All too quickly, I'm reeling, tripping over the precipice of sanity. Sensations mix with adrenaline. Horny thoughts turn dark and in this moment, I'd let Jasper do whatever he likes.

Writhing under his assault, Jasper whips away just as quickly as he started. Strolling around the bed, he grabs my wrists and drags me over to the edge. My head hangs off the mattress, giving me a cracking view of the underside of his thick cock. Prying my mouth wide, Jasper guides his purple head directly into the back of my throat.

Using the position to my advantage, I drag my nails up Jasper's firm thighs, covering him in a network of red lines while he fucks my mouth without relenting. His balls slap against my forehead, his hand curling around my throat to feel the outline of his dick pumping against the inside. Gliding further south, his hands close around my breasts, massaging thoroughly.

My own hands journey upwards, sliding to the point behind his balls. Noting Jasper shaved, I tickle his gooch while deep-throating his thrusting cock the way he likes. Jolting away from me sharply, Jasper exhales deeply in an attempt to steady himself. Good old gooch tickle works every time. Twizzling me around, my leg is pinned against Jasper's chest as he thrusts his cock into me with no resistance. I'm soaking wet, greedy, accepting him all the way to the hilt. Jasper fills me, stilling in his attempt to tease but the pained look on his face says that plan is quickly backfiring.

"Don't hold back Jasp. We have all night for rounds two, three, and then some." I bite my bottom lip, curling my other leg around his back.

"I hope we have a lot more than that," he replies hopefully and my lip pops free. Erm, yeah, about that...Deciding to change tactic,

I whip over the leg that was resting on Jasper's chest, smoothly turning onto all fours without his dick needing to leave me. If anything, the twisting motion lets his erection curl deliciously and I settle myself back on him with a pleasured groan. This is better. No optimistic glances or sweet words. Just fucking.

Getting the memo, Jasper shoves my face down into the mattress and goes hell for leather on my desperate cunt. Slamming home on every thrust, lifting my ass higher with harsh fingers. His balls assault my clit, filling the hotel room with the slapping sound that's overshadowed by my cries. Every time I think I must be used to Jasper's girthy size, from that very first time trapped in the bus's baggage compartment, the beating his dick provides proves me wrong. From my clenched toes to my strained neck, I feel him everywhere. His hands, his ability to dominate me, his constant presence.

Scraping his fingers across my ass, Jasper presses his thumb into my ass. Scrunching my eyes tight, black and yellow spots shimmer across the inside of my eyelids, my head a mess of heady desire. Using the said thumb to keep me firmly in place, I can only hold on a little longer until the starting tremors of a climax slam through me like a volcano. Coaxing Jasper over the edge with me, we cry out together, my hands cramping from fisting the covers.

Only once the glorious spasms raking through my body ease does Jasper flop forward, dragging me into a snuggle with his chest at my back and dick side pulsing inside me.

"I know you don't want to hear it," Jasper mutters, and I instantly know he's right. "But you've become everything to me. Everything I could have ever dreamed of." Yep, I'm out. Attempting to move, Jasper's arm winds around my middle, holding me flush to his sweat-coated body. Yet his words are out there now, already penetrating my thoughts and preventing what should have been a sex-induced slumber.

"I need to clean up," I say too harshly, fighting to be freed. This time, Jasper lets me go, and I dash into the bathroom, switching on the shower faucet. My chest is panting for a whole different reason now, sheer panic rising within and threatening to strangle me. Jasper appears in the doorway, his still semi-hard dick bobbing as it slowly settles. Looking at either side of him, I jump into the shower, almost slipping over as I slam the glass door closed.

"Don't do that," Jasper grunts, opening the door and stepping in. Shit, now I'm cornered. He's a criminal mastermind. Gently planting a hand on each of my hips, his green eyes wait for me to stop looking elsewhere. "I'm not trying to trap you, love. I care, that's all. And I can tell when there's something wrong. When you're hurting, it hurts me too," he tries to coax me into his body. Fat chance now, my heart feels like it's about to shoot out of my recently-fingered ass. There are enough juices down there for it to just slip out. Not the way I planned on dying, but it would make a pretty good newspaper story.

"Why?" I challenge, keeping my jaw tight. No one implied I was 'hurting' as Jasper claims; in fact, I'm living my best life here. Getting back to my roots when my instincts ruled and emotions didn't confuse the fuck out of me. It's easier that way. "Why would you invest your compassion in someone who can't reciprocate it?"

"Because," Jasper runs a hand through his dampening blonde hair. It's sticking up in all the wrong places thanks to not being dried properly the first time and having me claw the shit out of it.

"Ahh fuck it," Jasper suddenly says, clasping his hands on either side of my face. "Because I love you, that's why." My eyes narrow into slits now, even more suspicious than before.

"You love me?" I ask through squished lips. Jasper nods, loosening his hold, and slides his hands to my neck, brushing his thumbs over my collarbone. The words stutter through my brain like a train with a track, chugging along until it inevitably gets stuck in the mud. "Like a grandma you love, so you get dibs on her inheritance kind of way, or like a sister you have a weird sex dream about and now it's super awkward kind of way?"

"In a forever kind of way," Jasper replies without blinking at my sister sex tactic to scare him off. *Forever*. That's a big word. Not literally, it's only seven letters, yet it refers to something far beyond the comprehension of the human mind. Unfortunately, it is a concept given to the finite expanse of the universe.

"Candy!" Angus barks in my ears. He pops up on one side of Jasper's slippery shoulders while Hamish takes the other.

"Stop distractin' yaself and answer the poor lad!" Hamish shouts deafeningly loud, causing me to wince. Between the pair of them, Jasper's green eyes are filled with optimism. Just for the rewarding smile, I wish I could give him what he wants. Yet, I have nothing to say. No response to give that would make the weight in the air around us lift so I can breathe properly again. I'm drowning in dread, uncertainty, and him. Jasper. The Jester to his Queen. But a Queen without a kingdom is just another self-entitled prick with an ego problem.

"I'm not asking you to say it back," Jasper finally breaks through the heavy silence, his chest falling heavily. "In fact, I'm not asking for anything other than you letting me stay by your side. Whether you're slicing loser's new assholes or running over chicks you wrongfully think would turn my eye, I just want to be there through it all." Angus whistles low, agreeing with Hamish that Jasper is quite the catch. Ignoring the pair of them, I focus on the gorgeous man trying to convince me he loves me the same night I struck him with a baseball bat.

"Again, why? I have nothing to offer. Except maybe my legacy apparently," my eyes lower to the fancy marbled flooring, and Jasper grunts.

"I don't want a single cent or any claim in your inheritance. We can get in the car right now, drive to the nearest cliff and toss your bank card over the edge for all I care." I pout further, not knowing where that leaves me. Money transactions I can understand, but the feeling churning in my chest is blurring too many lines.

My lungs constrict again, and my head sways with wooziness. That's it, death is coming for me. Jasper continues, either oblivious to my impending stroke or fully aware and trying to prevent it.

"Offer me your crazy thoughts, your wild journeys, your insane antidotes. Bless me with your incredible pussy, this stunning body, and your raspberry-flavored lips. That's all I want." Angus and Hamish slither away, giving me no more distractions to blame. When Jasper puts it that way, it really doesn't sound like much sacrifice on my part other than allowing him to love me. I nod once with furrowed brows, failing to see the catch.

"Okay, I guess. I can do that."

JASPER

"Are we there yet?" Candy asks for the millionth time from the Lambo's passenger seat. Like all of the other times, I leave her question unanswered - mostly because she hasn't specified where 'there' is. My instruction this morning was to drive until we found where we were going, along with the insistence we'd know it when we saw it.

A yawn stretches at my mouth, which Candy mistakes for a gesture for food. Tossing a gummy bear sweet into my mouth, it flies to the back of my throat and I choke, barely keeping my grip steady on the wheel. Peering through slitted eyes, I quickly pull into an empty bay at the side of the road, punching myself in the chest to cough the sweet up.

"Hey! You found it!" Candy exclaims while I recover. Turning to question her, I find the passenger seat empty. Having jumped from the open top, she's halfway down a dirt track, heading towards a skatepark at the other end. I check around to see if it's safe to leave the Lambo here in plain sight, gauging the quiet gardens in one direction and the edge of a small town on the other. Chasing after her, I catch up just in time to open the metal gate for her to enter, acting every bit the spontaneous and attentive gentleman she says she doesn't need.

Unlike its surroundings, the skate park is heaving with people – mostly teens huddled in small groups and not actually skating. Their boards are propped against the half rails while they smoke weed and peer at us with side-eye glances. Candy isn't bothered though, striding directly for the group with their pants laying low over their boxers. I reckon they couldn't skate if they wanted to, judging by the great pools of material puddled around their sneakers.

"Hey guys, mind if I borrow this?" Candy nudges a board with her foot, so it falls to the ground. Her tattooed cleavage has most of them stuck for a response, not that I can blame them. Taking their silence as a yes, Candy reaches over to pluck the joint from the youngest's grip.

"And this," she smirks, popping it in her mouth and speeding away on the neon green wheels. Approaching a steep ramp, Candy's powerful strides shoot her skyward as she ascends to the top and performs an impressive kick spin in the air. Unlike everyone else in the park, I'm not surprised. Candy attacks every aspect of her life with the same ease that allows her to flip the board around in mid-air, never faulting once. Seizing their conversations, the teens crowd around to watch the incredible girl I've laid claim to. Ever since that first time we met in the baggage hold, I knew she'd be mine. But first, I needed to make sure I was worthy.

Zipping past, Candy outstretches her arm to pass me the joint and I find my place hitched on the fence. Smoking and watching her wow the crowd with her catalog of tricks, my eyes track her every movement, from gripping the board to her feet in one hand and blowing me a kiss with the other to skidding across a half pipe at lightning speed. Pride fills my chest when the teens cheer and whistle after her, noticing how versatile Candy is. She owns every situation she's thrown into without a moment's hesitation.

Pausing at the top of a ramp, Candy propels the board over the edge, exhaling before pushing herself forward. She sails down the death drop, veering up the next to flip in the air. Her head is mere centimeters from the ground, her pink hair brushing the concrete, but my heart doesn't pause a beat. I knew she'd land it before her wheels slam down hard and she skids to a stop. The smile plastered across her face is everything. Beaming and bright, her chest falling heavily in her baggy vest that exposes all of her side boobs in a stunning navy lace bra I'm all too familiar with. She's paired her top half with my olive green shorts, opting for maximum comfort for traveling and not giving a shit about what anyone else thinks. I probably admire that the most about her.

"Where did you learn to skate like that?" I ask when she walks between my legs, taking the joint from my mouth. Taking a long time, her eyebrow hitches at me knowingly.

"Life on the street, *love*," she mocks me. "Learning to skate is as integral as learning to hot wire a car. Makes for an instant getaway in places others can't follow."

"Least you have no reason to need a getaway now," I try my luck, pushing for her to acknowledge what I said last night. I've never told a woman I loved her, aside from my own mother. Jack was the real mummy's boy, but I learnt a valuable skill in the bitter world of jealously. It doesn't pay to trap people against their will, which is why I'm eager to help Candy see that's not what our future holds. Leaning in close, she blows the smoke from her mouth into mine, sealing her heady gift with a kiss.

"I wouldn't be so sure," she smirks and I groan. Here we go again, always with the swings and roundabouts. "Come on, your turn," she pulls me from the fence. I protest, not that she cares. Following her lead, the teens run to grab their boards, suddenly interested in using the skate park for its intended purpose. At least they're not all standing around to watch me fail. Flicking the board up with her heel, Candy uses the illusion of holding my hand to lead me to a smaller ramp and hands over the board.

"It's just like riding a motorbike, standing upright without the handlebars," she shrugs.

"Yeah, that's exactly the same thing," I grumble. It's not the board or falling on my ass that bothers me, but the desire to live up to all her glory. Wobbling slightly, I manage to get my balance before Candy shoves me down the ramp, and it all goes to shit from there. My arms flail wildly, the board skidding aside to abandon my feet. Toppling aside, Candy is right there, running alongside to grab me as I tumble. Her arm around my neck saves my head from smashing against the concrete, her legs sturdy enough to hold me like a dancer being lowered at the end of a waltz.

"My hero," I jest, tugging a strand over her hair behind her ear. Her raspberry lips lift in a cocky smirk I want to kiss right off her face.

"What did you expect? You're too pretty to let fall." I laugh, biting down on my cheek to resist telling her just how hard I've fallen for her. Righting me, Candy moves towards the board and kicks it upwards into her hand.

"Have your fun love, I'm happy watching," I shoo her away. She catches my fingers and draws my hand up to meet her lips, continuing the role reversal in our corrupt Cinderella story.

"Meh, I'm bored. Let's find somewhere to hold up for the night and you can make it up to me for your terrible skateboarding skills." This has my eyebrows bobbing as we leave the skate park together, the board still firmly in her grip. Pulling Candy under my arm, she takes full advantage of shoving her free hand down my sweatpants and scoring her nails along my dick. I groan, quickening our pace, and by the time we've got to the car, I'm ready to take her then and there. If only a group of kids wasn't on our tail, yelling for their board back as I speed into the nearby town, hunting for the first place to stop. It presents itself in the form of Candy's favorite venue – a motel.

Pulling around the back, so as to not draw attention to the Lambo itself, I head for the reception while Candy branches off. A flickering vending machine has caught her attention. Giving a fake name and a wad of cash in return for a night's stay, I struggle to take my eyes off the girl that's got me hornier than a dog in heat.

Dropping to her knees, she wastes no time in shoving her arm inside. Her ass tilts up in the air as she tries to pry some goodies from the metal prongs. Wishing her good luck with that, I head for the matching door number to the key held in my hand. I can always set up without her.

Making it two steps inside the door, my burner phone begins to vibrate in my pocket. I frown, dropping our overnight bag on the plastic dining table and fishing it out. No one except the attorney has this number, and I seriously doubt he's working this late at night.

"Jasper? Is that you?" A frantic voice sounds as I answer and press the device to my ear. It takes me a moment to recognize it, especially through the layer of desperation I never expected to hear.

"Malik?" I ask, pretty sure my mind is playing tricks on me.

"Oh, thank fuck," he heaves out a breath that causes the line to crackle. "Tell me Candy is with you? That you're keeping a close eye on her?" I scoff, moving towards a musty-looking double bed.

"Caging her was your downfall Malik, not mine. Worked in my favor though." I smirk to myself. After the day I've had, a bit of mockery and a long bath is exactly what I need.

"None of that matters now. I need to you listen to me-"

"Personally, I think my days of listening to you are well and truly over. The last time you called me, I obeyed like a good little pup, and within the hour, you were blaming me for attacking Candy. I won't be so naive again." My voice is harsh, hardened by the truth of the betrayal I've barely thought about in a week.

"Jasper, wait! It's Jack, he's-" I end the call before any more of his lies can filter into my ears. I wondered how long it'd take Ace to track down our burner phones. How long Malik would last before his jealously tore him apart enough to beg me for her back. The door opens before I've had the chance to pocket my phone or wipe the satisfied smile from my face.

"Heard you talking. Who was on the phone?" Candy asks, setting down the many packets and soda cans clutched in her arms.

"Oh, no one," I dodge, drawing her into my arms. After the

evening we've just had, now's not the time to bring Malik and his latest ploy to take back what's mine – whether she'll admit it or not. "Just a wrong number," I grin.

"Okay," Candy smiles back, placing a quick kiss on my cheek. Pulling away from me, she swings her hips side to side, moving towards the boxy TV sitting on a wonky dresser. Lifting the remote and assessing its weight in her hand, she then rears back and smashes the blunt control into the screen.

"What the fuck?!" I gasp, rushing to catch the TV as she does it again, dislodging it from its already precarious position on the edge of the dresser. It's pointless as the shattered screen hits the floor, and Candy slams her boot into whatever remains. "Will you stop that?! I thought we were done playing bipolar bitchtits for today."

"This? Oh, it's nothing," Candy says nonchalantly. "Just a lie, since that's what we apparently do now." I stand back as she wanders into the bathroom, and a moment later, the sound of the mirror shattering fills the motel room. Pinching the bridge of my nose, I exhale before going after her.

"Okay, okay! I get it." Grabbing Candy's blooded fist as she raises it again, I yank her back against my body and trap her there with my forearm. "I'm sorry," I mutter in Candy's ear. In the mirror's shattered border, I notice the sheer rage burning from Candy's eyes before I recognize the tightness of her posture. She's not just annoyed; she's pissed as hell. "It was Malik on the phone. Obviously, he's looking for you, but I thought you'd react like this so-" Candy's head flies back so fast, I'm blinded by the searing pain that explodes through my nose.

"You're lying again!" Elbowing my ribs, she twists out of my grip and shoves at my chest. I topple into the bathtub, landing hard on my ass with my legs up by my head. "You didn't want to tell me because you were scared I'd run back to him. At least be man enough to admit it," she cries. Cradling my nose, I squeeze my eyes shut in an effort to get my pain under control. Candy's shadow hovers over me, the shattered rasp of her voice echoing around my head.

"You're the one person I could depend on never to lie to me, so don't start now." Opening my mouth to respond, a jet of icy cold water shoots from the overhead shower. My clothes instantly cling to my body, coating me in a frosted blanket until I drag myself over the lip of the tub. The front door slams closed, leaving me alone with the thundering water hitting the base of the tub. Fuck my fucking life. I pull myself up into a sitting position, ready to put an end to today at last. Fuck knows I'll need a decent sleep for whatever Candy decides to bring on next. It's lucky I like crazy, and it's even more fortunate I'm madly in love with her.

CANDY

Flying down the middle of the road, a long line of vehicles blare their horns behind me. I flip them off, pushing my foot along the tarmac beside the stolen skateboard. When headlights shift, signaling an overtaking, I serve the board side to side, taking up this whole side of the road. Angus and Hamish are clinging onto each of my legs, chuckling until they spot a sign on the left up ahead. '*Marley's gentleman's club.*'

"What do you think boys?" I ask my gummy sidekicks. They nod quickly in the headlights, their tongues hanging out like a pair of dogs. At their request, I jump off the board with a small run, so as not to fall on my ass, saluting the trusty plank of wood goodbye in the hopes it finds its way back to the kid I stole it from. As soon as my feet hit the smooth concrete before a pair of tall iron gates, the tightness in my lungs finally eases. Time to get back to my roots and cause some havoc.

It doesn't take long or too much effort to hoist myself over the gates, pausing to blow a kiss at the surveillance camera. Landing heavily in my sturdy biker boots, I straighten and dust down my PVC trousers and lacey see-through corset. A black bra underneath hides the goods, but otherwise, my tattooed chest is on full display, the way I like it. Who said you can't break and enter without looking gorgeous? Someone ugly, that's who.

On top of a tilted driveway, a manor house sits beneath an open, starry sky. Lights project over the entrance, casting a glimpse at the expensive cars parking in a line leading around the back. As I stride closer, delicate vines become visible, carefully stretching up matching trellis panels on either side of the main doors. Rumbling laughter catches my attention as I drag myself up one of the panels destroying dozens of potential rose buds on the way. Crawling over the roof tiles, I slip inside the first unlocked window I find and then exit the lavish bedroom in search of some fun.

I find it in the form of tipsy men all crowded into a games room. Books line every wall, gathering dust on rich walnut shelves. A cocktail bar is being manned by hired help, two smartly dressed young men who eye me suspiciously as I enter the room. I wink, keeping my back straight, and smile in place all the way to the hordes huddled around either a poker or a snooker table. Weighing out my options and maybe avoiding the area that reminds me more of the Monarchs, I opt for the snooker table.

"My turn," I state, pushing through the onlookers and ignoring their grumbles about a queue system. The man bent over the table doesn't seem annoyed by my announcement, however. Surprisingly younger and in shape compared to the older men suited and booted around us, his face lights up at the sight of my cleavage. Funny that. A flop of dark hair sweeps over his brow like a boyband wannabe, his cheeky grin showing he's good looking, and he knows it. Straightening, he lifts the plastic triangle from his carefully placed balls.

"Excuse me ma'am," a security guard interrupts. "This is a closed event."

"I know. I'm your entertainment for tonight. Or maybe, you're mine," I bob my eyebrow at the wannabe. Smirking, he waves the security guard away and chucks me a cue.

"Think you can handle breaking?" He asks, gesturing to the

balls. I scoff, sharing an indulging look with Angus, who has jumped onto the edge of the felt table.

"You could break off his dick and use it to make him a new asshole," Angus drawls. Nodding, I take position at the end of the table, making a show of chalking the tip of the cue and blowing away the excess. Bending over the table with my PVC ass tilted in the air, I line up my shot when a crash sounds over by the cocktail bar. The cue goes wide, ripping a hole in the tabletop, and I scowl over my shoulder.

"Who the fuck is making more racket than me?" I ask no one in particular. A girl around my height with gangly legs flies into view through the turned heads, vaulting over the bar and landing heavily in a pair of stunning black and gold studded ankle boots. Holy. Sole. Sister.

A pinstripe jumpsuit clings to her slender body, stretchy enough for her to parkour across the room and look damn good while doing it. A thick band of black leather is strapped around her neck with a steel ring hanging at the base of her throat, and further up is where it really gets interesting. Vibrant purple hair creates a mane around her face, which is artfully painted like a sexy clown. Pink lips with a thin, black line continuing the smile up to her cheeks, a painted button nose, and streaks of pink and black striped over her eyes. Those eyes flick my way, stealing the air from my lungs. One iris is icy blue, the other fluorescent pink.

Another crash sounds from behind the adjoining door before two hooded figures barrel into the stunned room. She doesn't waver though, nodding at me before hopping up onto a windowsill and disappearing from sight. No way is she going to leave me standing here like that. When adventure comes calling, I'm the first to answer.

Dropping my cue, I'm automatically drawn towards the assholes taking chase. One of the black hoodies rushes forward, and I promptly stick out my foot to trip him into the poker table. The other grabs me from behind, tossing me aside. The floor meets me halfway, slamming my elbow into my ribs and jarring both in pain. Extending my good hand out to push up from the plush carpet, my fingers curl around the pool cue, and a smile graces my face. Game on.

In one fluid motion, I'm on my feet and the hefty stick in my hand is connecting with the black hoodie's back. It snaps on impact, giving me a much sharper weapon to brandish in his face as he spins on me. Yet it's not a face I find there, but a mask. Electric blue crosses for eyes, and a built-in smile catches me off guard, giving the creep and his friend time to disarm my jagged cue and dig a gun into my sternum.

"For everything that's holy, pull that trigger and give me something to really climax about," I dare him. The black hood hesitates, tilting his head towards his friend long enough for me to twist the pistol from his hand and snap his wrist all at once. Silly fucker should have known just by my appearance; being threatened with a gun is a regular occurrence in my calendar. His bellowing scream is drowned out by me emptying his gun into the ceiling. As much as I wish it were his chest that was riddled with a tea strainer right now, a little voice in the back of my head tells me Jasper would not be all that impressed. Damn Jasper and his effect on my actions, even when I'm mad at him. Especially when I'm mad at him.

The other hood tries to grab for me until I slam the butt of the gun into his mask, cracking it enough for the LED lights to splutter out. Then, I run. The entirety of stuck-up fuckers hoping for a simple night of snobbery are now quivering against the bookcases, giving me a clear path to the open window and beyond. One of the red Tesla's I noted earlier flies across the tarmac driveaway with an uneasy swerve, a familiar purple-haired girl clutching at the wheel.

"Hey! Wait for me!" I yell over the hollering from the window behind me, running across the tiled terrace. Her head whips my way, noting the two hoodie men stumbling out onto the rooftop. I don't wait for her invitation, noting she's slowed enough for me to use a marble column like a fireman's pole and drop onto the ground. Then, I propel myself through the open passenger window.

Her manic laughter fills the cab along with the screech of tires shooting us toward the iron gates. They open helpfully, probably to save the wreckage we were about to cause and allow us to fly onto the main road. Somehow, I managed to get my head over my ass and plant myself in the seat with a relieved chuckle.

"Didn't expect to have company today," she quips. I spare a glance her way, noting the awesome color of her eyes again. They must be contacts, and I know what I'll be using Jasper's Prime account for when I eventually return to his sorry ass.

"I'm in need of some excitement, and you've got that written all over you," I reply. The girl's brows tighten briefly, and she looks over her arms and chest in confusion. "Never mind," I brush off, preferring to hang out of the window. All that driving in the open-top Tesla has ruined me for having a roof prevent the wind from sweeping through my hair. My impromptu chauffer keeps the speed at almost 100 mph while the road is straight, veering around cars with jerky movements. As soon as an intersection appears up ahead, she slams on the brakes, and I have to stop myself from going through the windscreen.

"Lassy needs some lessons," Hamish states from the back in-between grunting. I look over to find him balls-deep in Angus again and I yell in disgust. What is it with those two and the motion of an engine? They're almost as easily turned on as me. Deserting the Tesla with me still inside, the pink version of Beetlejuice hops out of the cab, making a beeline for a darkened alley nearby. I rush to catch up, taking long strides to remain by her side.

"So," I start, adding a skip to my step just for fun. I'm wild like that sometimes. "We've got some time to kill before those masked baboons catch up with us. How about I show you how to break their necks with a plastic spoon?"

"Seems counterproductive," she mutters, leaping over a gate. "There'd be no one to chase me if they're dead."

"Ahh, you're one of those," I nod. Her curious gaze slides my way, and I wave off her concern. "The chase is all the fun. Once it's over, you have to live with the consequences." Angus grumbles something about my own consequences awaiting my return, but a nearby bar tunes him out. I stop to curtsey at the bouncers before catching up to the roaming wanderer. She has no clue where she's going but the determination in her painted features is commendable.

"Well, what do they call you?" I try instead, curious as to who this fluorescent imp is and where she came from.

"Kelsii, with two i's." We slink from an adjacent alley, strolling up the sidewalk and forcing others to duck out of our way.

"I'm Candy, with four limbs and a magical pussy," I outstretch my hand. Kelsii sprays it with a burst of laughter and gives me an awkward sideways high-five. Up ahead, a pizza delivery guy is loading up his bike with four steaming boxes. The smell drifts to me, causing my stomach to grumble on cue. Tapping his pockets, he darts back inside for whatever he's forgotten, and I relieve him of the hassle of delivering one of said pizzas.

Kelsii watches me closely, her arms relaxing by her side as she mimics my stance. Theft can't be a new concept to her, considering she seems to be on the run, but I'm well aware others aren't as capable of taking what they want and not give a shit about the consequences. Spotting a park nearby, I guide her towards it in search of a bench where we can pop the box and enjoy our impromptu meal in the moonlight. This is what I love. Living for the moment, never knowing where it's going to take me or who I'm going to be with.

"Does it top knowing you're going to wake up next to those who adore you and hang off your every word, though?" Angus asks. I hunt for him, spotting his jelly butt sitting on the back of a duck in a nearby pond. I scowl, mentally berating him to pick a damn side and stick to it. A skid sounds from the road closest to the open gates, a burnt orange truck stopping beneath a street lamp.

"Here we go again," Kelsii says with a hint of delight, her legs already braced to run.

"Cool it Kels, that's not your entourage; it's mine," I roll my eyes. From the driving seat of the truck I know too well, Ace jumps out, his hands held high in defense.

"I'm not here to toss you over my shoulder and spank you all the way home," he says, slowly approaching. He spares Kelsii no mind, probably because we're sitting mostly in the dark, masking her interesting appearance.

"Shame," I pout, stuffing the last slice of pizza into my mouth and tossing the box aside.

"I merely came to ask if you'd accompany me to the hospital," Ace wisely stops a little distance away. His hair is a mess of cowlicks from where he's ruffled his hands through it, while a crumpled baggy tracksuit hangs from his muscled frame.

"Fuck's sake," I roll my eyes, standing and stretching on a yawn. "What's Spade done now?"

"Not Spade, it's Jack." And with those four words, my feet are moving without my consent, leaving my new friend to her own devices.

MALIK

Numb. That's all that's left. Once the anger subsided, and the misery had also deserted me, only the numbness remained. What I thought would be a single night of hunting soon turned into days filled with self-loathing and from there, time was lost to me. I'm not alone in my turmoil, nor will I be left alone by those forcing me to remain hopeful. True to their word, the Monarchs have proved their loyalty. Yet now, it all seems pointless without her to complete us.

Sliding my hand into my jacket, I withdraw the hip flask stashed in the hidden pocket and pop the cap. Downing a shot of whiskey, I shove the flask out of sight before a nurse walks into the private room. Her suspicion at my jerky movements is quickly replaced by the routine she's been following every day since we arrived here. Noting the stats from a bleeping machine, scribbling down notes, checking vitals. All the while, the man I consider a brother lies limp in the bed.

Jack's blond hair appears darker against the stark white cushion, his muscles becoming leaner. My gaze flickers over his face and away again, preferring the view of the shiny lino at my feet. I've resigned myself to sitting in the armchair by the door since I can't leave, nor can I see Jack in such a pitiful state for too long. Still, as the nurse makes a pleased sound in the back of her throat, I find myself perking up to see what's caught her attention. Her withered hands have rolled back the blanket and are inspecting the healed gash on his sternum. It's puckered and pink but healed nicely in a simple line among the bruising.

The stab wound Tanya inflicted was deep but easier to manage than the coma Jack slipped into when his head connected with the concrete. Luckily, nothing else was broken when the taxi backed into him, but enough damage was caused to be touch and go for a few days. I could have murdered that bitch a thousand times by now if it hadn't been for Ace and Spade talking me down. Once Jack is better, it's his right to seek revenge. All he needs to do now is wake the fuck up. Although, I have my own suspicions at this point that it's not the coma that is keeping Jack down but his own desire to check out. I can't blame him for thinking it just doesn't seem worth waking up.

A figure fidgets across the room, peering out of the blinds for the thousandth time. Spade stands tall, his shoulders taut and jaw tight. Like the rest of us, he's not bothered to upkeep his appearance. The dreads hang loosely from the top of his head, the curled growth at the sides and back starting to blend in. The jeans encasing his legs haven't been changed in a few days, and neither have the special edition sneakers that tap impatiently. His agitation reminds me of why I started drinking at the early hour of 9 am.

With that thought in mind, I finish off the rest of my hip flask, uncaring if the nurse sees me or not. She tsks and places Jack's notes back in the holder before leaving the room, and we three Monarchs to our melancholy silence. Not that Jack's been particularly chatty lately. In the end, the repetitive bleeping of the heart monitor gets too much, and I crack.

"I don't understand what's taking so long. Ace left two days ago. If it were me, I'd have dragged her by-"

"But it's not you," Spade cuts me off without looking my way. "We agreed as a group it would be better if you stayed here." His dismissive tone rubs me the wrong way, even if I know he's right. I'm in no state to be around anyone, least of all Candy. One wrong word, and she'd have been lost to us forever. Pushing to my feet, the whiskey hits me all at once, and a hard sway knocks me back into the armchair. Spade only looks around when the wooden feet scrape against the floor and upon seeing my head loll to the side, he turns his back on me again.

"She could have been it, you know," I mumble to myself. Seems my brain is bored of keeping the self-destructive thoughts on the inside. An orderly wheels a cart past the open door, pausing to hand me a breakfast tray. I spot the nurse over his shoulder, giving me a pointed look to get some substance in my stomach other than alcohol. Lifting the satsuma, I feel its weight in my palm before squeezing tightly.

"The one who could have changed everything. Too bad the only way I know how to love is to suffocate." Juices pour down the length of my arm, disappearing beneath my suit jacket and shirt cuffs. Doesn't matter; I can't remember the last time I showered or changed. In fact, the citrus freshness is a welcome change.

"It's too late for regrets now," Spade says from the window. "She's here." My heart lifts and seizes all at once as I shoot upright, slamming the breakfast tray down on a nearby table. Crossing the room on dead legs, I spot Candy's neon pink hair just as she disappears into the entrance two levels below. My eyes catch Spade's blue ones when his hands grab my biceps and start to shove me aside.

"What the fuck?!" I yell, fighting lazily as my vision swims. He backs me into the en-suite bathroom and switches on the light. "Spade, I need to see her," I warn in a low growl. He briefly turns to pick up a black duffle bag and throws it at me.

"Mmhmm, and she doesn't need to smell you before she's even entered the room. Shower and change, then I'll let you out." The door is slammed closed and locked from the outside as I try to barge my way through it. Catching sight of myself in a mirror, I grimace at the state of my reflection. Sunken dark eyes stare back at the greasy mess of brown hair and crumpled suit I didn't realize was so stained. Spade's right; I need to sort myself out.

Switching on the shower, the temperature struggles to rise much above freezing, but I take it. Stripping, I make quick work of pumping a shampoo and shower gel combo that's clearly going to bring out a rash from the wall dispenser. I scrub my body and scrape my scalp hard enough to leave my skin reddened before wrapping myself in an itchy towel.

All that's in the bag are t-shirts and gray sweatpants, two pairs of sneakers, and a small wash bag. At least Spade thought to pack us all a toothbrush in his one-armed haste before we left for the hospital. Only Ace has returned back to the Devil's Bedpost, which has remained closed without notice, to access his computer and track down our girl. Once my teeth and hair are brushed and I've dressed, I knock heavily on the door for my keeper to let me out. The pause makes me nervous that Spade never intended to release me, but then he swings open the door to a similarly empty room.

"Where is she?" I ask, pushing past him. "Did I miss her?" Spade's hand slams in the center of my chest, halting my impending panic attack. Just then, with my mouth open, ready to tell him to get fucked, Candy swans into the room with a doctor in tow. If I thought a quick shower and fresh set of clothes were enough to prepare me to see her again, I was extremely mistaken. My chest squeezes, my mouth has gone dry. Even in the baggy tracksuit that she seems to have got the memo about, her pink waves bounce with vitality and her telltale biker boots are firmly tied upon her feet. I can't find a single word to describe how good it feels to see her again.

But it wouldn't matter either way. Candy's face purposely avoids mine and Spade's, her full attention focused on Jack. Snatching up the clipboard attached to the base of his bed, she skims over his notes, pretending to understand while the doctor puts it into basic English for her. They'll continue to do tests in the hopes of bringing him out of his coma, despite the jump start they previously tried to no avail. Dismissing the doctor by tossing the notes back at him, he looks between us and Ace, who has blocked the doorway with his size, before edging his way out slowly. After allowing the doc to pass, Ace steps in to the room and reveals Jasper lingering in his shadow. Looks like the whole gang's here, I muse to myself.

"You stupid bastard," Candy mutters, dropping down on Jack's bed and taking his hand in hers. I realize Spade is still holding me back, so I shove him away, standing tall on my own. It's safe to say the whiskey has well and truly left my system, doused by the realization that this big reunion won't be as glorious as my brief dreams hoped. Tension thickens the air between us, every eye fixed on Candy and trying to preempt her next move. Will she blame us for Jack's predicament? Will she listen to the whole story or jump straight to ripping Tanya's head from her neck? I wouldn't stop her. Hell, I'd help her. Fuck waiting for Jack to get his own back; that bitch needs to stop breathing. Now.

"Who did this?" Jasper speaks for the first time. Ace leans down to mutter in his ear, not that I'm sure the words are registered before he shuffles forward on heavy feet. His green eyes are haunted, framed by the scar lining his cheek. A defense streak slices through me, wanting to protect Jack from all harm, but I don't truly believe Jasper would hurt him.

Still, the divide between *them* and us makes me uneasy and my fists curl just in case. Jasper stops just short of Candy's side, his hand reaching out to touch her shoulder. She snaps around at the contact, glaring daggers and huffing a warning breath through her nose. Releasing Jack's hand, Candy then stands, head held high, and walks straight out the room. The fuck she is.

I follow, dodging both sets of hands and ignoring the calls that try to stop me. Candy doesn't get to swan in, refusing to look at any of the men who laid down their lives for her and leave. The man in me finds her boldness sexy, but the monster in me has awoken. Candy is quick, using the length of her long legs to her advantage but she can't escape me. Not twice anyway. I stalk her all the way to the nurse's station, where she whistles for the older nurse that made sure I had breakfast.

"Room 2B, you have a pest control problem you might want to look at," Candy states. She reaches over the desk, grabbing a pen and notepad. "Call me when he wakes up." Instantly committing that number to memory, I lean my forearm on the counter, blocking the way to the exit and forcing her to look at me. Of course, she doesn't. Spinning away, Candy hunts for anywhere I'm not and finds herself at a dead-end with me right behind.

"Are you going to look at me?" I ask in a low voice, standing close enough to see the hairs rise on the back of her neck. Leaning past her, I'm able to hear the breath catch in her delicate throat as I twist a nearby door handle. Swinging it wide, I use my body to crowd her inside the empty hospital room.

"I'm not doing this," Candy snarls, twisting sharply in an effort to leave before I slam the door closed.

"Doing what?" I respond just as sharply, pushing at her shoulders. Again and again, I shove at Candy with all the pent-up frustrations I've been holding onto for her. If she'd just stayed in her room, let me handle Tanya when I had the chance, none of this would have happened. Or if it had, she'd have been here under my protection.

"I'm not playing this game anymore. You had your chance, you fucked up." For the briefest moment, glinting in the stream of light piercing the paper-thin blind, a spark of vulnerability captures Candy's face. I still, a lump lodging in my throat, refusing to let another breath pass. Perhaps I misread the situation, believing Candy's ignorance was just that and not because she was so deeply hurt by our actions. Maybe I could-

Her fist lands in my gut, catching me off guard. As does her swift elbow to my jaw as she tries to duck under my arms and escape. Yeah, fuck everything I just thought. Candy is a stubborn ass who deserves everything I'm about to throw at her. Catching her around the waist, I drag Candy back through sheer determination, tossing her onto the hospital bed.

"There's so much you don't know," I grit out, struggling to pin down her arms and legs at the same time. Luckily, the sweatpants Spade provided me do a much better job than one of my fine suits, and in no time, I'm sprawled out, locking each of her limbs down with mine.

"And I don't want to know it! I gave you more than I've ever given anyone. I trusted you, but thanks for the reminder of why that's a really fucking stupid thing to do." Candy's hand wriggles free, and she lands a slap across my face before I can catch it. Once re-pinned and forced to lie flat beneath me, Candy does the one thing I couldn't have predicted. She scrunches her eyes shut and holds her breath with puffed-out cheeks.

"Look at me," I growl, giving her a rough shake. When that doesn't work, I rack my brain for the best way to approach this. To get through to her. "Candy. Please look at me," I whisper, lowering my forehead onto hers. Growling low in the back of her throat, Candy finally opens those chocolate browns, and something inside me melts. I hate myself for it, but I also can't deny all I need is her. Right now.

Slamming my mouth onto hers, the same sparks fly as the first time we kissed. Nothing has changed, even though my passion is laced with a bitterness I need to expel. Forcing Candy into the hard mattress, my grip on her wrists turning bruising. I can't get close enough. My dick grinds against her core, my chest pushing down too hard, yet I can't put any distance between us. From her soft lips with a raspberry hint, her smooth curves hidden beneath the baggy clothes and yearning to be marked. And then there's the sassy attitude that waltzed in here, trying to make out I'm the one who hurt her. I'd have died to protect her if only she'd asked, but no. She ran away. A hunger lying dormant inside roars to life, burning through me with the force of a tornado. I need her. I have to have her.

Releasing her wrists, I grip Candy's head and tug at her hair. Whatever it takes to get the response of her breasts and hips rolling against me deliciously. She smells just the same, like gum and danger, and fuck if it doesn't make me instantly hard. Grabbing her jaw, I pull her mouth open to delve my tongue inside and run the risk of her biting it clean off. She thinks about it, the scrape of her teeth lining my tongue but doesn't. In fact, her whole body goes limp, and that's when the warning siren blares in my head.

The door opens, giving enough distraction for Candy to sandwich her leg between us and jerk her knee into my balls. The adrenaline of our kiss spares me some of the agony that would have floored me, but still, I roll onto my side, cupping my throbbing nuts. Jumping out of the bed, Candy storms across the room to a panicked-looking Spade.

"You want some of this?" Candy gestures to herself. Spade slowly covers his privates with both hands.

"No, thank you," he shakes his head. Smart man, but even in her most furious state, I find it impossible to resist Candy. Glutton for punishment, some might say. Flicking her hair over her shoulder and flipping me off, Candy's voice reverberates around the hallway, calling for Jasper to say his goodbyes. I manage to raise a shaky finger at Spade, putting as much malice into my order as I can muster.

"Do not let her leave."

CANDY

A hand snaps closed around my wrist, not tight enough to hurt, but I stop anyway. Glaring at Spade, I meet his impassive stare head-on.

"Don't make me shoot you again," I threaten. A surgeon walks by, halting before looking Spade up and down and deciding he can fight his own battles. It's not just the Monarchs I'm eager to get away from right now, it's this hospital. Anyone would think I'd be at home here among the dying, but I prefer my corpses at the end of a weapon gripped in my hand. No, fucking hospitals remind me of icky things like prodding gloved fingers and rape test kits. Officers that don't listen, doctors that judge. Being a thirteen-year-old runaway with a knack for pickpocketing does not mean I'm 'asking for it.' Stupid, uptight, judgmental pricks.

"Candy babe," Angus pops up on my chest. Half of his body is still trapped beneath the neckline of Jasper's sweater, but the top half is able to give me a swift slap. "Leave the past where it belongs. You're strong and feisty, so come back to the present and give these shitheads hell." I nod, feeling that steely ballsiness I pride myself on filling my veins. Before I can snap Spade's hand clean off and fuck him with his own shattered forearm, a deep voice sounds from behind.

"We just want to talk," Ace states coldly. At odds with his tone, his muscled torso presses against my back, crowding me into Spade's front. A few weeks ago, this precarious position would have been enough cause for a three-way. Now I have a double-ended dildo I call Space (Spade + Ace = you get it). Removing my wrist from Spade's hold, I extract myself from the body heat I could become all too comfortable in.

"Talk fast then. The sunset isn't going to ride into itself." I spot Jasper lingering by Jack's doorway, still peering in as if his twin is going to jump up and shout 'Psyche!'. I put him out of his misery, grabbing the back of his hooded denim jacket, which I'm totally stealing by the way, and dragging him into an empty waiting room. Call me clingy or whatever, but Jasper has become a security blanket for me. That one constant I'm pretty sure I can depend on, although my trust is shot thanks to Malik and his cronies.

True to his nature, Jasper pulls me back against his chest, winding his arms around me for strength as the others enter the room. Malik included. Although the tremble to Jasper's arms suggests it's not me he's hoping to bolster, but himself. I wonder what the deciding factor was; seeing Jack in the hospital bed, the guilt of not being here sooner, or that after everything he's been through, he's still not standing on the Monarch's side of the divide.

"Well, get on with it Ace. Apparently, you want to talk, despite being oddly silent during the car ride over," I give him an impatient look. He grips the back of his neck and rubs it, avoiding my gaze.

"I daren't say the wrong thing and have you diving out the window halfway down the freeway," he mumbles back. Now standing straight again, Malik steps into the center of the room, commanding everyone's full attention. It isn't lost on me how Ace and Spade remain at his back, and Jasper stays at mine. When two leaders face-off, that's when you tend to see whose side their minions take. Unfortunately for Ace and Spade, they haven't chosen the winning team.

"There's no time for this pissing contest," Malik growls, back to the asshole I first met. I merely stare at him, noting his face front-on for the first time. Heavy bags hang under his bloodshot eyes, thick stubble lining his jaw that's probably considered a full-on beard by now. He seems to be studying me just as close until I yawn widely, leaning back into Jasper's hold. His scoff is music to my ears, but his next words are not. "Your safety is all that matters now. Kiss goodbye to your vacation. From now on, you'll remain with one of the Monarchs at all times. Wherever you go, we go until the threats against you have been dealt with."

A harsh laugh bubbles from my lips, which spreads into the widest smile. That was it? The big sale pitch? Malik might as well save his breath than spew that possessive shit at me. He forgets I've been reminded of what freedom feels like, so now especially, I'm not going to bow down and be his bitch. Tugging Jasper to my side with his arm left around my waist, we prepare to leave.

"What Malik means," Spade sidesteps into the doorway, "is that you were right about Cherry having an ulterior motive, but the last we saw, she was being dragged away against her will. Ultimately, Tanya is behind all the recent strikes against you. I know this is a lot to take in, but you're Leicester's daughter, and Tanya wants pretty much everything that title comes with. Now you've returned, you need to remain in sight of one of us at all times."

"She's been fine with me up to now," Jasper's chest rumbles, perking his head up. His grip tightens on my waist protectively, and I shrug him off too. You could cut the testosterone in this room with a cake knife.

"Don't listen to their lies, Jasp. They have no idea what they're talking about," I grin, knowing that'll hit them where it hurts.

"Get fucked," Ace pitches in, his angry streak flaring. "All we've done these past few weeks is look for you so we can keep you safe."

"Oh, I'm well aware of the lengths you'll go to in the name of keeping me safe. You left me locked up and bound in a dark room, remember? Lying is just your latest tactic, it would seem."

"Okay, this isn't working," Spade rubs a hand over his face. "Candy, let's go somewhere else, just the two of us. I'll take you to a shooting range if that's what it takes. You'll know I'm not lying when aiming a rifle at my chest." He rubs at his shoulder, swallowing thickly at the thought. Trust Spade to appeal to my inner-sadistic nature, but I'm afraid I'll have to pass. I have plans of my own.

"I'm only leaving this hospital with Jasper or in a wooden box. I don't care which." My chest flutters, but I push the notion down, catching Angus' eye on the row of chairs. He holds a chubby finger to his lips and I give him a tiny nod. Malik, however, isn't so good at concealing his emotions anymore. With nostrils flared, he turns his narrowed eyes on Jasper instead.

"Talk some sense to her since she seems to be loyal to you alone," he grits out. I don't try to bite back the smile that spreads over my face at the hurt in his expression. Poor Malli-Moo isn't used to being fucked over; he just shits on the world and expects us to lick his ass in hopes of another taste. The giddy feeling at his pain flees when Jasper follows Malik's instruction, pulling me aside for an intervention.

"Don't you dare," I warn him. There's a purity in his green eyes, so open and honest that he's hard to look at. Jasper really cares for me, and I don't deserve it.

"I only want what's best for you," he breathes, and I grunt.

"Then get the fuck out of my face."

"I'm on your side. I made a promise to listen to you, and trust your instincts. So tell me why you think they're lying. I'm listening." I stutter at having his full attention, feeling uncomfortable in my own skin. Jasper reaches out to take my hands, deepening the threat of betrayal seeping through my body. Taking a steady breath, I relish Jasper's touch while I still can.

"Well, for starters," I say loud enough for the others to hear, "Tanya isn't capable of wiping her own ass, and secondly, they said they haven't seen Cherry since the night I left. Seems a little strange to me that she happens to be in Jack's room." I point through the pane of glass separating the waiting room from the hallway and towards the window cutout in Jack's closed door. All four men rush to crowd my personal space, trying to get the same vantage point I've had this entire time. Flame red hair leans over Jack's still body, a bunch of chrysanthemums in a dainty hand. A moment of panic fills the waiting room before they suddenly scatter, bursting into the hallway. Jasper is with them, leaving me utterly alone.

"So much for staying with a Monarch at all times," I smirk to Angus and Hamish on the plastic seats. They share my evil grin, hopping down to waddle by my ankles. While the guys are distracted by trying to force the locked door open, I slip into the hallway and exit the ward. Hitting the back stairwell, I throw myself over the metal railings until landing on the concrete level at the bottom.

Ducking into the shadows beneath the stairwell, I quickly wriggle out of these sweatpants, peel off the sweater and remove the black beanie hidden in the lining. Taking an extra second to make sure my hair is covered, I smooth down the long-sleeve black top before pushing free from the fire exit. My boots hit the paving slabs guiding the way back to the parking lot, which I make a run for in skinny jeans. A taxi cab skids to a halt by the pavement as I approach, the passenger door popping open for me.

"Ew," I comment as I throw myself into the leather seat and slam the door closed. "Tell me this isn't the cab that ran Jack over."

"My resources were limited," Cherry mumbles from the driver's seat, throwing the cab into gear. We speed from the parking lot, leaving the hospital as merely a reducing image in the rear-view mirror. Blowing out a harsh breath, I send a silent apology to the Monarchs. Keeping up the pretense of hating them, especially when their hands were on me, took an Oscar-winning performance. But ultimately, just like they said, I need to keep myself safe. This is why affection doesn't work; someone always gets hurt.

"I hope you're right about this," Cherry remarks. I snort, telling her I'm right about everything, despite the uncomfortable tug in my gut. I've had to harbor this scheme ever since spotting Cherry hiding out by the restrooms in that sleazy bar and creating the riot that would give us a few precious moments to converse. At first, I was going to add her to the body count, but then she told me everything. The truth, for once.

"Who knew Tanya's old wig collection would prove to be so useful? I do hope they don't go too hard on the decoy," I chuckle. Cherry's brown eyes catch mine with a strange sympathetic look, and I realize what I just said. "There's cameras and panic buttons all over that hospital. They can at least drag her outside before breaking her neck and remember to scatter her body parts across multiple states." The look of horror crossing Cherry's face is much better.

Pulling onto the freeway, Cherry follows the signs for the airport. I pop the glove compartment, flicking through the fake passports and tickets she's procured. A banged-up suitcase packed for us both is laid across the back seat, which Angus and Hamish have decided to park their jelly butts on. If it keeps them off the upholstery, I'm fine with that. Cherry used the motel key I dropped for her while shoving my tongue in Jasper's mouth by the Lambo, giving her access to my clothes and the stash of cash beneath the motel bed. I have to say I'm impressed by Cherry's resourcefulness, yet with each passing mile, the finality of our decision hits home. This isn't some girly retreat; we won't be coming back. The further the distance, the more my chest aches like someone has taken a sledgehammer to it.

Yet, at the time, this seemed like the best option. The Monarchs can go back to their life prior to me hijacking it. Tanya is my problem. I need time and space to think rationally, and catch her out without my feelings playing havoc with my thoughts. My only regret is deceiving Jasper. Not to mention beating the shit out of him for lying, when I was doing the exact same thing but I had to make it convincing. At least I had the decency to let Ace 'catch' me by leaving my burner phone on and insisted he picked up Jasper on the way over. He's a Monarch through and through, it's only right they're all together. I'm growing soft in my old age.

"You're thirty," Angus drawls. I pointedly ignore him, already knowing I'm over halfway through my existence. Leading Cherry around by leaving a trail of breadcrumbs, aka gum wrappers with instructions scribbled inside, was a stroke of genius I'm putting down to aged wisdom, and Angus isn't going to take that away from me. Congestion up ahead forces us to slow and Cherry to wind through the traffic in an effort to keep going.

"Last chance to back out," I warn as Cherry indicates for the airport. A huge plane veers over the top of the taxi, temporarily stealing the daylight. She doesn't reply but takes the turn, so I have my answer. Leaving a life behind isn't a natural specialty to others like it is for me, yet even I can admit this time feels different. Heavier, unclear.

"What about Zak?" Cherry's voice wobbles as she pulls into a waiting bay for cabs and switches off the engine. Twisting in my seat, I meet my old nemesis face-on. Until recently, the hate burning in my veins for Cherry could have powered a small oil factory, but all of that washed away when I realized she's as much a victim of Tanya's jealously as me. At least she says she is; I'll still hold all the cards before we start braiding each other's hair.

"A certain Chief of Police I like to call Captain Knobstick, who has a particular taste for his secretary, owed me a favor. Your son and sister have been placed in a safe house. It may not seem like it yet, but you did the right thing coming to me. I may be slightly unhinged, but threatening kids is where I draw the line." Moving to get out of the cab, a soft hand touches my arm.

"Thank you," Cherry breathes. "For believing me. And forgiving me." I give a sharp nod, wanting to remove myself from the smushy situation asap.

"Tanya's downfall is that she can't predict me, but she does have the advantage of connections. While I took Big Cheese's lectures for granted, she was listening. Watching. Learning. As long as I have an entourage, I'm too visible. It's time to catch this bitch in the web of her own doing."

Taking our case from the back, Angus and Hamish hitch a ride as we abandon the cab and any hopes of redemption. There's no turning back after this, and I wouldn't want to anyway. Call me selfish, call me spineless. I'm saving myself and the ones I… tolerate. That's all that matters.

SPADE

"We should have done this fucking weeks ago!" Malik bellows, leveling his fist into one of the wood panels on his wall. I leave him to his tantrum, remaining in the doorway of his suite to ensure the safety of the nurse. Her eyes flick my way, regretting the choice to volunteer as our health care professional, but I reassure her everything's fine.

She checks over the equipment wired up to Jack before tightly tucking the cover into the sides of his body. The decision to move Jack here came right after Candy's disappearing act and Malik snapped. Maybe snapped is putting it lightly. We've officially been banned from Milligan hospital, and Jack's care had to be provided elsewhere. Since he's not going to wake up anytime soon, coming home seemed like the best option at the time.

"I will return every day to check on him. Call me if there are any developments," the nurse tells me as I escort her out. Softly closing Malik's penthouse door, a crash immediately connects with the other side, and the nurse screams.

"Don't worry, he won't do anything to Jack," I tell her. "Once he's calmed down, it'll be a good focus to remain at Jack's side while we handle…everything else." A sigh reverberates from the base of my chest, but I manage to keep it together until I see her safety out the front door. Locking it back in place, I press my forehead against the brass frame. I saw the hospital surveillance just like everyone else, watching her master plan unfold, yet I'm still perplexed. Oh Candy, what the fuck have you done now?

"Sounds like it's going well," Ace comments dryly behind me. From the stool where he's taken residence, his back is hunched over the bar, and fingers curled around a beer. I curse, no longer wondering why we're all so fucked up if alcohol is always our go-to when emotions hurt that bit too much. Crossing the room I never thought I'd see deserted, I round the bar and pluck the drink from his hand. What hasn't been covered in white sheets is coated in a thin layer of dust, meaning one of us will have to stand and wash every glass we own. Dibs not me, no backsies.

"Maybe instead of looking for her in the bottom of that bottle, you hippity hop up to your computer and find our girl."

"She was never ours." Ace swipes the bottle back and downs the rest. "We were her play things. She set up a whole plan to escape us; I say this time we let her go."

"Speak for yourself," Jasper replies, walking through the connecting door to the bar. With nowhere else to go, he hitched a ride back with us, and rightly so. He should never have left in the first place. I don't know at what point being a Monarch meant throwing shit at a ceiling fan and taking the hit of whatever came flying back. Dropping onto a stool next to Ace's, Jasper leans on his elbows and puffs his cheeks out the way he does when he's thinking. "I've spent every single day by her side, trying to be worthy of being there just to be ditched as well. I deserve answers."

"Oh yeah?" Ace chuckles. "Since you know her so well, please enlighten us. Where would she have gone?" Jasper looks away with a small shake of his head. I'd call it quits there but apparently, Ace is done remaining quiet. Weeks of walking on eggshells around Malik will do that to a person. "No? You're telling me you didn't microchip that bitch the second you stole her." Jasper flies off the stool, planting his fist into Ace's temple.

"Don't be mad because you fucked up your chance!" He topples Ace onto the floor with a loud crash, swinging punches into his gut. Ace fights back with the same vigor, his added bulk giving him the upper hand on Jasper. I let the two scrap while reaching for a jug. Placing it in the basin, I switch on the cold water and peer over to see if either has knocked out the other yet. Apparently not if Jasper's split lip is anything to go by.

"That's enough, both of you," I shout, tossing the bucket over the bar to douse their irritation. Joint screams fill the air from their impromptu shower before Jasper dives aside in time for the tin to bounce off Ace's forehead. An instant red mark appears, but I'm not sorry. "Malik is already losing his last shred of fucking sanity up there. We need to remain united." As I hoped, the pair help each other up and settle it with a fist pump. Airheads. Ace even picks up and dusts off Jasper's stool with his wet hand.

"How's he doing up there?" Jasper asks. A question I'd been dreading.

"Crushed," I confess, leaning on my forearms. Losing Candy the first time sent Malik spiraling inward. If it weren't for me, Ace, and the thought of what Jack would say when he wakes up, Malik would have forgotten to eat. Not to mention his personal hygiene. But this time, I just don't know how it's going to go. "He's absolutely crushed."

"And unpredictable," Ace chimes in unhelpfully. "Let's hope he doesn't flay Jack and wear his skin to drink tea and sing Spice Girls songs."

"What the fuck is wrong with you?" I say at the same time, Jasper groans, "I hate everything you just said." The three of us pause, staring at each other, and for some unexplainable reason, all burst into laughter. Not because anything is humorous, but at the sheer unfunniness of what's become of us. Bickering and fighting in the closed-down bar, Jack having an extended nap, Malik's lost his fucking mind and we've just lost Candy for the second time. I can't pick which disaster to start with and strangely long for a quiet day of playing poker with my once-best friends. No drama. Just a hand of cards, a cold drink, and the knowledge that wherever Candy is, she's happy. That's the best we can hope for at this stage.

Ace comes back down to earth first, finishing his drink and tossing the glass into the trash can beside me. I try to catch it mid-air, yelling at him that it's not the recycling but fumble. The glass shatters on impact with the inside of the can and I sigh. That's not a battle I'll be conquering today. That's it; I'm getting the playing cards. Popping into the back room and returning, I don't ask if the boys would like to play or not, dealing them each a hand. They follow my lead, placing down pairs for our game of goldfish to begin.

"One thing I can't figure out," I say after stealing all of Jasper's fours.

"Just one?" Ace chuckles, and I nudge the arm he's resting on. Off guard and slightly tipsy, his head falls and he just manages to stop himself from face planting the bar. I pay him no mind, directing my question at Jasper.

"What did we do that was so bad? I know we acted rashly, we probably shouldn't have locked her in her room, but we were trying to keep her safe. The way she looked straight through me at the hospital," I look away, deciding maybe a beer is the way to go. "She really hates us." Popping the cap, I hand one to Jasper and another to Ace before having one myself. The deep sigh Jasper releases as he places down his cards says it all.

"In our terms, it may not seem like a big deal. But to Candy...," Jasper pauses, looking for the right words. "You've triggered some long-term repressed memories she's been running from all this time." He takes a long swig, our game forgotten as I move around to drag a stool next to both of the men. Even Ace spins to hang in Jasper's rare insight.

"I don't think she knows how much she says during her nightmares, but it was bad. Bloodcurdling screams bad. It would make you want to take a screwdriver to your own ears just to avoid hearing it bad. Whatever you guys did, it took her back to another time where she was bound and trapped."

"Shit," I curse. Although, deep down, I had already come to pretty much the same conclusion. We can try to downplay our roles that night, and paint ourselves as the saviors. We can pretend not to see the cracks in her facade and move on, taking everything in her stride and leaving no fucks behind for the rest of us.

But from Candy's point of view, we left her out, plain and simple. Once again, there was an issue, and instead of acquiring her help, we shoved her aside. I know without a doubt if she'd have been there, Jack wouldn't have gotten hurt. If she'd been there, I'd still have my girl.

CANDY

The wheels touch the tarmac, thrusting us forward in our economy seats and allowing Cherry to finally release my damn hand. For someone who mapped out this plan, I'd have thought she'd make a point to avoid flying if she's so damn terrified of it. We may have fucked the same guy, making us some sort of screw sisters, I suppose, but this is another level of intimacy.

Shaking out my sweaty palm, I peer down the walkway to see if the dude a few rows in front with the most incredible afro has woken up yet. He has, but not enough to notice the array of pretzels I enjoyed frisbeeing into his hair. It wasn't entirely my fault; Angus wanted to play truth or dare. It's the girl with a buzz cut who should really be worried.

We roll to a stop in the airport bay and I've had enough. Jumping up before the seatbelt sign switches off, not that mine was ever on, I pull Cherry after me to be first at the doors upon opening. Angus and Hamish manage to wriggle out the hatch before me though, running along the corridors like a pair of raving dickheads, waving their arms in the air and screaming in a high enough pitch to make me wince.

My biker boots eat up the hundreds of twists and turns on the way to baggage reclaim, except for the flat escalators built into the floor. Those I sat on with my knees pulled up to my chest, cackling my craziest laugh at everyone who passes by. Got to amuse myself somehow. Cherry's not the most entertaining of traveling partners. She's barely said a word. It's only after we've passed customs, collected our suitcase, checked the contents are intact and exited does she finally speak. Not to me though.

"Tanya," Cherry grunts into the receiver of her cell. The instant she turned it back on, it began to vibrate insistently. "I can't talk, I'm on Candy's tail." Cherry's brown eyes slide to mine, nodding to confirm the narrative we agreed on. That Cherry is chasing me across the country, awaiting her next order while we can hatch a plan of our own. I'm like Dr. Evil, sassy, stunning, schemey, and shit. The voice on the other end of the phone makes my stomach roll to the point where I stroll away. Approaching a gap-year traveler with the biggest backpack created, I pull a stick of gum from the pack he's just pulled out of his pocket, gifting him a wink.

"Understood. I'll be in touch," Cherry walks up behind me and taps me on the shoulder. Jerking her head, we leave the vicinity on foot.

"Did Tanya say anything interesting?" I drawl, presuming not. That woman hasn't manufactured an interesting thought or sentence in her entire mundane life.

"Just to stay close to you. She's too busy trying to find her missing cabbie and Nick at the moment." I snort, imagining Tanya chasing her tail and panting like a tired doggy. I wasn't too surprised about the Devil's Bedpost employees cutting themselves a slice of the action that tends to follow me around. To most people, getting tangled in mafia affairs will be the highlight of their miserable lives if they live to tell the story. And the others are swayed by the promise of money they'll probably never receive.

"What's she got on you anyway?" I ask the question that has been niggling at my mind during the entire flight. Cherry avoids my gaze and shrugs, muttering about it being personal, so I drop it. I hold enough secrets of my own not to need anyone else's.

The suitcase wheels scrape along the sidewalk, drowned out by the continual flow of traffic rushing towards the airport. The sun beats down, seeping through the same black long-sleeved top I've been wearing since the hospital. Let's not even mention the twatmuffin that wore jeans to go on the run. *Jeans.* Like I'm an amateur. Sweat drips down my back, my biker boots beginning to drag lazily. My tongue feels thick in my mouth, aching for the sweet taste of an ice-cold gin and tonic while reclining naked in a pool. Specific, I know, but striving for high standards ensures one never becomes comfortable just lemoning around. Cherry is suffering too, starting to lag behind, so I take the suitcase and slow my strides for her.

Spying a parking lot for the Coupon Karen's who refuse to pay the airport's parking fee, I slink over the road and duck beneath the barrier. Time to teach someone not to be such a cheapskate. Settling on the red Mini, I pick the lock and make short work of hot wiring the engine. Cherry is left trying to shove my abandoned suitcase in the trunk, mumbling around the size before dropping into the passenger seat.

"Really? A mini?" She asks, a hint of sass returning.

"Seemed like the best option," I shrug, easing the car out from between a Land Rover and a Jeep. My companion falls silent, allowing me to pump up the radio and catapult us onto the freeway with no destination in mind. We'll just drive until the gas runs out.

Turns out, the Mini had a full tank, and the endless stretch of road was becoming tedious. Especially when my passenger has decided to become a mute that's trying to hide the single tears that randomly roll down her cheek. Shifting my hands from the wheel, I drum a tune on the base of the leather, formulating a plan.

The cunning mastermind I am takes the next three billboards we pass as a sign of fine intervention. Yellow Box Storage, the Chippendales, the Blur Royale Casino – in that order. Except for the fact I need to shit, shower, and shave before I let a well-oiled guy dry fuck me up on stage. The next sign is for a motel, the word 'vacancies' flashing insistently. Thank you, Opportunist Jesus. Veering into the next lane without looking, a long line of cars blare their horns, so I slow right down to a crawl. The horns grow louder, mixed with screeching tires as vehicles swerve around me and the grinding metal of a collision.

"Reckless drivers," I mutter, taking my exit. Cherry is silent in the passenger seat, and when I look over, I find her white knuckles knotted around the seat belt at her chest. Luckily, the motel has an open parking lot not too far down the road, used by most of this tiny freeway-adjacent town and the best place to stash a stolen car. Unfortunately, the motel's prime position for visitors doesn't mean it's anything more than a dingy shithole. How quaint.

Darkened windows loom over the graveled car park, where not even the sun wants to shine. Rats run the length of the building, burrowing into holes in the crumbling brick. Any visible guests seem to be conducting business in their rooms; if the scantily-clad prostitutes and overdressed businessmen exiting their 22-plate vehicles are anything to go by. The anorexic guy in the reception either didn't notice or actively turned a blind eye, accepting our cash without taking any details.

"Next time we go on the run, we're hitting a 5* resort in Hawaii," Cherry grumbles. She heaves the suitcase awkwardly over the gravel, looking nothing like the well-groomed woman I was first introduced to. Chipped nails, greasy hair that's lost its vibrancy. Hints of old bruises linger beneath her skin, adding to the frailness hidden beneath a navy t-shirt and cargo pants. If anything, the loose outfit and her hitched movements make it seem like there may be some internal damage. The swelling on her mouth has reduced, but she still hisses every time her tongue rolls over the tender split there.

"Hawaii is overrated. If Jasper hadn't tied up most of my money in one of those stupid bank accounts, we'd be dancing with leprechauns in Ireland by now." Bucket list item numero uno. Letting us in, I take one look around the dusty bedroom and clock the open bathroom beyond.

"I'll hit the shower first," I tell Cherry as she flops the suitcase heavily onto the double bed. "Choose something to change into from my clothes."

"What? Where are we going?"

"Out to party," I shrug. Heading into the tiny bathroom, I spot Cherry standing still, frowning at my reflection in the mirror. "Hey, you said you'd keep a close eye on me; you can keep a close eye on my ass grinding against some of the country's finest specimens." An image of the Monarchs flashes in the forefront of my mind, and it takes a thorough scrub in the shower to scour it back out.

Instead, I wonder how daring Cherry will be with her outfit choices. Maybe someone else might be cautious about leaving a recent nemesis with stacks of cash but not me. If Cherry wanted to do a rob and run, she could have done it back when packing in the first place. Now she's stuck across the country with me for companionship. Lucky girl.

As it so happens, Cherry's idea of dressing for a night out is covering all her best assets. I don't know if she found the black poncho in my clothes or robbed a nunnery, but it just won't do. After a fashion intervention and more than a little fighting, I manage to shove Cherry back into the Mini as night falls. I rasp my knuckles against the boning of her corset, figuring if there is internal damage, the ribbon binding should keep everything in place for the next few hours at least. I can sense her disagreement, the rigidness in her posture having nothing to do with the outfit choice, even after we've arrived in the city. Rounding to the passenger side, I reach over to unbuckle her belt before bopping her on the nose. Her scowl makes me chuckle more. It's not like she's in a skimpy, skintight catsuit and heels like me.

"Maybe we should go," Cherry hedges. She's back to walking on eggshells around me, not having the balls to say get the fuck in the driver's seat and take me away from here.

"I can't imagine you have survived this long by being a pussy shit," I counter, leaning on the Mini's roof and blocking her exit. Blinking up at me, there's nothing but earnest in her solemn face.

"It's easier to be the baddest bitch in the room when you're not around," she admits, visibly steeling herself. "Besides, I wasn't being a pussy. I just figured we should be saving money," she argues when I force her ass out of the car. I roll my eyes, tossing the keys to a valet I don't intend to collect from.

"Living for today is the only way," I reply over my shoulder, quoting a fortune cookie I got once. Some guy that owed Big Cheese money had ordered Chinese takeout before I'd snuck through his kitchen window. He happened to be dead before the delivery boy turned up, and it seemed a shame to waste good food.

Popping my gum, I spot a scalper lingering back on a nearby corner and suddenly turn to approach him instead of the flashing booth attached to the theater. He smiles a mouthful of decayed or missing teeth, leading me back into a darkened alleyway to do our deal. Pulling a note out of my back pocket, he places two tickets for tonight's Chippendale show into my other hand. At the last minute, I clench my fist closed around my cash and punch him square in the face. His silhouette stumbles back, dropping onto his ass. Cherry gasps behind me, her curiosity getting the better of her.

"Happy now?" I ask, shaking the tickets at her. "I just saved us $200." Her answer is drowned out by the scream of fans rushing towards a hummer that's pulled up by the sidewalk. A topless hunk steps out, shirtless and shinier than a glitter fart. He puts on a show of flexing, stopping for selfies, and signing all the tits being shoved in his face. He's handsome I guess; chiseled face with a strong butt chin, smooth black hair curled at the front like a stripper version of Elvis, but he's not doing it for me. Cherry neither apparently, her eyes downcast and a sigh leaving her chest. Linking my arm in hers, we walk inside and head straight for the bar.

"Two vodka and limes, and keep them coming to…" I look around, spotting a booth with a perfect view of the stage, "table seventeen in the center there." Cherry's eyes follow my pointed finger, mumbling something about people already sitting there. Weird, I didn't see anyone, and even if there was, they sure as shit scattered when I secure our tickets to the table with my penknife. Right on cue, the drinks are delivered by a shirtless waiter in a bow tie. The lights go down and the music hypes up, signaling the start of the show. Yet Cherry hovers on the very edge of the booth, so I drag her backward, planting a glass in her hand with a harsh order.

"Drink."

"Maybe one of us should stay sober to make sure we can get back to the motel in one piece?" Cherry offers. Even in the hottest outfit I own and her jet-lagged, smudged panda eyes, she's tentative to let loose and enjoy herself. I can't tell if she's trying to be my friend or if she's stressed, but I want the feisty bitch who tried to kill me back. She was much more fun.

"You're rolling with me now. Shit like designated drivers doesn't matter anymore." I clink my glass against hers and tip up the bottom, forcing her red lips to part and accept the sharp taste of our cheers. Yet her face hasn't changed after a decent gulp, and it's my turn to sigh. "Look, as long as we're stuck together, you might as well enjoy the ride. Follow my lead and I'll show you a life you'll never want to leave."

"But I do want to leave. I'm done with the schemes, the fighting, even the promise of money. As soon as Tanya isn't a threat anymore, I'm taking my son and getting far away from all of you."

"Even Jack?" I dare ask, not even sure if I want to hear the answer. Cherry's face lights up with humor, but not the good kind as she twists to face me properly.

"Let's be realistic. Even after I went rogue and tried to win him over for real, the truth was blatantly obvious. He only has eyes for you." The first act strolls onto the stage, a bearded lumberjack in red plaid and an axe in his hand. I ignore the tugging in my chest from Cherry's statement, spinning her by the shoulders to enjoy the show and avoid her knowing stare. The crowd around us roars their approval as the man on stage lifts his axe above a staged tree trunk.

"There's no fucking way he's up there with a real-" Angus

starts, appearing on the table to see the man clean cut through the trunk with unmistakable realness. "Well, hot shit."

"Yes sir," I nod, relaxing back in the suede seat. For a little while, the lumberjack chops his wood while sporting a girthy trunk of his own in his white briefs. Wiping his brow, he rips his plaid shirt clean in half, causing the horde of thirsty women to scream in unison. Me however, I'm twisting in the booth to wave over the bartender with another round. I want to join the hype, but something is holding me back. I can't put my finger on what it is exactly, just that the chasm inside my chest where adrenaline usually thrives feels dull. Annoyingly dull. Maybe I'm also jet-lagged, or maybe Cherry's words are eating away at me. I hope not because sewing her mouth shut is an inconvenience neither of us needs. Whatever it is, I need to drink it away before anyone notices I've lost my mojo.

The show moves along slowly, probably to give people value for money, but I just slouch further into the booth. Cued by the shift in lighting, from white to red, and the dip in music to a saucy number, the lumberjack steps aside, making way for a man in a suit. I saw this on a poster on the way in – the 50 shades edition. I roll my eyes, muttering for some divine spirit to give me a break. Malik could break Christian Grey like a toothpick, and now my mind's back in the place I'm trying to keep it away from. Leaning on my elbows, I pry my eyes open, willing myself to focus.

More characters don the stage – a sexy doctor, a welder brandishing a massive tool, and a fae elf combo coated in blue, sparkly paint for the book-sterbaters in the audience. Bodies roll, gyrate and full-out fuck the floor while I suppress a yawn. The gummy bears to my right are having the time of their lives, jerking off vigorously and squirting candy worms all over the table. Dirty bastards. I take Cherry's second drink and down it, giving myself a sharp slap. I can do this. I can find the vitality that carries me through each day. Yet still, my eyes shift back to the man who has lost his suit and is now standing in just boxers and a tie. Running his hand through his hair, he pops his bicep, pouting a kiss at a woman in the front.

"Argh, this isn't working," I sigh in exasperation. I thrust the glass into Cherry's hand while shoving past her. She tries to grab for me but I'm too slick, darting and weaving through the tables. My feet hit the steps to the stage and already, my adrenaline is making a reappearance in the base of my chest. Yes. It's actually working.

Sliding into the choreographed routine, I take center stage just as they all drop to the floor, rolling the length of their bodies along the ground like well-oiled snakes. My eyes flutter closed, allowing the vibe of the music to invade my movements. Reaching my arms up high, my hips roll from side to side like a professional belly dancer. Suddenly, five hot bodies press against me, closing in from all sides. They slip and slide against my catsuit, filling my senses with a much cheaper cologne than I've grown accustomed to. It's not enough. I need to chase the horny high, I'm comfortable with or I'll lose myself in a whole load of shit I might not survive.

With my eyes squeezed closed, the press of muscles rings blissfully familiar. The knot in my heart lessens, and a relaxed smile graces my lips. Behind my closed lids, flashes of piercing blue, emerald green, puppy dog brown, and the deepest pits of endless black find me. I'm captivated, fully enthralled in the husk of my imagination. In time with the bassey music, defined abs and well-endowed groins grind along with my movements, taking me where I need to be. The safe place locked away inside.

Suddenly, rough hands seize me, dragging me from my fantasy and sharply back to reality. It's only then I realize the music had stopped, allowing worried murmurs to echo around the silent club. Eyes filled with sheer panic are on either side of me, and following their stares, I see why. My hands are wrapped around the waistbands of two dancers, hoisting them into my hips with undeniable strength. Added to that, my nails are embedded into their erections, threatening to decapitate their plump purple heads if they jerk away too quickly. My boots are heavily pressed on their bare feet, securing them in a web of my own creation.

Security guards have donned the stage, ushering the dancers to a safe distance. Who knew coming up here uninvited with the intent to force the dancers on me isn't deemed acceptable. With fingers braced on their tasers, the security guards stretch out their free hands like they're caging a wild lion. Closing in on me, I catch the eye of a dancer at the back, the suited one that set me on this darkened path to the stage. He doesn't look scared, but cocky as shit, pursing his lips that mouth 'desperate whore.' That's when I flip my switch from play nice to get fucked.

"I'm not going anywhere until I've had a face full of dick!"

"You could have had that every night at the Devil's Bedpost if you hadn't run away," Angus mocks from his spot sitting precariously on the axe sticking out of a splintered trunk door stage left. Releasing the two dancers with a sharp shove, the hot doctor gasps, moving away before checking the condition of his prized possession.

"That's not helpful!" I scream, lunging through the guards to get to Angus's smug face. My hand wraps around the axe's handle instead, so I swing it violently, warning everyone to get back.

"Play the music! Hit the strobe lights!" I shout into the crowd. Brandishing the axe with a steady hand, I point it in the direction of the dancers, who squeal more than the women sitting below. "Either you lot smush your dicks in my face, or I'll slice them off and do it myself." For some unknown reason, that above all else, causes chaos to irrupt. An array of taser wires slam into my body, leveling me flat on the floor. Electricity ripples through my veins, igniting a new sense of pleasure I've been missing. Gripping the axe close to my chest, the wooden handle nestled between my cleavage, I lick the steel blade before it's wrestled from my grip.

Next thing, I'm being tossed onto my front. The pussyfuck that's manhandling me must be gay because he ignores my up-tilted ass in favor of slapping a pair of handcuffs on my wrists. A feeling I know all too well. My upper arms are seized as I'm forced upright and dragged on lazy heels down the steps and swiftly out of the club. A swat van pulls up at that moment, whipping their door open for a pair of uniformed officers to storm out in full riot gear. Damn, that was fast, maybe because they've apparently left most of the team elsewhere.

"Report of a disturbance with a dangerous weapon," the first states through his helmet. The security team are more than happy to toss me into their grip. Cherry rushes out, calling my name and the second swat member makes a grab for her too.

"Hey! I didn't do anything! Let me go," she struggles against the hold. Together, we're shoved into the van and sealed inside. In the tinted green lighting, I notice Cherry visibly relaxing against the side bench with a strange look on her face.

"All good back there?" A familiar voice asks as the swaties slide into the front. Lurching forward and driving through a red light, the pair take turns to hold the wheel and remove their helmets. Floppy brown hair springs free, and knowing brown eyes catch me in the rear-view mirror. My breath hitches until I realize who I'm actually looking at. Nick- Ace's sneaky lookalike. Cherry drops down to the floor, picking the lock on my cuffs free with a knowing grin.

"I called them when I saw things escalating. They were nearby anyway, tracking my phone," Cherry shrugs. The cuffs pop free, and I rub my fists, moving up onto the bench to join her side. A row of bulletproof vests knocks against the side of my head when we turn a corner, causing me to raise a brow.

"And the whole swat team get up?" I ask, still wrapping my head around what just happened.

"We knew it wouldn't be long until you got yourself in trouble," the second guy answers. The one I'm going to presume is the missing cab driver. "Just didn't think it'd be within hours of arriving." The other three share a chuckle, and I realize the ache in my chest doesn't hurt so bad. Could it be as simple as having people around me once again, or is it that those people are regarding my crazy nature with ease like the Monarchs did?

ACE

Okay, curiosity got the better of me. That's the only reason I'm doing this. It absolutely wasn't Spade's insistent nagging that forced me to power up my trusty PC and scour the hospital surveillance footage again for missed clues. Candy's escape was too well-planned to execute alone. Never mind the fact Candy couldn't coordinate a surprise party for someone with amnesia. This time, I go beyond just watching her duck out of the waiting room and into the fire escape. Using various cameras on different levels, I manage to track Candy's movements all the way to the back door, where she slips into a taxi with a very familiar redhead behind the wheel. Motherfucker.

Shifting my search to Candy's apparent accomplice, it takes no time at all to locate the cell phone registered to her name. Most interestingly though, is the phone call that pops up on my screen at that exact moment, allowing me to tap into the call.

"You'd better get here quick. Candy's about to get herself arrested."

"Shit," a voice I can't quite place responds. *"Tanya will be scouting police records. Candy will give us up before we've even got started."*

Alarm bells ring in my mind at what the man could be

implying, but then I wonder if his intentions are sinister at all. It's clear he doesn't want Tanya to find them, whoever 'they' are, but is his plan to keep Candy out of jail to help her or to ensure she's running around free for an attack? Another male's voice sounds in the background, stating they're on their way and the phone call dies. Less than thirty seconds - too short for a wiretap if I hadn't been fortunate enough to see the call pop up at that precise moment.

Typing furiously at the keyboard, my interest now piqued, I manage to hone in on a cell tower before the signal goes dead. It's not exact, but it's something, I think, as I shove away from my desk and go to hunt for the others. I know Spade will be downstairs, passing off his physiotherapy as working to get the bar back up to scratch. There's no news of when or if we'll reopen, but he's going stir crazy around here. I peer into Jasper's pink and fluffy room, spotting a light on through the adjoining bathroom. Heading next door instead, I look inside Jack's room to find Jasper lying back on the central swinging bed.

"Come inside, close the door and lie next to me," Jasper says. I still at his strange request, wondering if he even knows it's me in the doorway. After a long moment, I obey, moving further into the room. With the door closed, I carefully lie back on the bed, causing it to swing back and forth.

"Holy shit," I choke out a laugh, seeing what Jasper is staring at. Above us on the ceiling, a monster face has been sprayed on in glow-in-the-dark paint. Raging eyes, a sharp jaw and square chin, a vein in the temple, and devil horns breaching the slicked-back hair. It's surprisingly well-detailed, a talent I didn't know Jack had. "How long do you think that's been there?"

"Fuck knows. It's obviously Malik though, which makes me think him being the first face Jack sees might not be the best idea," Jasper says. The thought strikes a chord with me, but not as much as the longing in his voice. He wants to be with his twin, to be there was he comes around. Shit, I think we all would if there wasn't a half-Arab guard dog pacing around the suite. Silence washes over us and I twist my lips, trying to think of what to say. I'm usually the last one to open up, but history shows suppressed feelings, and unvoiced thoughts are our downfall. I need to try harder.

"How are you holding up? Must be weird being back?" I ask weakly. Jasper's chest rises and falls deeply in a white t-shirt, his shrug causing the bed to wobble again.

"I'm under no illusion my being here will only last until Malik realizes he has a stow-away. It's hard to feel like I've returned home when the king of this castle still hates me."

"He doesn't hate you," I reply, although my voice betrays my uncertainty. When it comes to Malik, I don't even think he likes me half the time. Jasper rolls his face my way, the disbelief clear in the shadowed hitch to his brow. I concede, rewording my response. "Malik's not himself right now and he's definitely not in control. If me and Spade want you here, then that's where you'll stay."

"And do you? Want me here?" There's a hint of vulnerability in his voice, one that makes me regret every bad thought I'd ever had towards him. Turning his head back to the ceiling, the quiet between us grows louder as I twitch my foot.

"The only thing that matters is Candy wanted you here. She fought for you, and I'm pretty sure the reason she didn't just take off one night when you guys were living the high life is that she wanted to bring you back to us. The least we can do is respect her decision."

"Wooooow," Jasper longs out, his smirk evident in a slip of light bleeding from around the doorframe. "The self-proclaimed woman-hater. She really did a number on you, huh?"

"She did a number on all of us," I chuckle, and we fist pump over our chests. Just like that, an invisible string of tension snaps between us and I could swear it's just like the old days. Where we would hang out, smoke cigars, drink the nights away, and share a woman on the odd occasion. Like the day we shared Candy before she ran to him in her hour of need, and I have built up a wall of resentment ever since. "I have a lead on her, by the way," I mutter, drawing myself back from those kinds of thoughts. "Question is, do we go after her or trust she has a plan?" Jasper snorts, confirming what I had already concluded.

"Candy never has a plan." He links his fingers over his chest, kicking off the floor to quicken the swing of the bed once more. I stomp my foot down, not just because it makes me feel dizzy as fuck. How did Jack ever sleep like this?

"Then we need to talk to Malik," I push to sit upright. I sense the hesitation lingering behind me, but I've made my decision. Grabbing Jasper's arm, I hoist him upright so fast that the bed swings back to karate chop us in the thighs. "Come on, you're with me. It's about time he saw the Monarchs are back together, whether he wants to be included or not." I don't wait for an answer, reluctantly dragging Jasper all the way to the door before releasing him. I may want to make a stand, but I'm not going to yank him the whole way like a scolded chIld.

Reaching the top of the second staircase, the door to the penthouse is slightly ajar, which means the nurse must be in. Malik wouldn't have unlocked it for anyone else and she refuses to be shut in alone with him. Easing the door open, I enter just as Jasper appears right behind. His green gaze displays exactly what I was thinking - it's far too quiet in here.

"Malik?" I call out, heading for the bedroom first. The nurse pops her head up from note-taking on her lap, a pair of glasses balancing on the bridge of her nose.

"He's on the balcony," she replies, going back to her scribbles. "Said something about needing some air space or throwing himself off it." Contrary to the first time she visited, the nurse no longer seems as fragile, which leads me to believe she's grown accustomed to Malik's dramatic ways. I spot his shadow beyond the curtain covering the balcony, confirming he's still there and leaving him to it. Walking to the other side of the bed, I take one of the dining chairs placed there and rest my hand on Jack's still arm.

"Studies show he'll be able to hear you if you talk to him," the nurse says without looking my way. Placing the notes down on the chair after she's stood, she collects her equipment and makes her exit. I slide my wide eyes to Jasper, who's lingering just inside the doorway, my shoulders lifting of their own accord.

"What the hell am I supposed to say?" I ask. Jasper puffs out his cheeks, slinking over to the nurse's chair opposite. He peers at his identical twin, leaning in really close to Jack's ear.

"Oi, fuck face!" He screams. "Stop faking, you lazy shit!" I rush to shush him, my eyes darting to the open doorway where I expect Malik to come storming in. He doesn't, luckily, so I quickly close the doors. Returning to my pew, I reach across and smack Jasper over the head.

"What's your fucking problem?!" I whisper shout. The Brit chuckles, sitting back with his arms folded. It's the most relaxed I've seen him since Candy made a run for it, and for that reason, I join in his easy smile. Kicking my boots off, I take it one step further, propping my feet up on the bed and crossing my fingers over my middle. "Tell me your favorite memory from when you were kids."

"Wow, the big guns, huh?" Jasper raises his eyebrows, slouching further down in his seat too. Anyone could think we were just three friends reminiscing together.

"Mmhmm," I nod. "Neither of you have ever spoken about your childhood. Not to me anyway."

"That's because we don't like you," Jasper winks. He drops his head back, the cogs in his mind visibly turning. After a long moment, he seems to come up with something. "Our father owned a pub in Southern England, a real traditional place named after a Duke who lived in the town 500 years previous. Rumor had it he suffered from terrible gout, so a specialist golden boot was created for him to wear. Only on one foot, mind you, and a normal shoe on the other. Well, our father kept this golden boot locked in a glass cabinet in the pub for all to see. It was his main attraction. People would come from all around to see it, until one evening Jack and I stole his cabinet key and crept down to see it up close. We only wanted to feel how heavy it was, try it on," Jasper smirks at his own stupidity.

"Turns out it wasn't as weighty as expected. Jack accidentally heaved the thing across the room, smashing it on impact with the floor. A chunk of gold skidded our way, a sticker saying 'Made in China' staring back at us. We thought the whole thing was hilarious, but now I reckon we could pinpoint that moment as when it all went to shit. Tourists stopped coming when a pair of shitheads graffitied 'fraud' all over the outside. Our father's mental health declined; he turned to drugs and spent the last of his money to ship us to boarding school over here. That's the last time we saw either of our parents."

I listen to Jasper's tale, sitting forward in shock. I had no idea the twins had suffered like that at such a young age, and it speaks volumes about why their forced separation by Malik cut so deep. Resting my hand on Jack's chest, I sigh with the weight of their trauma. A deep inhale rocks through my palm, and the next second, Jack jolts upright with a strangled gasp. A girly scream sounds and I blush, realizing too late it came from me. Covering my outburst with a manly cough, Jasper jumps up to ease his twin back into the pillows.

"Jack? Is that you, brother? Talk to me," Jasper pleads, panic and elation flooding his green eyes. His twin blinks against the harsh sunlight. Attempting to shield his eyes, Jack soon realizes the feeding tube is embedded in his forearm and tries to yank it out. We dive on him, forcing him back into a reclined position holding his wrists in place.

"Take it easy, bro. Let's leave that shit for the nurse to deal with," Jasper tries to joke, the bob of his eyebrows urging me to do the same.

"Yeah fuck that shit man. Don't sweat it; we'll stay here until she arrives." Just out of sight of Jack's eye line, I grab my phone out of my back pocket and shoot the nurse an SOS text message.

"Jasp, I have to tell you something," Jack speaks at last, his voice croaky. Loosening his arms, we steadily release him, and Jasper drops onto the side of the mattress.

"Whatever it is can wait. You're awake, that's all that matters right now." Shaking his head, a tear leaks from Jack's eye and pools in his ear.

"No, it's important," he insists in his hoarse tone. "The graffiti on Dad's pub, it was me. I did it." I brace myself for an attack that will likely send Jack straight back into his coma, preparing to lunge between them, but Jasper merely chuckles.

"Yeah, I know, you idiot," Jasper lightly shoves Jack's head aside. "You interrupted me, and I hid around the corner in the freezing cold until you finally left. Like I said, a right pair of shitheads." The twins grin at each other and I drop in my seat, tutting at how similar they really are until Malik throws the door open with a face of thunder. Oh shit.

CANDY

The swat van pulls to a stop in the dead of night after trailing around for hours. In that time, Nick and Cabbie Tom have filled me in on what they've been up to since escaping the mansion. And a little bit before that too, including their recruitment and what's been going down at the mansion. Mainly in the cellar. I'm starting to see a fuller picture now, and realize why we're slinking around in the shadows because of one shady bitch. Tanya is not all she seems to be.

Whipping the side door open, Cabbie Tom holds out his hand to help me step onto the road. Hooking the handcuffs through my catsuit strap, I stretch my back and peer around for a hint of where we are. Just above us on a hill, a rickety old house sits with every single light still on. Each of the two stories is clad in wooden panels, topped by pointed turrets. There are no other buildings visible along the rocky road, no other vehicles either. Just us, the moon, and the house that must have survived generations of death. The wind carries an eerie whistle that has Angus ducking behind my legs.

"Where the hell are we?" I ask, following Cherry to the base of a thousand stone steps. Fuck my life.

"This is where we are staying tonight. A manor turned inn by the old woman that owns it. Subsequently, said owner is Tanya's last living relative," Cabbie Tom tells me with a sly look. He's a middle-aged man, gray strands just starting to shine through his thinning dark hair. I got a better look at him in the van than I can see out here, but nothing gives me a reason to think he isn't just a simple Cabbie with an unfortunate mole above his right eye.

"Thanks to you, I hear," Nick smirks, slapping me on the shoulder. I glare at him and tilt my head like a crazy person to make him quickly retreat. Then it's my turn to laugh. Ascending the stairs, a crow caws nearby, freaking everyone else out except for me. Takes more than a superstitious bird to ruffle my feathers. Growing agitated by Cherry's slow footsteps, I move onto the adjacent grass and use wide strides to overtake her. The ground is slippery beneath my heels, although the pointed heel helps me to stick in place rather than tumble all the way to the bottom again. Reaching the crest of the hill, a door decorated with metal bolts and a flourishing brass knocker greet me.

"Should I knock or-" I ask when the door peels open of its own accord. Behind, a frail, petite woman stares back with a wide smile. Oooh, I get it now - a rickety old house for a rickety old spinster.

"There you are! I was worried you may have gotten lost." Her pale eyes regard me closely, her smile not faltering. I frown, fairly sure beyond the mask of crinkled skin, I recognize her. The woman ushers us inside, creaking the door closed as we peer around her home. Reaching my chest height, her leathery hands lightly touch my arm and guide me into a large drawing-room.

"It's lovely to have you here," she says. Okay, now I have goosebumps. "I haven't had guests in quite a while, and it gets so lonely up on this hill." The house is as spacious as the outside would suggest and filled to the brim. Random objects that speak of a life well-traveled litter every inch of the walls, making it nearly impossible for the aged, floral wallpaper to peak through. Abandoned olive green sofas sit around a Persian rug and coffee table, but it's the matching armchair that's withered with use.

"Any reason no one has stayed here recently?" Cherry asks, rubbing her own arms to warm up. The temperature isn't cold, but it seems we all feel the chill that comes with the spooky surroundings. The old woman's smile takes on a sad edge as she nudges aside the long, gray plait that rests over her shoulder.

"Ever since the new freeway was built, bypassing this part of town, there's been no reason for anyone to venture this way. I don't mind about the money, but it's the company I miss. The whole reason I opened up my home after my husband passed was to have someone to talk to." Her face turns to a full portrait above the fireplace. Another set of washed-out eyes stare back from the frame, watching our every move. A thin comb-over sits over a stern brown, a no-nonsense expression cemented on his painted face. Freaky. Not what I'd have on my wall. I'd have the bust of a stag made entirely out of dildos.

After a long moment of reflection on the painting, the old woman forgives us for her manners and takes our tea order. She tots off into the next room, clanking about while we try to relax in the space. It could be lavish, minus the layer of dust coating most surfaces. Small pawprints mar a glass coffee table and white hair prickles the carpet.

"Someone want to fill me in on the plan? Or are we going to drink this old witch's voodoo tea and never make it out of here alive?" I ask, dropping into the well-worn out armchair. Springs prod me in the butt, and I smirk. Dirty old bitch staring at her husband's portrait and getting her horny on.

"This is the plan," Cherry answers, opening a sideboard drawer to peek inside. "Call it a recon mission if you like. This woman is the only connection we have that can enlighten us to who Tanya really is."

"Right," I roll my eyes. Even if this OAP is related to Tanya, the chances of her remembering anything of use is a long shot. Tanya's lived at Big Cheese's mansion for as long as I've known her. "And how do you propose we happen to bring up that seed of information without looking suspicious?"

"This may help," Cabbie Tom says from across the room. I crane my neck, spotting a photo frame in his hand. Pushing myself up, with the help of Angus and Hamish's chubby little hands, I abandon my heels and pad barefoot across the tattered rug. Cabbie Tom hands me the photograph tentatively as if the image is supposed to mean something to me. All I can see is a couple on their wedding day. The man is sharply dressed in a pale blue suit, cravat, waistcoat, the whole setup with a cane for appearance's sake. The woman is in a white dress that would have suited a window rail better, long brown hair flowing down her back and a broad smile on her face. In her arms, she's cradling a baby.

Cherry shuffles in closer to pry the frame from my hands and gasps, seeing whatever I'm missing. Just then, the old woman returns, a tray of cups, saucers, and a tea pot clinking together in her hands. Nick swoops in, saving her from breaking a hip, and places the tray onto the coffee table.

"Forgive me for prying," Cherry starts and I snatch the photo from her grip.

"Who's this?" I ask brazenly when no one else was going to. The woman waddles to the mini table by her armchair, almost tripping over my heels, to retrieve her glasses. Squinting closer, the smile regrows across her wrinkled face.

"Ahh," she breathes after the longest minute. "My beloved granddaughter and her husband." We all watch her stroke a crooked finger down the white dress in the photo, her movements filled with care. "Such a shame. Quite the scandal back in the day." Putting the frame down on the table, we all take a step closer.

"Really? How so?" Cherry asks first, her interest thoroughly piqued. Something about her eagerness goes beyond a recon mission, but I ignore the thought for now.

"Their marriage was an arranged one, meant to bring our families together," the woman looks to her dead husband wistfully. "I warned my granddaughter to remember it was merely business, but she was besotted. And he took her for granted." The smile has disappeared from the old woman's face, replaced with a hard scowl. "My Tanya was with child before we could get her down the altar, as you can see." Gesturing to the photo with her bony digit, my limbs go slack.

"Oh silly me," the old woman gasps, returning to the present. "I forgot the milk. I'll be right back." She trots off, leaving me frozen in place, my eyes fixated. No wonder I didn't recognize Tanya in the picture since I've never once seen her smile so genuinely. On closer inspection, the sharply dressed man in the photo could be Big Cheese, but who does that make the baby? Cherry's eyes slide to mine, and I shake my head vigorously.

"You can get fucking fucked. My mom is my mom. She's a dirty slutty stripper, but she's mine. I know where I came from."

"It's not you," Cherry breathes, hanging her head. "I think it's me."

"Tanya, is your mom?! Ew. How often did you have to scrub your skin of her genes before you felt like suicide wasn't your only option?" Nick gives me a weird look, and I brush him off.

"I was raised by my half-sister, the same one that is now caring for Zak. Shortly after he was born, I was diagnosed with post-natal depression. I thought if I found my birth mother and got some answers, it might help me find my own way. I tracked Tanya down, posed as a new recruit," Cherry turns away bashfully. "I just wanted to get to know her, but then the jobs started rolling in, and I was making good money. Before I knew it, I was fully fledged in Leicester's gang, and I've been trying to escape ever since. You were meant to be my last job."

"I've heard that before," Angus laughs at the irony of it all. The diamond heist that put me on the Monarch's trail was meant to be my last job too, now look where we are.

"Does Tanya know?" Nick asks quietly, running his hand up and down Cherry's back.

"I don't think so, but I couldn't be sure."

"So your secret mom is my ex-step mom. Heavy shit." I shrug. To be honest, nothing can surprise me after the Krabby Patty formula was leaked online. Everyone check on your seahorses; they're not okay.

"The woman said they married; she never said they divorced," Cabbie Tom points out, becoming quite the sleuth.

"That would make sense," Cherry nods, and I raise my hands, palm-side up for her to elaborate. "It can't be a coincidence as Leicester and Tanya became estranged; she grew more obsessed with the safe only you could open. Leicester must have changed his will to cut her out, and the only way she'd benefit from his money was if you are dead."

"And hence why you're really still on this crusade hunt," I nod in understanding, causing Cherry to frown. "You could have escaped a thousand times since we made a run for it. Except for half the inheritance I claimed should also be yours." There's no judgment in my voice. I learnt long ago money makes the world churn, so I chose to depart and live in a figment of my own imagination.

"I've come from nothing, just like you. The care system hasn't been kind to either of us before my sister was legally old enough to take me on, and you have no idea how hard it is being a single mom." Tears well up in Cherry's eyes and for some unexplainable reason, I pull her into my chest. Angus and Hamish frown at me from the armchair, but I've committed now to squish Cherry's head against my breast and pat her back. All this talk of mom's reminds me I need to check in on my own, especially now I might have some insight into why she's been acting so shady. No doubt Tanya's made her intentions to kill me known.

"Erm, I don't mean to break this up ladies," Cabbie Tom's voice travels from the kitchen. "But the old woman's not here." Cherry breaks away from me and we rush over to him. "I thought I'd see if she needed any help, but she's gone."

"Maybe she ran out of milk and went to fetch some?" Nick suggests unhelpfully.

"Yes, that frail woman thought she'd skip to the 7/11 in the middle of the night to fetch the strangers in her house some milk.

Or maybe she's got her own cow tied up out back and went for a midnight milking sesh," I slap him around the back of the head. Agreeing to split up, I take the next door into a regal study. The furnishings are all made of the same walnut wood, and unlike the rest of the house, there's not a speck of dust in here. No little old woman either, so I turn to leave until something on the bookcase catches my eye. A book is popped out from against the others, giving me full haunted house vibes. I yank on it, hoping the bound leather pages reveal a trap door. They do not and the book drops onto my toes.

"Motherfucker," I curse, grabbing it with the intention of tossing it in the fireplace. A photograph drops out, fluttering through the air until I grab it in my fist. Uncrumpling the image, I find the face of the old woman looking back with fewer wrinkles. In her arms, there isn't just one, but two babies with an inscription underneath. Cherice and Candice. Fuck. That. The pullback of a gun sounds from behind, and I turn to find the woman standing there with an LMG in her hands.

"I knew it wouldn't be long before the pair of you came here. Suppose you want the rest of the story, Candice?"

"Don't fucking call me that," I seethe, but she ignores me.

"It just so happened my Tanya's betrothed had another woman on the side. A whore who was pregnant at the exact same time. Leicester took you in briefly, and wanted to raise you and Cherice together, but Tanya was furious. She did whatever it took to lose you in the care system, making it impossible for you to be found. In turn, Leicester started divorce proceedings and did the same to Tanya's child as payback. Somehow they reconciled down the line, but the two of you were untraceable until you came of age."

"Who knew I was so interesting," I smirk, relaxing under the scrutiny of the barrel. After hearing about my epic story, I reckon dying at the shaky hands of a trigger-happy OAP seems like a worthy ending. Crashes sound from somewhere else on the lower level, giving me a chance to dive out of the way of Granny Gunnut. Bullets spray across the bookshelf where I was just standing, her reaction too delayed to catch me. The door bursts open before I make it there, revealing Cherry with a pistol in hand.

"Candy, duck!" She shouts, and then shoots away. The blowback catches her unawares, knocking her off balance for the bullet to sail just over my ducked head. I feel it wisp against my hair and whistle all the way to strike the old woman in the chest. She lets out a weak gasp and falls back like a feather lost in the wind. A frail little waif crumbling under the weight of a hefty machine gun.

"You shot your grandma," I praise, giving Cherry a standing ovation. She looks horrified and tosses the pistol at me as if that'll make the shot my fault. Whatever, no skin off my back. Twisting, I pop another bullet into granny's neck and regard Cherry with a bright wide.

"Now we can share the blame just like we share a daddy," I beam. The brown eyes opposite widen, Cherry's skin a shade too pale and a shudder raking through her spine. "Too soon?" I pout as more gunfire explodes through the kitchen. Winding my arm around her shoulders, I draw Cherry through to a hallway I haven't ventured into yet. I'm kinda liking this big sister shit because I'm absolutely the bigger and better sibling in this scenario.

A masked gunman twists into the hallway in an effort to escape whatever is happening in the drawing-room, coming between us from the front door. Still, it gives me an idea. Plucking the handcuffs from my halter neck strap, I sneak up behind him while he's distracted by trying to shoot back at who's around the corner. Pressing the cold metal of the pistol into the back of his covered head, I hand Cherry the cuffs. Taking his chunky wrist in my free hand, I smash his fingers against the wall until he's forced to drop his gun. Then, wrenching that arm behind his back, Cherry takes the hint to grab the other, securing them in place.

"What are we doing?" She hisses at me, flinching at every sound around us.

"We came here for answers. Since granny isn't talking anymore, we might as well grab one of her henchmen." The man struggles, shouting in another language until I slam the butt of the pistol into his mouth, shattering a few teeth. The gunfire in the drawing-room stops, hushed whispers seeping our way. "Nick, Cabbie Tom, is that you?" I call out, and suddenly, two men rush out into the hallway. Their faces look just as relieved as ours and as I shove my new prisoner forward, I can see why. Multiple men are lying dead on the floor, or are as good as, while the shadows of more pass outside the windows.

"The sideboard doubles as a weapons unit. There's rifles, daggers, a spear; you name it." The smile on my face grows malicious. Oh, fuck yes, this is what I was made for. The man yells out, throwing a knee into Nick's side until I bring the pistol down again, this time into his temple. He crumples against me, blood already spewing through the cotton mask attached to his head. Swapping the pistol for the machine gun Nick is holding; I shove the bad guy into his and Cabbie Tom's hold.

"Take him and get back to the van. I'll meet you there soon." I usher Cherry to go as well when she hesitates. Recent history has proven she isn't made for the battlefield. Heavy boots trample through what I imagine is the back door and I whip around the drawing-room corner. Ducking into the sideboard's shadow, the lid is popped open to reveal an array of shining weapons beneath the wooden surface. Granny had style. While the men whisper hushed commands, I reach up to pluck out whatever comes to hand first. A spikey ball of metal lands comfortably in my palm, and I thank whoever is watching up above for blessing me with tonight.

"Who knew this rickety old house would provide such rickety old fun?" I ask Angus who's ready on crouched legs. Painted lines border his chubby cheeks, and a mini Candy Crusher is clutched in his jelly fist. Hamish steps forward on his other side, fully donning a tartan kilt and matching beret. "Where's your weapon Hamish? This is war."

"Right 'ere ma laasy." Reaching beneath his kilt, he pulls out a chunky metal-tipped spear, and I nod in appreciation. That is one hell of a girthy weapon. Assisted by the sweet melody of bagpipes, the three of us storm forward into the center of the room. Machine gun in one hand, a grenade in the other, the men behind the kitchen counter fall silent and gawk at me through the serving hatch. Their heads drop out of sight as I spray a round of bullets from one end of the wall to the other until one brave fucker steps into the doorway, warning me to stand down.

"You're surrounded! There's no way out of this!" Feet shuffle in behind me, all clad in black and armed to the teeth. I throw a glance at each one, remembering their eyes for my sweet dreams of carnage later.

"How did you know gangbangs are my style?" I smile. In one swift spin, I've taken out most of their legs with the bullets raining from my firearm. My ballerina moves have put me back by the arch to the hallway, the furniture taking the brunt of bullets meant for me. Those in the kitchen grow ballsy, trampling forward with their weapons raised. The only assassin left standing on my end runs at me, so I do the only logical thing that comes to mind. Yanking the grenade pin out with my teeth, I toss it at him.

"Hot potato!" He quickly skids to a stop, stupidly catching the metal explosive to knock it back my way. Oh, henchman wants to play. The grenade sails through the air as I line my machine gun like a bat, swing and knock it out of the park. Well, directly into the kitchen crowd those who can't scramble out of the way fast enough. My finger twitches on the trigger, taking out my pitcher as I dive behind the hallway wall. My body hasn't hit the floor before the grenade detonates, propelling me further towards the front door. The walls shake, with the one closest exploding completely. Plaster rains down as I scramble for the open front door where the newest gunmen had entered, my slick catsuit taking the brunt of the wall chunks and a cackle bubbles from my lips. I'm not usually so Bonny and Clyde, but this shit sure is fun.

Breaching the cool night air on an army crawl, I don't bother with the stone stairs. Instead, I throw myself down the grassy slope like a battered burrito, collapsing in a heap at the bottom. Tender hands ease me to my feet, Cherry's horrified face waiting there.

"Holy shit! Are you okay?" Behind me, the house is still

crumbling, thanks to the integral supporting wall I seem to have targeted.

"Never fucking better," I grin, tasting blood. Cherry helps me into the van where our kidnapped henchman is tied up, still out for the count. Straps have secured his body to the grate between the back and the cab up front where Nick is checking me over. Or checking me out, who knows these days. Cabbie Tom hits the accelerator as soon as the door is closed, jerking me into my abducted friend. His revealed bald head rolls aside, his bulky chest too inviting. Curling up in his torso, I sigh, the smile permanently etched into my face.

"We're gonna have so much fun," I breathe just before sleep takes hold of me.

JACK

The pounding headache that's kept me company since the moment I came to is still there, thumping away, squeezing away each fleeting thought. As if that wasn't enough, every time Malik raises his voice on the other side of his closed door, I feel like smashing myself over the head with a tray and slipping back into my coma. It's been nothing but shit news after utterly shit news since I woke up anyway.

I manage to draw the darkness of the room towards me, sinking further into Malik's memory foam mattress. His pillows are unbelievably soft, enveloping around my head as the first snore is torn from my mouth.

"Jack!" Malik shouts, suddenly standing over me. I squint just in time to see his hand flying towards my cheek, delivering a sharp slap against my face.

"Jesus Christ, Malik!" I shout, throwing a weak punch into his chest. It hurts my knuckles more than anything else, bouncing off his black t-shirt. "I was only taking a fucking nap." Malik mumbles an apology, trying to rub my cheek better, but I swat him away. The damage is done now, and you guessed it, my headache has become a full mind-fucking migraine. Looking sheepish, Malik reaches for the lap tray resting on the end of the bed, a full plate sitting untouched upon it.

"You need to eat," Malik says, struggling to keep the sternness out of his voice. I sigh, pushing myself upright as he lifts a forkful of mashed potato towards my mouth.

"Ew, Malik. Fuck off," I slap his hand away, smearing potato all over his Egyptian cotton bedsheets. "I'm done; get me out of this bed." Without taking no for an answer, I whip the cover off and attempt to slide out of the bed. My legs are like jelly, but luckily Malik's there to help me stand. This time, I don't refuse his help. It's slow going, but we manage to make it into his bathroom, where he finally leaves me be. For a while, I just stare at myself in the mirror, familiarizing myself with the shadow of the man I've become. Too skinny, too pale, too weak to give a shit.

Making my way over to the shower, I manage to flick on the faucet before slowly sliding down the slickened tiles. Resting my head against the wall, I lazily wash myself in Malik's stupidly expensive shower crème. Water pounds off my crippled body, sinking me in the misery of my existence. The woman I thought I might have a future with turned out to be a lie. The woman I pushed away is missing. A bunch of drama I don't fully understand happened in between those two events, and I missed it all. While Tanya was escalating her plans, my brothers were forced to hang back because of me. I wish they'd let me die, in all honesty, because this is a new low point I didn't realize I could sink to.

The door bursts open and I flinch, spotting a figure through the glass divider, speckled with water droplets. I moan at Malik to fuck off when a blond quiff flicks around the divider.

"Jasper," I groan. "I'm fucking naked." His green eyes that match mine roll, and he steps inside the shower, fully clothed.

"Get over yourself, brother. It's nothing we haven't seen before."

"We?" I question as Jasper reaches over to pluck the shower

head from its holder. He bends down, soaking his jeans to wash out the rest of the shampoo I slapped into my hair as Ace appears at his back. I don't bother trying to cover myself now, resigned to being the 'patient' for the foreseeable future. Once Jasper is done, he pats my shoulder and steps aside for Ace to swoop down and collect me in the cradle of his arms. And from there, it just gets worse. Sitting with a towel bunched over my dick, Jasper dries my hair while Ace forces a banana into my mouth.

"Okay, that's it. I feel much, much better now." I push myself upright. Faking my newfound strength, I attempt an easy smile and hope I pull it off. Either way, I leave Malik's suite with the towel held in place and my bare ass on full show. I almost trip down his stairs twice, but I thankfully make it in one piece. Letting myself into my room, I sigh happily at the familiar sight. Thank fuck no one decided to make over my space while I was out in la-la land. Dressing in a pair of sweats, I just about make it into the elevator before I slump against the side mirror. Fuck taking the stairs again.

"Jack! You're up!" Spade shouts, running from the kitchen area to grip me in a bear-hug. I can't hold in my groan of pain, although I wanted to. Finally, someone who isn't treating me like I'm about to break or fall asleep and never wake up again. Meeting him with a grin, Spade helps me into the bar area and over to one of the plush sofas. His arm around my middle doesn't seem as condescending, his worried glances laced with affection. "I've missed you man."

"I didn't technically go anywhere," I jest, lowering into the cushions. The smell of musty polish drifts through my airways, and I finally relax. There's no place like home.

"Yeah, I know. But seeing you so still, it wasn't the same as seeing you smile or hearing your laugh."

"Jesus, I didn't know all of you were harboring such unrepressed love for me," I roll my eyes. Although deep down, a warm, fuzzy feeling starts to spread. Spade sits opposite, hunching over with his elbows on his distressed jeans. The tightness of his short sleeves shows how in my absence, he's been hitting the gym twice as hard. The last time I saw his hair, it was braided back, whereas now, the top section has been twisted into dreadlocks with the sides and back still shaved short. When Spade's piercing blue eyes linger on mine for too long, I tilt my head to the side knowingly. "Go on, whatever it is. Spit it out."

"I have a confession to make," he admits, and I huff out a laugh. I knew it. Another beat of silence passes before Spade swiftly stands. Disappearing behind the bar, he grabs a large cardboard box and returns to drop it on the table between us. Metal clanks inside, but I make no move to open it. Mostly because I think I've exceeded my exercise limit for today.

"Things have been...weird," Spade sighs, running a hand over his dreads. "Sometimes, when I came back from the hospital, and I had the whole building to myself, I just didn't know what to do. I didn't know how to process everything, so I thought - what would Candy do?" His blue eyes slide to me sheepishly, and I'm sure there's a blush coating his cheeks.

"Ahh Spade, what have you done?" I force myself to sit upright, needing to prepare myself for whatever is coming next. Reaching into the box, Spade pulls out a range of items one by one, laying them across the table before me. A carburetor, greased chain, spark plugs, headlights. It's the fender that gets me, sky blue with telltale white stripes.

"Is that..." I breathe, comprehending what I'm looking at.

"Pieces of your bike. Yeah," Spade rubs the back of his neck. "I warned you if that helps. Before I left the hospital, I'd whisper in your ear that I was going to dismember a piece of your bike for every day you were asleep. Turns out, I ran out of parts," he winces, and my eyes widen. My...whole...bike. Then, a laugh escapes my mouth. I laugh so full-bodied, I have to grip my stomach as a stitch forms there and a tear rolls from my eye. That really is something Candy would fucking do.

"She's really messed with all our heads, for better or worse," I chuckle, trying to focus on breathing. My head has gone all light, and now I'm worried passing out in front of Spade will see my entire bedroom dissembled. "Get me a fucking drink, then put my bike back together, and we'll call it quits."

"You've got it," Spade grins, his shoulders sagging in relief. Striding away, he grabs a pair of beers when the connecting door reveals Ace, Jasper and Malik. Ace ducks behind the bar to assist Spade, carrying over four beers and one bottle of water. I moan, slumping back into the sofa. Still, as Ace pulls out a pack of cards from his low cargo pocket and deals out to each of us, the irritation in my chest eases. Jasper nestles into my side, his body propping me up so he can draw cards and place them down for me. Also means the cheeky fucker can see my entire hand and play to his advantage, but I let it go in favor of enjoying time with my men.

Games roll from one into the next, the laughter flowing easier, and by the time Malik brings out his fancy whiskey, Spade even manages to sneak me a beer. I know it's short-lived, but I can't remember the last time we all sat down together like this, and that's not because I'm suffering from amnesia. Having Jasper firmly beside me, his support not faulting for a second means more to me than he'll ever know. But still, as the night draws in, it becomes all too obvious to me that someone integral is missing.

"So when are you guys leaving?" I ask as I fold in my next hand. The smiles around me die sudden deaths, replaced with furrowed brows and frowns. I met Ace's eye, relaying the information he told me after I first woke up. "You said you wanted to be here for when I came to, and you were. I'm awake and I'm fine. So when do you all leave to go get our girl back?"

"Our girl?" Jasper chokes in question, throwing his arm around me. I feel all eyes swing my way, hunting for my answer. Or maybe it's my approval they want. I was the one who rejected and tried to replace her. I was the one who lied to everyone, especially myself. After all, without Candy, Jasper's stubborn ass would have never forgiven Malik and vice versa. If that's not a reason to admit I'd loved this crazy girl the moment she stole Malik's bike, I don't know what is.

"You back on the Candy train, brother?" Jasper pushes when I don't reply. He's not going to stop until I say it, and a part of me really wants to. As if that'll solidify the Monarchs once and for all, with her in it. I can sense the held breaths around me, so I smirk, putting them all out of their misery.

"You say that as if I ever really left."

CANDY

"Hey Candy, are you back here?" Cherry's voice sounds as she pushes the motel door open with her foot. Brown, paper bags crumble in her arms, the contents overflowing onto the floor with her abrupt stop.

"Thing of beauty, ain't it?" I smirk at her stunned expression. Remaining wide-eyed in the open doorway, I swing a weapon around in my hand. The Candy Crusher is hidden in the shower, so she can't see me cheating on her with this cheap store-bought bat. As much as she has served me well, smashing out teeth and shattering bones with finesse, today called for something a little more rough around the edges.

Muffled cries from the man strapped on the table between us jolt Cherry into action. She rushes inside and slams the door shut, eyeing the rusty nails I hammered into the bat while the screaming asshole on the table took a little concussion nap. He's wide awake now though, craning his neck and pleading through his gag for Cherry to set him free. He manages to draw my roomie closer as he wanted, but not to his aid.

"What the fuck is going on in here?!" Cherry whisper shouts, checking there are no gaps open in the paper-thin curtains. I resist telling her there's no need since my captive has been screaming for the best part of the day, and no one has come to investigate. It was the third nail-bat strike in his chest that really set him off and he hasn't shut up since.

"You remember our trigger-happy friend from Granny Gunnut's house right? He looked a little banged up, but he's not beyond recognition yet." I prod my finger into the open wound in his chest and send him squealing like a delusional pig again. "While you were off with Nick and Cabbie Tom, I thought I'd get started on our interrogation."

"Okay..." Cherry nods, sidestepping around the table in the center. "I get that. But why isn't he wearing any pants?" My eyes drop to the highly unimpressive, limp penis hanging between my victim's legs. Somehow it seems to be retracting further inside his body with each blow of my bat, and at this point, I'm fully invested for scientific reasons. Grabbing the rope I've looped over a wooden beam lining the ceiling and tugging hard, his bound feet shoot upwards, creating a V with his legs and exposing his hairy asshole to me.

"It's ribbed," I tell Cherry, giving the rusty nail-bat a shake, "for pleasure."

"I'm no expert," Cherry turns away from the table, and I scoff. Locking me out until 2 am, just to fuck her electric toothbrush, begs to differ. "But I don't think that'll feel very pleasurable."

"I never said it was for *his* pleasure," I roll my eyes, lining up the bat with his back alley. "It's for mine." Bracing one hand on the table and adjusting my grip, I tell the big guy to stay calm while I sort out his piles problem for him. Flexing my shoulder, a soft hand touches my forearm, and I frown at the concern in Cherry's brown gaze. "What? If you don't have the stomach for some basic torture, feel free to wait outside."

"It's not that," Cherry reels back, feigning offense. Huffing, I take a step back, tossing the bat onto the dresser and releasing the rope for my victim's legs to slam down hard on the tabletop. He sags back on a gagged sigh of relief, writhing against the thick ropes tied in a star pattern over his chest and linking beneath the table. Narrowing my eyes at Cherry, I will her to spit out whatever it is that can't wait until after this douchebag is singing like a canary.

"I just…want to make sure you're doing this for the right reasons." Her eyes slide to the disappearing act that is the magical, shrinking penis and back. Reaching out for my blood-stained hands, Cherry draws me over to the bed shoved against the far wall. I resist, of course, refusing to be treated like a kid with a sugar problem. Instead, I cross my arms over my black corset, cementing my feet in a pair of platform, knee-high boots. Aside from that, I'm only wearing a black thong - my usual torture outfit. It's empoweringly feisty, and any fucker that looks at my ass uninvited only adds to their sentence.

"I know these might be uneasy times-" Cherry starts, and I blow through my pursed lips like a horse.

"Look around you sis," I hold my arms wide. "These are the best of times! We can go wherever we want, eat what we like, screw or torture whoever comes along. No one lording over your every move, except maybe me. It doesn't get better than that."

"Mmmm, I'll take your word for it," Cherry replies, looking unsure. "Call me conventional, but have you ever thought your need for…spontaneity is because you've never stopped running?" The man tied to the table has either passed out now or is listening intently to see if his piles will live to see another day. Spoiler alert, they will not.

"And what, in your expert opinion," I fake a bow, "would I be running away from?" Cherry catches a glimpse of my mocking smirk on the way back up, my fingers drumming against my bare thighs to get back to business.

"Yourself." Cherry holds my unimpressed gaze, daring me to argue. Instead, I brush her off, turning and heading back to the dresser with an eye roll. I've never understood the need to analyze my lifestyle choices. Maybe I'm biased, but I've always thought those who have to pass judgment on my life are clearly seeking help in their own. The notion of freedom shouldn't be confined by conventional constructs. If schools taught the lessons I had to learn on the streets; I reckon the whole world would be a happier place. I should write a manual called 'Finder's Keepers,' and then a sequel titled 'Freedom Can't Be Owned.' Number one bestseller, here I come.

Returning to Mr. Trigger happy on the table, I scrape one of the bat's nails over his teeny dick. He immediately starts to scream through his gag again, showing that he was just being nosey. Weirdly, giving this guy an anal tear has suddenly lost its appeal. Damn, I can't let something as stupid as words mess with my head. Keeping Cherry in my eye line, I lift the bat high when a thought filters into my head.

"Rewind," I say, slamming the bat down into the henchman's chest. He jolts and screams, but I leave my weapon embedded in his flesh while speaking to Cherry over his body. "You said you wanted to make sure I was doing this for 'the right reasons.' How is hunting for answers, not the right reason?"

"Because you don't give a shit about searching for answers. You never have. Sometimes it's easier to focus on being angry rather than dealing with the issue that is in here," Cherry reaches across the screaming banshee between us to point at my chest.

"Ohhh, it all makes sense now," I agree. "The issue is my esophagus isn't large enough to take-"

"No. No, no. I meant your heart. The truth is your heart is broken, and no amount of speared rectums will fix that. You miss the Monarchs," Cherry sighs. I swallow past a sudden lump in my throat, singing the Macarena in my head to drown out her words. Turning away from me and strolling over to collect the dropped groceries, she dumps the lot on the end of the bed before climbing across the mattress. I watch Cherry kick off her shoes and recline, throwing one arm over her eyes and waving the other one in the air. "Enough revelations for today. Proceed with your interrogation."

Glancing at the man on the table, our eyes connecting for a

strange moment, I shrug and wrench the bat from his chest. All that remains of his t-shirt are battered pieces of cotton, barely strung together and soaked in blood; his torso a riddled mess of oozing holes. Every pound causes more blood to splatter over my face until I'm wearing the warm liquid like a sheet of gory armor. Feelings can't find me behind here. Especially ones that twist my heart in knots and fill my head with pretty fantasies that can never be. People lie, men cheat, and lovers betray. Those are the facts I need to remember.

"Shouldn't you try asking him some questions?" Cherry muses in-between more strikes, these ones venturing lower. I stop between his belly button and crotch, tossing the bat aside. I'm bored of using that now. Digging through the bag of supplies I bought, I pull out an electric drill. "You know, before he bleeds out."

"You ready to talk yet?" I ask the asshole on the table. He nods his head vigorously, dislodging sweat from his pale brow. "No? If you say so," I smirk. His following screams are drowned out by the rev of the drill pulsing in time with my finger flinching over the button. This is going to be a long night."

JASPER

"You sure this is the place?" I ask Ace, peering over at his laptop. Jack is sandwiched between us in the back seat, his narrowed gaze glaring at Malik behind the wheel of his truck. After Jack had insisted on coming with us but was still slightly fragile, we knew we couldn't board a plane to track down the red flashing dot on Ace's screen. So without any other option, stalking by road it was, and Jack has criticized Malik's driving every single mile.

"Well, it's where Cherry is," Ace confirms, closing his laptop and stashing it away. "With any luck, Candy is still with her."

"And if not, we can kill the bitch and call it a good day," Malik replies. I share a look with Spade in the rear-view mirror, seriously wishing the others had listened when I suggested we ditch him at a gas station. I get he's protective, irritated, and as sexually frustrated as the rest of us but sheesh, that guy needs to sort his shit out. He's going to send Candy running before we've even stepped inside the door.

"Let's take it easy asshole," I bite the bullet when it seems no one else will. "Our priority is bringing Candy home." I reach forward to slam my hand down on Malik's shoulder. *"Willingly."* He shrugs me off, grunts, and exits the truck.

"He's going to fuck this up," Jack sighs, trying to nudge me out too. I hold him back easily with my hand sprawled over the chest of his black tee.

"You're not going anywhere little brother," I tell him. Ace and Spade take my lead to dart out of the truck and slam the doors closed. Malik is quick to press the lock on the key fob, leaving Jack pounding on the glass and yelling from inside.

"Take it easy!" Spade cups his mouth to yell. "We'll be back in no time. Have a nap or something," he chuckles, nudging us to move. As a group, our feet are moving across the main road, through the parking lot, and to the entrance of the rundown casino on the other side. There's a decent amount of vehicles around for midday and a steady flow of people entering in jeans and t-shirts. Not the type of casino I'm used to, where you wouldn't get far in less than a tux and dress shoes, but we are pretty far out from civilization. This club must be the most exciting building around for hundreds of miles of farming land and a single Applebee's down the road.

"I think we need to go in with a strong plan," Spade nods, trying to draw us into a huddle. Ace and I oblige, but the blearing alarm from Jack's insistent movements inside the truck distracts us. Hysterical laughter bursts out of my mouth at the sight of my brother's stupid face pleading to be let out of his automobile prison. However, said laughter is short-lived when I notice Malik has slipped away. Asshole.

"Plan is, whoever sees Malik first, knock him out and lock him in a cupboard. Then find Candy and-" Ace starts, but I interrupt him.

"And let me do the talking," I finish. I can understand the glares I receive at that, but we've only got one chance here. It's not that I don't trust the men who were once like brothers to me, but I like to think I'm formulating the trick sheet on understanding her. I hope.

Heading inside, somehow the overriding stench of farmland follows us. Worn carpets are caked in mud, trodden in by the sea of cowboy boots all around. Retro slot machines create a pathway down the center, straight to the bar at the far end. I'm pleasantly surprised to see a number of decent brands of alcohol stocked against the mirrored back wall, much like the Devil's Bedpost. Not that I'll be drinking.

Behind the slot machine dividers, the space has been split into poker and a zone for race betting. A large flat screen postured on the wall is currently playing a rerun of an old horse race, which one crafty fellow seems to have remembered the results for. The crowd around him groans and he pumps his fist in the air, taking his ticket directly to the betting booth to claim his prize. Only one other door covered with a frilly, red curtain would suggest at a nightclub area, but otherwise, that's all there is to see. With the open-plan view, I scan the crowd for a pop of fuchsia and come up empty.

"I'll check the perimeter. They might have seen us coming," Spade states, in full G.I Joe savior mode.

"I'll check the restrooms," Ace adds, weaving his way to the edge of the room. I watch him go, a head above everyone else and smirk. The women in the restrooms are about to get a nasty shock. Instead of thinking rationally, I put myself in Candy's mindset and a thought dawns on me.

"Excuse me," I stop a passing waitress with hands full of food. "Do you have any private rooms? Maybe one with an impulsive chick that has a nasty gum-popping habit?"

"To the left of the bar," she jerks her chin, hurrying off to serve a cowboy who's calling for his chili cheese fries. Keeping my eye open for Malik to intercept me at any moment, I make my way across the floor to the bar. A door to the left opens as I approach, a butch guy storming out, red-faced and cursing beneath his heavy mustache. Bingo. Ducking past him, I grab the door and slip inside before it slams closed, concealing my entrance.

A poker game is in full swing between the remaining players.

Five men, much like the cowboys outside with large white hats covering bald spots and cigars cemented in their mouths, grimace and groan at the shitty luck on their hands. Taking them for everything they've got in the form of chips, cash, watches, and a random cucumber piled in the center of the table, Candy sits with her back to me. And holy hell, what a backside it is. Having spun her chair around the wrong way, I have a stunning view of her ass tilted upwards in a tiny skirt that barely stretches around the seat itself, a black corset laced tightly along her spine.

"You found it yet, love?" I ask, sliding into a vacated seat from the recent departure. A flash of panic widens Candy's eyes, but she quickly masks it, plastering on a smirk.

"What do you suppose it is I'm looking for? From where I'm sitting, I have everything I need." She flashes me her hand. A royal flush in hearts. How fitting. The gentlemen around the table watch me closely as I lean in, resting my chin on Candy's shoulder.

"The rush that's begging you to go all in because you don't really want to win."

"Is that right?" Candy's brown eyes slide my way, her cocky smile cracking at the seams. "Then tell me Jasp, what do I want?"

"You want to hit rock bottom. You want to crash and burn so hard, nothing is left but an empty husk of who you used to be." I anticipate her next question of why anyone would want that and cut in to answer. "Because it'll prove knowing us didn't make a difference. That despite everything we promised you, nothing changed, and life is still the chasm of shit you've mastered climbing out of."

Every breath in the room is on hold, waiting for Candy's reaction. Keeping her best poker face in play, she pushes the rest of her chips into the center of the table, announcing she's 'all in.' The men look at each other uncomfortably, one by one placing their cards down to fold.

"Pussies," Candy growls, reaching for her winnings. With nothing else to play with, the men begin to stand until Candy snaps her fingers, pointing for them to sit back down. Keeping close to her ear, I slide a hand over Candy's thigh, her open position allowing me easy access.

"You can reinvent yourself all you want love, but it won't work. We tainted your sick little heart, and now the only thing you crave is us. The challenge we provide, the heat of our bodies, the risk of losing yourself to something no one else gets to experience. It's all yours for the taking."

"They betrayed me," she ducks her head towards me and whispers weakly, causing my smile to widen.

"The chaotic, crazy Candy I knew didn't hide behind weak excuses. Give in already, and I'll make it worth your while." Without being able to resist each other for one more second, our lips connect, cementing my promise. Holding back my groan at the raspberry taste I've missed, I push my hand higher to the apex of her thighs, squeezing firmly. My indestructible girl crumples for me, pouring her soul into my mouth the instant her tongue pries it open. I fall under her spell, not used to the openness of Candy's passion. Her tongue commands my full attention, luring mine into a false sense of security. Under the surface, our connection snaps back into place, and all grudges I held against her ditching me disappear. She's an evil sorceress like that.

A hand on the back of my collar wrenches me back, swiftly followed by a shove to my chest, sending me toppling off the chair onto the floor. I barely have a chance to shout before Malik's taken my seat, his hand possessively clamping down on the back of Candy's neck.

"Enough of the bullshit. You're coming home with me right now," he threatens. Contrary to the throat punch I thought Candy would have delivered to him; she simply twists to blow and pop a bubble of pink gum in his face.

"You want me back? Play me for it." Reaching for the cards, Malik's other hand slaps down on her wrist, halting her movements.

"Why would I bargain for something that's already mine?" I roll my eyes at Malik's cocky attitude, knowing he'd fuck it up for us. Pushing myself to my foot, I catch the eye of each remaining cowboy, an uneasy plea in each one.

"Everyone out," I growl, flashing the gun tucked into my waistband at the gawking spectators. They scramble, rushing out of the door which I lock from the inside and lean against. Malik twists, his mouth open in protest, but I cut him off.

"There's no way I'm leaving you alone with her in this mood," I tell my ex-nemesis. Malik doesn't take kindly to anyone telling him what to do, especially me. Luckily, Candy is here to provide an entertaining distraction. For me, at least.

"Well, I'm not going anywhere. I came here for some fun, and I'm not leaving without it," she shrugs. Grabbing for the cards again, Candy begins to shuffle while Malik stands to lord over her.

"Mmmm," he nods beside her pink hair. "Because everything is one big joke, right?"

"Only you," Candy looks up to flutter her eyelashes, and I see the last shred of Malik's patience snap. Gripping the belt bordering her ass, Malik lifts Candy clean from her seat. Veins ripple through his arm as he tosses her face down onto the poker table. Chips crash to the floor like hail stones, skittering in all directions. Candy is quick to flip over, planting a boot in Malik's chest to hold him at bay. There's a fight for dominance happening, and at this stage, I'm not sure who I'm rooting for. Candy in all her spunky, pissed-off glory is a sight to behold, but I do understand Malik's enragement. After everything we did - no fuck that. After everything *I* did to keep her safe and happy, she ran.

Shoving her boot away, Malik swoops in like a demon of darkness. Grabbing her knees, he pins them closed between his thighs. A risky move, in my opinion and as much as I'd love to see Malik crying about his burst testicles, I cross my arms in apprehension. Candy doesn't buck the way I'd expected though, momentarily distracted by Malik tugging off his shirt. She stills, transfixed, allowing Malik to pop the clasp of her belt buckle with one hand and smoothly slip its length from her.

"I'm going to strike you for every week you left me sitting in that hospital, not knowing where you were or if I'd ever see you again." Tightening the leather in his hands, I sway to the side for a look at Candy's passive face. The fight has fled her, leaving a lifeless shell that nods along. In fact, she twists onto her front as soon as Malik releases her legs, her ass tilted up in the air. The skirt just about keeps her covered as she leans on her forearms, ready and waiting. Thwack. I jolt, the sheer volume of the whip ricocheting through me. Malik groans, stretching his neck as if the strike physically soothed him.

"Every scar you receive will be a reminder of how I felt," he states coldly, devoid of emotion. I take a mini step forward, wondering if I should intervene before this goes too far. Yet Candy isn't fighting, so for now, I hold off.

"Furious," he says, slamming the belt home against Candy's upper thigh with an almighty whack. "Betrayed. Confused. Alone." The whips crack through my eardrums, but I hold back my winces. When Malik shifts, I see angry lashes from behind her knee to the under crease of her ass. White welts begin to emerge from the redness, already starting to swell as Malik flips her over and plants her on the edge of the table with a hiss.

"Every time you sit down from now on, you're going to remember exactly what happens if you fuck with me again. I've given you more of me than I thought possible, and in doing so, you now have the ability to destroy me. That's not a power I'm going to let you escape with so easily." Then his mouth is on hers in a fiery display of dominance.

The door handle rattles, Ace's voice calling through the wood, so I pop the lock. He, Spade and Jack storm in, about to cuss me out until they spot the exhibit in the center of the room. The fight goes out of Jack, not that he'd have had the energy for more than a minor tussle. Easing the door closed behind them, the four of us slowly move further inside, each taking a stand around the table. I push a chair Jack's way, but he flips me off, his eyes engrossed in the clash of tongue and lips before us.

Ace reaches forward to untie Candy's corset ribbons delicately with his sausage fingers. Malik cracks an eye, his tongue still fully invested in Candy's mouth, permitting Ace's assistance. Once the corset pops off, and Spade reaches for her breast however, Malik rips away from their kiss to smack Spade's hand away.

"You can all stay, but this time, she's mine." He growls, threatening Candy to disagree. She doesn't make a single sound, just sits ramrod straight and awaiting Malik's next move. Warmth spreads through my chest, realization settling in. She knows he's at breaking point. She's giving him exactly what he needs to heal. The question is what the cost will be later.

Pushing her shoulders back onto the felt table, Candy lies flat in the center of the Monarchs posted at all sides. Malik's front becomes visible, and I gasp, my eyebrows shooting to my blond hairline. The others have spotted it too, apparently for the first time, and Jack now accepts that seat. Across the expanse of Malik's chest is a caricature tattoo of Candy. Pink wavy hair frames a cheeky winking face with a lollipop between her raspberry pink lips. It's a stunning piece that must have taken a full day's work, but it's so much bigger and more colorful than anything I've ever seen Malik get. Oh man, Candy's not the one who's whipped here - it's Malik all over.

I bite my lip against laughing while pointing a finger in his face, too enthralled with the tension rippling around us. Candy lays still, open to our hungry gazes. Her pink hair flows around her shoulders, in stark contrast to the greenness of the tabletop. The colorful tattoos on her chest line the tip of her full breasts, her pert nipples perfectly round. A sight I'll never tire of seeing. Malik pops open the button of her skirt, only to loosen the waistband and shove it higher over her toned stomach. She's completely bare underneath, and an anguished groan resonates through us all.

Ordering her to spread her legs, Malik loosens his slacks and frees himself, not that any of us are looking. We're too enthralled by the anguished cry that leaves Candy's lips as Malik slams inside her in one firm thrust. That spanking must have had her dripping and ready, although I don't think anything could have prepared Candy for Malik's punishing strikes to her G-spot. She screams each time, her voice filling the private room while we merely stand there in awe. Flushed chest. Clenched eyes. Her fingers scraping over the felt. I've seen Candy break for me many times, but never like this. I'm not jealous; I'm beyond enamored. She's fucking stunning.

When it grows too much, Candy tries to buck away from Malik and scratch at his recently tattooed chest until we step in. Following suit with a Monarch grabbing each of her ankles and wrists, I close my hands around her forearm forcefully. Stretched out, she's left to Malik's mercy, but with the tension comes something more toxic altogether. It may be Malik fucking her, but it's all of us punishing her. For running away, for lying, for not believing we could help. In fact, the more Candy screams, the more I want Malik to take from her. My blackened heart beats in time with her pants, the need rising to see her break for us.

Twisting her wrist in my grip, Candy's hand locks around mine, squeezing tightly. At that moment, it's not the woman pinned to the table who breaks; it's me. The façade that I need her pain shatters, stripping me back to the truth. I just need her. Entirely and wholly, not this half-assed version that thinks she can ditch us at any moment.

A strangled cry rings out as Malik grips Candy's hips, dragging her further down onto his dick. I sense the moment he pushes her over the edge, his jerks becoming even more savage. She holds onto me, being pulled under the spell of a climax claiming her entire being. Tremors rock the length of her flawless body, covering her in a shade of crimson red. As a unit, we ride those waves with her, so in tune with her guttural noises, it takes me a moment to realize Malik has pulled out and turned away to clean himself up. He didn't finish, drawing confused looks from the rest of us.

It's glaringly obvious now this wasn't about Malik's pleasure or staking a claim over his girl. This was to teach her a lesson. To show her a hint of how we felt. I was only without Candy for a few days in comparison, so I can't even imagine how the Monarchs suffered all those weeks I had her to myself. She's flushed, panting, and exposed between the five of us. And for now, Malik seems content with that.

CANDY

Pulling my skirt down over my sore upper thighs, I sit on the edge of the poker table. Fingers clenched on the edge, a sigh tears from my chest. The air in here is stifling, and with every eye trained on me, I can't form a coherent thought, never mind what I should say.

"Meet me at Applebee's in a few hours," I grumble roughly, standing to leave. A strong hand grips my upper arm, but it's not Malik like I'd expected. It's Spade.

"How can we be sure you won't make another run for it?" I level him with a glare, twisting my arm out of his grip. Barring allowing Malik to rid himself of the demons that were clearly riding him into a state of insanity, I'm quite done with being manhandled.

"You don't. But either I have time to clear my mind, or I walk away for good." Looking over my shoulder, fear runs through the twin's green eyes, and Ace ducks his head. I don't need to look Malik's way to feel the anxiety radiating from his very being. I don't think at this point I could look at him anyway. When no one responds, I pick up Malik's discarded white shirt and pull it over my arms. Fastening one button in the center for the sake of the shirt not blowing off my tits mid-stride, I exit the room without looking back.

I make a beeline for the fire escape around back, heading straight for the blue van sitting on the edge of a delivery route and fenced field. The boys spent all night stripping the van of its Swat team vinyls in order to dispose of the body decaying in my motel bedroom. I'd wanted to play with my gunman friend for much longer, but alas, his heart wasn't up to the challenge. He wasn't talking through his gag anyway.

Whipping open the side door, Cherry squeals, shoving Nick off her with a guilty look. I frown at the pair of them and their matching swollen lips before deciding to sit in the cab. Cabbie Tom is stretched out, asleep across the seats, until I shove his legs aside and take the driver's seat. Sitting down with a wince, I speed away from the casino, trying to put as much distance between the Monarchs and my clouded judgment as possible.

"Candy?" Cherry probes through the mesh divider. "Is everything okay? Did something happen?" I scoff, unable to open that can of worms at this moment in time. A stupidly naive part of me reckons if I voice any of the thoughts rocketing around in my mind, I'll burst into tears and drive us all into a ditch.

"We've gained the upper hand again. We need to regroup and discuss how to move forward," I state coldly. Inside, I'm wondering if these three would even want to stick around if the Monarchs are back in the picture. Not to mention it could be slightly awkward for Jack after his ordeal. Angus and Hamish appear on my lap, leaning into squish me in a bear-hug sandwich, and that's when I know I'm really fucked. Angus has never hugged me, nor have I wanted him to.

I drive erratically, switching lanes and nudging vehicles out of the way in a bid to reach the motel in half the time it would usually take. Those who refuse to be bullied threaten me with small swerves, which I mimic, causing our vehicles to scrape together with a cringe-worthy sound. Nick curses from the back, but I prevail, forcing the cars to back the fuck off and give me a wide birth. Winding down the window to flip the other drivers off, my cackle trails behind in the rush of air. I just wish it was filled with the genuine humor that it would have before Malik re-entered and fucked with my mind.

"Do you have any idea of what you're going to do?" Angus asks, peering up at me. I toss him a patronizing look. If I did, he'd know it long before me. Just as I was getting back into the swing of being free, the Monarchs had to crash back into my life. I wanted to leave them behind, and continue the only way I feel comfortable. It would have been so much easier that way, but it seems like they won't let me go, even if it is for their own benefit.

A small bell above the door announces my arrival, not that the five pairs of eyes trained on the entrance would have missed me. My chin tilts upwards, my loud footsteps hitting the lino floor confidently. The Monarchs are stretched across the back three tables, all sitting in a line to face this way. In the center of the middle table, a large strawberry milkshake with extra cream and sprinkles awaits me. I resist smirking at Jasper, not wanting to lose my nerve. Sneaky fuck. Behind the milkshake, Malik is propped upright with his crossed fingers on the table. He's found another shirt, this one safely nestled underneath a tweed jacket that is far too overdressed for our venue.

"You came," Malik states. It wasn't a question, and the answer is obvious, so I take a seat, placing the folder in my hands on the surface.

"Before we start, I want to ask you one question," I tell him, temporarily losing myself in the black spiral of his irises. Damn, this man must be beautiful to radiate such toxic beauty in the shitty lighting of a chain restaurant. "Why couldn't you just let me go?"

"Because I love you," Malik replies instantly. The Monarchs

heads turn swiftly to their once-leader, all except for Jasper, who looks anywhere else. Ignoring the inward shiver that tries to seize my lungs, I scoff.

"You guys pass that word around too easily."

"No, we really don't," Malik counteracts, waiting for me to make the next move. Steeling myself, I replay the lengthy conversation Cherry and I had prior to me coming here. For the first time in my life, I had someone who just listened to what I had to say. From deranged rants to insistent whining, Cherry sat cross-legged on the bed, letting me vent every damn thing that's been playing on my mind and then helped break it down into factions. Now though, with the Monarchs seeming so close yet so far across the cheap tables, I'm struggling to remember what my point was. The whore in me just wants to fuck across these tables to avoid the awkward silence filled by the Spice Girls crackling through the speakers.

"Anyway," I roll my eyes, directing my attention at Malik. "It's obvious you're not going to let me go, nor do I wish to be trapped in a life of your creation. So I've made a list of demands." Sliding the folder towards him, I scoot another chair around to prop my legs up and take my milkshake in hand.

"We've having a business meeting? In an Applebee's?" Malik breaks a half-grin, seemingly impressed but not moving to take my well-thought-out proposal. He'd better. After giving Cherry far too much insight into the way my brain ticks, I boycotted the anorexic receptionist's computer, typed up and printed the damn thing. I've never been so prepared for anything in my life. The others peer over at the folder curiously, but it's clear who's back in position as head douche. Soon, the anticipation proves too much.

"Read it then," I snap around my striped straw.

"It's my turn to ask a question," Malik cocks a brow irritatingly. "In an ideal world, what's the end game here? How do you see your future playing out?" Oh, Jesus Christ. All I wanted was some quintuple dick fun and I've landed myself an overbearing daddy.

"The future is overrated, but my demands are right there if you just open the cover," I scowl. Malik's amused eyes flick down, then back up again.

"No."

"No?" I echo, my mouth hanging open. Shoving at the prop chair with my boot, it skids away with a painful screech that stops all the other diner's conversations as well. Spade bristles from his seat on the far end, shooting up in outrage.

"What the fuck, Malik? Hand over the file so we can negotiate some terms already." He dives across Ace, grabbing for the folder until Malik slams his hand down on top. A scrap breaks out between the two, hands slapping and mixed shouts drawing more attention our way while Ace remains trapped in the middle. Getting caught up in the hype, I throw the contents of my milkshake over the pair, coating them in a layer of pink slush. My precious file comes off worst, so I snatch it back from Malik's slickened grip.

"This is stupid. I don't even want you to read it now," I growl. Storming away, I toss the file into the trash can and shove through the exit. What a waste of fucking time that was. I hit the road on foot since Nick told me to call if I needed a ride, and now I'm too pissed to do anything. Some air is the safest bet, or I might lash out on one of the several hundred cows milling about in the next field. It's not the cow's fault I bore my soul on a piece of shitty paper that my former…whatever the fuck he is wouldn't even read.

Feet jog up from behind, and it's no surprise when Spade and Ace step in from both sides in front of me, blocking my path. I glare at them to get out of my way until I spot the stained piece of paper in Ace's hand. The very one he must have retrieved from the folder I tossed in the trash.

"Candy," Ace pities me, "this is-" I snatch the paper, crunching it up and stuffing it into my cleavage before a shadow appears over Spade's concerned gaze. A flush is blazing through my cheeks as I spin, throwing my fist into Malik's unmoving chest.

"Let me explain," he states calmly. Me however, I'm the opposite of calm.

"Let me rearrange your stupidly perfect face," I lash out. Malik catches my wrist, spinning me in one swift motion to face Ace and Spade again. I feel the embarrassment crawling under my skin with every passing second they stare at me, but Malik's words in my ear give me a welcome distraction.

"I don't need a list of demands because I already know what you want." I choke out a bitter laugh, struggling against his hold on my pinned arm. I really wish these shitheads would stop telling me what I do and don't want or need. Malik's chuckle reverberates from his chest into my back, despite the very real possibility my shoulder is about to pop out of its socket. Malik remains oblivious, his voice laced with humor.

"Endless supplies of gum, free access to the bar's inventory, the freedom to leave for undisclosed periods of time without notice, copious amounts of sex, and a funeral for Sphinx. How'd I do?" The last one got me, and I stop struggling. In all my buried regret and pain, Sphinx's memory is hidden deep down there. I may not have had him long and hated his hissy guts, but a girl doesn't forget her first pet. Biting the inside of my cheek, I twist my head into Malik's neck, drawing comfort from the source of my anger.

"I put a lot of thought and effort into this detailed document; the least you could have done is read it for yourself," I grit out.

"None of it matters anymore," I feel Malik shrug against me. Jasper and Jack appear at last, completing the circle just in time to witness my further humiliation.

"My demands don't matter?" I scowl, bucking to catch Malik off guard. His chin takes a knock, but I reckon I hurt myself more than anything. His free hand smoothes my hair from my face and trickles down my collar bone.

"You don't need demands because as of two hours ago, I put the Devil's Bedpost up for sale." All mouths go slack this time, and with one last tug, Malik releases me into the rest of the Monarchs.

"You did what?" Spade gasps.

"Did you feel like consulting us on any of this?" Ace crosses his arms and frowns. The twins remain quiet and I sidestep towards Jasper on instinct. Not because I'm in the business of picking favorites, but because I have some sucking up to do, and not in the fun sense. He gave me everything, and I tossed him aside to handle my shit alone. It's clear the guys won't allow that, so I'd better get back in his good books.

"It's no secret each of us wants to be with Candy, but it's also clear she can't adapt to a stationary living arrangement," Malik addresses everyone, straightening his jacket. He looks ridiculous with strawberry milkshake splashed across his fine attire, but at least he smells nice. Turning his knowing stare on me, Malik offers his hand, and the sappy idiot in me accepts.

"And now you won't have to. I've been searching my whole life for something to fill the void that's been slowly consuming me, and then I found you. Your list of demands doesn't matter because from now on, I'm at your mercy. You call the shots, you tell us where to go. We can go sailing, live in an RV, get on a plane and never come back, whatever you decide."

A truck zooms past us, the horn roaring and driver shouting for us to get off the road, yet no one moves. My hair whips around in a tornado until the air settles again, quelling the long-standing torment in my soul. Here we are, in the middle of nowhere, with my hand in Malik's. He's selling his pride and joy, handing over control and submitting to me. I struggle to process what it all means, although the gummies postered on my back are screaming some kind of 'L' word at me.

"And the catch?" I ask, blocking out the squeaky shitbags who both know I'm not ready to comprehend that heavy shit. Hell, I might not even be capable of it.

"This is my only condition," Malik replies, and I laugh. Knew it. His eyes narrow and his lips purse before he's able to catch himself. Old habits die hard, I guess. "Return today and let us protect you until Tanya is dealt with. I need to settle matters with the bar, and I can't do that while worrying about you. I'm proposing to start a new life of your choosing, something that puts me far out of my comfort zone. All I'm asking is we start it properly without always looking over our shoulders."

Flicking my gaze from one Monarch to the next, they each give me an agreeing nod. Then my eyes land on Jasper, and his face softens. He can't stay mad at me. Reaching out my other hand, I knot my fingers with Jasper's.

"Okay." A collective sigh rings out around me, any annoyance at the whole selling-their-home bombshell dissipating. A full beaming smile sweeps across Malik's face before he swoops in, crashing his lips against mine. Passion radiates through his kiss, empowering me with positive notions that this is the right choice. This is where I belong. Angus and Hamish have gone strangely silent as my inhibitions are being swept away with the motion of Malik's tongue slipping into my mouth.

In a flash, he withdraws, and another mouth replaces his. The insistent need of these full lips lets me know it's Spade without needing to look. Fuck how I've missed Spade. With his hands flat against my back, his chest presses me into a capsule of desire. I can taste his desperation, his swelling cock against me from just one touch. His mouth claims mine like it's the first time, stirring an odd sensation in my chest. I want to screw him into tomorrow, but there's something else. Withdrawing, Spade plants a kiss on my nose tenderly, a smile reflected in his blue eyes before he turns me into Ace.

"Oh, I see. It's pass the parcel, and I'm the prize," I smirk.

"Fuck yes, you are," Ace grins. His lips take me hostage, showing no mercy in a cruel twist of passion. He wants me, but he's not going to let me off easy for my decisions. And I really don't want him to. By the time Ace releases my mouth and leaves me panting, I turn around to find the twins have already departed. Huh. I don't spend much time thinking about that, preferring to watch Malik, Spade, and Ace all readjust themselves so they can walk away with a modicum of dignity.

Hanging back, I withdraw the squished piece of paper stuffed between my tits. Apparently, all that hard work digging deep into my own psyche, which is a scary motherfucking place, wasn't needed after all. Moving closer to the fence, I smooth out the page and glance over the single demand I wrote there before feeding it to the closest cow.

I want to come home.

MALIK

'Because *I love you.'*
I looked her in the eye, and said those words and she didn't even blink. In fact, she dismissed me. Spanking Candy and forcing her to come for me has done wonders for the anger I have trapped inside, but it's not enough. That much is evident by the way I'm squeezing her abdomen, my cheek stuck to her nape. With only five seats in the truck, and no one comfortable with splitting up, I took the passenger seat and nestled Candy firmly on my lap. Fuck looking whipped; I need this girl to feel alive. It's Jasper's turn behind the wheel, leaving the muscle squishing Jack in the back.

"Uno," Spade announces, proudly holding his single card. I sigh, inhaling Candy's raspberry scent. Being stuck in this confined space when all I want to do is show Candy how much I've really missed her is driving me insane.

"Pick up four, cock munch!" Ace exclaims, leaving a grumbling Spade to take from the deck Jack is stuck holding in the middle. The game continues back and forth while I change cheeks, preferring to watch the traffic pass out the window instead. We're back among civilization, judging by the BMWs and Mercedes racing by at top speed, but that doesn't relax me as much as it should. If anything, the increasing cell towers and expanding towns are causing more anxiety to ripple through my being. I was the one who asked Candy to return with us; I just hope I'm not putting her in more danger by doing so.

"Ah-ha! I win!" Ace cries out, breaking through my thoughts. A slap and grunt sound before the rippling of cards cascading to the floor. Turning back, I see Jack holding his thigh where Ace must have slapped him and his torso where he must have jolted too sharply. Meeting Ace with a warning glare, Spade tosses his last card onto the floor with the rest.

"Well, I was runner up, so she can suck my dick while you take her from behind," Spade mutters.

"Of course, you're the runner-up; we're the only two playing dick-knuckle," Ace responds. Fucking idiots, the pair of them.

"You're both complete wankers," Jasper mimics my thoughts. I cock a brow at him, not expecting Jasper to have been the voice of reason. "It's been so long, the first person Candy graces with her glorious pussy will finish in seconds. Best to jerk off before getting your turn." And there it is; I shake my head to myself.

"The feminist in me should have a problem with this," Candy muses from my lap. She's been suspiciously quiet and as I peer around her, I see why.

"Stop reading those magazines," I grumble, grab the wad of glossy paper she picked up at the last gas station and toss it out of the window. "They'll rot your brain." Candy twists her large, brown eyes on me, blowing a bubble of gum in my face. I gnash my teeth into the pink sphere, popping and stealing half before she can retreat it back into her mouth. In spite of all the stress weighing on my shoulders, it's all about the small moments where her smirk makes me forget about everything else.

"It's a little late for feminism now," Jasper breaks through our bubble of peace. "Didn't you once blow a guy for a turn with his remote control helicopter?" Candy's eyes drift out of the windscreen, a pleased smile on her face.

"Totally worth it," she nods.

"And yet we had to venture across the country and make a massive gesture just to convince her to come back," Jack huffs dryly.

"Ignore him. He's salty you wouldn't let him play sex-dibs UNO," Ace chuckles.

"I'm absolutely fine," Jack scoffs, sounding the opposite. "But if we're being realistic here, I've been through the worst of it these past several weeks, and I need to reconnect with Candy the most. I shouldn't have to play for pussy dibs."

"That's very true, but you did also sleep with my sister," Candy reminds him, and the truck erupts with 'Oooooh's' and a bout of laughter. Behind his flop of blond hair in the rear-view mirror, Jack's face flushes pink, and his words are flustered.

"She's only your *half*-sister," he rushes to say, as if that makes it better. Spade nudges his shoulder playfully while Ace scuffs up his hair. Neither of which Jack likes. "Look, if I'd known who she was, I wouldn't have-"

"Slept with my sister?" Candy finishes for him, and I join the others cackling with laughter.

"Half-sister!" Jack protests. I almost pity him, but then I remember he didn't embrace Candy the way the rest of us did, and this is the first time I've laughed properly in too long.

"Ohhhh. So it's my fault you slept with my sister?" She questions, spinning on my dick to raise a brow at him.

"Stop saying that!" Jack shouts in exasperation. Spotting her taunting grin, he relents with an eye roll. "Okay fine, I was an idiot, and I have a lot of groveling to do. I was confused and... uncomfortable with my feelings. Everyone have a good laugh at my expense." Turning his attention to the window, the hysterics die, and a chill sweeps in. To some extent, we all pushed Candy away at first, and now there's much more, so much more at stake than just winning her heart. There's making sure she lives long enough to realize she's already given it to us.

"Are you sure we can trust Cherry to come through?" I ask the question everyone is thinking, but no one else wants to voice.

"Haven't you learnt to trust my intuition yet?" She tosses me a knowing scowl, and I back off. Thankfully, Candy didn't insist on bringing Cherry home with us, but I still don't like the fact she's part of our latest scheme. While we head back to keep Candy safe at the bar, Cherry, Nick, and some guy named Tom I don't know or trust are hanging back to keep Tanya off our trail. Cherry swore to falsely feed her boss information on Candy's whereabouts as long as her son is kept safe. It's a tangled web I still don't quite understand, but I'm trying to suppress the control freak inside. I'm relinquishing to Candy's decisions from here on out.

"You know what. We should probably take this sex-fest elsewhere. The Devil's Bedpost won't be very marketable while dripping in cum," Jasper smirks, trying to lighten the mood again. Ace and Spade perk up in the back, seeming to agree.

"Do we have time for a detour?" Ace asks hopefully, his eyes sliding to mine in the mirror, and I shake my head.

"I just want to get our girl back, no more delays," I reply, resisting the urge to add 'and my word is final.' We're not far off now anyway and I'm still coated in milkshake. My shower is calling, and the way my hands drop to the heated center of Candy's thighs, I won't be going in alone.

"I agree," Candy nods, surprising us all. She must be just as home-sick as I am and eager to make the most of the time we have left in the bar. Turning herself to straddle me, her chest presses into my face so she can address the others. "We have business to attend to. Besides, dripping in cum only adds to market value." Rocking my crotch forward, I groan into her cleavage, drowning in my own slice of heaven. Amen to that.

CANDY

The truck smoothly pulls into the garage and my boots hit the concrete floor before we've even fully stopped. My legs are restless, my body aching and my mind reeling. Stretching out, I head for the open garage hatch, throwing a smirk back at the boys just getting out the cab.

"See ya," I salute, ducking out into the setting light of the day.

"Wait, what? But…I won?!" Ace calls after me like a wounded puppy, and I chuckle.

"You may have won *your* game, Ace, but we play by my rules. You want me, you'd better find me first." With that, I take off into the Devil's Bedpost, using the key I slipped out of Malik's pocket to gain entry first. Cutting through the kitchen, I leave the lights off in favor of sneaking around in the shadows. It's eerie being here without the usual employees milling through or the punters in the bar getting rowdy. I hit the staircase, entering my room first and locking the door behind me.

It's just like I left it, even though the smell of Jasper lingers in the air. My fluffy fairy lights hang limply, and the motion-censored recording of Spade's voice has been disabled. My eyes drop to the floor, looking at the spot where I writhed around screaming for someone to come back. Raising my hand to touch the spot of dried blood on the corner of the dresser where I cut my cable ties free, I quickly slap myself around the face. It seemed like something Angus would do, so I figured I'd beat him to it, snapping myself out of the temporary funk that took hold of me.

Heading to the window instead, I open it wide and peer out. Beneath the orange and reddish sky, the Monarchs are standing in the center of the parking lot, hanging around and doing nothing.

"What are you guys waiting for?" I call out, grabbing their united attention. "This pussy won't fuck itself."

"Giving you a head start, love," Jasper grins. "There's no fun in winning at an advantage."

"That's very honorable of you." I reach back inside to grab a monster-sized black dildo from the drawer on my nightstand. "But don't wait too long because I'm going to get myself off at least twice before you find me." I wave the dildo out of the window, and the men scatter, more than one of them shoving Jack backward to give him the biggest disadvantage. So predictable. Waiting for the rest of the Monarchs to disappear from view, I hold a finger up at Jack when he looks my way longingly. This pity-party shit doesn't do it for me, and there's only one way to fix that. Crawling out of the window, wiggly willy in hand, I wriggle across the tiled outcrop covering the entrance of the bar.

"Here, catch," I whisper shout, tossing the dildo at Jack. He doesn't move out of stubbornness, his face remaining highly unimpressed until the giant dildo slaps him across the face. It's a hefty fucker and I won't be surprised if he has a black eye tomorrow, the thought making me roll with silent laughter. My body tips off the edge of the outcrop and I grab the guttering at the last moment, swinging my legs around to clasp onto a support beam. Shimmying down, my feet land in an overgrown shrub that itches like a motherfucker. From there, I duck low, grabbing Jack's hand on my way past and dragging his stubborn ass back into the garage where no one will look. Silly ninnies can chase their own tails.

"This was your plan all along?"

"Well, my plan was to hide behind a curtain in the hopes Jasper and Ace would get bored and start sucking each other off, but this works too." Jack balks, so I draw him around to a high stool left over from the bar's restoration and settle him into it. "What? Do I look like the kinda girl who would let a bunch of men play for me? I fuck who I want when I want." Angus appears on the hood of the truck, stretched out like a catalog model to remind me that's not strictly true anymore. My list of 'fuckable' partners has whittled right down to five. Whatever.

"Okay, so you've got me here. What now?" Jack asks, crossing his arms over his chest defensively. He thinks I'm going to hit him. It's not a bad idea - take out some delayed pent-up anger I've been holding onto, but life's way too short for that shit. I do flick him on the temple and get some satisfaction from his resulting flinch though.

"Get out of your head Jacky boy and kiss me."

"You want me…to?" He hesitates but I'm done talking. Actions are the best language. Planting my mouth on his, I commit the taste of the Brit I've missed to memory. It's been way too long. He may look like his twin, but he feels like something else entirely. For a start, it's refreshing he doesn't hang off my every whim and calls me out on my shit. But behind his reservations, Jack's lethally addictive. I want to please him, to make him crave me, and I'm worried about the lengths I'd go to in order to make that happen.

Continuing to force myself on him, Jack parts his lips, allowing me full access to his mouth. I roll my body against his in an attempt at seduction, but the longer he just sits there, the more my confidence wavers. I'm sure Jack wants me, but now he needs to show me. After a full minute of taking my brutal kiss like an oral rape, something clicks, and Jack grabs the back of my neck roughly. Our teeth clash in a bid to dominate, his fingers digging into my skin possessively. I sink my teeth into his lip, and he bites back on mine twice as hard, besting me this time.

"I want you to say it," Jack breathes between licking my now-tender bottom lip.

"Say what?" My eyes flutter open to find his emerald green ones staring back. They glisten in the garage's artificial light, holding so much more than the desire for a quick fuck.

"That you forgive me. That you'll be my girl." Rounding his hands to my face, he cleverly pins me in place when I try to avoid his gaze. Fuck, always with the heavy shit.

"I'm not into that possessive bullcrap," I dodge, trying to lean in for another kiss which he deflects.

"Just fucking say it. Let me believe, just for now; you're all mine in body and soul." Now I understand his open stare. It's despair, torment, and a dash of self-loathing. If I needed any more confirmation that Jack is truly sorry for trying to block me out, this is it. Not that I would hold the need to experiment against someone, it's human nature to explore, and I never had any doubt Jack would come back to me in the end. All part of the magical pussy. It's the gift that keeps on giving. So just this once, I relent and tell the gorgeous man what he wants to hear.

"I'm all yours Jack, for as long as you show me you want me." To prove my point, I lift my low-V t-shirt over my head, revealing my bare chest underneath. Then I wriggle out of my hot pants before helping Jack with the button on his pants. Shifting his jeans and boxers down just past his balls, his girthy erection springs up to greet me. I lick my lips, immediately drawn to the plump purple head. The guttural groan that leaves Jack as I take him all the way to the back of my mouth is pure music bouncing around the walls of the garage. His hand knots in my hair, holding me down for a beat to savor the feeling.

"Holy fuck, how did I ever think you weren't the girl for me?" He moans as I rise up and take him again, just as slowly. I've missed this. Not just the feeling of a throbbing cock in my mouth, but the feeling that comes with completely enthralling a man. Movies like to depict the woman as the submissive, but this is true power.

Swirling my tongue around Jack's tip, I tug his shirt as a signal to get it off. He obeys, and as I glance upwards, I'm temporarily distracted by the pink scar in the center of his sternum. I've heard the story of what happened, and I read the doctor's notes, but this is the first time I've seen evidence of what Tanya did. Jack notices my focus has diverted and begins to pull his shirt back down until I growl around his dick, sinking my teeth into the base of his shaft.

"Okay, okay!" Jack relents, yanking off the material and chucking it across the room. Then I go back to choking on his dick until he groans that's enough. I obey, releasing him with a pop, but only because I want him inside me, right now. Stroking my nails up his thighs, I grip Jack's hips and pull him off the stool so that I can sit on it backward. My breasts push against the backrest, my ass tilted off the edge to give Jack easy access. He draws his fingers through my wetness before sinking his dick into me just as the side door opens.

"Motherfuckers," Jasper growls, closing the door behind him. "I knew you better than to keep running around that damn house." I cut Jasper off with a groan, too distracted by the blunt head stroking my G-spot deliciously. Jack slides in and out of me lazily, his thumb toying with my asshole. My nipples rub against the backrest, turning into fine points that ache to be played with. Cue Jasper. He grabs the stool legs, gently dragging it forward, so Jack has to walk to stay inside me.

"Fuck off Jasp, I'm busy here," Jack growls dangerously. Jasper ignores his twin, pushing himself up on the workbench and putting his crotch directly in front of my face.

"If you're good enough, it won't matter if I'm here or not." With that, Jack hits me hard in the uterus, and I cry out, not expecting the increased vigor of his thrusts. He slams into me, sending my eyes rolling back in my head as Jasper fiddles about with something from a nearby drawer. Water sounds from nearby, gushing viciously. I moan louder, tilting my ass so Jack can hit as deep as possible, branding his mark within me.

"Here," Jasper says and I look up just in time to see him hand Jack a washed, hefty screwdriver.

"I don't need it," Jack protests but accepts it anyway.

"You don't, but she does." Meeting my eye with a wink, Jasper reaches out to stroke his thumb over my lips. "So fucking beautiful," he murmurs as Jack lines the rubber end of the screwdriver up with my ass and slowly twists inside. The sensation is everything, spiraling me into a sudden climax that nearly rocks me off the stool. Between Jack's stiff cock and the pressure pushing into my back passage, my cries grow into screams that tip Jack over the edge too. He stills, pumping his hot cum inside me on a strangled shout and all the while working that screwdriver into a smooth rhythm. By the time I come down, my head lolls to the side to see our audience has now grown by two. Spade palms his dick through his gray sweatpants while Ace's hungry gaze captivates mine.

"You ready for the next two, Crazy Girl?" Spade taunts. A layer of sweat coats my skin, but the challenge ignites a fresh wave of adrenaline in me.

"I'm always ready for two," I shoot back, leaning over the stool. Jasper tosses Jack a clean hand towel that's stashed away for when the boys work on their bikes, allowing him to withdraw and clean me up as the others swoop in. Stripping off his pants, Ace lifts me with ease and takes my spot on the bar stool. His tip is already glistening as he lowers me straight onto his solid cock, Spade taking up the rear. Ace and I have been in this pleasurable predicament before, except the green eyes blazing past the side of Ace's head aren't the ones appreciating my tattoos from behind this time.

Holding Jasper's gaze, I lower my head to take Ace's mouth. He rocks inside of me, strategically making me gasp so he can seize my tongue. I allow him to take me hostage and render me immobile as Spade's fingers also push inside my pussy, coating himself with my juices. Using them to slicken my asshole, his thick dick slides gently but firmly inside. I try to keep up with his kiss, but in the end, my head topples onto Ace's shoulder, and I lose myself to their combined rhythm. I can't remember feeling so full, to the point where I can't comprehend how my next climax crept up on me so fast. All I know is what felt like a snug fit is now squeezing both Spade and Ace so tightly, that there's mumbled concern about lack of circulation.

Gripping my sides, Ace lifts up and lowers me back down slowly to let me ride out my orgasm and release them both from the dick-jail I'd created. Finding the stool's rungs under my feet, I help him, putting the smile back on my face. Spade stands still between Ace's open thighs, his hands reaching around to massage my tits. Fina-fucking-lly. He plucks at my nipples, tweaking them between deft fingers as I ride their two dicks in unison.

Resting my head back, I crane my neck for Spade to capture my mouth for a searing hot kiss. Ace increases my speed, tactically breaking me away from Spade to ride all three of us to the finish line. A concoction of magical things happens in my lower region, causing me to groan the loudest. Spade swells first, Ace following right behind. I feel their every ripple, every pulsation, every groaned spurt filling me until cum is spilling down my thighs. Stars burst behind my eyes, and it's not even my orgasm.

Reaching over to sandwich me in the center, Spade plants a hand on Ace for stability. It's short-lived though, as a gloriously naked Jasper plucks me from their confines. Pressing my chest into his, my legs lock around his waist. Cum drips from me, smearing over the pair of us, and I couldn't be hotter for it. Jasper plants my ass on the hood of Jack's truck, stretching me across the glossy orange. His hand slides up the length of my torso, between my breasts, and settles over my neck. With the other, he grabs one of my ankles and plants it over his shoulder before slamming home inside me without warning. I cry out, still tender but deliciously wanton.

Jasper wastes no time, working my body like a well-greased machine. Out of all the men here, he knows me best. From the clasp on my throat to the angle of his hips on each thrust, Jasper owns my every scream. His body is in reaching distance for my nails to scratch long, angry lines down his perfectly muscled torso. Abs flexed, his head cocked, and stunning green eyes watching my every movement. Relenting to the pleasure and sinking into the light-headedness Jasper's grasp on my throat is causing, my head lolls and my eyes flutter closed. Suddenly, a hand grips my chin, yanking me back to the present. Without realizing he had entered, Malik is there, his dark eyes swimming like pools of lust.

"Watch him break for you," he orders, twisting my head to see his hold on the back of Jasper's neck too, forcing his face closer to mine. "Watch us all break for you." A pained expression crosses Jasper's face as if he wants to hold on, but the tension is just too much. A deep crimson flush coats his chest just as he explodes, carrying me over the ledge with him. We both groan, writhing to draw every scrap of pleasure from our bodies. His groin rubs against my clit roughly, his balls slapping against my ass.

I come down, gasping for air and clawing at Jasper's hand to release me. When he does, I inhale deeply, noticing the others have also stepped forward to spectate my undoing. In this moment, I'm an open book for all to read, stripped bare of my cocky attitude and simply…theirs. Five pairs of eyes watch me closely, five solid chests heaving with excitement. Jasper pulls out, stepping back to join the others which allows the cum pour from me down the front of the truck. I prop up my leg on the grate, laying languid for them all to take their fill from the view like the empowered boss bitch I am.

"I suppose it's your turn?" I smirk at Malik lazily, my eyes fluttering shut briefly. Shuffles of movement sound around me, not that I bother to see what's happening. Whatever it is, I'm sure it'll be electrifying.

"Not yet," Malik replies by my ear. He brushes the hair from my face tenderly. "First, we're going to get you cleaned up, fed, and rested. I want you at your best for when it's my turn to take you."

"Yes Sir," I smirk as Malik lifts my naked body into his arms and carries me from the garage, lulling me into a blissful sleep before we've even made it past the door.

MALIK

A murmur. A twitch. A rising awareness of the edge of my subconscious rouses me from a death-like sleep. Beneath my arm, the smart-mouthed woman I've invested my heart in shudders violently. I pull the cover higher, concealing her nakedness as she curls up into a tiny ball tucked against my chest. Settling back into a peaceful state, her strangled scream jerks me upright, alarm overpowering my limbs. I hunt for an attacker in the dark, only realizing after her next cry for help, that this particular assailant is in her head.

"Why would you do that?" I blink through the dark, soothing my hand over her back. Her vulnerability taps into my protective nature, the desire to demand answers clawing at my chest. I have to remember that's not the way to help her and that all Candy really needs is comfort. "What…what did he do wrong?"

My brows twitch, my thoughts lost to the shadows. As much as I want to ease her troubled mind, I want to know more. Candy doesn't reveal her past - no doubt for a good reason – but a selfish part of me wants a sneak peek into what built her into the person she is. Learning how to handle Candy is like learning a new language without any assistance, and this may be my only shot at deciphering the key.

"I trusted you. You've destroyed me." Dread races through me, leaving an ice-like coldness in its wake. Images assault my mind, ones I hope are pure fiction and will probably never know either way.

"Shhh," I soothe, stroking her sweat-covered forehead with my thumb. "I'm here. I'll save you."

"Can't save the dead," Candy mumbles back. Drawing my hand down to cup her cheek, wetness pools in my palm, and that's when I can't stand it anymore. Winding my arm around her back the next time she arches upward, hissing as if in pain, I draw Candy upright into my lap in a shift motion. Quick enough to shock her awake, locking my arms around her when she tries to lash out with a strangled scream.

"It's Malik. You're safe now; nothing's going to happen to you."

"Too late," Candy's whispered answer comes, her face turning into my neck. As her body slackens, my heart splits itself in two. Half beats with the primal need to heal Candy's scars, the other half disintegrates for the horrors it must have taken to break my beautiful girl. Cradling her against my body, we remain for as long as Candy allows, losing ourselves to our thoughts. Mine are filled with regret and promises of redemption, while I can only guess what dark path Candy's are tumbling down. Feeling the shift in her posture from arched to stiffening, I move first, refusing to let her walls fully re-erect just yet.

"Come with me," I coax, drawing her to her feet. Candy allows me to take her hand and lead her into my en-suite bathroom. The lights above the basin provide a low, orange glow, highlighting the smashed mirror underneath. Just like the various holes in the walls around my suite, Candy says nothing, leaving my dignity intact. It's bad enough I have to see the visual reminders of how I lost myself to fits of anger while she was gone without having to voice them too. Switching on the bath faucets, I tip in a healthy dose of bubble bath and turn to find Candy right behind me. Her breasts brush my chest, her lips close enough for her breath to fan over mine. But it's her eyes that entrap me. All-seeing and unwavering.

"Forget everything you heard," Candy warns me, her threat lost by the vulnerability marring her features. I loosely rest my hands on her smooth hips and shake my head.

"If it's a part of you, I want to know it."

"Not this," Candy shakes her pink head in defiance. "My secrets are buried for a reason. A stupid nightmare doesn't change anything." Brushing Candy's nose with mine, a heavy sigh rocks through my core.

"Every piece of you is incredible to me. Where you see weakness, all I see is strength. Every man under this roof would have fallen at less." Seemingly assuaged, Candy sidesteps my body to enter the large jacuzzi tub, her hand tugging my wrist down behind her. Happy to obey, I've barely slid into the bubbles before Candy is back in my lap; much like the cuddle in bed I didn't think she'd accept again anytime soon.

"One of these days, I want you to tell me who hurt you," I mutter against her ear, stroking my fingers along the length of her smooth skin.

"It's hilarious you think a single fucker that's ever wronged me isn't in an unmarked grave somewhere forgotten." Lifting her hand full of bubbles, Candy blows them at my proud grin. Why I ever worried over Candy's safety is a mystery, although worrying is how I show I care. A fact Candy will have to accept one day, like how I've accepted she's branded on my soul as clearly as the caricature tattoo permanently marked on my chest.

"What about Tanya?" I ask, trying to keep the judgment from my tone. I'm done with telling Candy what to do. Her way of thinking simply fascinates me.

"Tanya is a blip in my universe," Candy pops any large bubbles unfortunate to float our way. "But I find her attempts at beating me mildly amusing. Once she really pisses me off, she'll know about it." I grunt, dropping the subject and hoping that time doesn't come once it's already too late. I know assuming the worst is a fault of mine, but that's where Candy counteracts me. If she's not worried, I need to trust that there's no reason to be.

We remain in the water until it turns cold, and my fingers drawing patterns across Candy's thighs are well-pruned. Kissing her forehead, I suggest we head back to bed. Candy hums, suggesting she was already halfway there. Rising, I grab for a towel to tie around my waist before helping Candy up. Not because I worry she'll get the wrong idea, but from experience that Candy will definitely try it on. She'll take any out to avoid her feelings and tonight, I'm enjoying her being exposed. She feels closer to me than ever before.

Carrying her from the tub, I place Candy carefully on the counter by the basin, quickly fetching a towel from the heated rack. Coating her in its warmth, her head lowers onto my shoulder and I still, merely remaining there. As far as I'm concerned, this night can never end, and I'd be a happy man. Our fronts press together, providing the connection for my heart to tumble straight from my chest into hers.

"Can I ask you a question?" Candy says into the silence, jarring me back to reality. Twisting her head, those chocolate brown eyes peer directly into my soul. "Why did you really tell the Monarchs they couldn't have girlfriends? The real reason, not just some controlling bullshit." I drop my forehead against hers, slinking my arms around to hold her close.

"The more people under my roof, the more risk there'd be that I couldn't protect everyone, and if anything happened, the blame would fall on me. It was easier to deny my men love than to see them broken by it, until you came along. The fierce woman who has us all by the balls and doesn't need anyone's protection. At least now, if you happen to crush one of us to dust, we'll all fall together."

Smirking, I press a quick kiss to her lips, praising whatever God brought this Crazy Girl my way. Alarms blare in my head, telling me not to ruin the moment, but there's so much I want to say. So many promises lining my lips, ready to fuck our utterly perfect moment into a distant memory. I know I shouldn't, but I reckon I'd regret leaving words unsaid more than Candy's expected reaction.

"I think every decision I've made in my life was unknowingly bringing me closer to you." I exhale deeply, preparing myself for Candy to shoot me down.

"I don't believe in fate," she shrugs and I raise my brows, having expected worse. "Opportunities arise every day; just some people are too chicken-shit to seize them. But I've traveled far and wide. I've done things in the name of survival you couldn't understand, yet I've never met a group of guys that can captivate me like the Monarchs."

Flutters burst to life in my chest as if Candy has just declared her undying love for me. In her terms, it's close enough, and I'm now riding the high of passion. Sweeping Candy off the side, I return us to the bed, now more than ready to end this night before she takes back her words. Tucking us beneath the covers, I press a kiss to her nose, the smile cemented on my face until further notice.

"I just hope there's enough of us to keep you entertained and that there's always someone you can always turn to if you ever do decide to let us in properly." Snuggling her into my chest, Candy's breathing evens out so quickly, that I'm not sure she heard me. But I heard me. As the dark weighs down on our cocoon, pulling me into its clutches, I mull over the overall lack of jealousy and possessiveness overriding my usual senses. I don't even care who she confides in, as long as she finds a way to cross that bridge with someone under this roof. This is about Candy healing more than picking favorites. At this stage, all I want is what's best for her, and I'm man enough to admit that won't always be me.

CANDY

The house is strangely quiet as I venture out of mine and Jasper's room in search of some entertainment. My hair is tied into two high ponytails, which swish as I toss my head side to side, playing hopscotch down the stairs. My boots almost slip a few times, adding a death factor to my game. Will I make it down, or will I tumble to my death, who knows? Angus and Hamish dance in and out of my legs as I go, jumping the last few steps with me with a 'weeeee.' Angus has been so much more fun since Hamish appeared. Even his eyebrows aren't tense all the time. The little guy just needed a good rogering and a companion, a lot like me, I guess.

Clattering sounds from the kitchen while I spot Jack standing against the two-way mirror. Spraying the surface, he proceeds to clean it while his gym shorts rub the clear outline of his cock against the glass. That way, I smirk to myself. Passing through the security door to the bar, I also find Spade up a ladder with a large duster in his yellow, gloved hands and Ace vacuuming between the tables.

"What the hell are you guys doing? Don't we have cleaners for this menial shit?"

"Malik won't let anyone he doesn't trust within a mile of this place. Except for the surveyor, who's due to arrive in an hour, and this place has to be 'spick and span.'" Spade rolls his eyes and finger quotes, almost tipping backward off the ladder. I make no move to catch him, but he manages to straighten before I was forced to step back and watch him fall, making me the asshole of the day.

"Is the surveyor a neat freak? I doubt he's going to check the rafters for dust."

"There's no arguing with Malik's logic when it comes to these things. He reckons hitting the road with you won't be a cheap venture, so we need the best evaluation we can get." Spade goes back to his dusting while Jack finishes the bar and grabs a mop to start on the floors. I don't know what Malik is panicking about. We can easily pick up work on the road, do some cash jobs at bars on different beaches, and a few wet t-shirt competitions on ladies' night with these guys - we'll be rolling in it.

"Well, you guys enjoy that, I'm going to sunbathe on the garage roof," I signal to Ace's headphones sitting around my neck. From the second I woke up, I decided today was a catching rays and chilling to music type of day, making the best of being on house arrest until this place sells. Malik will argue I'm not technically 'in' the house, but he'll have to settle for keeping me bound to the property line. Any less than that makes me claustrophobic.

"Um, have you looked outside?" Jack asks. I swivel towards the revolving door and the thundering downpour of rain pelting against the other side. Thanks to the fan I had on to sleep and Ace's vacuuming, my dreams just popped like a bubble of gum. Fuck! I'm out of gum too. Worst day ever.

"Are you fucking kidding me? The one day I want to enjoy the sun, and it's fucking raining. The world is actually against me," I curse, always having suspected, but the proof is now slamming against the porch.

"I mean," Jack says, pausing to lean on his mop, "technically, it has to rain sometime. Precipitation, evaporation, and all that. What goes up must come down."

"Thank you very much, Mr. Weatherman, but what do you suggest I do with this?" I drawl sarcastically, opening my Monarch leather jacket to reveal the glittery pink bikini top underneath. The matching thong is poking out of my mini denim shorts with the button popped open and strings pulled high over my hip bones.

"I can think of a few things," Ace suddenly shuts off the vacuum and straightens. Like the others, he's opted for baggy sweats and gym wear for his domesticated cleaning look. I'm more interested in the hungry look in his puppy dog brown eyes though, and not for the same reasons. Ace is hungry for me, whereas I'm hungry for excitement.

"Yeah, so can I," I smirk, striding towards the revolving door. Whipping off Ace's headphones, I toss them onto a table, flick the lock and push my way out into the rain. Anyone who was chasing me halts in the doorway, whereas I run down the steps and stomp in the closest dirty puddle. Kicking wildly, I splash slick mud over the front of the Devil's Bedpost in great, big slashes.

Saluting goodbye to the guys now screaming curse words at me, I run around the back of the parking lot and let myself in the back door. Jasper is there, drying the last of the washing up and putting everything back in its proper place. Lost to the tune he's singing to himself, he doesn't notice me approaching until I pluck the blender from his hands.

"I fancy a shake, don't you?" I grin, kissing his cheek. The surprise in his green eyes subsides, replaced with the warmth of his smile.

"Oh, sure. That'd be nice," Jasper agrees. He moves over to the refrigerator, retrieving the milk and an array of fruit for me. All the while, I keep my muddy boots out of his eye line by moonwalking around the kitchen island. Accepting the milk alone, I tip the contents into the blender and hit the power button just as the three guys from the bar run inside.

"Wait, no!" Jasper cries out about the lid, but I manage to duck away while four bulky men fight to get to the power button first. By now, half the room and all of the present Monarchs are coated in frothy milk jizzed out by the open blender. That was stupid; someone really should have put the lid on it.

Darting back up the stairs, I recently played hopscotched down, feet and shouts pounding after me. Laughter bubbles from my lips as my mind struggles to pick where to go. I'd head straight to Malik's suite if the big bad wolf wasn't yet to be seen, meaning I can't gauge his mood. Setting on Spade's room, because it's always Spade, I lose precious time messing about with the handle before racing inside. I manage to get one leg up, preparing to hop up on Spade's bed and jump dirty tracks all over that fucker, when an arm hooks around my waist. Lifting me clean off the ground, I'm wrestled back into the hallway, where Spade and Jasper grab a foot each to pry the boots off my feet. Kicking and screaming, Ace mumbles at my back, drawing me back downstairs when Jack is waiting with the mop.

"Here, you can start with the floors," he pushes the mop into my hands. "Then Jasper will oversee you fixing the mess you made in the kitchen."

"Okie dokie," I smile sweetly, waiting for Ace to release me. Swaying my hips, I dance around, moping up the muddy footprints across the floor under the scrutiny of four narrowed gazes. I don't know what they're so worried about, it's not like I'm going to do something reckless.

"Oops," I twist, 'accidentally' knocking a vase of flowers off the sideboard in the games room. A collection of gasps sound, and it's Jasper who jumps forward first, catching the vase before it hits the ground. Unfortunately, the flowers inside were fake, so there's no added water inside. Serves the Monarchs right though - they've never bought me flowers, fake or real. What's the surveyor going to care for a bunch of tulips? Moving into the kitchen again, I spot a small tub of paint sitting exposed on the side. Hello, my beauty.

"Don't you dare," Spade says, spotting the paint the same time I do. The lid is slightly askew, the color on the side matching the skirting board Jasper must have been touching up before needing to chase after me. No one moves, no one even breathes at that moment.

"See, the thing is Spadey," I announce. "You just dared me." Spinning around, I whack the paint pot with the end of the mop. The guys all race forward, saving most of the kitchen from being splattered in burgundy red paint. Instead, it's coating their faces and t-shirts. Ace's shoulders sag, his fucks forgotten as he spits a wad of paint onto the floor.

"Why are you purposely trying to piss Malik off?" Jack groans, trying to wipe his eyes clean. He fails, smearing the paint more like a superhero mask.

"Because it's fun, and I've made it my life's mission," I shrug as the guys part to reveal our missing member.

"Mission succeeded," Malik hisses, the vein in his temple pulsating. I like the danger seeping from his dark eyes, his hair slicked back perfectly to mirror image the sharp edge of his jawline. The smart suit snapped back to his body like it never left has one single speck of red point on the shoulder that I dare not point out.

"I vowed not to order you around anymore, but you'll have to forgive me on this one. If this place has a spec of mud by the time the surveyor arrives, you lose all sexual privileges. From all of us." I smirk, popping my hip and calling Malik's bluff. The others, though, cross their arms sternly, their tensed jaws seeming to agree with Malik's threat.

"Well shit," Angus muses from the counter, failing to keep the amusement from his gruff tone. "Looks like they're serious this time." Grumbling, I stalk away to pick up the paint pot and start cleaning like some domesticated housewife. A few months ago, I'd have walked out this back door and never looked back. Now though, I've been ruined by five massive dicks in all senses, and my magical pussy would never forgive me if I gave that up for the sake of some scrubbing.

SPADE

A low snore rattles through my bed frame and into the base of my skull. I lie on my back, staring at the ceiling and willing the sun to come up. Thanks to the surveyor pointing out all of the renovations needed in Malik's suite, he has commandeered Ace's room. And while Candy is also in there, she has yet to see daylight since she went in a few nights ago, Ace is stuck camping out on my bedroom floor.

Another snore grinds through me, and I twist to look over the edge of my mattress to see he's rolled into the bedpost, hugging it like a splinter-infested teddy bear. At first, I think about suffocating him with my pillow, but then Candy would kill me in the most brutal way imaginable and I quickly dismiss that idea as not worth it.

Instead, I fling back my cover and leave the room before I do something I'll regret. The house is silent, everyone enjoying their full night's sleep in their own comfort. Lucky bastards. In just my boxer shorts, I slip into the gym, hoping to burn off enough energy that I could sleep through the apocalypse. Picking up a set of wireless headphones, which we leave in here for times like this, I push the little buds into my ears and scroll through the playlists on the wall panel. I settle on some Five Finger Death Punch, preferring to keep the lights off and power up the treadmill.

Glimpses of light from the street lamps we had installed outside ruin the illusion of running through a darkened woodland, but with just enough imagination and sleep deprivation, I still manage it. This is my happy place, where I go to when I need an escape. From snoring, from Malik's mood swings, from life, anything. I just wish I could feel the night's air on my skin, soothing the sweat I soon break into. I could head out and do it for real, but wandering away, alone and in the dark, is just asking for trouble.

Instead, the music fills my mind and the thunderous pound of my feet banishes the stress from my limbs. Imagining the shadows of thick trunks around me, I set my sights on the mirage of a spunky imp with bright pink hair. She runs, goading me with smirks over her shoulder that draw out the predator within. Like the first time I really fell for her, cocooned in the basement as I witnessed her vulnerability, I tumble through the steps needing to be closer. Needing to have her in my arms at all times. Turning up the treadmill's speed, I go all out, pumping my arms in sharp strikes. The mirage ducks behind a tree and reappears with horns protruding through her pink hair, the lower half of her body coated in fur like a goat.

I'm so caught up in the fantasy my mind has conjured that I almost miss the flash of red light shifting across the wall opposite. Craning my neck back to the window, I misstep and fly off the treadmill, crashing into a heap by the kettlebell stand. Still, with adrenaline rushing through my limbs, I hoist myself up and sprint to the window just in time to see a car skidding away down the dirt track. The hallway light flicks on, my fall having finally woken Ace.

"What the fuck's going on in here?" He yawns, rubbing his eyes. His hair is a sweaty mess, but I don't have time to mock him for it, barging past to run down the stairs.

"There was someone outside," I whisper back, hearing Ace pad after me in the shadows. Peering around the corner, I don't see anything usual but grab a concealed handgun from underneath the poker table anyway. Ace grunts in surprise, but he doesn't know the half of it. I've been hiding weapons all over the place since we were so easily trapped last time. A mistake I won't be making again. A 'ding' sounds before the elevator doors slide open, revealing the twins slumped against opposite walls inside.

"The fuck you guys doing," Jack mumbles incoherently, stumbling into the games room. Jasper spots the gun in my hand, shining from the elevator's temporary light. His eyes snap open, his back straightening.

"What is it Spade?" He asks all business.

"I saw a car driving away through the gym window," I tell him, not trusting the others in their lazy states.

"You sure it wasn't someone getting lost?" Jack sighs, heading for the kitchen's coffee machine. My blood boils at his nonchalant attitude, the real urge to shoot his hand off as he reaches for a mug coursing through me.

"This place is a long way from anywhere - that's why we chose it. No one just 'gets lost' up here at stupid o'clock in the morning," I snarl. A hand pats my back, Jasper's gaze catching mine to give a nod in solidarity. At least one person is taking Candy's safety seriously. I'm mostly surprised at Jack, but maybe after everything he's been through, he doesn't think an ambush would happen twice. Let's just hope he's right.

Ordering the others to do a sweep of the lower level, Ace and I take the bar while I spot Jasper slap Jack upside the head just as he's about to take a sip of steaming coffee. I bite the insides of my cheeks to hold back my smile, keeping my mind focused. Looking into the bar via the two-way mirror and spotting nothing unusual, I enter through the steel connecting door, keeping my gun raised. I'm in full Combat Karl mode, ducking low to span the outside of the bar when the lights overhead flicker on, breaking the illusion.

"Whatcha up to?" Candy asks, popping a bubble of gum loudly. I turn to shush her and stutter, my mouth going slack.

"Holy hotness," comes out instead. Contrary to usual, Candy's wearing makeup, except both her pink and blue eye shadow and red lipstick has been smeared. Below a studded choker, only a pair of heart nipple covers and tiny leather pants sit beneath her Monarch-branded leather jacket. On either side of her head, a ponytail completes the look with her beloved bat resting over her shoulder. Ace releases an appreciative whistle, and in no time, her presence has attracted the twins too. "We...erm...why are you dressed like that in the middle of the night?" I ask, unable to concentrate.

"Malik and I were watching Suicide Squad on Ace's computer," Candy shrugs. "I wanted to get in the mood, and it turns out Malik has quite the dirty fantasy for all that comic book stuff."

"I think we all do now," Ace agrees, his eyes glued to her chest. Realizing I'm still crouched with a gun in my hand, I straighten and place it on the bar. "Where is he anyway?"

"Mmmm?" Candy flicks her eyes back towards us after her gaze has wandered. "Oh, he's washing off his makeup. Didn't want you guys to see my craftsmanship, apparently." Wide smiles break out on all of our faces, our eyes lighting up with the same idea. We've got to see this. Rushing towards the connecting door, the four of us become squished, all fighting to squeeze through first, when Candy's voice makes not just me, but all of us fall dead still.

"Aww, you guys got me a present!" She's skipped away, and suddenly, we're all retreating to catch up with her. I manage to catch her wrist first, yanking her a step back from what's caught her eye. Outside the revolving glass door, sitting on the porch is a gift hamper. Safe behind the glass, I lower myself down to get a better look. Encased in glittery cellophane with a huge pink bow, the oversized tag reads 'Welcome Home.'

Jack curses under his breath and I scowl over my shoulder, wanting to stamp 'I told you so' into his forehead. Standing with a sigh, I turn to my brothers, preparing to state the obvious. *Click.* Candy unlocks the door and pushes her way out before any of us can stop her. I rush out, using my body as a meaty barricade when she reaches for the handle.

"Are you insane?!" I ask, earning myself a sarcastic glare.

"Okay, rephrase. We can't just pick up a random gift basket. This must be Tanya's doing. It probably has a bomb inside."

"Spade. It's a teddy bear and a bottle of wine. There's no bomb in there," Candy points past me, reaching for the handle again, but I shoulder her arm out of the way. Tutting, Candy shoves me aside and I topple over, careful not to touch the hamper on my way down. I yell at Jasper to do something but it's too late. Candy's picked up the gift basket and is walking down the porch steps.

"Seems a shame to waste good wine," she calls back. "But if it'll put your mind at ease, Spadey, I'll prove it to you. The things I do for my Monarchs," she mumbles, kicking over a traffic cone that we keep for the busy nights. Well, when we used to have customers, that is. Placing the basket on top of the cone, Candy takes her power stance, rearing back her bat. My hand wraps around her waist just in time, yanking her off balance and into my chest.

"Humor me," I beg, walking her back towards the porch. Her ass in those tiny shorts presses against my boxers, her ponytails tickling my chest. Trailing my fingers along the length of her arm, she releases her beloved bat, and I quickly hand it off to Jack. Jasper waits for us to be back under the safety of the porch before raising the handgun he's still clutching. He shoots once. Nothing happens except my relaxed sigh as he shoots again and again. Easing Candy into Ace's hold, I lean in to kiss her smeared lips when heat suddenly explodes across my back.

Both the fear and force of it throw me into Candy's body, bringing her down to the ground beneath me. Ace drops beside us, throwing his arm over my back protectively. All around, shattered glass rains down onto the porch's overhanging roof like hail. A flare of orange burns my retinas, causing me to hold a hand over my eyes while pushing myself upright. Candy merely lies there, staring in awe.

"Huh," she remarks. "Suppose it was a bomb after all." I huff, leaving her in the cocoon Ace creates in my absence. I shake my head, pulling Jack and Jasper up to investigate with me. Charred remains of the basket lay all around the parking lot, along with blackened balls of stuffing from what used to be the teddy. Incinerated straw fills my nostrils as the three of us inspect the remains. It couldn't have been a large bomb, and whether Jasper's bullet or the damaged clock face I spot set it off is a mystery. Either way, a bomb just tried to blow up my girlfriend and someone is going to pay for that in blood. Tanya or Cherry, as I'm undecided whose handy work this is.

Calm and collected as ever, Candy props up her head on her hand, popping a bubble of gum and wriggling her fingers in a wave each time I look back. Rolling my eyes, I wonder why we are trying so hard to protect someone who has no regard for her own life. Yet to do nothing would look like we don't care at all, and that's so far from the truth even Candy can't deny it anymore.

CANDY

Turns out, this face paint wasn't as washable as the label suggested. I don't mind personally; the smeared eye makeup brings back fond memories of Kelsii at the gentleman's club, but Malik had a thing or two to say. He cursed me out a million times over as I scrubbed his face red raw in the bath and only managed to shut him up by sitting down on his dick. I'm a people pleaser like that. Dragging on a pair of Ace's gray sweatpants, I roll the waistband over several times and leave my upper body in just a sports bra. It's not like I'm going anywhere any time soon.

On that depressing thought, I skip down the stairs in search of something to do. Jack walks past on the other side of the two-way mirror, a case of scotch in his hands. Perfect. Entering the bar, Spade is there too, looking super fine in a tight vest and baggy shorts, while boxing up the alcohol and clearing out the cluttered area beneath the bar.

"What you guys doing?" I bang my hands down on the bar, causing the pair to jolt. Spade places down his box, smirking like today's entertainment just arrived, whereas Jack watches me tentatively. Clearly, a screwdriver in the ass wasn't enough to cross the bridge he'd built between us. Maybe a wrench would do it, or a hammer perhaps? Either way, he needs to loosen up and so, a plan hatches in my mind.

"We figured now's as good a time as any to start packing up. It's not like we're going to reopen and the realter has some viewings booked in the next few days," Spade shrugs. I close the distance between us, leaning over the bar to rescue his box from that stupid idea.

"Let me rephrase the question – what the fuck are you doing 'packing away?'" I awkwardly finger-quote around the box. "Alcohol is for consumption, not collecting dust. Pop some bottles, and let's have ourselves a goodbye party." Placing it down on Ace's prized chestnut table, I pull out two bottles of Ejaculating Unicorn gin and eye the glitter floating around inside. A corkscrew presents itself, attached to the tattooed arm of my old road buddy.

"I'm down, love," Jasper bobs his eyebrows. Grease mars the front of his lime green t-shirt, along with the smears over his emerald eyes suggesting he's been working out in the garage. A figure moves through the revolving door just over his shoulder, and my smile widens. "What about you Ace? Feel like a daytime drinking game?" My not-so-broody tech genius slings his arm around me, pressing a kiss to my temple.

"Candy, drinking and games? There's nowhere else I'd rather be," he chuckles and warmth spreads through my chest. Weird, I must be catching a fever. Nothing I can't drink away. I take Jasper's offered corkscrew, popping the gin lid and lifting it to my mouth. A hand snaps out, relieving the bottle before I make it to my lips and I scowl at Malik, standing there with a large, rounded glass filled with ice.

"If you're serious about drinking our inventory, we're going to do it with class," he says, pouring a large measure. Spade appears on his other side, opening a can of tonic to add in and with Jack lowering onto the sofa nearby, it looks like the whole gang's here. I accept the glass, taking a seat beside Jack to plant my legs over his thighs. The others stalk away to grab their drinks of choice while I sip mine, watching Jack closely. His blonde hair is flopped forward, shielding his dazzling eyes from my stare. Placing his hands onto my calves, his thumbs move in small circles and I sigh.

"Can we fast forward to the point where it's not weird between us? I'm too highly strung to not rape you at any given notice."

"I seriously doubt you jumping on my dick will feel like rape," he smirks, flicking his hair aside to give me a humored look.

"If you don't drop the pussy-foot bullshit, it'll be my strap-on ramming your virgin asshole you should be worried about," I reply earnestly. Jack's cheeks pinken, his eyes darting to Spade, and I gasp, almost dropping my drink. "I knew it! You guys totally-"

"What game we playing?" Jasper interrupts, handing his twin a whiskey glass. The bottle goes on the table separating the four sofas framing it. Ace joins his side while Malik reclines on another, crossing his ankles on the leather. Spade is last to join, rounding the back of my sofa and leaning in to mouth-fuck my face in an obvious show of dominance. I fucking love it, like a dare for the next to do even better. Means I'm a winner every time. Pulling away with a knowing smirk, Spade takes the last sofa, holding his drink up in a toast.

"How about 'Never have I ever?'" he says, and I snort.

"Way too broad. I'll have done shit you guys couldn't even comprehend. Let's play 'Would you rather?' If you disagree with the person choosing the question, you have to drink." Muttered agreements sound, and I sit upright, nestling the heel of my foot against Jack's cotton-covered dick. "I'll go first. Would you rather sleep with your ex or your boss?" I smirk, my head snapping to Jack's. With Malik sitting opposite, the atmosphere thickens as I announce I'd take my ex any day. The only boss I've ever had turned out to be my father, and I don't have any ex's, so it's a no-brainer on my end. For Jack, Jasper, and Ace though, it's mildly amusing watching them knock back their drinks, working hard to avoid Malik's stunned stare.

"Moving on," Ace clears his throat. Leaning forward, he refills his whiskey before doing the others and rests back in his seat.

"Would you rather die alone or with everyone you love?" For some reason, all eyes move to me, and I chuckle.

"I'm taking down every fucker stupid enough to love me," I raise my glass and down the gin and tonic in one long swig. No one else joins me, some silent conversation happening around me and the tension growing heavy. The opposite of what drinking games are all about.

"Okay, my turn," Jasper interjects. "Would you rather lose all of your memories or your money? I vote money." Sounds of agreement ring out from all of us except Malik, the cogs in his mind visibly working.

"A few months ago, I'd have said take my memories. A lot has changed since then," he muses, drinking his whiskey and dropping his head back to stare at the ceiling. Puffing my cheeks out, Jack nudges me with a small smile.

"How about this one then, Malik. Would you rather be handsome and dumb or ugly and rich?" Thankfully the friction around us lessens, and I add a mental score in Jack's column for later. Rolling his head around, Malik runs a hand through his dark hair, an easy smile taking root on his chiseled face.

"Why you asking me? Spade's the pretty boy here without much going on in the old medulla oblongata," he taps his temple. Chuckles ring out, even from Spade, who doesn't deny the accusation.

"Ouch Mal," Jasper chuckles. "You'll need to use simpler words if you want Ace here to understand. He's been sparring with me a bit too hard lately." Ace elbows Jasper, causing his drink to spill over the rim of the glass.

"I'll remember that next time you need the dark web scanned or a drone to swoop in and save your asses." Lifting his glass to drink, his middle finger sticks out in Malik's direction.

"Don't listen to them big guy," I smile at Ace. "They're just jealous the coke-can monstrosity in your pants fills me more than both of them combined."

"Wanna test that theory, hot stuff?" Jasper straightens, looking intrigued. It doesn't escape my notice that Malik remains quiet, his interest also piqued. The mental image flaring to life in my mind is appealing, while this game is proving not to be. Major bummer when I'm looking to lose myself for a few hours and hear the hilarious tales of what I did afterward.

"I appreciate you want to distract me from the fact you guys suck at drinking games. I could have had more entertainment with a bunch of nuns diving into their wine stash. Where's the dirty fun at?"

"We have that game of Twister from the 90's night in the basement," Spade suggests. I shoot upright, my heel crushing down on Jack's dick with a pained grunt.

"Why didn't you say that in the first place?! Get your fine, dumb ass down there so the real excitement can begin!" I smack Spade's butt on the way passed, starting to limber up for the best game of Twister these guys have ever seen. Being an indoors person has never been my forte, but with enough games, liquor and taut muscles, I'm sure I can survive this hiding away thing for a little longer.

ACE

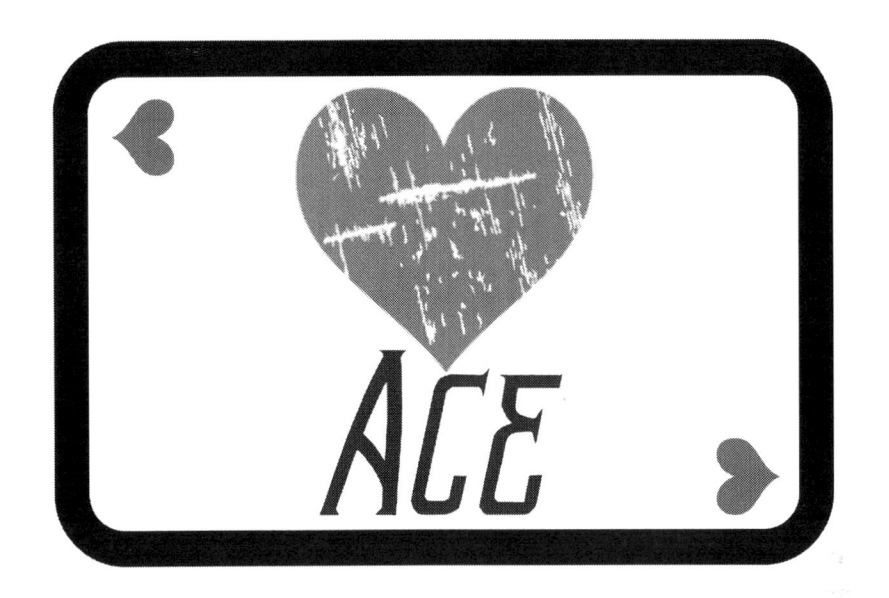

"Thanks man, have a good one," I tell the pizza delivery driver, accepting the stack of boxes he hands me. Nodding his cap, he disappears into the darkness, and I push through the revolving glass door, the booming music from inside seeping out to disturb an otherwise calm night. In the Devil's Bedpost, however, it's a spectacle of grinding hips, body rolls and prowling predators circling the dance floor, waiting for their turn. Malik is with Candy now, holding her flush against him, and he won't be releasing her anytime soon. Swaying slightly, I make my way towards the bar, handling my drink much better than those wobbling around me.

"You wanna know something weird?" Spade throws himself at me, nearly knocking the boxes from my hands. He's completely trashed, and I blame Candy's version of beer pong for it. Every cup was a mix of various drinks that basically burnt the shit out of our throats.

"Always," I chuckle easily, nudging him back onto a bar stool while I plant the pizzas on the bar top. I don't know who left Candy in charge of ordering, but I'm pretty sure she ordered one of each item on the menu. Spade grabs my face, twisting me to face him. Our noses are too close, but he refuses to let go, seriousness bleeding from his blue, hazy eyes.

"I should hate having to share the one girl that's captivated me with you cock-muffins. But I don't. I secretly," he pulls our foreheads together to stare directly into my eyes, "*looooooove* it." Erupting in laughter, I shove a hysterical Spade away and then quickly grab his arms when he nearly topples off his stool. He isn't fazed, babbling away like a teenage girl. "I mean, how lucky are we?! Eventually, we'd have all settled down and grown distant. Maybe only see each other at funerals and weddings, or not see each other at all. But this way, we get to remain together. We get to share the best girl in the world instead of destroying each other by fighting over her."

"Yes well, thank you for that Dr. Phil, but please get off my fucking arm." Spade looks down at the bicep he's taken to nestling onto, releasing me with a jerk.

"Pass me my pizza. I need to sober up," he grunts, swaying in his seat. It's my turn to laugh, slapping him hard on the back. Deep down, I hear what he's saying, but the macho man in me doesn't want to say it out loud. I've spent too long burying my feelings to voice them so freely. I'll leave that up to drunken Spade and the rambling twins that descend on the food, muttering in some made up language they both find hilarious.

"Oh fuck yes. Anchovies and beetroot. How did you know?" Candy praises, stumbling into the bar and stealing a box at the far end. The question rings out too late as she bites into the slice in her hand before I stagger over and slap it away. In turn, Candy slaps my cheek, hugging the box close to her chest. "What the fuck, asshole?! Get your own," she pouts, but I'm too busy prying the box from her death-like grip. Inspecting it, I find nothing out of the ordinary except a crime against pizza toppings.

"Who put in the pizza order?!" I shout over the music, getting nowhere with the giggling hyenas around me. Malik is still in the center of the dancefloor, swaying around with a sex doll in a pink wig I didn't see Candy swap herself out for. Taking the box with me, Candy leeches herself on my ankle before dragging behind me as I cross the dancefloor to kill the music. The sudden silence is filled by Candy calling me a 'cunting pizza thief' and Malik mumbling words of love to the sex doll. "Guys! Snap out of it! Who ordered the fucking pizzas?!" I shout, fear dousing the alcoholic high I'd been riding.

Holding each other up, the twins point at each other and then frown in confusion. Spade looks like he's passed out over the bar, the rhythmic snore radiating through each deep breath the only reason I'm not panicking about him right now. I have issues of my own, with Candy clawing her way up my body to grab for the pizza in my outstretched hand. I hold it out of her reach, shoving her face away when she makes a move to sink her teeth into my collar bone.

"Malik! Back me up here," I plead, finally getting his attention. His dazed eyes roam over the doll, telling her he'll be right back before dumping her in a heap on the dance floor. "We don't know where the pizzas came from, and Candy's was her favorite order," I try to explain to him as he staggers over. Some of what my widened eyes and stern face are trying to convey must sink in, resulting in Malik's index finger being held out.

"Party'sssss over. We're all too drunk to…um, check. Ride, on wheels I mean. But we can do a perimeter swoolaloo on foot while Ace checks the cameras." Malik grins, super proud of whatever the fuck he just said.

"What? No!" Candy shrieks in outrage, shoving angrily at my chest. Her brown eyes blaze with fury, not even resembling someone who's been drinking all damn day. "No ones passed out and pissed themselves while we draw dicks on their face yet; this party hasn't even gotten started!"

"Spade has," Jack announces excitedly, poking a finger into Spade's side. Sleeping Beauty snorts and grumbles while I let my guard down to squeeze my eyes shut, hunting for the last of my patience. That mistake costs me as Candy jumps, knocking the box from my hand. In a flash of movement, Candy's dropped to the floor as soon as the pizza slices have rained down, dragging her tongue across the toppings before I can heave her away. Limbs flailing, she screams and tries to scratch every inch of my forearm until I toss her safely behind the bar and block the entrance.

"Ignore them, love," Jasper smirks from across the bar, reaching out for her hand. "It's about time to take this fiesta upstairs and leave the Mr. Serious to his brooding." Jasper pouts his lips, making weird kissy noises at me.

"Count me in. I'm not missing out on throuple fun with some twin telekinesis," Jack gestures between his and Jasper's head, swaying into a sleeping Spade.

"You mean telepathy," Jasper snorts, pulling his twin upright for the pair to bob their eyebrows at Candy. She's not paying them any attention, preferring to stare at me with the rage of a tasered bull. I brace myself for the impending attack, refusing to back down on this one, especially when I'm the only one able to access the rational part of my brain.

"Stop thinking with your dicks for once," I growl, turning to face Malik when he approaches the bar to join this fight. "Who knows what drugs are already entering her system. We need to get her to a hospital."

"I'm right here," Candy growls, shifting into a rugby tackle stance in my peripheral vision. Malik leans on his elbows, tapping a finger on his cheek in thought.

"Poison doesn't seem like Tanya's M.O. She's put too much work into besting Candy. She'll want to see her success personally." My chest falls heavily, glad the real Malik is starting to peek through but a really bad feeling is choking me from the inside.

"Still right here…" Candy reminds me, and I can sense my time running out. She's going to attack me any second now.

"Unless this is Tanya's end game. To make us watch Candy suffer. I say we get to the hospital and they can test-"

"That's it," Candy snarls, her hands fisted. "Whether Tanya launches a nuclear missile at my face, or I just don't wake up in the morning, I'm all about living for the now. I'm not going to spend my life looking over my shoulder or passing up my favorite pizza. Trust no one and never stop running."

With that, Candy stomps her foot down in an effort to run at me but doesn't quite make it. I see the life leave her eyes and her body starting to crumple in slow-mo, diving forward to catch her before she hits the ground. My body takes the brunt of the pain, but it's the sudden shudders that seize Candy's entire body that has my full attention.

"Call 911, now!" I bark at whoever is aware enough to listen. The tremors worsen, a seizure claiming Candy until a thin line of white foam bubbles from her lips. My heart jackhammers in my chest as I simply hold her to me, not knowing what else to do. Fuck, fuck, fuck. Where's all that first aid training when you need it the most? My lips press against her cheek, her pink waves grasping onto me desperately in a beg to do just…something. Tears gather in my eyes at the sheer uselessness I can't handle until suddenly, Candy goes limp in my arms, her head knocking against mine, but at least she's still breathing. For now.

"Back again?" A familiar voice breaks me from my spiraling thoughts and I shoot upright in the tiny waiting room seat. The nurse who attended to Jack hovers in the doorway, trying to hold an amused smile, but I don't miss the way her eyes dart from one Monarch to the other, quickly doing the math.

"It's our girl," I sigh, seeming to be the only one who's noticed her appearance. "She's been p…partying too hard," I grind out. The lie tastes bitter on my tongue, but I can't divert from the witness statements we gave the cops. They were quicker to swing in here with accusing stares than the doctors were able to pump Candy's stomach clear of whatever poison she'd ingested. With none of us being able to prove our relation to Candy, not even after Malik flashed the portrait on his chest, we're being kept in the dark.

"I see," the nurse nods slowly. Glancing at the watch hanging from her pocket, she catches sight of a colleague and prepares to leave.

"Hey, wait," I stand and close the distance between us. Not too close, as I'm sure the cameras and lingering police are watching, but close enough for her to hear my low voice. "Would there be any chance you could let us know how she is? The doctors won't tell us anything, and we're all the family she has," I lie, not wanting to get into that tangled web now. The nurse's eyes flick side to side as she steps back into the hallway, her mouth set in a tight line.

"I'll see what I can do," she mutters and whisks away. My forehead automatically leans into the door jam, cursing myself for ending up in this hospital again so soon. I'm not confused about where we went wrong, just pissed as all hell we're still sitting here moping around.

"I'm going to finish this. No more waiting around," I growl low enough for my words to be drowned out by the busyness in the corridor but loud enough for the Monarchs to hear me. This time, all heads raise and meet me with understanding yet unbelieving gazes.

"We can't risk leaving this hospital until we're taking Candy home," Spade says optimistically. I groan, slamming my fist into the wall and stomping back over to the row of chairs. "After a second attack has happened at our bar, the police will be especially interested in our movements over the next few days. I'm as ready to kill that bitch as you are, but I'm not spending my life behind bars while you fuck my girl." Spade raises a brow, trying to lighten the mood but it fails miserably.

"I'm not so sure there would be any fucking going on," Jack pitches in. "Candy would have all our balls if any of us tried taking her revenge away, so jail might be preferable." Agreed mumbles ring out, except from Malik. He's yet to say anything since he reappeared from the bathrooms, forcing himself to expel every ounce of alcohol from his system. Needless to say, he's wallowing in guilt for getting himself into such a drunken state.

"It's not like Candy is able to tell us what she wants right now. I say we take care of this now and deal with her consequences later," I say, anxious to get out of here and do something productive. Sure, this goes against everything we've been trying to establish with Candy, but I'm starting to understand Malik's burden. Someone has to make the tough decisions.

"You guys still don't get it, do you?" Jasper sighs from the row of seats behind, scrubbing a hand over his face. "We're hers, but she's not ours. Candy will do whatever the fuck she wants and she won't let anyone else make decisions about her life. If we play the game right, we'll be all she needs but never feel comfortable. We could lose her at any minute, and that's not something I want to risk by slapping on the dominating bullshit." Standing, he paces over to the glass wall, peering down the corridor we last saw Candy be wheeled down.

"It's not good enough for me," Malik says, his voice croaking from the recent vomit train that passed through his throat. "I can't keep falling for her if being protective means she might just disappear again."

"Give her an ultimatum and that's exactly what she'll do," Jasper replies, not looking our way.

"This is bullshit," Jack shoots up, a mix of resentment and misery gripping his features. "How are we supposed to be with someone if we can't keep her safe? There's no give and take; just her decision and she's not always right." Jack glares, daring me to disagree but I can't. I hear his words deeper than I let my face show.

"Get creative," Jasper replies for me, strolling back around to address us all. "Nothing's black and white with Candy. Decide exactly what it is you want and find a way around it."

"I want Tanya's chest caved in beneath my fist," Spade growls as a small sound comes from the doorway. The nurse blinks several times, visibly trying to pretend she didn't just hear that.

"Um, Candy's awake and asking for you," she says

"Which one?" Malik asks blandly, everyone standing to join my sides.

"All of you," the nurse shrugs, doing her best to understand the situation. All it'd take is one look at Candy to understand one man would never be enough for her. "She's over on the next ward. Head over whenever you're ready." Following the nurse out, we navigate the brightly lit corridors and stop at the reception to locate Candy's bed number. An elderly matron warns us visiting hours are nearly over for the night as we stride away, and I chuckle under my breath. As much as I'd like to see security try to kick us out, Malik will have Candy in a private room before she can place the call.

In a room with seven other beds, the paper-thin blue curtains have been pulled around Candy's. I swallow thickly, steadying myself for whatever I'm about to see in the bed. I can still see Candy convulsing in my arms at the forefront of my mind, a lump lodging in my throat. Her eyes rolled back, her lips frothing. Those images will continue to plague my nightmares for a long time yet. Reaching out, I curl my fingers around the curtain and prepare to ease it back.

"Wait," Malik whispers, halting my hand. "Jasp, you understand her better than any of us. Will you convince her to let us deal with this? Make her see reason?" There's a hushed plea in Malik's tone, the anguish of passing over control clear for all to see.

"No," is Jasper's swift reply. I sigh, wishing they'd settle their differences once and for all. Jasper's green eyes hold each of ours, lingering on Jack's the longest. "I can't talk to Candy alone because she's a Monarch. We deal with Monarch business together, as a family." A shift in the air has my hand dropping altogether, and I turn to complete the circle with my brothers. Malik holds Jasper's eye, understanding dawning with a small nod. Reaching out, Jasper clasps a hand on Malik's shoulder, drawing him closer to rest their foreheads together and finally build the bridge that's been long overdue reconstruction.

"I get this is especially hard for you. At least with there being five of us, she'll always have someone to turn to. Without realizing it, Candy has ensured she'll never have to be alone again."

CANDY

A shiver rolls from my ear perking up at the sound of my Monarchs, all the way down my drugged spine. *'Never be alone again.'* The nausea shifting in my gut has nothing to do with the recent poison that flooded my system and everything to do with my capabilities to comprehend those four words. Doubling over, I expel my guts onto Angus and Hamish on the shiny floor as they scream and flail. Angus slips over, sliding out of sight as hands seize my body. I flinch, realizing too late that the hand rubbing up and down my back, and the fingers pulling my hair out of my face, aren't trying to harm me.

Fuck, I'm a mess. Not just in my current circumstances but in general. How far must a person fall to be completely at ease with a drug attack yet flinches at the first sign of affection? I used to think my ability to remain emotionless was my armor, but now I'm not so sure if I was trying to keep others out or myself in. What if the only person that truly is against me is me?

"It's okay Crazy Girl, we're here," Spade soothes. Once my stomach is emptied onto the hospital floor, a wet cloth wipes my face clean, and I'm pulled into a pair of strong arms. I know by the firm chest at my back and coconut scent it's Ace, but I don't open my eyes to look. I've hit the rock bottom of Soberville with a crash landing, and I can't bear the pitying looks waiting on the other sides of my eyelids.

Instead, I choose the illusion of sleep that pulls me into an internal conversation with Angus. He's waiting there, in the privacy of my mind with a wide grin that's at odds with his angry eyebrows. I try to shy away from him, knowing whatever he's about to say isn't going to give me any reprieve from those huddling around my body right now. How much weight can this bed even take before it collap-

Remember what Jasper said in the hotel. Angus cuts off my train of thought. Okay fine, my self-induced distraction. Rolling my eyes behind my lids, I think back to the night Jasper rocked my world in the fancy suite and then rocked said world straight off its axis. He was glistening and gorgeously naked, adhering to my every whim and bringing me to the brink almost instantly. He also told me he loved me, in the forever kind of way.

They all do kiddo, and spoiler alert, you love them too. Angus nods menacingly as if he's thoroughly enjoying my mental breakdown. Irritation flares through me, itching at my skin from the inside. I want to lunge out of the huddle I've found myself in, eager to break free of the consequences of letting these guys remain close. People associated with me get hurt and even if they didn't, a kid raised on hatred doesn't know how to love.

Yeah, you do. That wriggly feeling in your tum tum, the cutterflies in your chest, the warmth you feel when they're nearby. How you pushed them away to save them the hassle of knowing you. It's all love. Angus grins as Hamish appears, taking a chubby, pink hand in his.

Well shit. I somehow accidentally fell in love, not just once but five times over. How the fuck did that happen? Angus gives me a knowing look, and I turn my face further into my pillow. Yeah, I do know how.

After my breathing has leveled out and my heart rate dropped back to normal, I slowly twist onto my back to alert the guys that I'm officially ready to talk. Dispersing from the nest they've created, Jasper helps to prop me up while Spade fluffs my pillow. Jack and Ace pull up chairs, and Malik prefers to hover, not knowing whether to sit on the end of the bed or stand with his arms crossed. In the end, I grab his bicep and weakly yank him down into the empty spot at my side.

"Well, this wasn't where I planned on waking up tonight," I fill the silence, not exactly sure what time it is anyway. It could easily be the following day from my last recollection, and I'm missing out on my daily lunchtime tequila shot. Malik shuffles in closer, drawing me under his arm and finally reclines back.

"I know this is going to be hard to hear, but since you're stuck in bed, now's the best time to say it," he says and I brace myself for what's coming. Fuck it, I'll beat him to it.

"We told you so."

"I love you too," I say at the same time. Shit on a brick. My eyes bulge and my cheeks blaze with heat. Inside, I die a little as all five pairs of eyebrows hitch, slowly joined by soppy smiles. Oh god, I've turned into one of those gooey girls I'd stab just for a taste of reality.

"Come again?" Jasper asks, his eyes crinkling at the corners.

"Fuck off," I tell him, trying to roll onto my side but Spade doesn't let me. Taking the other side of my bed, he nudges me to remain upright when all I'd like to do is go die under a rock somewhere. So I do what any semi-rational woman would do and close my eyes in the hopes they all disappear. They don't, judging by their amused chuckles and slowly, a smile graces my lips. Great, I'm a giddy teenager too. When I reopen my eyes, Angus and Hamish are sitting on my legs, brandishing a banner that says 'We <3 The Monarchs.'

"That was unexpected," Ace smirks, but there's something hidden behind that smile. Something he either doesn't know how to say or has decided it's not the right time. I'm distracted by the soothing touch of Malik's fingers stroking up and down my arms.

The once unshakable force that ruled the Devil's Bedpost with his strict rules and quick temper is a distant memory. He changed for me, and the least I can do is give him what he wants. Snuggling into Malik's side, I sigh with the weight of every misguided belief I've been holding onto.

"Since we're sharing," his chest rumbles beneath my head as he refuses to let this go. "We should all voice our peace and then we can leave it here." Agreed mutters ring out, and I roll my eyes.

"Before you say something stupid like 'we'll be making all your meals in-house from now on,'" I mock Malik's voice and he presses his mouth into a thin line. "I'll take a crate full of poison pizzas over your spinach smoothies any day." The humor around the curtained area pauses for everyone to share a concerned look. My whole body aches as I try to get comfortable, although no amount of muscled cushion or shifting on the mattress will ease my discomfort. I feel like a scalpel has been taken to my insides, carving out all the bits I don't really need. Clearing his throat, Jack demands my attention and then immediately looks shy at receiving it.

"We're in a relationship. You with...all of us," he nods and I raise an eyebrow.

"Great start. Continue," I smile, deciding this is way more fun than I originally anticipated.

"You might have no regard for your own life, but you're one of us now. That means you need to live for us," Spade nudges my side. My smile drops, the good feeling gone. Ace leans forward to take my hand.

"We'll follow you to the ends of the earth, do whatever it takes to protect you," he says in this weirdly rehearsed speech.

"But in order to do that, we need you to promise you'll start looking after yourself. Loving you means losing you isn't an option anymore," Jasper finishes strong, his green eyes filled with such adoration. Adoration for a girl who stupidly just got herself poisoned for the sake of some beetroot, anchovies and a dash of stubbornness.

"Relationships are about give and take," I nod slowly, accepting the truth I didn't want to hear. But it's out there now, and there's no denying it feels damn good to acknowledge. These beautiful, broken men love me. They want me around, and for that reason alone, I have something to live for now.

JASPER

Thanks to the new tech Ace installed on all of our phones and around the building for extra security, a notification flags the instant movement is detected outside. I shoot upright in Jack's hanging bed, causing him to groan at the sharpness of my movements as the scar lining the center of his chest is tugged. He rubs it and I bat his hand away, telling him to let it heal properly. I didn't mean to fall asleep here, but we'd been reminiscing until late while giving Candy the space to recover in the room I now share with her.

Insistent pings sound from both of our phones, so I reach over Jack to grab mine. The live feed shows a delivery van pulling up outside, instantly jolting me from the swaying mattress. Forgoing a t-shirt, I shove my feet into Jack's timberlands and grab the rifle stashed in his wardrobe on the way out. Spade and Malik are already there, jogging down the hallway with a similar firearm in their hands. Jack skids into the elevator behind us just as the doors slide shut, snatching his rifle back from my hands. I let him, preferring the satisfying crunch of bones beneath my knuckles anyway.

The doors slide open, revealing Ace on the other side. In full camo, his phone is clutched in one hand and Candy's bat in the other. He must have been on his way out for a jog before receiving the same notification as the rest of us, but Candy won't give a shit about how accessible her bat was if he damages it. Whether we save her life today or not, she'll have all our heads in that instance.

Rounding the kitchen counter to where the truck has pulled up outside, Malik gives silent instructions, which we gladly follow. Leadership is as much his forte as his major fault, yet I don't mind now we have a common goal. Bracing his hand on the door handle, Malik uses his fingers to count down before whipping the door wide and aiming the beefy machine gun at the oncoming delivery guy. I pop up at the window with Ace while Jack and Spade mirror us on the other side. Everywhere the balding middle-aged man looks, the end of a barrel is facing his way.

"P-p-parcel for a Miss O. R. Gasm?" the man balks, trembling around the cardboard box in his hands. Malik barks at him to place it on the ground slowly, not noticing the growing wet patch in the crotch of the man's trousers. I lower my weapon, scanning the area instead of intimidating the man, who is clearly a pawn. Movement shifts by the tree line, disappearing before I can get any clarity as Candy strides through the kitchen.

"Cool it hound dogs; I placed this order myself." Malik makes a grab for her wrist and somehow, even in her recovering state, she manages to slam her elbow into his ribs and nudge him aside. Approaching the man, Candy accepts the package, wishes him a lovely day and retreats unscathed. Spade rushes to slam the door closed, double locking it just in case while we all peer over the box she puts on the kitchen island.

"Not more sex toys is it?" I joke, trying to lighten the mood. Candy bobs her eyebrows at me over the table, an easy smile spreading across her face. If I wasn't already sold on this girl, her impenetrable resilience would have done it at this moment. She puts the rest of us to shame.

"No, you might argue this is even better." Now I'm thoroughly intrigued as she uses a knife to cut the box open and pops the lid for us all to look in. Among the excess of brown paper stuffing, a box labeled 'The complete tattoo machine starter kit' sits next to a bag of love heart sweets.

"You know when you have the best dream and wake up like, 'holy shit, I need to do that?'" Candy beams, immensely proud of her latest purchase. "Pussy up boys, I'm branding you all today."

"Do you know how to…tattoo?" Jack asks, sounding unsure.

"No better time to learn," Candy shrugs, abandoning her box in favor of fetching a drink. Malik's chest puffs outward against his hastily buttoned shirt, releasing his breath with the grim nod of acceptance. I'd flick my wrist and make a whipped sound if I wasn't in exactly the same boat. Spade reaches inside the box, emptying the contents to set it all up.

Returning from the games area, Candy is carrying a glass of water she must have brought down with her. I've never seen Candy drink water, but I suppose permanently marking people is sober business, and I'm glad to see she's taking a task seriously for once. Hopping up on the counter in one of my baggy t-shirts and nothing else, she watches Spade's movements intently. I pull up a stool, settling myself between her legs to listen in on Spade's crash course on how to use the gun. The sight before me is too intriguing, however, and soon enough, my mind wanders as I brush my thumbs up the inside of her thighs.

"I trained as a tattooist's apprentice straight out of college. Wanted to make a career out of stabbing people and being artistic. Suppose I have, just not in the ways I'd imagined," Spade says, sparing Malik a brief glance. Our stoic leader has crossed his arms, making himself a pillar for Jack to sneakily lean against. Whether he needs it or just wants comfort, I'm not sure. Come to think of it, it might not have been an accident Jack kept me talking in his bed until I fell asleep. Maybe he craves the solace of having us close again. By the time Spade is done with his tutorial, Ace is spraying a cotton pad with sterile spray and brushing it over his left pec.

"Whatever you want to brand me with Sweetness, I want it

right here." I admire his bravery in going first, accepting her practice attempt over his heart. I hope he doesn't live to regret it. Although, crazy shit like this encapsulates the whole gist of being one of Candy's boyfriends – going along with whatever she has in store for us because that's what living for the moment is all about. Candy scrubs a hand through my hair like an eager puppy, flipping her leg over my head and giving me a stunning view of her glistening pussy. As quick as it appears, it's gone, and I'm left to join the back of the apparent queue by Jack.

"I won't judge you if you cry," Candy smirks, pushing Ace back onto the island. He chuckles, cockily resting his head on his hands. I watch Candy with interest as she retrieves her bag of love heart candies abandoned in the box and rips them open. Climbing up onto the island, she then straddles Ace's sweatpants and tells him to stick out his tongue. He does as she asks, for her to pop a love heart onto the end of his tongue and laugh to herself. Then Spade pulls gloves onto her hands one by one like an evil surgeon smirking at her next victim.

"What colors do you want, beautiful?" Spade asks, setting out pots by Ace's shoulder. I grin, already knowing what's going to come out of her pretty mouth by her scoff.

"Pink, obviously." Ace's brown eyes flick our way in panic and Jack breaks into laughter first, dragging me off the hysteria cliff right after him. Spade bites down on his bottom lip to hide his smile, pouring the hottest pink available into one of the pots. Starting up the tattoo gun, he hands it to Candy and guides her to dip the new needle into the coloring.

"Er-" Ace shudders as Candy raises the gun over his chest. "We're not drawing out a stencil or…anything?" Without answering him, Candy eases the needle down, pressing too deep if Ace's jolted scream is anything to go by.

"Press lightly, try not to drag as you draw out what it is you're thinking of," Spade advises her. The laughter on our end has died out as we realize soon enough, that it'll be us at Candy's mercy.

Ace's hisses lessen as Candy gets the hang of drawing over his skin, blocking in the pink. Following her orders, Spade dishes up some black and white, remaining over her shoulder to offer advice now and again. It's not long before Candy accepts Spade's disinfectant spray and a dressing to bar the rest of us from seeing the final product.

"When everyone's all done, we'll do a big reveal." Candy announces coyly. Fisting my hands, I step forward to go next, knowing the anticipation will kill me long before Candy's needle does. Patting the clear island counter once Ace has vacated, I fall into the trap of Candy's brown doe eyes. She's the image of calm, giving the illusion she's a pro.

"Where do you want it?" She asks, her eyes dropping straight to my crotch. Yeah, no thanks.

"Am I gonna like it?" I counteract her question with a cocked eyebrow. Instead of answering, she peels back one of her gloves to take another love heart from the pack beside me. Looking it over, a wide grin spreads across her face and she nods. Fuck it, I think, tilting my head to the side and tapping my neck.

"Go on then, hit me with your best shot." The excitement that thrums through the beautiful, insane chick before me is the instant reward I needed for my sacrifice. What's a patch of skin if I get to be in her good books for a while longer? No doubt I'll fuck up some time and this visible reminder that I'll do anything for her might just work in my favor. Popping the sweet in my mouth, Candy's lips crash onto mine for a quick, heated kiss. Caught completely off guard, the mix of her raspberry lips dominating mine and the bitterness of the sweet dull my senses, leaving another hidden taste in their wake.

With me trying to catch my breath, Candy takes a large drink of water, replaces her glove and starts the tattoo gun up once again. This time she starts with the black, drawing an inky outline while asking Spade to fetch some green. She starts higher than I'd anticipated, the scrap of the needle edging the line of my jaw beneath my right ear. I concentrate on studying her face while she loses herself in her work. At some point, her tongue pokes out of her mouth, and I swoon for her like a giddy teenager. With each stroke, her confidence grows, and by the end of our brief tattooing session, my hands have curled around her hips as she stands between my legs.

"It's an honor to be stabbed by you," I smirk, "and a huge turn-on. When you've finished, I'll be dragging you upstairs to stick something in you."

"We'll see," Candy muses, handing the gun back to Spade. Peeling the plastic glove down the length of her hand, she quickly whips it into my dick. I hiss at the sharp sting, cupping my groan and half rolling off the island. Candy nudges me aside the rest of the way to give Jack my seat. While Spade makes quick work of switching out the needle, Jack argues about having his ink somewhere hidden, but Candy isn't having it. Gripping his hand, she wrenches Jack's forearm upward and takes the gun back to press the fresh tip into his wrist.

"If you move, you'll fuck it up," she warns him, and my twin relents with a sigh. Catching onto the big idea, Spade takes a love heart, flashes it to Candy and proceeds to force it into Jack's mouth. The scene is as ridiculous as it is hilarious, watching Jack's face scrunch up with the sourness hitting his sensitive teeth and then contort with a hiss of pain from his wrist. Taking Candy's drink, I raise it to my mouth, too distanced by Jack's unanticipated, girlish squeal to realize how much liquid passes through my lips. The sudden burn of alcohol blazes a trail down my throat, causing me to splutter and spray the rest into the basin.

"This isn't water?!" I choke, catching a glimpse of Candy's smile as she continues to work on Jack.

"I never said it was," her sweet voice muses. "My regular tattooist always said vodka steadies the shakes. Mind you, he was an eighty-year-old man with Parkinson's." Jack's cries turn panicked and I pat my hand on his shoulder to keep him still. Candy glares at me in warning not to look at what she's doing, so I keep my eyes averted. I'm just here because I know what a pussy Jack is for needles. Fuck knows how he survived being stabbed. All the while, Malik remains by the opposite counter, a stern expression on his face as he saves himself for last. If this isn't some gang-on-girl bonding time, I don't know what is.

Once Jack is bandaged up, he slides from the counter and into my underarm. Drawing him over to a stool, I note his paleness as Ace slams a plate down on the counter. Jack takes one look at the food and retches, but I won't let him off that easily.

"You can't be sick if there's no food in you. Eat, it'll do you good," I tell my mirror image. When he doesn't move, I lift his bacon roll and stuff it into his mouth, laughing at his feeble attempt of a protest. Ace delivers another plate for me, taking it upon himself to make breakfast for us all while Candy bands us in the same room. Talk about teamwork. I take my roll and move to stand by Malik, noting that Spade has disappeared. Candy fills her time, shifting through love hearts and looking for the one she wants until he reappears, having clean-shaven the side of his head. Taking a pew on the island, he lies back and rolls his head our way, an entertained grin on his face. Well shit. Candy thrums with eagerness, dipping the gun into the white ink. Steering clear of his dreadlocks, she uses the white to outline Spade's darker skin before shifting so I can no longer see. Figures.

"Can someone pour me some yellow?" Candy asks, and I'm more than happy to assist. Wiping my hands down on my sweatpants, I tip the contents of the yellow bottle into a new pot. Passing it over, my hand accidentally knocks the bag of love hearts, sending them crashing to the floor. Shit, I curse under my breath, bending down to scoop them up. Ace is there in a flash, his hands hovering over the sweets at the same time as I see what has him frozen in place. Picking up one of the small hearts, my heart stops beating. What. The. Fuck.

Scrambling for the discarded delivery box, I pluck out the invoice receipt and mouth the item to Ace. 'Crude love heart candies.' Our widened gazes lock, dread seeping through me until a steady smile grows across Ace's face. Reaching over the mound between us, he then plants a sweet in my hand, his mouth moving but no words coming out. 'For Malik.' Reading the message on the candy, I have to bite my inner cheeks to resist from blurting out a laugh. Nodding, we hastily clean up the rest of the sweets just in time for Candy to announce Spade is all done.

"You're up Malimoo," she calls, and I slip the love heart into her hand.

"Do your thing, love," I whisper into her ear, kissing her neck in the same place she's permanently marked mine. After Spade has refreshed the gun's needle one more time, the gun whacks back into vibrating and I have to leave the room. Ace bundles out right behind me, along with a confused-looking Jack. I fill him in with muttered whispers, and as a trio, the three of us descend into silent fits of laughter. Tears stream from my eyes and my legs give out, just thinking about Malik's face in the next five minutes. Never mind what's on my neck and Spade's head, it'll be Malik's response that will make it all worthwhile.

Ace topples down beside me, the laughter racking his body feeding the flames of mine. Jack has slumped into a chair around the poker table, his smile wide but his eyes flicking back to the dressing on his wrist every few seconds. Poor fucker, but that's the joys of spontaneity. A foot kicks mine and I breathe to calm myself as Spade stands over me, announcing it's done. Damn, Candy sure learns fast. Helping me up, the four of us return to the kitchen, where Candy stands proudly next to a normal-looking Malik. The same black t-shirt and sweatpants are covering his stiff body, not a dressing in sight.

"Where is it?" I ask, giving him a visual pat-down. "Don't tell me you backed out."

"That's none of your damn b-" Malik starts until Candy yanks down his waistband, revealing the perfectly placed heart on his groin. Clasping my hand over my mouth, Ace's choked gasp says it all.

"Okay guys, line up. Let me take a look at my handy work all together," Candy beams, standing us all side by side. She rips the dressing off Ace's chest, then removes Jack's with softer movements. Her hand lingers in his, amusement evident in her eyes. "Take a look," Candy urges. Jack's green eyes drop to his wrist at the same time mine do. In a pale blue love heart, the words 'Eat Ass' stand out in bold, black lettering. Ace gets a good look at the side of my neck, bursting into laughter as I twist to spot the image on his chest. 'Dad Bod' sits in the pink love heart, and I put my fist in my mouth. Ouch, that one's going to hit him hard. Turning my attention to myself, I hunt for any reflective surface and settle on the microwave. Craning my neck, I struggle to read the inscription backward until it suddenly becomes so clear, that I can't unsee it.

"Tell me that doesn't say what I think it says," I tell no one in particular. Ace answers anyway, barely able to speak through his laughter.

"I Love Cock." I cringe at hearing it out loud, wondering just how random Candy's selection process was when it came to picking out our tattoos.

"It could be worse," Spade joins my side. "You could have 'Tiny Dick' on the side of your head." My smile returns with a vengeance as I spy the yellow love heat etched into his scalp. Yeah, he's right, it could be so much worse. Returning to the huddled group, I see we've moved into a circle around where Candy is holding Malik's waistband down, urging him to look already. His love heart is actually nicely shaded from the darkened purple around the edges to a soft lilac in the center. Candy learned quickly in her practices, but the colors don't distract from the words in the center. The very words that Ace and I picked out for him. 'I Have Crabs.' His dark eyes meet each of ours before slowly sliding downwards, the tension in his jaw tightening.

"What the fuck?!" Malik explodes, nudging Candy's hands away to grip his own boxers in his fists. Doubling over and groaning at the sight just beside his dick, the rest of us succumb to the laughter we can no longer hold in. Tears fill my eyes again, blurring the funniest moment of my life playing out before me. The louder Malik shouts, the louder our hysterics become, filling the entire kitchen with their echoes. Spade bumps my shoulder, his chin jerking towards a very impressed-with-herself Candy edging out of the room.

"Don't blame me. Your fates were left up to the Candy Gods. My usual type of love hearts are just roofies I write on with sharpie pens," she shrugs and strides away. I slip through the crowd, grabbing her hand in mine before she's able to make it out of the door.

"I have to hand it to you, love. No one else could brand us as you have and still live to see another day." A proud smirk takes residence on her face, her nonchalant stance not fooling me one bit. She thought she could do us dirty and make a run for it, but she's sorely mistaken. "But not even you can get off without a consequence."

Candy's smile suddenly drops, and my grip tightens on her hand as she tries to pull away. Shouting for Spade to prepare the tattoo gun one last time, Ace and Jack appear to help me drag Candy towards the island. She struggles, but not as hard as I reckon she could.

"See, the thing is," she attempts to reason, "I only trust one person to ink my body."

"Yeah, we heard, a vodka-loving old dude with the shakes. I'm sure you'll be fine with us," Spade chuckles, holding out the machine for me to take. I don't though, twisting my head towards Malik.

"Want to do the honors?" I ask, securing Candy's ankles to the countertop. An evil grin spreads across his face, not dissimilar to the one Candy was wearing after the package first arrived.

"Hell fucking yes," Malik agrees, striding over to accept the tattoo gun. Once freed from the machine he clearly did not want the responsibility of using, Spade then moves to help me pin down her other ankle as she tries to kick out.

"Make sure it's something she'll really hate," Ace adds and we all nod in agreement. Malik looks thoughtful for a second before grabbing a pen to hastily scribble on the side of the cardboard box. Showing his design to the rest of us, we immediately approve.

"Oh, fuck yes," I agree with a wide grin. "She'll hate it."

CANDY

Beneath the dressing on my denim-covered ass cheek, the tattoo Malik gave me itches like a motherfucker. I reckon not from the ink settling but with the anticipation of seeing what's underneath. After flipping me on the island counter, the Monarchs chuckled enough to make me think all manner of things could be on my ass now. Something cliché, no doubt, like a fucking fairy or shooting star. Not that I care much for my own body but point-scoring, I care a shit-ton about that. Not to mention how annoying the continued muffled sniggers that ring out every time I forget and drop onto my backside are. In conclusion, this whole situation is really starting to grate on my cheesy nipples.

"I don't like being on the outside," I growl, leaping up from the porch swing. Spade grins, twisting his head back from where his forearms are resting on the railing.

"Or you could say, being the 'butt' of the joke." He laughs, along with the twins on the swing and Ace leaning against the outside of the building. Thinking he's some kind of comedian, Spade's blue eyes flick from my face to my ass, and I promptly punch him in the face. He cries out, grabbing his cheek but I'm no longer paying attention. Being laughed at isn't my only concern right now.

"Hey," I ask quietly, postering myself by Ace's side. "Have you heard any news from Cherry yet?" The humor in his face wilts away, replaced by concern. Not for my half-sister, that's for sure. Probably for me.

"Signal from her phone hasn't been active in a few days. I couldn't say where she is or what she's up to." I scowl at Ace and his vague insinuation that Cherry must be 'up to' something. I thought old dogs were able to learn new tricks, but apparently believing my intuition isn't a trick the Monarchs are able to master. Pushing that aside, my chest does that weird twisty thing again the more I think about why Cherry might have fallen off the radar. Is she in trouble? Should I go searching for her? I may be untouchable, but she had no idea of the kind of world she was thrusting herself into.

"Look sharp," Ace jerks his chin. "They're here," I don't try to hide my unimpressed huff or the dull stare of my eyes. By 'they,' Ace is referring to a stuck-up realtor and the first of today's viewings for the Devil's Bedpost. I understand that in order to sell the bar and free us from all physical ties, people need to actually have a look around the place, but I can't help to feel somewhat territorial.

Homes aren't easy to come by when you're an unwanted orphan. Neither is a loving family and even though the Monarchs are coming with me, this building holds an odd sense of familiarity to me. I have my own room here. I learned to love here. I mastered the art of double penetration here. Nope. Despite what Malik said, I can't wait outside with the others. I need to scout out and see if any potential future owners are worthy enough to take on such a legacy. Shrugging off the coarse hands that have taken up residence on my hips, I dodge Ace's grip and rush to meet our visitors at the top of the porch steps.

"Hello there," I greet them before the Monarchs can stop me. Beside the suited kid that doesn't look old enough to manage his own morning glory, never mind sell a property, a couple stare at me wide-eyed. Sure, she's cute in a bleach-blonde hair past her blouse-covered boobs kind of way, and her legs look never-ending in tightly-fitted pants. On her slender arm, a tall dude with a man-bun and slickened beard hides behind his large shades. They seem to be a long way from the Snob Convention, but still, I put on my best smile. "Come on in then. There's plenty to see."

Ignoring the unsure stares across the patio, I push through the revolving door with our guests right behind. Malik stops mid-stride in a fine suit, the vein in his temple popping out to say hello as well. How thoughtful. Vexed by my appearance, I watch his rigid posture flee in favor of a resigned sag. I could almost laugh in his face at thinking I'd stay outside as requested. Who else is best to show around our special guests? Not Mally McMoody pants, that's for sure. Linking my fingers with his, I pull him aside to let the realtor babble a bunch of useless info from the paper in his hand. Seriously, who cares about the ceiling's structural integrity? Deciding his bland voice isn't doing us any favors, I plant my boot on the central low table.

"Make sure to appreciate this stunning piece made in-house by our own handyman," I catch Ace's curious eye through the window and wink. "Only the best waxed and varnished chestnut. It's the least we could do in our rebuild after the fire."

"Fire?" Blondie asks, steering my way with interest piqued in her baby blues.

"Oh yeah, quite recently in fact. My dead mob boss father's estranged wife has dipped to new lows in her efforts to kill me. Hopefully, she gets the memo we've moved out before she tries again." Silence follows while I maintain a fixed stare with Blondie. Her face has drained of color and as she takes a few steps away, her man grips her hand tightly.

"Umm....moving on," the realtor ushers our visitors through the bar, pointing out stupid shit like ample storage and a new speaker system. Malik just stands there, staring at me with his mouth gaping open. I frown, wondering if he wants me to shove my tongue inside or if he's just taken to mouth breathing all of a sudden.

"What? I was just being honest." I tut, leading him after the others. The trio pass through the connecting door, entering our games room and heading to peer inside the kitchen.

"Decent size, am I right?" Smoothing my hand across the island, the couple nod politely, their smiles rather tight. Maybe they need convincing what a luxury a marbled surface like this is. "There are enough stools around the island for all your friends and family to come for parties and a big enough space in the middle to slice up the homeless man you procured for dinner." Gasps ring out all around, and Malik lunges forward, trying to slam his hand over my mouth. A quick fist to the balls deals with him long enough to finish my sales pitch.

"And when you're done, you can drag the remaining carcass down to the basement and crush him into one of the chest freezers. No one will suspect a thing." Winking at Blondie, she covers her mouth like she's going to be sick and runs out the back door, her partner right behind. Oh wow, morning sickness. "Congratulations!" I call after them, but Malik is on me in a heartbeat.

"Seriously," he seethes, pinning my body against the counter. The realtor slips out of sight as Malik crowds my vision with his furiously dark eyes. "What the fuck was that?"

"Nothing I said wasn't true. And besides, the Devil's Bedpost has a reputation to uphold whether we're in it or not. The new owners will need to be prepared for any old rivals that come looking for us." Seeming somewhat satisfied, Malik releases his tight grip on my waist as the realtor's voice sounds from near the back door.

"The next viewers are already here. Shall I let them in or-"

"Let them in," I interrupt with a beaming smile. When he doesn't immediately step aside, I plant a kiss on Malik's lips, using the power of surprise to slip away from him.

"Let me do the talking this time," he growls, barging past me to reach the back door first. I shrug, remaining behind to ask Angus what I did while the next lot of victims, I mean viewers, enter from the rear. Once again, the realtor's voice fills the kitchen with useless facts until I've dropped into a chair, not bothering to hide my yawns. Preferring to start with the upstairs this time, we're all led towards the golden-door elevator opposite the games room.

"The elevator goes all the way up to the suite on the third level," Malik says, making a show of pressing the button.

"Don't forget to mention it can hold up to 1700 kg," I pitch in. The realtor looks relieved like I might have said something stupid. "That's the equivalent of eighteen dead bodies, just to put it into perspective for you. Although, we managed to jam over twenty in there, right Malimoo?" The echo of silence follows and weirdly when I turn around, only Malik is still there with me. Huh, more weak stomachs I suppose.

"You're gonna make me do this, aren't you?" Malik breathes, his voice low and husky. I bite my bottom lip, reading the signals wrong when he speaks again. "Candy. Go to your room." Angus pops up on Malik's shoulder, his face the picture of shock. Running my tongue over my teeth, I slowly pat Malik's chest.

"Fine," I agree, stomping up the stairs. A suspicious hum follows me as if Malik didn't believe I would go so easily, but that's okay. I'll work on a revenge scheme later. For now, I slip into my room and head straight for the dresser. In the top drawer Jasper has filled with all sorts of shit, the stark yellow contact lenses I ordered sit at the top. Kelsii's stunning eye combo has been on my mind, leading me to purchase a range of contact colors, all in vibrant neon. Sticking with my dark jeans, I fish out a black baggy jumper and tug it on, all before slipping into the hidey-hole Jasper showed me. The same one I was tear-gassed in, but at least it's not locked this time.

"Is this the plan?" Angus pipes up once we're secluded in the dark. I shush him, focusing on applying my contact lenses in the dark. It's not as easy as it sounds. Poking myself too hard in the eye more than once, I blink rapidly, pretty sure they're in place before pressing my ear against the wood.

"Lassy's lost her mind," Hamish grumbles. A screech similar to leather stretching sounds behind me, quickly followed by repetitive squeaks like two dog toys being bashed together. Clenching my jaw, I curse myself for the day that grouchy, horny little lemon appeared to fuck my conscience whenever I need him. Instead, I draw myself back to the task at hand. Bracing my upper teeth over my bottom lip, I countdown before uppercutting myself. The impact of my fist into my jaw works a treat, my teeth swiftly sinking into my lip. Warmth rises to the surface as blood pools along the seam of my mouth. Using my fingers, I swipe the blood across my chin just as muffled words seep through the wooden door. It's go time.

"Mewwwwww," I hiss through the slats, scraping my nails across the wood. The voices stop, wait a moment, and then continue discussing the options of converting my room into an art studio. Fuck that. "Mewwwww," I say again, pulling the neckline of the jumper off the back of my head. As a shadow steps in front of the slats on the other side, I vault myself from the hidey-hole and grab the closest leg.

"Mutated rats!" I scream, bracing my teeth around the slender ankle in my grip and peering up at the stranger with a crazed look in my yellow eyes. She's screaming and kicking me off with her sandal before I can even make out her features, fleeing the room with the realtor right behind. Pussy. Malik remains though, his feet planted firmly beside my bed and arms folded. "The mutant rat is coming for you," I grin, using my gravelliest voice. Army crawling along the floor, Malik doesn't shift, not even when I wipe my bloodied mouth across his dress shoe.

"I'm going to squirrel away in your butthole," I choke on a laugh, thoroughly entertaining myself if no one else. Instead of kicking me away as anticipated, Malik lowers himself down onto the floor and pulls the length of my body up his. He doesn't try to avoid the blood smearing across his shirt either, as a heavy exhale shifts beneath my cheek.

"I'm confused," he admits in an open tone. "Do you want the bar to sell or not?"

"Well, yeah," I mutter, indecision gnawing at me. I know selling is what has to happen for us to be free, so my only explanation for acting out is boredom. "Just to the right people," I confess. "You've put so much work into this place. It can't go to just any asshole that won't care for it. And besides, we have unfinished business here."

"Oh yeah? What would that be?" Malik asks, tilting my head up to brush noses with his.

"We can't sell until you've fucked me on every. Single. Surface. And that bar downstairs is lying in virgin territory. With me at least," I smirk, knowing in my gut some drunken brotherly love must have gone a bit too far down there. Rolling his eyes with a devilish grin, Malik brushes a thumb over my split lip.

"If that was the issue, all you had to do is say so."

MALIK

"Just follow my lead," I tell my men with a final nod. Their reactions are mixed between grumbling and unleashed excitement as we file in through the entrance of the bar. Having cleaned herself up and removed the contact lenses, Candy is eagerly awaiting on top of the bar in only a set of lace lingerie. Even from here, her heightened position allows me to see the crotchless opening of her panties as she tries to find a comfortable position around the tattoo I gave her. Just the thought of what's under that dressing makes me grin. Although perhaps it'd be a better use of my time planning my own funeral than reveling in the fact I've finally got a strike on our point scoring system.

Stripping out of my suit jacket, I toss it onto a nearby sofa and begin to roll up my sleeves. The vibrating wand I took from Candy's beside table sticks out of my pocket, knocking against my thigh with each step. The guys at my back follow suit, peeling off their t-shirts to ascend on Candy like vultures on a carcass. In that scenario though, I'd be the lion that gets first pickings. She's giddy with excitement, laying herself back across the bar and knocking the staged beer glasses off in the process. We let them fall, honing our sights on the stunning feast before us.

"Seems you've been a bad girl, love," Jasper breaks the silence first, his fingers trailing over her hip bone.

"Yes I have," Candy grins like the Cheshire cat. Digging into the other pocket in my slacks, I pull out four reams of bondage ribbon, also commandeered from Candy's room. Wrapping the combined length around my hands, Spade's eyes sparkle with anticipation.

"And being bad deserves a true punishment," he adds, winking over me to Ace.

"Oh yes it does," Candy wriggles, begging for more of us to touch her. Waiting for Jack and Ace to round the bar, my four men grab an ankle or wrist in unison, pinning Candy across the polished surface. Catching their eyes with a malicious nod, I start with Spade, tying Candy's wrist to his. Once convinced it's secure, I move over to bind her ankle to the outside of Jasper's thigh. It's not lost on me the way his crotch jolts as I smooth the ribbon between his legs, but that's a story for another time. Then I do the same for Jack on the opposite side and finally, Ace with her other wrist until she's well and truly bound to us.

"I hope you're ready for this," I say, leaning my forearms on the bar beside Candy's head. An arrogant twitch to her eyebrow frames the rich, chocolate eyes that swing my way.

"I was born ready. Give me your best shot." Acting out an uncaring shrug, I lean close to her ear, brushing away the pink hair so she can hear me clearly.

"I love you," I whisper, noting the instant her body stiffens. "We all love you. Your insane ideas, your scheming mind. You're perfect to us." Skimming a kiss over her cheekbone, I silence Candy's protests by claiming her mouth. She tries to bite me until I grip her chin, holding her in place to accept the love I'm determined she will receive. Sweeping my tongue into her mouth, the coppery taste of her split lip mixes with the raspberry gum I know will be stashed between her teeth and cheek. Feeling the shudder of her limbs, I crack an eye to see the other Monarchs pressing light kisses over

Candy's entire body, except for the areas she'd want their lips the most. Torture at its best – Candy style.

Every touch is kept light, every lingering kiss filled with the longing of the feelings she won't accept. Writhing beneath us, Candy wretches her face away from me to shout in a pained tone.

"No! Not that! Anything but that!"

"I thought you wanted to be punished, *my love*," I mock, grinning wide into her panicked eyes. Leaving the others to their assault, I smooth my hands down the side of her face. So beautifully damaged. So blissfully original. So ours.

"Please stop," Candy's voice comes out small and suddenly, my heart tugs. Have I misread the situation, and unknowingly created another scenario like the night we locked her in her room? A frown hitches between my brows as Candy turns her eyes on me, larger than usual and filled with tears. Fuck. Telling my men to stop, I bend over Candy to reassure her we didn't mean any harm when she jerks upwards, headbutting me in the nose.

"Psyche!" She shouts through the blinding haze of pain that crushes my face inwards. Grabbing for an old bar cloth, I pinch my nose as blood pours out without a sign of stopping. There's no remorse in her cackle and by the time the spots have cleared from my vision, she's managed to jerk her feet free to kick both of the twins in their dicks. They fall to the floor, howling, while Spade and Ace are quick to rectify her outburst. Using the sailor's knot attaching Candy's wrist to theirs, the pair slam their hands onto the bar top far above her head. Interlocking their fingers in a death grip, Candy's arms are retched upwards without hope of escape.

Too enraged with the blazing pain pulsing through my nose, I turn away to breathe deeply. I can't afford to lash out again like at the casino, although fuck knows Candy deserves more than just spanking by belt this time. No one plays the puppy dog eyes trick on me. Using the two-way mirror behind the bar, I check my reflection for any sign of a break as Jasper drags himself upright. Snatching Candy's ankle, he grunts for Spade to hold it tight before passing a still-incapacitated Jack to hand the other ankle to Ace.

The breath I was trying to steady saws out of me, and I turn to see Candy's legs spread wide in a V. Snatching the vibration wand from my pocket, Jasper switches it to the highest setting and jams it against Candy's lace panties. I don't bother telling him it's exactly what she wanted because the screams that leave her mouth quickly become what I want too.

Bucking against Ace and Spade's iron-clad grip, Candy moans louder and louder, her abdomen jerking with the intense vibrations rippling through her sensitive clit. Slowly, I help Jack upright and draw him around to the end of the bar, where we get the best view. Between the missing crotch in the black lace, she's glistening and ready, although we won't be done torturing her for a while yet. The dressing of her tattoo is tucked inside the French trim, reminding me who the real winners are here.

In no time, a cry is ripped from Candy's throat, and her orgasm is a glory for us all to watch. Only once her body is pulsating and chest heaving does Jasper relent with the wand, although he doesn't turn it off. Reducing the vibrations to a lazy rhythm, I push Jack forward to do the honors. I would love to get in there first myself, but he needs to rebuild his confidence around her. It's not lost on any of us how tentative Jack seems when Candy is present, still trying to find his way back from denying his feelings for her. Besides, getting to Candy last when she thinks she's all done and drawing out that last climax from her is an art I'm happy to perfect.

This time, however, he doesn't show any tentativeness. Jack plunges two fingers into Candy's soaking cunt, catching her unawares. She gasps as Ace promptly drops Candy's leg over Jasper's nearest shoulder and then clamps his free hand over her mouth. A smirk pulls at his lips as he nods for Jack to continue, which the Brit complies with immediately. Pumping his fingers into Candy, Jasper works the wand over her clit in small circles. Unbuttoning the buttons of my shirt, I toss the cotton material aside with the blooded rag in favor of joining my topless brothers and proudly display the chest piece I had tattooed in her honor. At least that should distract from the state of my face.

"More," Candy begs, tugging against the holds on her wrists. Jack looks back to share a shrug with me and then steadily adds another finger, then another. He works her juices around his digits, pushing Candy to arch her back and groan louder. I remain at the end of the bar, leaning my hands on the wood and gripping tightly. Watching Candy break for me is the closest I get to having control these days. It's the balm to my tormented soul, the band-aid to the festering wound that is my subconscious.

Noting his twin has worked Candy into a frenzy where she greedily accepts Jack's entire fist, Jasper ramps up the wand again. On cue, Ace and Spade drop to take Candy's nipples in their mouths and I'm treated to my own show. My dick strains painfully against my boxers, anticipating the moment I swoop in to take over. Not yet though. For now, I'm happy watching Jack fist our girl into another crashing climax that I get a front-row seat for. Streams of creamy cum drip from her open slit, soaking the lace panties. Pushing off the countertop, I ease the wand from Jasper's grip, switching it off and tossing it into the closest basin.

"Looks like she's ready for two, don't you agree?" I ask Jasper, sliding my eyes over to Jack. Both pairs of green eyes ignite with excitement, checking each other carefully for reactions. Although, they needn't bother as Candy answers for them.

"Fuck yes!" She shouts, fist pumping the air because Ace and Spade allow her to. "Twinning is definitely winning." My eyebrows rise, some unwritten bonding code being forged at this very moment. Ordering the twins to strip, I peel Candy's soaking wet panties down her long legs. As a unit, we lift her stunning body for Jasper to slide underneath, his dick bobbing up in-between her legs. Remaining tied to Ace and Spade restricts her upper body movements. Once Jack has used a stool to mount the bar, there's an awkward pause as he looks down at Jasper's dick and then gestures to me.

"Shove it in then," Jack tries to tell me what to do and I scoff.

"If I touch Jasper's cock, he'll explode before Candy's even felt him," I roll my eyes and cross my arms. Jasper moans about that not being true, but I'm not an idiot. I've seen the types of books he reads. Jack purses his lips, fisting his own erection to keep it away from his brother's.

"Well I'm not touching it," he groans and Spade laughs.

"You'll be touching it when it's inside her."

"That's not like it's my hand though," Jack persists, drawing a humored laugh from me.

"Oh for fuck's sake," Ace grumbles, pushing Jasper's dick into our girl. She merely lies there and giggles when Jasper jolts, telling Ace not to be so heavy-handed. "Do I have to do yours too?" He asks Jack, who promptly shakes his head. The instant he eases his dick into her eager pussy, all joking is forgotten. Even Candy's usual bullshit is stripped back as the twins fill her and begin to move. The bar echoes with pleasured groans from the trio as Ace, Spade, and I are able to take a step back. Spade goes as far as to pull up a stool, his tied hand slacking to toy with Candy's breast.

There's something to be said for watching your girl being double fucked, and to not feel an ounce of jealously. Trivial bullshit between our gang doesn't matter anymore. Candy's pleasure is our pleasure, and seeing the flush of pleasure coat her skin is all the payment I need.

CANDY

S tretching out across the mattress, I flop aside to find myself completely alone. It takes a moment to even remember whose bed I'm in after our bar sexcapades turned into a drunken sex fest that's lasted...well fuck, I don't know what day it is either. Spying the camera stand and spotlight tucked into the corner, I grin, remembering just what brought me into Ace's room. Once the delicious ache gnawing deep inside me subsides, I reckon a popcorn and homemade movie night is in order. There's no better gratification than watching yourself rule the big screen.

Rolling onto my back, resting my head on my hands, my smile starts to slip. That after-sex high I crave dissipates, opening my mind to a whirlwind of thoughts I'd been ignoring.

"You know what you've got to do," Angus berates me, appearing on my chest. Knocking him aside, I force myself upright, a plan forming in my mind. Yeah, I do know what I need to do. I need to sort my shit out and roll on this movie date. Can't overthink when I've got a dick in each hole and one in each hand.

After getting my head in the game, I dash across the hall into my room and dress hastily. Leaving my hair in a style I like to call 'sexed-out lioness bedhead,' I stop by the bathroom to clean my teeth. Catching sight of myself in the large mirror, I stop to appreciate how well my randomly chosen outfit has panned out. A black top with a high collar and teardrop panels cut out from neckline to bust clings to my curves, riding the edge of some skinny dark blue jeans. Nodding at myself, I'm convinced more than ever today's the day to sort out some important business, and this is the outfit to do it in.

Satisfied I'm ready as I'll ever be, I go hunting for the men that will protest my every decision along the way. I never bore of watching them try, even though their success rate is in the minuses. As predicted, I find the whole gang in the bar area, although they're not lounging around waiting for me as I'd hoped. Instead, there's an insane amount of flapping and rushing going on, boxes being pushed around, and furniture moved aside. Spade approaches me with the whole cashier in his hands, asking if I can hold the door open. I leave my foot wedged in place but don't move out of his way as he struggles to slip through, planting a morning kiss on my lips just as he manages it.

"Where's the fire?" I ask when no one pays me any attention.

"The realtor called," Malik pops up from behind the bar, his hair as erratic as his darting eyes. "Apparently, your attempts to frighten the viewers away didn't work. Someone's puts in an offer with the intent to sign the papers as soon as possible. Whoever it is, they want us out." There's an ominous notion to Malik's tone, one that Jasper and Ace both clock onto with sly side-glances.

"Hmmm, well, count me out. I'm going to get my roots fixed today." I spread the parting in my hair, clearly demonstrating the need to cover my three-inch growth of shit-brown. Nasty stuff. Malik's vein that I've taken to calling Dr. Temple Popper, pulses as he tries to hide his disapproval. Leaning on one hip, I cross my arms, daring him to disagree.

"I'd feel much better if you took…someone with you," he finally grumbles, his eyes shifting between the others.

"An escort, you mean," I tsk. "What's Tanya going to do? Give me a perm?"

"Don't look at me," Ace quickly ducks his face. "I went last time. Two hours of being ogled by old women in curlers." He visibly shudders, busying himself with bubble-wrapping glasses. Jack pulls himself upright from where he was unhelpfully lounging on the sofa, offering to go while Malik gives Jasper a pointed look to say 'Jack isn't up to protecting me on his own.'

"I'll come too," Spade agrees helpfully, reappearing from the adjoining room. "I could do with going to Home Depot anyway."

"Perfect," I clap my hands together. "You guys take the truck, and I'll head to Shepperton on my quad." My chest warms with that sentence, both from the acceptance of owning something so beautiful all to myself and the anticipation of her thrumming to life beneath me.

"What?" Malik jerks in confusion. "Why would you go there? Marystone is much closer."

"Oh, excuse me Colonel Time-Keeper. Marystone doesn't have Polly-May, the incredibly talented artist that can transform my hair while being a mom of five who's living out of her van and snipping split-ends to provide her kids with a decent education. Fuck's sake Malik, where's your humanity?" Malik raises his hands, mumbling about being careful and backing away. I feel like petting him like a good boy but somehow, I don't think he'll approve.

"Shepperton it is," Jack shrugs, winding his arm around my back. No quad ride today it would seem - sorry pretty lady. Leading me outside towards the garage, I give in to Jack's tender hold and lay my head on his shoulder. The soft cotton of his t-shirt smells like coconut, filling my mind with a distant memory I can't quite grasp. Snuggling further into his neck, I'm debating whether I can put off today's errands in favor of hitting replay on our garage sex-sesh as Spade opens the door for us to enter. Jack's green eyes tip my way, seeming to read my mind, and I drag my face away. Not now, but soon.

"Next time you take me out in this truck Jacky, we're going somewhere far away, just the two of us."

"Deal," Jack agrees, popping the passenger door for me. Spade swoops in, spinning me by the waist and tucking me into his side.

"Not today though," he chuckles, stuffing me into the backseat and then crowding me with his body. Pushing my back flat against the leather, his chest pins me down. Not that I'm complaining. Even when Jack tuts and revs the engine, I'm encapsulated by the piercing blue eyes hovering over me. Spade's dreads hang over one side, creating a curtain around us.

"I'll never know what I've done right in this lifetime to deserve you," he breathes against my lips. My chest flutters as his body gives me no room to squirm away.

"More like what you did wrong. I'm karma's consolation prize for fucking up every opportunity that's ever come your way."

"Then I'll continue to make every bad choice and commit every wrongdoing just to keep you around. If you'll have me, that is," he smirks like the confident fuck he is.

"I'll always have you Spade," I whisper, catching myself too late. A blush floods my cheeks which I hope is hidden by the shadow of this stunning man closing the gap to take my lips captive. Fiery passion leaks from his very being, filling me in a way I'm unfamiliar with. Every sweep of his tongue leaves me even more breathless, not that I need to breathe anymore. Spade will live for me.

A rough swerve and screech of tires break through our hypnotic trance. I smirk, catching Jack's jealous glare in the rear-view mirror as I sit upright. Slowly running my tongue over my top lip, Jack jerks at a nearby car horn, just saving himself from swerving into the next lane.

"Do you need me to drive?" Spade asks, barely containing his stifled laughter. Jack flips him off, keeping his eyes strictly on the road the rest of the way to my chosen town. It's a small and modest center point for the suburbs circling it. Vibrant bouquets burst from the florists. Delightful smells emanate from the farmer's market. There's a long line of people waiting outside the butchers, taking full advantage of his BBQ specials as advertised on a propped-up chalkboard. It is the perfect day for a family cookout, I muse to Angus when he smushes his face against the window and leaves a tongue trail of slobber there. Pulling up alongside the salon, aptly named Cuts To Dye For, Spade leans over me to peer at the sunny yellow sign above the doorway and tries to pop the door.

"Hey, woah, cool it. I don't need a minder while I'm trying to get my girl-time on. I'll meet you in that restaurant in a few hours," I point to an Italian Bistro over the road. Beneath a green, white and red striped canopy, a waitress dresses the outside tables with cloths, cutlery, and breadbaskets. Usually, a place like that would have been my first point of call if I were in a thieving mood, but my bank card is burning a hole in my back pocket. The best type of payback for Tanya right now would be to not only spend my inheritance but to blow it on the most menial things. I could return home with a pet jaguar at this rate.

"I'm not sure…" Jack starts, but I'm already out of the door.

"Two hours. Dinner's on me and dessert is me," I wink, pushing against Spade's chest when he tries to follow.

"I like the sound of that," he beams, his hand clutching mine long enough to kiss the back of it.

"Mmmm, alright," Jack scratches his chin. "Two hours or I'm coming to carry you out. Just so I know - which one is Polly-May?" he asks, squinting through the glass wall behind me.

"How should I know? I've never been here before."

"But you said-" I slam the door shut, skipping inside the salon. A bell dings above the door, announcing me to the three hairdressers who are busy attending to their clients. A receptionist straightens, pulling a lollipop out of her mouth. Freckles patter across her cute button nose, her youthful skin, brunette ponytails, and innocent brown eyes appear barely out of college.

"Do you have an appointment?" she asks sweetly while I follow the lines on the swirly resin countertop with my finger. Shaking my head, she taps the screen, listing available slots, when I notice the pair of scissors poking out of her cardigan pocket.

"Are you a hairdresser?" I interrupt her, drumming my nails on the counter now.

"Oh um, I'm in training. I sweep the floors and make the coffees mostly until we find willing models for me to practice on," she shrugs. A large grin spreads across my face, and I spread my arms wide.

"Well, here I am. I need a fuchsia top-up, and I'll take that coffee too."

"Err, I wouldn't feel comfortable. I don't have much of a portfolio at the moment," her wide eyes dart around, looking for assistance. Or maybe permission from the stern hairdresser in the back who is shaking her head.

"No better time to start building it up. Plus I'll pay you $500 if you get me in that chair in the next two minutes." No longer paying attention to her boss, the teen whips a black cover with backward sleeves over me and fetches the coffee in no time. Dropping into the seat with a magazine I picked out of another client's hands, the teen removes her cardigan, revealing a name tag stating her as 'Clara.' She triple checks a sheet of paper, instructing her how to mix up my shade as pink before getting started on me with shaky hands.

"Relax," I tell her. "I once dyed my own hair while high on opium. Came around a few days later to realize my head was caked in enamel wall paint." Clara gasps, only laughing along when I do.

"What did you do?" She asks, separating and clipping my hair into sections.

"Shaved it all off," I shrug. "Rocked the Britney look for a while. Wish I could say I learned my lesson, but that'd be a lie." Much more relaxed now, Clara gets to work applying the fluorescent color on my roots while I complete each questionnaire in the magazine on her. By the time she moves onto my duller lengths, we've deduced her TV double from the Office would be Pam Beesley, she knows every type of Starbucks coffee and her sex IQ is sitting at a healthy 80%. Sorting my hair into perfectly placed foil strips, I shake my head like a robotic poodle, impressed by her handy work. The girl has potential.

"That's all done for now," Clara announces, thoroughly impressed with herself. "I'll come back to check on you in about 45 minutes. Would you like another coffee?"

"I'm good thanks. I actually have an errand to run. I'll be back before my hair fries," I reassure Clara, although her face looks anything but. She stutters as I remove the fancy apron and head towards the back door. Pausing on the outer stone step, I suddenly remember my manners.

"Oh, and if any hunky sex-gods come looking for me, tell them I'm getting an anal wax in the back room and I'll double your fee." Without waiting for a reply, I jump off the step and bolt through the alley. The wind rustles through my foils as I go, keeping vigilant of the Monarchs lurking around any corner. Angus is right beside me, vaulting from trash cans to street lamps and phone boxes. Just like he said this morning, I know exactly what I have to do today, and my hair is not the only priority on that list.

JACK

Shutting the trunk of my truck, I check the time on my phone. Again. It doesn't matter how much effort goes into an idea if no one is here to see it. Tapping on the contacts, my thumb hovers over the call button as a scuffle sounds at the garage door. Rounding the truck, I spot Candy stumbling inside in just a baggy hoodie, rubbing her eyes and yawning. I rush over to grip her waist, steering her away from Ace's worktable before she bumps into it.

"What time is it?" She mumbles, leaning her head forward on my shoulder. In fact, her entire body leans into mine until I'm the only reason she's still standing.

"Early," I answer, temporarily losing focus as her lips trail along my neck. "Come on. Before the big bad protective wolf wakes up and refuses to let you out." Guiding her to the passenger seat, she finds the pile of clothes I placed there; pre-empting texting her to meet me before daybreak would require a fresh outfit. She tosses the clothes into the back, climbing in to curl up in the seat. After leaning over to secure her seat belt in place, Candy's hand fists my t-shirt.

"I'm baffled that you guys still think Malik has any say over my actions," she mutters almost incoherently, and I can't resist placing a quick kiss on her temple. Her vibrant hair still holds a freshly-dyed and expensively conditioned smell I inhale deeply.

"Actually, I meant Jasper. It's impossible to get you away from him these days." Seeming satisfied, Candy releases me and I shut the door, cursing my leechy brother under my breath. Although, I'm unable to breathe easy until I've peeled the truck out of the garage and put some distance between us and the Devil's Bedpost. Candy's snoring before we make it out of the dirt track, but it doesn't stop her from sleep-talking.

"Okay Mr. Chew. You can take me to marshmallow land, but keep your jelly jizz to yourself." I huff a laugh, reaching out to rest my hand on her thigh. It's not been easy keeping my plans to myself and sneaking around while the others command her full attention, but the further we travel, the lesser my chest feels like it's compressing in on itself. It's been a long time coming for Candy and I to reconnect properly without her being distracted, and I'll be damned if I let anyone get in my way this time.

Dipping in a pothole on the craggy backroad, Candy wakes up with a start. Her arm flies over her eyes, protecting her from the onslaught of daylight she didn't see rise.

"Fuck, where the hell am I?"

"I thought you thrived on adventure," I smirk, feeling ten thousand percent more myself without the stress of competition hanging over me. It's hard to stand out when my actions already had me on the back foot, the need to prove myself tearing me apart. Veering into a makeshift parking space on the side of the track, I turn off the truck's engine and twist to grab Candy's clothes. It's only a pair of high-tops, denim shorts and one of my vests I grabbed on my way out, but Candy looks good in anything. With the back-end of fall threatening to steal the last of our warmth, now's as good a time as any to work on our tan.

Accepting the clothes with a hitched eyebrow, Candy peels off the hoodie, leaving her completely naked in my passenger seat. My mouth goes dry. From her pert nipples to her hairless pussy and then some, she's flawless. The colorful tattoos lining her chest only add to her appeal, complementing the dangerous edge that keeps us so enthralled.

"Shall I get dressed, or do you want to just stare at me all day?" Candy smirks, her eyes dipping to the jerk behind my zipper.

"Trust me, I won't be just staring. But there's champagne in the back so-"

"Sold," Candy shouts, hopping out of the cab butt naked. A lorry flies by, blaring its horn in appreciation, and Candy grabs the clothes as an afterthought. I tuck away the protective streak that flares up in me, having learned by watching to let Candy do what she wants. As long as she's in one of our beds at the end of the day, what's the use in trying to cage her any more than that. Retrieving the hamper from the trunk, a dressed version of Candy joins my side and leans her forearm on my shoulder.

"So, other than getting drunk and the promise of some one-on-one action, what are we up to today?"

"Take a look for yourself," I point to the scenery towards the horizon. Starting a few feet in front of us, massive fields of wheat sprawl all the way to the skyline. Hundreds of miles of nothingness, except for the intricate patterns of crop circles spaced evenly apart. I remember seeing this place on the news once and never had the inclination to visit it until now.

"Damn," Candy remarks, her arm slipping, so she's just leaning her body against mine. Linking my fingers in hers, we take in the view in a rare moment of silence. Not just verbally, but a mental silence I can feel emanating from Candy, and that in itself was worth the drive. "I've never seen crop circles in person before."

"I figured they're weird and wonderful, just like you," I blush. Dating clearly isn't my strong suit, but luckily, taking a compliment isn't Candy's either. Her body stiffens against me, her mouth usually silent. "Not to mention mysteriously cryptic and they appear out of nowhere." We share a knowing grin, washing away all awkwardness in an instant. Drawing Candy forward, we venture into a manmade path among the corn, kissing the world goodbye. For today at least. My Timberlands meander, one foot in front of the other lazily.

After a while, we break free of the first crop circle, creating a burnt orange maze for us to navigate. We venture directly for the middle so I can set the hamper basket down and finally pull Candy into my arms the way I've been wanting. The first taste of her raspberry lips, the way she slots into my body like she was created to be there. A soft moan leaves me, faded out by a gentle breeze shifting through the crisp corn.

Needing to have more of her, my hands delve into Candy's pink hair, holding her still for my tongue to slip into her eager mouth. She accepts me greedily, fighting back for the dominance I refuse to let her have. No more pussy-footing, no more begging for scraps. My dues are paid, and I'm ready to take back my prize. My tongue overpowers the strong sweep of hers while my fingers grip her so close; that there's no space left between us. Where I end, she begins. Her hands travel up my t-shirt, soothing over the abs I need to work on reviving.

Reaching higher, her fingers dip into the crevice of the scar sitting centrally in my abdomen and suddenly, our kiss pulls back to something softer. A gentle mix of longing and desperation tainting the scrape of my lips over hers. The point where her thumb smooths over my scar aches, but not physically. From shame. Releasing her, Candy refuses to let me step away, tipping her forehead against mine. Regret spreads through my chest like a poison, churning up the shame I've been struggling to come to terms with.

"Where did you go just then?" Candy breathes, softly begging for my truth. And so help me, if nothing else, I want to give it to her.

"I knew you'd leave," I finally voice the words I haven't been able to admit to anyone else. "I knew something would push you away, probably Malik. So I tried to protect myself from that. But the longer you stuck around, the more confused I became. All I knew was...I didn't want to be alone, and I wanted to save myself the heartache that would destroy the Monarchs for good."

"You were never alone. You had the others," Candy tries to console me, not disagreeing with the inevitability of her ruining us all. Pulling back to take her hands, I draw us down to spread out a picnic blanket and sit together with a united heavy sigh.

"The love I have for my brothers is not the same as knowing the irresistible, undeniable love I've grown to have for you. You've united us, but you've also saved each and every one of us individually. I have no idea how you've done it, and I don't know if we'll be able to repay the favor."

I catch a glimpse of vulnerability in Candy's chocolate brown eyes before she looks away, knowing she understands. Demons follow Candy. They torment her in her sleep without her knowledge. Yet while awake, she'll never confront the truth long enough for us to free her. I came to that realization long before anyone else and reconciled with the fact she doesn't need rescuing from her past. I'll settle on being here to preserve her future. Cupping Candy's cheek, I bring her attention back to mine before my courage flees and the need to voice my thoughts is swallowed by the embarrassment of sounding desperate.

"You have the power to ruin all of us now. But not loving you is so much worse than waking up from a coma to find you gone anyway." Sealing my words with a brief touch of our lips, I preempt the shift of Candy's limbs and provide her with the escape she now needs. "Tag," I say, shoving her onto her back to give myself the advantage. Her choked laugh rings out as I duck behind a wall of corn, the trample of her high-tops taking chase behind me. The baggy shorts I opted for allow me to dash around sharp corners, barely evading Candy's outstretched hand. Exertion burns through me quickly with the lack of recent exercise, but I press on, twisting into an alcove and stilling for Candy to run past in a pink whirlwind.

I remain there, only tiptoeing out of my hiding space when I'm sure Candy is a good distance away. Rounding back, I trace my steps to the hamper. I reckon I could eat and have a nap before she's managed to track her way back. Spying the crumpled picnic blanket, I flatten it out as a body collides with mine, rugby tackling me down with surprising force.

"Tag!"

"Motherf-". I crash down hard, pinned beneath Candy as she straddles me. Leaning forward, she crushes her boobs in my face to reach into the basket. I effectively flop back and enjoy her assault until she's found what she was looking for. The bottle of champagne. Her hand curls around the cork and I buck aside, tossing her to the ground.

"Don't celebrate yet," I warn. Removing the bottle from her hand, I place it back in the basket before slamming my palm down on her forehead. "The game isn't over until you're pinned and begging beneath me, and tag by the way."

"No sneaking off to relax this time!" Candy's words chase me despite her remaining in the center of the crop circle. I hear the pop of the champagne bottle anyway, figuring she needs some bubbles to spur her on. Then the corn beside me shakes as Candy volleys herself through the center, almost catching me straight away. I skid sideways, changing course to run full speed down the adjacent pathway. Unlike the cheater on my tail, I stick to the pathways, veering left and right in an attempt to shake her off. Fingers graze my neck, announcing me as 'tagged' and so the game continues.

Whipping back on myself, I slow in favor of listening for movement before running around like some wild ostrich. Silence weighs heavily, so I creep to an intersection in the crop circle. I spotted the one we're in from the truck, noting the mix of squares and triangles rotating in a pattern through the circle, giving Candy plenty of sharp corners to hide behind. A crow swoops overhead, tilting its head this way and that in search of food. With a loud flap on its largely spanned wings and a caw, he disappears from sight just as the corn to my right rustles. A smile hitches up the corner on my lips, my Timberlands treading carefully not to give away my position.

Rounding the next corner, the white material of the vest disappears from view, and I dash forward after her. She's as fast as a whippet, evading me every time I think I'm closing in. Coming out at the same intersection, if the random boulder I keep spotting is anything to go by, I stop long enough to hear the crunch of shoes behind me. She's following around in circles, effectively making me chase my own tail.

Pretending to dart away, I wait for the shadow to appear in the patch I was just standing in before throwing myself into her body. We fly into the corn, flopping down hard in the alleyway parallel. If it were anyone else, I'd worry about how hard we hit the ground, but nothing can bring Candy down. Except for the flash of red that catches my eye registers too late, and the next thing I know, the undeniable crack of a gunshot blasts next to my ear.

"Jesus Christ!" I scream, rolling off the body beneath me to grasp the side of my head. The shine of the pistol seeps through my cracked eyelids, so I quickly grab and toss it into the corn somewhere. Lying in the fetus position, I wait for the ringing to mostly subside before taking in my surroundings. A pair of glazed brown eyes peer out from a wash of flame-red hair, shifting through the heavy pants leaving her busted lips. Bruises stain her visible skin, her arms trembling as they rest against mine. Confusion fills my mind, like a bad dream coming to life, but as Candy steps into view, I realize this isn't a dream. It's a fucking nightmare.

"Cherry?" Candy asks, dropping to her knees. I fight the urge to dive over Cherry and draw Candy in my arms, not trusting the woman who happened to turn up on my crop circle picnic with a gun, but Candy would probably throat punch me. Drawing myself up into a sitting position, I rub the scar in my abdomen, noting that I fell harder than I intended to. But my focus isn't on myself. It's on the pair of miserable eyes that keep sliding my way, no matter how much I try to avoid them.

"What are you doing here?" Candy asks, scooping Cherry into her arms. The whole scene is surreal. My current girlfriend is attending to my ex, who happens to be her long-lost sister. I reckon I'll need therapy after this.

"How did you find us, more like," I grumble, although the answer to my question is sitting right beside me. Cherry's phone must have skidded out of her hand when I tackled her to the ground. A now-cracked screen lies face up, showing the bleeping red pin of her tracking...me. I curse, yanking my phone out of my pocket and switching it off. If Cherry can find me in a field of corn, nowhere is safe.

"I needed to speak to you in person," Cherry tells Candy, barely standing on shaky legs.

"Come this way; you can join our picnic and fill me in on what the hell happened," Candy offers. I scowl at the intruder high-jacking my date, not caring how Cherry obtained her mass of bruises or why it looks like she hasn't eaten in weeks. This woman is the reason I was tricked, stabbed, and slipped into a coma. But above all else, the thing that really pisses me off is that she looked me in the eye and promised she'd never lie to me.

CANDY

With a battered Cherry tucked beneath my arm, I shift her back towards the center of the crop circle. It's a good job I dropped a trail of strawberries, so I didn't lose Jack again. The broody Monarch is dragging his feet after retrieving Cherry's phone and gun, his disapproval palpable in the air. Not that it matters; Cherry is hurt and has come all this way to find me. I need to know why. Entering the middle of the circle, I settle her down gently on the picnic blanket and fish a bottle of water out of the basket.

"Careful," Angus pops up from between the crackers and cheese. "It's starting to look like you care." I frown, shoving his squishy head back down.

"For your information, I do care," I whisper, giving him my best evil eye. He glares right back, only his angry eyebrows and pink eyes visible. I slam the basket shut, not knowing what's got into him. Or maybe, what's got into me because the last time I checked, I wasn't capable of affection. Dare I say, while straightening out the Monarch's issues, they have rewired some of mine. I burst out laughing, placing the bottle in a concerned-looking Cherry's shaky hand. Jack joins us at last, settling down on the edge of the blanket, and protectively pulls me into his side. I roll my eyes at the distance now put between myself and Cherry but let it go in favor of assessing her injuries.

"Cherry, tell me what happened," I coax, letting her down a decent amount of water before pressing her with a stern look.

"Tanya was onto us the whole time. I kept falsely reporting your whereabouts like we agreed, but then a group of thugs appeared and...and..." Cherry's voice breaks and her gaze drops to her feet.

"And gave you exactly what you deserved?" Jack offers, and I thump him. Blinking up with large, tear-streaked eyes, Cherry looks at Jack for the first time.

"I don't expect you to hear me out, but there was a point where you stopped being a job and I genuinely-"

"You're right, I don't want to hear it," he grumbles, turning his head away. And people say I'm childish.

"I know," Cherry tucks her face back into her shoulder. "I'm sorry. I did try to get you out, but Tanya's always one step ahead."

"That's because you work for her," I respond in a non-judgey tone. "She knows what your next move will be because she trained you that way. Whereas, with me, she can never see me coming. It's infuriated her for years, and now I know why." I hold my sister's gaze, wondering how it must have felt to find out Big Cheese hid her in an orphanage just because Tanya did the same to me. It's a shitty reason for a crappy upbringing. "Now, back to the problem at hand. What did the she-witch do now?"

"Nick and Tom are dead," Cherry croaks, a fresh tear rolling down her cheek. Looking away at the reams of corn shifting in the breeze, I hide my regret with a mask of indifference. I never even got to drunkenly backseat drive in Cabbie Tom's taxi and throw up all over his upholstery. Although something tells me it's Nick that Cherry is mourning for, her fingers fiddling with a new love heart necklace around her throat. It's always baffled me that women can go from man to man, hopelessly looking for love, but I guess not everyone is as comfortable with themselves as I am.

Aside from the lack of unblemished skin, thanks to the bruises in varying sizes disappearing beneath her scruffy white t-shirt, there's something missing. Cherry's spunk. Her determination to see our plan through to the end. This isn't the woman I first met, nor is it the one I left behind to hold the fort for me. Cherry has been broken in the short time since I left her, raising the question if I should have insisted on bringing her with us.

"Tell me everything," I demand this time, pushing off Jack to give Cherry my full attention. For the next however long, Cherry sniffles her way through an ambush at the motel room.

The first downfall, I note, is that she stayed too long in the same place. The second was building a routine that was easily traceable. Sounds like gunmen similar to those who attacked us at Granny's house were able to follow Cabbie Tom back to the parking lot and shot him down in broad daylight. Nick fought back as much as he could, gallantly diving over Cherry to save her. Then, the men just turned and left. Cherry reckons they must have believed the bullet went straight through Nick's chest when she collapsed, but I'm not convinced. Tanya doesn't leave anything up to chance.

"It's going to be okay," I soothe, patting my hand on her shaking leg. Pulling the hoodie off Jack's arms, I slide it around my sister. We share a hidden smile when Jack grumbles about being invisible, and I rub her arms in an effort to soak some warmth into her frail limbs. "Come on, the truck has heating. You're coming back with us."

"Like hell she is," Jack replies, challenging me with his green glare. Tilting my head to the side with a direct stare in the way people usually find uncomfortable, Jack's raised chin refuses to back down.

"I'm in charge, and I say she's coming," I grit out.

"And I say she's a fuckton of trouble. I'll give you the world Candy, but I'm not budging on this. She's not entering the Devil's Bedpost ever again." After a beat, I lunge at Jack, flattening him on his back. Pinning his forearms under my knees, I shove my hands into his pockets, not so carefully knocking his dick aside in my hunting. Finding his phone, I twist the screen to use his face ID and permit me access.

"What are you doing?! There's nothing on there you need to see," Jack tries to snatch the device back. I roll my eyes at the wallpaper of a naked body before realizing the tattoos are rather familiar. I don't know when he snapped this shot of me in the shower, but I look good.

"Relax. I'm not interested in your secret stash of stalker photos. I'm calling Jasper." This seems to make Jack even more determined to grab his phone back as we roll off the picnic blanket, fighting for the upper hand. His hand locks around my throat in an effort to toss me aside, but I just grind my hips over his dick and call him daddy. Pressing the call button, the dial tone rings once before Jack punches the phone away from my ear. It scatters into the corn, and I scowl, shoving Jack down hard by the chest.

"You're only a fifth of the deciding vote!" I shout when he elbows me in the ribs and scrambles away. Grabbing his ankle, I drag myself up the length of his body until we're standing nose to nose, glaring at one another. "Is this because you don't like Cherry or because you don't want me running to your twin?"

"Candy. I'm...warning you," Jack bites out, his nostrils flaring. "She's not..."

"Here," Angus finishes, having hopped up onto the basket. "She's not even here." I whip around, noting the area where Cherry was sitting is now completely empty, and shove Jack back a step. Both her pistol and phone are still in the spot where Jack left them - two items she wouldn't have left with if she was leaving willingly. A dent in the corn behind where Cherry was last seen has my eyes narrowing, and if that wasn't confirmation enough, a familiar cackle echoes across the sky.

"Oh, stepdaughter!" Tanya calls, mocking me. Not even Jack can stop me this time as I grab the handgun and flee what should have been our romantic picnic spot. I was planning to have Jack for dessert and take an after-sex nap under the cloudless sky. Instead, I'm running through sheets of corn in search of the voice I could easily never hear again. Shadows flicker on the edges of my vision, Jack's voice closing in from behind as he takes chase.

"Candy! Come back here, it's a trap," he tries to warn as if I didn't know that already. But I've failed Cherry once, I'm not about to do it again. She's the only person in the world who actually depends on me. To fail her now would be such a waste of my talents. I was literally born to piss Tanya off and have made a successful livelihood out of escaping death.

Twisting around corner after corner, I search the crop circle until I've run out of new ways to turn. Whoever I'm tracking the muddy footprints of is doing a great job at staying out of sight. So instead, I stop dead still and wait. If I'm the target here, they can come to me. In no time, footsteps crunch up the path behind me and I spin, raising the gun and knocking off the safety in one smooth move.

A hefty man all in black is fast enough to grab the barrel and twist my wrist sideways, sending the shot wide. Wrenching my arm behind my back, he gives my shoulder a sharp tug before disappearing through the corn. Jack hears my pained yelp as he appears at the opposite end of the pathway, calling for me. Instead of responding, I drop to my knees, hunting for the gun while a humored cackle causes a bunch of birds to disperse overhead.

"You can't run forever Candy! Just give me what I want, and I'll leave you be. You don't want the money anyway!"

"But I do want to know I've pissed you off every single day," I yell towards the sky. Patting the ground, my hand closes over something cold and curved, but it's not the gun. Tanya steps forward from the sheet of golden yellow, my hand still clasped around her leather boot.

"I suppose I'll just kill you now then." Lifting my head, I look down the barrel of the gun I was trying to locate and rise slowly.

"Go for it," I shrug, holding my arms wide. Jack's shouts are muffled by the gloved hand covering his mouth, his arms held immobile by a guy twice his side. The same one that has my wrist flaring with pain and shoulder screaming to be reset. Remaining nonchalant at her threat, Tanya's muddy glare narrows on me, her chest heaving beneath a see-through mesh top and laced black bra I'm sure were mine. Plastering a smirk on my face, I look my copycat up and down, running my tongue over my teeth. "Although, killing me still won't get you your money."

"What are you talking about?" Tanya spits, refusing to falter. Although the curiosity in her eyes already gives her away. "You have no one-"

"Except I do," I laugh, knocking the gun aside. "Release Jack, and I'll tell you what you want to know." Folding my bad arm under the other in a cocky I-won't-take-your-shit and I-need-a-sling kind of way, I then pop my hip, not letting Tanya's henchman think for one second my gut is churning inside. I've turned my back on a gun many times, but the panicked flash in Jack's eyes has me second-guessing that choice. Maybe it's not my time to die after all, so as the henchman releases him; I give Tanya the information she wants.

"Jasper signed the legal papers at the solicitors, naming himself as my next of kin." The resulting expression on my stepmother's face is hilarious, and I let her know it. Holding my bad arm in place, my body shakes with the hysterics this unforeseen moment has brought. Even as Jack is shoved into my side and I hiss in pain, humor still thrums through my veins. Right up until I look around to see both Tanya and the henchman have gone, and I'm no closer to finding Cherry.

Drawing Jack along, it's not missed how he's holding his chest, struggling with the exertion but refusing to quit. In fact, his strides are longer than mine as we storm through the crop circle, hand in hand. Hunting around each corner and inside every alcove, I realize too late Jack isn't searching for Cherry at all. Instead, he's leading me straight from the fields and back to his truck. Scowling, I yank my hand free and refuse to take another step.

"Relax," Jack rolls his eyes, taking my good hand back. "This is the best vantage point for us to look over the landscape for a hint of red hair." Easing my tense posture, I stand by his side, scanning the fields. There's nothing. Not a single person, redhead or otherwise.

Cherry's slipped away as easily as she appeared, like a crimson ghost fleeting between Earth and the spirit world. Clenching my jaw, I throw my fist down on the hood of the truck, forgetting too late the injury that's already starting to swell there.

"Hey! Watch it!" Jack shouts, but I'm too distracted by the hot pink imprint my hand just left on the paintwork. Following the trail of paint, Jack rounds my side just as I spot the message sprayed across his windscreen, causing him to lose his shit.

When you're ready to end this, you know where to find me. T.

"End it?" I chuckle, pulling up the sleeves of my hoodie. "But the real fun is just about to begin."

SPADE

"I don't like any of this," Malik announces for the third time and yet again, it falls on deaf ears. Leaning back in his seat, Jasper lifts his feet to cross his ankles on the games table. Usually, Malik would have snapped at that alone, but his attention is fully directed at a nonchalant Candy leaning against the elevator shaft. She's invested in rotating her bruised wrist and pointedly ignoring him. At least Jack has the right to look spooked, his hands fisting his t-shirt as if an impending panic attack is on the way.

Shoving the letter the postman just handed me on my way back from a jog into Malik's chest, he grunts, scrunching it up in his fist. In Candy's absence, I decided to head out for a run while Ace disappeared into the garage and Jasper checked inventory in the basement. We're all back together now though, and the tension that rippled through us at finding Candy missing this morning has returned. Malik briefly scans the typed words on the page before tossing it aside.

"That's not important right now," he scowls. I roll my eyes, picking up the piece of paper to keep safe. I think a letter from our solicitor to say an offer on the place we call home has been accepted is important, but I'm not the boss. Neither is Malik anymore. We're all slaves to Candy's rule now. Noting Jack's breathing is escalating, I throw my arm around his shoulder and guide him to sit down.

"Breathe Jack, it's going to be okay." His green eyes roll, his chest heaving rapidly. When Jasper doesn't immediately pitch in, I knock his feet from the table roughly. Groaning, Jasper rounds to Jack's other side and snaps his fingers in front of his twin's face.

"Jack, focus," he snaps. When it doesn't work, Jasper puts his fingers in his mouth and whistles in a high pitch. "Remember what we used to do. Name five things you can see," Jasper commands. Struggling against his own breathing, Jack points while fumbling out hushed words.

"Table…glass…paper, chair…." Jack moves his index finger to jab Jasper in the chest, "cunt." The three of us laugh, Jack's hyperventilating easing. I've heard the pair mention Jack struggling with anxiety after the time they discovered their parents had passed, but I haven't known him to have any since living under this roof. Recent events and the close call earlier today must be hitting him deeper than he's been letting on.

"Stop worrying. We're not going to lose anyone else," Jasper tells him, in all seriousness now. Settling his green eyes on Candy, Jack nods slowly while I wonder just how many panic attacks he had behind closed doors after Jasper left. Oblivious to it all, Malik is still pacing around, his face filled with the thunder of the storm brewing within. Here it is - the side he's been suppressing. The one he thought he could hide until it no longer existed. Opening his mouth, preparing to blow, Ace jogs down the stairs and cuts in between Malik and Candy.

"Checked the traffic cams. Couldn't make out much through the blackened windows, but I managed to track one of Leicester's old Mercedes from a town near where Cherry was taken, all the way to the mansion. I would call that evidence enough, but it's not my call," Ace says, turning to face Candy with his arms crossed. She peers up from her nails, noting the silence in the room for the first time.

"What are you all staring at me for?" She asks, blowing a bubble of gum and popping it loudly. Malik shudders with barely contained rage, his jaw tight enough to crack itself.

"You're in charge, remember. We're waiting for your orders," I reply when no one else is going to. Candy swings her chocolate brown eyes my way, an impressed hitch to her brows.

"Huh, you can teach old dogs new tricks," she muses to herself. Straightening, her pink hair bobs as Candy shifts her head from side to side, visibly weighing up her options. "Well, I've got my info. You lot can go back to your own business now. Don't you have a bar to pack up?" Attempting to stride past, Ace is the first to catch Candy roughly by the forearm.

"And where do you think you are going?" he asks in a threatening tone.

"Where do you think? I'm going for a nap. Jack wore me out reallll good," Candy winks at the man beside me, trying to twist herself free, but Ace holds fast.

"Bullshit," he seethes. "You're going to jump out the window and visit the mansion without backup. It's not going to happen like that." The rest of us stand, acting as backup.

"That's the stupidest thing I've ever heard," Candy laughs, stepping into Ace's body. Her free hand wraps around his back as she tiptoes to kiss him. To his credit, Ace stands strong but clearly not enough as Candy whips the pistol from the back of his jeans with her good hand and jabs it into his groin. A strangled groan leaves his throat, his hand releasing her immediately. I'd have done the same because there's no doubt a cornered Candy is an erratic Candy. Walking backward, she knocks the safety off the gun and raises it higher to aim at Ace's chest. "I was going to use the back door."

At the last second, her arm veers aside, and a shot rings out somewhere around Ace and Malik's heads. They dive for cover, and just like that, she's gone. I don't bother chasing after her until I hear the click of the back door shut back into place. Malik helps Ace up and as a unit, we cross the kitchen to find the door inevitably locked. The key is missing from the lock, and the spares are scattered in our own bags or discarded jeans.

"At least we know where she's heading," Jasper tries to placate Malik when he spins on us with fury in his gaze.

"Do we?" He questions, the vein in his temple popping as he locates Jack. "Tell me again what happened. Don't miss out a single detail." Jack sighs, gently leaning into my arm. I don't move, letting him take whatever comfort he needs.

"It's like Candy said. Cherry popped up out of nowhere. She'd tracked my phone and conveniently distracted us long enough for Tanya to sneak in and attack." Jack runs a hand through his sandy-colored hair. That's not exactly the version Candy gave, but it's close enough.

"And then...she just got away and wrote a message on your truck?" Malik continues, disbelief lacing his tone. I look past him to the smeared windscreen outside, only the leftover smudge of red Jack had to rub off in order to drive home. He took a hundred pictures of it first though, from every single angle, before calling Malik to relay the bad news.

"It was strange," Jack admits, frowning at the ground. "One minute, Candy and Tanya were fighting, and the next...Tanya just left. Right after Candy said something about you being her beneficiary," his eyes slide to Jasper in realization.

"Motherfucker!" We all shout in unison.

"Well, that's you out," Ace announces, shoving Jasper in the chest for his ass to fall onto a nearby stool. He argues but I agree. Jasper is now Tanya's last resort to get her money; he needs to remain here.

"You too Jack," I add. "You're not in the right state to come this time. Keep Jasper company until we bring our girl back safely," I try to assuage him. I notice Jasper has stopped grumbling, his eye catching mine with a small nod. Who's babysitting who is up for debate but the two of us know the answer.

A sharp beep sounds from somewhere behind us, slicing through the thinly-veiled plan we had falling into place. Heading back as a unit, I'm as shocked as everyone to see Candy on the other side of the two-way mirror. She can't see in, but she's waving with a huge smile on her face, anticipating us being there. Pressing her lips to the glass and leaving a smudged kiss, she lifts a bottle of tequila from the bar and skips out of the front door. Rushing after her, Malik punches in the keycode for a red light to flash. Again and again, he tries, long after the rest of us have sagged back in defeat.

"She's changed the fucking code," I growl, irritation crawling up the length of my spine. Not giving up, Malik grabs for the chair Jasper was about to drop into, causing him to collapse on the floor. Raising it high above his head, Ace and I both raise our hands as our former leader loses his mind.

"Wait!" I shout. "The bar just sold, we can't go around smashing it up now."

"Fuck the bar," Malik curses, and the whole room freezes. This bar was his life, his legacy and although he's attempted to play it cool these past few weeks, losing this place will cut him deep. At least, I thought it would, but the determination in his eyes now makes me question everything I once knew about him. "What we need is a solid plan to save our girl when she inevitably gets herself stuck in a whirlwind of shit."

"Thanks for the visual," Ace adds, striding into the kitchen. He reappears a moment later with a hammer, passing it over to Malik just as the pink flare of Candy's quad bike flies past the front of the Devil's Bedpost. "Come on then, let's go stop her from doing something stupid."

CANDY

The sweet hum of my beloved quad bike vibrates between my thighs. The slick, pink paint shines longingly as the sun dips towards the horizon. Impatience is clawing at me to accept Tanya's welcoming invite, and not even the Monarchs were going to hold me back any longer. They'll be behind me somewhere, tearing up the roads in an effort to catch up. I smirk, pulling on the throttle and blazing a trail all the way to the mansion I used to frequent. I pull into a parking bay a few streets over and use a well-practiced route of jumping hedges and creeping through loose panels in fences until the wall bordering Cheese's land stands tall before me. Or, my land, I suppose.

Tracking the shrubs to a point southeast of the main building, I lower down to remove the clumps of mud and leaves I use as camouflage for the hole I once hammered into the wall. Rule number one, always have an out.

"I thought rule number one was trust no one," Angus asks, popping out of the shrubs. I ignore him and my tender shoulder, wriggling through the hole and quickly filling it in again behind me. There's a reason I chose this exact spot as my escape area, thanks to the cross-over in cameras above my head creating a blind spot. Pressing my back against the wall, I stay crouched in the bush on the other side, peering over to look for anything suspicious.

Across the expanse of perfectly green grass, the ostentatious display of wealth still stands as proud as ever. A spotless white exterior, and an array of sparkling glass windows overlooking the glimmering swimming pool. At least Tanya's been looking after the place, but only because she hopes to one day own it officially. Tough luck. The sprinklers across the lawn switch off on cue, and I stand upright, hunting for movement elsewhere.

This is the first time I've seen the mansion since discovering the truth, and I wish I could say it feels different. That being close to the mansion helps me feel closer to Big Cheese, or feel anything really. Alas, it's still a white-washed pile of plaster and brick that is the cause of many recent attempts on my life. Hard to connect with a building under the circumstances.

My feet begin to shuffle forward when a shout makes me freeze, mostly because it came from the other side of the wall.

"Candy!" Ace calls sternly. I tut, resting my back against the stone once again. Shoving the mud and leaves aside, his head pops through the hole, swiftly locating and scowling at me. I kick a bit of dirt into his eyes, making him splutter and retreat. Serves him right for stalking me when I left the Monarchs behind for a reason. Suddenly, Ace shoves his open laptop through the hole and then shifts his own body through the gap as if some speed might slicken his approach. It does not, but surprisingly, the bulky bastard manages to wriggle his way through and pop up beside me.

"You're a pain in the ass, you know that?" Ace grumbles, hitting a few keys on his laptop. I almost knee him in the dick just to give him a reason to stay behind, but the cameras overhead whirl, their blinking lights dying out. The devices lower limply, like children being sent to the naughty corner, and I smirk.

"Huh, you do have your uses," I wink. Closing his laptop, Ace ignores me in favor of tucking it safely away. My heart lifts when I spot the handle of my Candy Crusher sticking out of his backpack, marred by the confusion of why Ace would encourage my recklessness. There must be a catch – or maybe he's collecting pussy points.

Once shifting the backpack onto his beefy shoulder, just to make a point, Ace puts his hand out sharply, fingers splayed. I wait a beat, making him sweat it out before linking my fingers in-between his. I'm not naive enough to see the gesture as any more than a sexy leash, but those weird razor-tipped cutterflies arise again, and my hoo-ha sings a little tune. At least it must have been because I wouldn't have made such a high-pitched, swoony sound.

Clearing my throat, I tug Ace along, sticking to the wall's edge. The pool is still, the grounds quiet as if everything around us knows to hold its breath. Trouble's brewing. The mansion will lose its mistress today, and then it'll be at my mercy. Once close enough, I whip around the back of the garage, yanking out the rear vent.

"Wait here," I tell Ace and duck inside before he can object. I return a few moments later, pulling a chainsaw behind me.

"What's that for?" Ace balks, clearly hoping for a clean gun fight if the pistol stashed in his back pocket is anything to go by.

"You'll see," I wink. Peering at the mansion, shadows approach from the east, where the paved driveway meets the garage. I shove the chainsaw into Ace's hands, opting for my trusty Candy Crusher instead. Slipping around the outbuilding, my swing is reared back and ready when Spade and Malik appear, their guns raised in preparation for an ambush. Motherfuckers. Lowering my bat, I walk out, uncaring to sneak around anymore. I catch Malik's eye and open my arms wide in a 'what the fuck Mistro?!' move. He has the decency to look sheepish, beckoning me over with a swish of his hand.

"No arguments," Malik says, not that I was going to protest. I'll take great pleasure in punishing him thoroughly later.

"At least tell me the twins stayed home," I narrow my eyes, and he nods. Thank fuck for that. No point in my best collateral tagging along for Tanya to kill us both in one night. Spade catches my attention, tiptoeing around the mansion like an action figure. He tries the patio door, finding it unlocked, and whistles for us to follow. No thanks. Raising the Candy Crusher, I smash out the kitchen window and ask Ace for a boost, chainsaw and all.

"What are you doing?!" Spade whisper shouts while I reply in a normal tone.

"Unlocked door? Really? Way too easy." With Ace's help, I clamber through the window, collecting up a few large shards of glass and tucking them into the buckled straps crisscrossing over my boots. You never know when extra weapons can come in handy, and if they don't, I'll just start a new fad. From the billiard room next door, the patio door slides open, quickly followed by a 'whoosh.' The entire room ignites in a burst of orange, and a flare of heat hits back through the open archway. Ace and Malik promptly throw themselves through the kitchen window, their faces biting back hysterics. Spade rounds the archway, his eyebrows a distant memory. But if they had been there, I bet he'd be making his best Angus impression.

"How'd that work out for y-"

"Just lead the fucking way," Spade growls, his fists in tight balls. Told ya, too easy. Tanya has been laying low for so long and now this evasive invitation? I can only imagine what she's been trying to set up, hoping to anticipate my every move. It's as if she never learns. Pausing by the cellar door, I listen through the wood for any hints of life downstairs and then dismiss it. Continuing into the hallway, I note it's too still. Too quiet.

"Where do you think she has Cherry?" Ace whispers by my ear. I force away the distraction of his breath coating my skin and the sudden thought of Tanya hiding out nearby, only to watch me have a four-way right here in the lobby. Nah, I'd rather strap her down in full view and do it, feeding off her discomfort like porn.

"The easiest place to get the upper hand," I reply to Ace, reaching behind to run a hand over his hardening crotch. Oh yeah, he'd so be up for it too. As a unit, we round the main staircase. The smell of gasoline hits me before I see the slickened shine to each step. Not just with one substance, but a mixture of oil and tar by the looks and smell of it. The fumes are overpowering, making the Monarchs choke, but I just crack into a smile.

"She's pulled out all the stops from her Candy playbook," Angus chuckles. I spot him doing a handstand on the flourished end of the railing. I'm inclined to agree until I spot Angus' little jelly dick flop over from his precarious position. Yuck.

"I think it's cute Tanya wants to play Jigsaw," I concur, drawing the Monarchs attention my way. Nosey buggers. "Too bad she has the imagination of a cactus and the personality of a weed."

"I've got this one," Malik states bravely. He hops up onto the railing, squashing Angus beneath his crotch. Not that the little pervert cares, releasing a pleasured moan rather than an annoyed curse. I tilt my head, watching Malik shimmy up the railing until he gets around halfway. One by one, the metal droppings of loosened screws hit the floor before the whole rail collapses aside, taking Malik with it. Pathetic.

"Malik!" Ace and Spade shoot forward, helping their brother out from under the wooden debris. Shaking my head at the display, I turn left and walk away. My eyes are super vigilant for the cliché shit Tanya's tiny, TV-poisoned brain would conjure up. Ace comes bounding up from behind as I approach one of the living areas, and I lash my arm out.

"Careful," I warn him. Taking the chainsaw from his hand, I swing the machine low, slicing through a barely-visible trip wire without the need to rev it up. Grabbing Ace's t-shirt, I yank him downwards as an axe swings across the doorway where our heads just were. The breath saws out of Ace, his wide puppy dog eyes captivating my bored ones.

"Holy fuck." The more the axe swings, the less traction it has until Spade is able to grab a hold and untie it.

"Okay, from now on, we follow Candy's every move," Spade nods sharply as Malik joins us, still dusting himself off.

"About damn time," I reply. With them right behind, I navigate around the furniture without touching a single thing, dragging the chainsaw and my bat along behind. Once safely in Big Cheese's old office, we take the winding stairs he kept for his own personal use directly into his master bedroom. Or at least it was. The stale scent of perfume hits me first, then the dirty washing strewn all over the place. You'd think when plotting an evil version of Home Alone, she'd have thought to pick up her panties, unless her feral crabs are all part of the plan – yeesh.

Tiptoeing around the clothing, I make it all the way to the door and crack it open the tiniest bit. A string is attached to the door knob on the other side, priming my beloved pink crossbow with a set of three silver-tipped arrows. I'll commend her for that one - it really is my style. Signaling for the guys to move aside, I whip the door open for the three arrows to sail past and hit home in a portrait of Big Cheese. It was a pretentious piece of shit anyway, but the arrows now implanted in his face just look pitiful.

The rest of the hallway is left untouched, ringing with a painful silence. Stopping outside a closed door, I pass the Candy Crusher to Malik and threaten his life if there's a single scratch on her precious pine when I get her back.

"Is she in there?" Spade whispers, insinuating Tanya. I gravely shake my head, leaning in close to his ear.

"I have a different type of business to handle. I'll be right back." Before he can ask any more questions, I boot the door open with a wood splintering crack and rev up the chainsaw. My arm judders with the power of its vibration, filling me with a burst of adrenaline I've been missing. Running into Jasper's old room, I take to his bed, intent on sawing it clean in half. Feathers fly from the pillows, the covers becoming torn and getting in the way. Dragging them aside, I hop up on the mattress, laughing evilly with the raw power of demolishing every surface Jasper and the wicked she-witch fucked in this room. The ottoman catches my eye, and I point at it.

"You're next, you suede piece of shit." The three men who accompanied me stand just inside the door, their eyes darting around frantically. There's no use worrying about Tanya; a) because I'm holding a fucking chainsaw and 2) knowing her, she'll sit and wait in her tower for me to arrive. Which I will do so in my own damn time. To their credit, by the time I'm satisfied the bed and ottoman are destroyed and run at the dresser with a banshee scream, the guys have relaxed into a mumbled conversation, slouched against the wall. Slicing into the dark, maple wood, the chainsaw splutters, evidently running out of gas, and I toss it aside.

"Shall we?" I ask, snatching my bat back from Malik and striding out, inspecting her closely. I pass my old room, knowing Tanya would expect me to take the awkward way to the attic. Instead, I wait for Ace to give me a leg up and yank down the attic door. A ladder extends automatically, settling onto the plush carpet soundlessly. "After you," I tell Angus, watching him leap from one rung to the next. Reaching the top, he looks back with a thumbs up and I'm satisfied. Lifting my foot up the first step, a hand wraps around mine as I reach for the ladder.

"Hey," Malik says, way too quiet. His dark eyes soften, mirroring a look Ace and Spade also take on over his shoulders. "There's no use telling you to be careful, but…we love you. That's all." Everyone's breaths hold, waiting for me to absorb the saying that still doesn't slide naturally into my ears. Instead, it shoots inside like a rocket and plays ping pong inside my brain until it explodes altogether. Gently twisting my hand from Malik's, so as not to hurt his feelings, I tap the area over his heart.

"Mm mmmm mmm mmm," I repeat back in a hum. Grinning like weirdos, the three allow me to turn away, their eyes fixed on my every move like kittens to a red light while I fight to get my head in the game. Angus is waiting at the top, tapping a watch that's appeared on his wrist, and I swing the Candy Crusher at him. No use rushing me now I'm already here. Ready to see whatever Tanya thinks will best me, and knowing it can't be worse than the awkwardness of staying at the bottom of these steps.

ACE

Taking the rear of those desperate to chase Candy up the ladder, I peer around the old-fashioned hallway for any signs of more traps we've missed. I'm not sure if Tanya thought she could channel her inner Candy or if she's just lost her damn mind, but apparently, I need to be ready for anything. When Spade whistles for me to hurry, I ascend the metal rings, popping up into the attic space.

The smell hits me long before I spot Cherry, postured up in the center of the room. Her hands are trussed to a fixture in the arched ceiling that I can't imagine was put there for any other reason. Blood leaking from her wrists score vein-like pathways down her arms, her face hidden beneath the curtain of her red hair. Other than the obvious, her body around the white t-shirt and jeans looks mostly intact, the shallow rise and fall to her chest signaling she's still alive, for now.

Circling the tattered boots hanging just above the wooden flooring is a thick line of glistening liquid that can't be anything other than gasoline separates us from Candy's half-sister. The fumes alone are enough to intoxicate a person stuck in this cramped space for too long. When no one moves, Candy shrugs and steps over the line, ignoring our rushed protests. We hold back, trying to remain vigilant, but it's difficult when we want to see what has Candy gasping. Peering over her shoulder, she's rolled Cherry's head aside to reveal the piece of tape stuck over her mind. More than that, the word penned in black marker barely registers in time. 'Gotcha.'

A click sounds as the room ignites in a blaze of orange with an audible whoosh. Heat explodes between the girls and us, causing me to stumble back. Spade's hand whips out to grab my shirt before I fall down the open floor hatch, pulling me upright. Covering my eyes, I peer over the wall of flames, relieved to see Candy is still okay in the center - but for how long? Darting for the hatch intentionally this time, I throw myself through the gap and land heavily below. Dragging up the aged rug, I quickly roll the dusty material and lift it up for Malik to grab. With the help of Spade, the pair heave it upwards while I push from below, making my way back up the ladder. Once cleared, we grip the corners and on a countdown, roll out the rug to flatten a patch of the fire.

"Candy! Come quick!" Malik shouts over the roar of cracking wood splintering all around.

"I'm not leaving without her," Candy replies, flicking a penknife from her boot. The rug catches alight as my heart jumps into my throat, seeing the knife isn't cutting the ties on Cherry's wrists quick enough. Groaning, I dart through the flames just before they close between us. Smoke invades my lungs, polluting my airways on spluttered coughs. Instead of trying to break the cable ties at her wrists, I grip the chunky chain holding Cherry upright and tug with all my might. On the second yank, the fixture rips from the ceiling, bringing a chunk of the wooden beam with it. I take the brunt of the hit with my back, crowding over Candy as she catches her sister's body. At this stage, I'm not even sure if Cherry is still alive, but I know for a fact Candy won't be leaving without her. Scooping the limp body up in my arms, I hunt for a gap in the fires to give us an escape.

"Over here!" I hear over the crackling fire, spotting Spade

waving wildly. Through the plumes of smoke distorting the view, I catch a glimpse of Candy's beloved bat swing back before Malik strikes it down on the machine embedded in the low vent spitting out fire. It looks homemade like a lawnmower engine turned into a flamethrower. He strikes it a few times, causing the flames to splutter temporarily, and I take my shot. Dragging Candy with me, we leap through, a few licks of the fire catching my ankles. Plowing into Spade, we all bundle down the ladder hastily, passing Cherry between us as we go.

Rushing back the way we came, Candy leads us through Leicester's room, down the stairs of his study, and through the lounge. This time, we take the front door, gunning for the bikes stashed in a nearby hedge. Grabbing Spade's for him, he throws a leg over the seat and rips the tape from Cherry's mouth. Her eyes burst open on a strangled choke, struggling to take in her surroundings.

"It's going to be okay," Spade lies. Nothing about this is okay. "I'm going to take you somewhere safe. Can you hold on?" Blinking up at him, Cherry tentatively raises her still tied hands for Spade to slot his head in-between. "I'll meet you back at the bar," Spade grunts, barely sparing me a glance. The pair speed off, leaving Malik and me to sigh in exasperation.

"Never a dull day," he mutters, and I roll my eyes up to the thick cloud of smoke churning from the mansion's roof. "We need to get out of here." Following Malik's orders as per usual, I step towards my bike when I suddenly realize it's too quiet. Hunting around for the reincarnation of trouble herself, I spot Candy kneeling down beside the house steps. Clawing her fingers in the mud, I jog over to ease her up.

"Candy, babe, it's time to go," I tell her as lightly as I can. Gripping a blue lock box in her muddied hands, her brown eyes sparkle with vengeance. Drawing her under my arm as I try to bury my concern, Candy lets me lift her onto the back of my bike, and with Malik at our side, we floor it the few streets over to where Candy has parked her quad.

"Do you know the easiest way to corner a rat?" She asks, easing over to her own vehicle. Settling on the black leather, Candy twists the combination lock on the box with her filthy fingers. Inside, a slim control with a single red button sits, seeming innocent enough until Candy prods her index finger at it. "Remove its hidey hole."

A thunderous ripple vibrates through the ground as if an army was storming the street before a series of blasts explode through the sky, one after the other. I flinch and duck on impact while Candy cackles from the seat of her quad. Speeding away, I share a wide-eyed look with Malik before we take off after her, not stopping once until we breach the Devil's Bedpost boundary. Slowing to a stop by the garage, the three of us leave our bikes to put away later as I grab for Candy's hand.

"Did you…I mean, was that-" I stutter, struggling to understand what happened back there. I've spent the whole ride trying and dismissing the thought that Candy is clearly so proud of. She's grinning from ear to ear, her chest puffed out.

"I've been hiding explosives around Cheese's property for years, waiting for the day the old man pushed me too far. Wish I could have blown it up with his whole crew inside, but this feels just as sweet." My brows touch my hairline as she turns to Malik when he pulls in, reminding me never to fuck over Candy. Holding her hand out, he pops his visor with a frown. "I'll take the Candy Crusher back now."

"Err," Malik pauses, pulling his helmet off. "I may have… dropped it in the attic when we were fleeing." I see the panic pass through Malik's dark eyes as we both wait for Candy's bitch-fit. When it doesn't come, I peer around her shoulder to see why. Following her eye line and spotting the Devil's Bedpost at Malik's back for the first time, my mouth drops. Lacking windows, sprays of bullets lodged into the exterior. Beneath the now-crooked overhang, a figure sits on the porch steps. His back is arched over to bury his face in his crossed arms, but the sweep of blond hair and preference for high-tops tells me it's one of the twins. Jack, I'd imagine by his deflated posture.

Malik shoots past, skidding to his knees. Prying up the twin's face, scores of tears line his puffy cheeks, a heavy bruise beginning to shadow his left eye. More dark purple marks have surfaced along the edge of his jaw, and upon seeing Malik, Jack throws himself into our past leader's arms. There, on the steps of the bar, Malik simply holds Jack while he cries, not once pushing him for information like I want to.

Even before Candy turned up and brought this crazy world right alongside her, Malik always had a fondness for Jack, not that he'll admit it. Through the cracks of his brooding armor, he always had time for Jack. The pair remain together while I twist out of Candy's steel-like grip and stride past.

The bar, or what remains of it, is a mess. Aside from the mirror Malik previously smashed, shattered glasses and broken stools cover each inch of the floor. The table I spent so long varnishing is splintered down the center, an axe still protruding from the center. Our DJ booth lies in a pile of ruin, and the inflatable cock Candy kept around for fun has been slashed to death. Glancing back at the trio outside, I spot another message written in lipstick on the only window left standing. Tanya's signature, it would seem.

Not so predictable after all.

My phone vibrates in my pocket, displaying Spade's name when I fish it out. Answering the call, I wander over to lean against the doorframe to see Candy has sunk to her knees before Jack too.

"Ace!" Spade shouts into my ear, panic lacing his rushed words. "Cherry's just filled me in on everything she's heard. It's a trap – this whole thing was a distraction to kidnap Jasper. you need to get to-"

"I'm here," I cut him off with a grave tone. "And it's already too late."

CANDY

"Knock, knock," I call through the metal door that sits on the back step of the Thirsty Kirsty strip club, stepping aside from the view grate when it snaps open.

"Who's there?" A gruff voice calls. I put my finger over my lips, silencing a guilty-looking Malik and Spade as they are the only ones left in view. Mouthing a reply for Spade to mimic, I catch Jack's blank stare across the other side and give him a solid thumbs up. Where he finds weakness, I'll be strong.

"Ben?" Spade answers, following my instruction.

"Ben who?" The gruff voice comes away, and I fist pump the air, so happy with how this played out.

"Bend over, or I'll shove my foot up your ass," I say, appearing from my hiding place.

"Ahh fuck," Mick grumbles from behind the grate, quickly followed by a radio for backup. He always was a pussy when it came to manhandling me, preferring others to do it after I bit his thumb off. In my defense, being my naive teenage self, I did warn him back when I still believed people needed some notice before I lashed out. Glad I snapped out of that annoying phase. A sudden attack is the best kind of surprise. Besides, he still has his other nine digits for fingering his boss' asshole like the suck-up he is. "Look," Mick drawls, finally meeting my eye. "She's not here. You'd better beat it before Art sees you."

"Yet I'm not leaving until I've swept the place myself. It's up to you if I do that quietly or if my boys here shoot their way in." Mick's eyes pass over Malik, Spade, and then Ace and Jack when they also step into sight as my menacing foursome. My chest squeezes at our missing member, but that thought spurs me on to get the answers I need. "Or fuck it, I could just do it myself?" Dislodging the shotgun from the strap at my back, I knock off the safety and fire a warning shot at the concrete doorstep.

"Okay! Okay! Here, for fucks sake," Mick opens the door, squishing himself behind it as I stroll inside. The metal of the gun drags noisily behind me until Jack removes it from my grip, securing it back in place on my back. We navigate the halls in no time, appearing from the beaded separator to emerge into the strip club itself. Nothing's changed, not even the lousy red lighting that was here the first day I walked into this place as a thirteen-year-old runaway. I'd been skittish back then, happy to hide behind those leading me astray – but that's a story for another time.

The stage is split three ways, each with a pole fixed in the circles at the ends. The catwalks sparkle with glittery lino that reflects in the spotlights overhead, casting the rest of the club in shadow. Clients can choose to sit between zones of sofas, hidden booths, or dining-style tables because who doesn't want a side of chili fries with their strip show? On the surface, the deep purple and burgundy color palette looks expensive but I know what an asshole the owner is for cutting corners. Half the flourishing gold fixtures on the walls are stolen, the other half are sprayed pieces of bent pipe he'd swear were hand crafted by Alexander Calder.

"I don't need a sign to tell me that would be Art," Spade signals to a man sitting off to the left beside the stage. I suppose his name is as pretentious as the fake Dolce and Gabbana suit he's somehow managing to still squeeze into. Aside from the pinched fabric struggling to hold in his beer gut, a ridiculous cowboy hat in the same ruby red is propped on his head where a gray comb-over used to be. I can't imagine his hair has lasted all these years since my last visit.

"The one and only owner, after he strangled his business partner. He likes to think he also owns the women that work here. Literally claims scouting them out is his 'art form.'" On cue with the music, two girls in bikinis fresh out of Uni take the stage in a choreographed routine. They branch off to separate poles, but their motions remain synced, as does the painfully forced expressions on both of their faces.

"I didn't realize blackmailing young girls into selling themselves is considered the work of a genius," Jack mumbles and I appreciate how quickly he caught onto my thought train.

"We could have been millionaires by now if we'd got the memo," I nudge him, and we share a smirk until Malik leans into my other side.

"You are a millionaire," he mutters, reminding me of what I've spent weeks trying to forget. I give him an evil side-eye, still insulted by such a statement. I've mastered living with nothing. To have everything now seems disgustingly ironic.

"So this is where you come from?" Ace asks, trying to change the subject. Settling himself by the bar, I slide onto the leather stool beside him and bang my fist on the polished surface.

"Not really. I'll write my life story one day and put that part in the prequel." A bartender appears, some fresh meat I feel sorry for. Ahh man, once you're in, you never get out. He's pretty hot too, ripped in low-riding jeans and a bow tie. Spade crowds my side, twisting my head to face him instead.

"There's not enough paper in the world to encapsulate your feisty spirit." He kisses my nose, and I let him off for that slyly possessive move. Five beers are placed in front of us since the alcohol here doesn't range much beyond that. We're not in an area that would care much for the drink. Anyone who is traveling to the dregs of downtown is only looking for one thing, a sweet and willing pussy. Lifting the beer to my lips, I spot a member of security striding over to Art and take that as my sign to get moving.

"Come on, before we cause a scene that my mom will have to pay for." Like he always does at the most inconvenient moments, Angus appears in the bar with an open mouth. Yes, okay, the Monarchs have scratched the surface of everything I kept bottled up, and now I'm caring about all sorts of people. Being in this place reminds me of why I shut off my emotions in the first place, but I'm not going there. Not now, not ever again.

Heading for a beaded curtain on the opposite side, I feel Art's eyes fall on me, the weight of his stare like a dagger in my back. Gesturing for the guys to go through the curtain first, I turn back to lock eyes with my Mom's prison guard. Beneath the tip of his hat, he grimaces at the very sight of me, or more like the girl he couldn't trap. Flipping him off, I slip through the beads, navigating the maze of private rooms that lead backstage.

Just like the many rooms on either side of the corridor, rich purple wallpaper lines the walls, enhanced by low mood lighting. Rich perfume is sprayed throughout the hall regularly to entice the clients to leave their inhibitions outside while the girls who are only supposed to dance do anything for a tip. Anything to save up with the illusion they can escape one day. Keeping my Monarchs close, we venture through the corridors as a perfectly synced unit. No door is left unopened, no room unchecked as we go, accompanied by the sympathy of shocked screams and cheating husband's fleeing. Yeah, I saw your face and your wedding ring Mr. I-have-a-fetish-for-schoolgirls.

"Suppose your mom isn't working currently," Spade says as we move towards the dressing rooms.

"Oh, she doesn't dance for clients anymore. She's the Madam who cares for all of the other girls. Ironic, right?" I chuckle, spotting Art still staring at me through the gap at the back of the stage. The girls have moved into swinging upside down with their legs spread wide for the measly midday crowd of spectators.

"But…I thought we were checking the private rooms for…" Jack stutters, a V between his brows.

"Nah, I was just being nosey." Linking my fingers in his because…well, I don't really need a reason, but with his twin not here right now, I think we could both use the added comfort. The dressing rooms are a stark contrast to the lavish areas for clients. Crammed, cluttered. Pokey holes in the walls where dreams are cried away, and souls crumbled to dust. Maybe I'm biased, but I've seen it too many times to deny.

My boots eat up the uncarpeted flooring, heading for the stairs leading to my mom's personal suite when a ruffle among the costume rails catches my eye. A brunette head is poking out from behind, drawing me into the oversized wardrobe. Bending low, I brace my hands on a netted nightie and a bunny corset complete with tail, whipping the hangers aside to reveal my mom.

"Jesus Christ!" She screams, dropping her handful of beads. Hitting the floor like bullets, the pieces of plastic shoot in all directions around the poxy room, most never to be seen again.

"Not quite, but I understand your confusion," I smirk at the woman who birthed me. Up until recently, I'd resented her for that fact. Now though, I'm not so bitter about it. Clutching her chest, Mom steps out from between the railing, her brown eyes darting over the men crowding in the wardrobe area.

"Did they find you?" Mom whispers, and I frown.

"Who are you referring to? These are my men," I lift my chin as various hands wrap around my mid-section. Taken aback, Mom sidesteps to shuffle behind the sewing machine stuffed in the corner. She's a short woman, at least a head shorter than me, with chestnut brown hair and matching colored eyes. Her body still resembles the slender sprite she used to be, back in the days when she'd throw herself around the pole and let men pay to bench-press her. You wouldn't know it now though, with a pair of baggy dungarees swamping her lithe frame and her hair tossed up in a messy bun. The most jarring thing is the pin cushion on her wrist, marking her as the in-house seamstress.

"How did you get in here?" She asks, powering up the machine before I can reply. Running my finger along the length of a feather boa, I pluck it out to wind around Malik's neck.

"Your security system is shit, that's how. Better question is, what the fuck are you doing in wardrobe?" I leave Malik to battle with the pink fluff to turn an accusing glare on my mother. Without looking at me, she rushes a piece of cloth through the machine, snagging the needle and ripping a hole in the pattern.

"I'm on house arrest thanks to a recent incident. Art's been good enough to let me work off the damage caused by fixing up costumes and other menial tasks behind the scenes." I roll my eyes at her tone, reading between the lines that the incident was somehow my fault. Everything always is around here.

"So you're here against your will?" Ace asks, folding his arms like he does when he jumps into protective mode. A bitter laugh tears from my throat.

"Unlike those out on stage, this is exactly where she wants to be. She's been under Art's spell since the very beginning." It's no coincidence my mom was promoted to Madam instead of tossed out on her ass when she fell pregnant with me. For any other 'employee,' that would have been game over, but not her. I've had my suspicions she's been screwing Art since the very beginning, which would explain where I got my magical pussy from.

"He saved me," Mom states, and I groan. Here we go again, round and round in circles, just like every time I visit. That's why I stopped.

"He broke you. You're just too naive to see it."

"No," my mom growls in a tone I haven't heard from her before. Slamming down the ruined outfit, she shoots up to glare at me. "Your father broke me. From the minute I found out I was pregnant, I was thrown into some mafia battle I have no interest in." I shift uncomfortably, not liking how much the Monarchs are learning about my lineage today, but I'm here for one reason only. Sighing, my mom yanks off the pin cushion bracelet and drags a measuring tape from the pocket over her breast.

"Judge all you like. I've had a good life here, and it's all I know. Art's been good to me. We can't all travel from state to state, living off scraps like you. Looks like you've done well for yourself though," she eyes my men, and I growl like a wild animal. Luckily, she lowers her gaze before I launch myself over the sewing table to throttle her with my teeth, true lioness style. Not even my own mother gets to look upon my pride of males with lust in her eyes.

"I might not have needed to live off scraps if you'd told me I was a millionaire," I retort instead, silencing her. Malik leans in, his stubble scraping against my ear.

"Told you so," he whispers. Whipping my head around so fast our jaws collide, I glare at him to shut it. Movement in front shifts as my mom pushes her way through the wall the Monarchs have made, trying to end this conversation. Hell no.

"Since we're in the mood for sharing," I follow her into the hallway, too focused on leaving out the word 'finally' to question the slight limp in her step. For once, I want to hear what she has to say rather than just get under her skin. "It's time to start talking. Tanya has taken something that belongs to me, and I won't stop until I get it back." The mention of Tanya's name has my mom's back straightening, and that's how I know there's more to this story.

"Let me guess, it's your stupid bat." I can hear the eye-roll in her tone as the six of us ascend her stairs. I would argue if Malik wasn't right behind to remind me how I stalked the Devil's Bedpost for my bat, but it all seems so menial now.

"It's the fifth piece of my soul if you don't mind." Passing through the door, I make myself at home on the brown leather sofa and gesture for the guys to do the same. Ace opts for the place I'm sitting, lifting me into his arms and dumping me onto his lap. The way his face buries in my neck resonates with how the others are looking at me, even my mom. I avoid her pitying gaze, looking at anything else in her mini apartment instead.

All of the furniture is second-hand - which I'm told is a polite way of saying upcycled from bits of shit or collected from dumpsters. It is amazing what people throw away, although personally, I prefer taking the items they'd like to keep. All bunched together in one long room, the sofas back onto a foldaway table with two stools. Dirty dishes cover the single kitchen countertop, and next a short person's refrigerator sits beside a single bed of crumpled sheets. It's supposed to fold away into the wall, but I suppose when you're not expecting visitors, I wouldn't bother tidying up either. The fist-sized holes in the wall are new though, and the curtain rail looks beyond wonky.

"Time to talk," I state, bored of the stale atmosphere. "And don't waste time on useless specifics. I only care about the locations of possible hideaways Tanya has up her sleeve."

"I don't know why you'd think I have any information," my mom starts, and I shoot up from Ace, accidentally kneeing him in the dick.

"You know so much more than you let on. Stop bullshitting me!" I shout, losing my shit. Nothing has had the capability to rile me in as long as I can remember, but I'm riled now. If this is my emotional coming-out party, then move over bitch, because I have arrived. "It's important," I say when no one dares to move. Releasing a long sigh, my mom moves to lean against the kitchen counter.

"You were barely a week old when Leicester took you from me. He wanted to pass you off as a twin with Tanya's newborn, but she wasn't having it. Last I heard, you were taken to some relative's house where a fake foster couple picked you up. There was nothing I could have done." Tapping my foot, I roll my hand in an effort to speed up her trip down memory lane. "So instead, I took the money Tanya offered me, monthly payments right up until you stumbled into this club at thirteen. After that, I was paid to keep tabs on you, and report back your whereabouts. As if that's an easy feat."

"What did you do with the money?" I scoff, not bothered about any other part of her sob story. "Lord knows you didn't need it living here, and none of it ever came my way."

"Remember the Harrington's?" Mom asks with a knowing tilt of her head.

"Subject dropped," I scowl, twisting away from where Angus has appeared on the kitchen counter to mimic her expression.

"Wait, who's-" Malik asks, but I swipe my hand through the air.

"Another story for another time." A shared look is passed between the Monarchs as if to acknowledge they'll never find out about it and they're right. That name strikes a cord directly into the hollow pit in my chest, although discovering my mom has been paying for my mistake all this time lessens the blow a minuscule amount. It's the one mistake I've always regretted until my emotional switch was flicked to permanently off.

"Tanya came here a few weeks ago, looking for you," my mom gives me an out from the awkward atmosphere filling the room. "Her goons tore the place up until they were satisfied I wasn't stashing you somewhere. Left me with a friendly reminder to report back if I should see you again." Lifting the baggy leg of her dungaree, an off-white bandage covers my mom's leg from ankle to calf. She knows better than to go to the hospital or alert the police, explaining why the strap is discolored and losing its elasticity. At least the holes in the wall make sense now.

"So you've got nothing of use," I purse my lips. There's no point asking if she will or won't inform Tanya of my visit, especially now I know the money is going to a good cause.

"One of the guys did take a phone call on his way out. He looked a lot like you in fact," my mom narrows her gaze on Malik. I step into the way, blocking him from her scrutiny and pressing her to carry on. "I don't remember what he said, only that one of the others comments on how loud he was talking. He mentioned something about speedboat engines at the triangle? It's not much but-"

"The triangle? I've heard of that before," Spade sits forward, locking his fingers together. "Pottersfield is an abandoned fishing dock on the east coast. There's a trio of old warehouses down there."

"Then it's settled," I clap my hands together, done with this convo, atmosphere, and family reunion. Jerking my chin, the Monarchs jump up to follow me out. No goodbyes or thank yous. My mom made her bed, or rather she didn't by the state of her mini apartment, and now she can stay in it. Jogging down the stairs, lousy security guards are waiting for us at the base. Notice how I just stormed my mom's apartment with four hunky men, and no one tried to save her. Some hero Art is. We don't stop for pleasantries, barging through the hallways like a gang on a mission.

"Seriously, who are the Harrington's?" Malik is on my back the instant we escape the Thirsty Kirsty, and I gulp in a breath of fresh air, unpolluted by modern-day slavery.

"Prequel, remember," I roll my eyes, locking that piece of information away to never see the light of day again. We have a lead to get back our final member, and I'm done playing games. Call me old, but I'm ready to settle down and have some six-way orgies without the stress of mafia wars hanging over my head.

JACK

The whole way back to the Devil's Bedpost, no one says anything. At least I have the drive to distract me, my knuckles white from the clutching the wheel. Pulling up in the parking lot, I leave my beloved truck abandoned across three spaces. Without needing to be told, we stride inside, past the shattered two-way mirror, and directly to the elevator. Malik pushes the internal button to take us to the top floor since that's where most of the weapons are kept. Except, when we breach his suite, Malik heads directly to his billiard room for the bottle of half-empty whiskey left on the edge of the table. Spade drops onto a seat at the dining table with Ace not far behind. That leaves Candy and me in the doorway, scowling at their lack of urgency.

"So when do we leave?" I ask impatiently, fiddling with the hem of my t-shirt.

"When we have a game plan and have rested up," Malik replies, planting the whiskey bottle in my hand to stop me from pulling the stitching out of place. "You know how every job goes. We don't go in hot-headed or without an escape plan."

"This isn't just any job," I growl, taking a swig of the drink anyway. "It's one of our own on the line."

"Exactly," Spade nods, rasping his knuckles on the tabletop. "That's why it's more important than ever we don't act rashly." Disappearing into his room for a moment, Malik returns to pass Ace a laptop, which he powers up straight away.

"I'll get on researching the dock now. We should have birds-eye views and a bigger picture of what we're dealing with in no time."

"We're dealing with a jealous cow bag who should have grown accustomed to losing by now," Candy tuts, stretching her neck out like she's gearing up for a fight. I might not be the beefiest of guys here, but I'd be right there by her side.

"Which is how we know she won't do anything too drastic to Jasper yet," Malik takes Candy's hand and draws her towards the dining table. When she refuses to sit, he settles for winding his arms around her waist instead. "This isn't just about the money anymore. This is cold-hearted revenge she won't exact until you're watching."

"If you're insinuating I should stay behind, you can think again," Candy raises her chin, refusing to return his hug. Malik doesn't falter, clinging on like a koala who's found his favorite eucalyptus.

"I wouldn't dream of it. All I'm saying is we need to be smart. I'm leaving that warehouse with all of my Monarchs and my girl, so no fuck ups. Then we're getting in the truck and leaving. Fuck selling the bar." The haze of my irritation lessens, allowing me to see clearer. Yeah, they're right - we need to treat this like any other job. Rounding the back of Ace, I widen my stance to watch him type furiously, switching from images to coding and back again. Taking another long swig, I pass the whiskey onto Spade, as we would have at previous meetings like this.

Loading up images from a satellite, the three warehouses Spade referred to come into view. There's nothing distinctive about them; stationary buildings of the same size with silver rooves and no sign of life nearby. The dock is a short distance away, branching off in a large arc of nothingness. Deeply-engrained tire marks lead away from the port to a dirt junkyard of abandoned boats that have been dragged from the water. Alongside the picture, Ace loads a list of info on the area. Pottersfield used to be extremely popular until a change in water levels saw profits dive-bombing. The maintenance cost too much to continue, leading to its closure. Looks like most of the hangers have been torn down and removed, all except for the three warehouses still standing tall. How suspicious.

Glancing up, I catch Candy staring longingly at me before she manages to duck her head. I swallow thickly, knowing all too well it wasn't me she was imagining then. For the same reason, I've been struggling to look in the mirror, preferring to brush my teeth and shower in the dark. All it takes is one misjudged glance, and the anxiety rising in my chest threatens to choke me out. At long last, she twists into Malik's hold and lays her head on his shoulder. Holding her close, his hand lowers to brush her ass, and a genius idea slaps me around the face.

"That's it!" I shout, causing Spade to spill his whiskey as he raises it to his lips. All eyes warily fly my way as if I've finally snapped. "Hear me out. Candy is able to best Tanya because she's unpredictable, which is exactly what we have to continue doing. What's the one thing we can do to ensure Jasper's safety?" Rounding the table, I pop Candy's shorts button and use my hand on the back of her neck to force her over the table. With her ass tilted in the air, I yank down her shorts, not surprised by the lack of underwear covering her perfect cheeks.

"Um, Jack," Malik places a hand on my shoulder in concern. "I don't think this is time." I roll my eyes, shaking him off. Pulling my phone out of my pocket, I open the camera to snap a picture of the tattoo we branded on Candy, which she's effectively forgotten about. Apparently, the others did too. Collectively, the three men around me suck in a sharp breath, their eyes flooding with panic. Ignoring them, I pull Candy's shorts back in place and toss my phone onto the table top by her head, screen side up.

Slowly rising, her gaze falls on the image staring back. A hot pink love heart with 'Marry ~~me~~ Us,' inside, permanently inked into her ass. We all watch for the hint of a reaction, our hearts laid out on the table for her to accept or stab into a thousand pieces. When the silence weighs too heavily, I catch Spade and Ace's urgent eye flicks to do something. Turning her by the shoulders, I bring Candy's dazed eyes back to mine.

"If you marry one of us, Jasper is no longer your next of kin. Then that person can sign another as theirs and so on. You'll both be protected by an anonymity of the inheritance being lost in a web Tanya can't untangle. She can't take us all out."

"I wouldn't be so sure about that," Candy finally speaks, a relieved breath whooshing out of me. It's not the tattoo she's freaked out about after all.

"Are you worried about us, Crazy Girl?" I smirk, knowing that'll strike a chord. Even now, as I'm effectively proposing to her, Candy struggles to admit she worries, cares and loves us. Not that I need her words, I can see it in the depths of her chocolate brown eyes. In her light touches when she forgets herself, how she crawls into our beds for comfort, how she puts her dominating nature aside so we can own her body, spirit and soul.

"Okay. Let's do it," her voice sounds small and despite the seriousness of the situation, despite my twin being in the hands of some jealous psycho, I chuckle. Ace and Spade stand to close in on us in a huge bear hug, hands shifting to get closer to her. For this one moment, aside from the impending doom ready to slam down on us, we bathe in our girl's very essence. The only question left is who marries her and how the hell are we going to decide.

CANDY

Closing Malik's door as softly as I can, I tiptoe down the stairs, only breathing once I'm safely back in my room. Holy fucking shit. I just agreed to get married. Oh of all the revelations that would come out of tonight, that's not what I thought would be one of them. Sliding down against the door, I dip my head between my knees, wondering how long it'll be until the guys stop arguing. What started as a simple game of rock, paper, scissors over who would walk me down the aisle turned rather 'competitive,' for lack of a better word. The last I saw, blood was pissing out of Jack's nose and Ace had just vaulted Spade over the sofa.

"Who'd have thought you'd go from an unwanted gutter rat to a bunch of guys fighting over marrying you?" Angus muses in his usual unhelpful way.

"What can I say – I've found my peoples," I reply, suddenly smiling and then hating myself for it. This isn't about marrying me really. This is about saving Jasper. If I hadn't been so laid back, toying with Tanya, I could have prevented all of this. Nick and Cabbie Tom would be alive, Cherry would just be some dick who tried to steal my man and my mom wouldn't be stuck sewing her way out of the dog house. It's fair to say the guilt train has finally arrived at its final station and it fucking sucks.

The more time that passes, the more I become convinced my absence has been noticed and they've decided to leave me be. Picking myself up from the floor, Angus and Hamish accompany me into the shower, washing in the suds I shake off. Tipping my head to rest against the cold tile, the steam closes in to create a fog. Lost in time, I stand under the scolding spray until it dips in temperature. Then it comes to me. I know what to do. Shutting off the faucet, I wrap myself in a towel and head back to find my cell phone. Jasper keeps it charged for me, not that I ever use it. Having a phone without any friends seems a bit redundant, except now I have a contact to tap on and call. A cracked voice sounds through the receiver, soothing my soul like a balm.

"I need you," I reply in honesty, sinking down onto the mattress.

"Tell me where and when. I'll be there," Cherry responds and dammit, a tear wells in my eye.

Throwing back the dressing room curtain, Cherry's face lights up at the sight of the dress clinging to my body. It's a classic ivory dress with a fishtail flare and sweetheart neckline, or so the bridal shop assistant tells me.

"Oh yes!" Cherry claps her hands, and I narrow my eyes.

"Absolutely not," I groan, whipping the curtain back into place. The assistant looks fit to cry at my latest rejection, rushing to help me out of it before scurrying away. I'm fairly sure she's not coming back since I've tried on half the store by now, my mood sinking to a new low. Dressing in the jumpsuit I came in, I shove my feet into the pair of Jack's high-tops I stole and make my way out to Cherry.

"This is stupid. I thought girls found shopping therapeutic. I'll just hit the courthouse like this," I raise my arms wide, only to slap my hands down on my thighs again. Lifting my Monarch leather jacket from the seat beside Cherry's, I'm starting to feel more like myself already, but my companion won't have it.

"Let's not be rash. We have at least," she checks her watch and grimaces, "four hours. We can find something in this mall to suit you."

"Just seems obsolete when I don't know what's happening to Jasper," I sigh. Thoughts flood my mind that I shouldn't have called Cherry or suggested wedding dress shopping. I should have kept my mouth shut and said my vows in secret.

"Now stop it," Cherry halts my steps, spinning me to face her. "Jasper's nothing if not capable. He'll be sweet-talking his way out of trouble right this minute. By the time you make it to the warehouses, he'll be sitting on top of a pile of bodies with Tanya's head in his hand." The sales assistant shrinks down behind the cashier and I smirk. Shouldn't have been listening in, Nosey Parker. "And besides, you're getting married! Regardless of ulterior motives, this is meant to be the happiest day of your life, and you deserve a dress." Linking my arm with hers, I draw Cherry from the store.

"I'm sure there's an army of people who would disagree with you about what I deserve," I chuckle.

"They wouldn't dare with us around," Ace mutters. My wall of bodyguards jolt away from the store's glass front and surround Cherry and I as we meander through the mall. My sister's eyes flick behind us uncomfortably, her relaxed demeanor having suddenly vanished.

"Ignore them," I tell her. "They aren't going to let me out of their sight until the deed is done." A grunt is echoed from one end of the Monarch line to the other. When I'd accepted the proposal last night, I didn't think Malik would have managed to snag a cancellation at the courthouse for 3 pm today. Or at least that's what he told me happened. I have no doubt he pulled a few strings or flashed a gun to ensure that slot had my name on it. Sooner is better, I tell myself, but considering a day ago, I would have laughed at the idea of tying myself down for life, it's going way too fast for the cutterflies in my chest. I'll be shredded to shit by the time we make it to the vows, no matter if I'm in a wedding dress or my birthday suit.

Spotting a pretzel stand, I gasp the same time Cherry does. We must be totally in sync. My tongue lolls out of my mouth as the smell hits me, just before Cherry yanks me away.

"This place is perfect!" She exclaims and I pout until spotting the store that has her so excited. Okay, maybe this time, she might just be right. A row of mannequins in the window are draped in a mix of black lace, PVC, and chains. It's like Goths 'R' Us and it's friggin' perfect. Allowing Cherry to drag me through the entrance, the Monarchs position themselves outside like they have done for the past six stores. As an afterthought, I realize they get to stand opposite the pretzel cart, and it's lunchtime. Twisting back, I barge between the mannequins to knock on the glass behind Spade's head.

"Get me a cinnamon one!" He gives me a two-fingered salute and smirks before heading over to where Jack is already placing his order. Then, I allow Cherry to usher me into the dressing room while she picks out dresses I'll be forced to try on. Last shop, I tell myself, kicking off the high-tops.

"And then the real fun begins. If you manage to convince one of the Monarchs that marrying you isn't suicide, that is." Angus mocks from the mini bench. My eyes narrow. I hate that little asshole sometimes, especially when his only purpose is to stir shit. But now my mind's reeling again around the million-dollar question. Or twenty-five-million in this case, if the numbers on my online banking are to be believed. Fisting my hands, I hiss at him through my teeth.

"You know what I think?"

"Obviously," he rolls his eyes and I press on.

"I think you don't want me to be happy. All this time I thought you were keeping me safe, but you've been keeping me miserable!"

Angus's black eyebrows lift, his mouth dropping open before he catches himself. Then, the anger sets back in.

"Oh yeah?" he shouts. "I'm surprised you noticed anything since you became too dick-drunk to realise you've changed. I thought you wanted to survive, not rely on some guy that'll grow bored of you one day."

"Well, it's a good thing I have five of them to keep rotating," I yell back, losing sight of what my argument was.

"Whatever," Angus dismisses me with his chubby hand. "I'm done with this. If I wanted to be ignored all the time, I'd have slipped into the psyche of someone who doesn't turn their back on their only friend to live a *normal* life." The way he says 'normal' as if it were a curse boils my blood to a fever-pitch. How fucking dare he! After everything I've been through, don't I deserve to be happy? To be…loved?

"Right. Like you haven't replaced hanging out with me for banging Hamish, you little *cockmunch*." A dress is flung over the top railing just then, the hanger almost puncturing the space between my eyebrows. Pushing my head through the curtain, I come nose to nose with Cherry.

"Are you trying to kill me so you can take my wedding slot to marry Jack?" I growl. Her shocked reaction brings my mood back to ground level and I burst out laughing. Never has anyone gone pale so fast or had the real possibility of their eyes popping out of their heads. "Oh man, you should see your face. Relax, it hasn't gone unnoticed the two of you are keeping as far away from each other as possible."

Popping back inside, I glance over the selected dress, my heart-stopping. The black fabric creates a perfect hourglass figure, even on the hanger, with panels of mesh curving along the sides. Spaghetti straps that hold the lowcut cleavage spiral around the shoulders to leave the back completely open. Then there's the skirt. Not my usual style, but the rivets of flowing material spiraling from the midsection shift through my fingers like water. "Hold up. Wait a minute," I call and hear Cherry's feet shuffling back.

"What's wrong? You don't like it?" Her voice leaks through the curtain, tinged with concern.

"I...love it," I gasp, never feeling so attached to a garment before. Surely that means this is it, *the* dress, and I haven't even got it on yet. "Get in here and help me put this thing on." Cherry's smile is beaming as she guides the material up my body, saying a mini prayer to herself that I decided to put on underwear today. Once she's smoothed the straps over my shoulders, we merely stand in silence, looking in the mirror. Wow. My tattoos stand out in stark contrast, like the princess of a gothic realm where gummy bears roam and men do as they're told.

"Okay, that's me sorted. Now it's your turn," I state, and Cherry's serene expression goes slack. I guess I didn't cover that part of the plan with her on the drive over. Probably because we weren't alone, and it's weird asking her to attend a wedding where her ex is one of the grooms, but she's my sister. Family has never meant anything to me because I've never really had any, but that changes today. Silencing her protests, I order Cherry to unzip me so I can shimmy out of the dress.

"Hold this, I'll be right back," I say, slipping out into the store in just my underwear. If this had been a normal clothing store, no doubt I would have gotten a few strange looks. But given its alternative nature, women in funky platforms with colorful dreads eye me with appreciation and pump fists in the air for women's rights. Somehow among the chains and buckles, I find a sweet skater dress that would suit Cherry perfectly. Fully black with golden geometric shapes covering the lower half, I pick out a pair of gold wedge heels and place them on the cashier's desk.

"We'll take these; she doesn't need to try them on." The punking awesome girl behind the counter with a nose ring smiles menacingly, whipping out a bag. She gets me. Growing bored of waiting, Cherry comes to find me with my jumpsuit and high-tops in one hand and the dress of my non-existent wedding dreams in the other. I dress hastily before whistling for Malik to come in and pay.

"It's official then. This is really happening," he mutters in a low tone, and a lump forms in my throat. Even as I accept the bag with numb fingers, the finality that comes with a simple dress settles in. I'm doing this, signing my life away to save another. I just hope it's not something I come to resent the Monarchs for later.

MALIK

Sitting on the courthouse steps in our matching-colored suits, my fellow men and I pass around a joint to calm the nerves. A pair of police officers are watching us through the windscreen of their vehicle, nodding in understanding. After all, the kid fresh out of the police academy is the one that sold the weed to us in the first place. The perfect rouse, using the drugs they confiscate to make some cash on the side.

Taking a long drag, I pass the joint over to Ace who's sitting in the center. Jack is leaning into his other side, Spade on the step below, everyone lost to their thoughts. It's not the way I would have planned to start my wedding service, nor is the venue at my back, but needs must. In less than thirty minutes, Candy will be wed to one of us, and selfishly, I've decided that person will be me. I have no doubt the others love her otherwise, I wouldn't be content with sharing, but my feelings go deeper than that.

Candy understands the monster lurking inside and has him purring like a kitten whenever she's around. She saved me from burying myself in my mistakes. I was in the midst of losing everything I'd ever worked for when Candy crashed into my life, slotting in like our missing piece to bring us all closer than ever. I hope, in turn, I've given her what we've both been looking for - a family. Damn, I fucking love this insanely incredible woman more than I thought I was capable of.

"She's ready," Cherry announces from the doorway, scrunching up her nose at the smell we're giving off. Ready in her black dress, she slips back inside with her head ducked as if this is a funeral. Sighing, I push to my feet, brush down my best navy suit and help up the others one by one. With my hand connected with Jack's, I stall to address my men.

"No matter what happens in there, her vows are meant for all of us," I nod. Ace and Spade clasp their hands around ours, Jasper's absence slicing even deeper. It should never have gone this far, and until he's back with us, we'll have the worry Candy felt forced into this arrangement. As a unit, we head into the courthouse; our heads lifted high. Being directed to room three by a smartly dressed redhead at the front desk, my heart swells more with each step, threatening to burst as we approach the civil officer posted outside.

"Do you have your marriage license?" The middle-aged man asks. He's tall and slender with rounded glasses and a beard that morphs into his brunette hair seamlessly. Ace pulls a piece of paper out of his inside pocket, handing it over. All fake, of course, but a good enough copy to fool even the trained eyes of the officiant. "And who is the groom?"

"I am," I state immediately, not letting anyone else get in there first. Murderous glares burn into the side of my scalp after we'd agreed to let Candy choose, but it's my name on the license, and we don't have time for umming and ahhing. We need to take action and make the most of our slot before we can retrieve our brother. Nodding, the officiant opens the door for us to enter, except we all halt in the doorway. Spinning our way, the stunning silhouette of Candy halts the very blood in my veins. Ace nudges me to shuffle forward, my heart in the back of my throat and mouth hanging open.

Thanks to a makeup kit and a curler Cherry brought, Candy blinks up at me through long lashes, her love heart face flawlessly contoured. Her glossy red lips are permanently pouted, her fuchsia hair pinned back in an updo with a few curled strands tickling her shoulders. Every curve is accentuated, and her waist is cinched in a stunning black number. Open-backed, low cleavage and framing her long legs that roll into studded biker boots. It's perfect, just like her.

"Shall we begin?" The officiant rounds us, a thick book in his hands. I clear my throat, suddenly parched, as I take a brave step forward. I expect Candy to laugh and kick me off my pedestal in favor of someone else, but she doesn't, she just stares through me like it doesn't matter who stepped up to the altar. "Did you decide on which version of vows you'd prefer?"

"The quickest ones," Candy replies, and my eyebrows twitch. Stepping up to the mark, I face my bride and take her hands in mine while the others sit to watch with a grumble. Cherry remains far on the other side, twitching with the hem of her dress.

"Very well," the officiant starts. Candy shifts us so all of the Monarchs are in her eye line, the only hint that she might actually want this. "Dearly beloved, you've come here today to join together in holy matrimony. In front of your witnesses, you will exchange vows and sign the marriage certificate, announcing you as man and wife. Before we begin, does anyone have any reason as to why these two shouldn't come together?" I pass a sly look back, daring one of the Monarchs to object. The clenched jaws and flared nostrils I get are response enough and no doubt something they'll hold against me for a long time to come.

"Then let's continue," the officiant says, not sounding convinced. Maybe it has to do with the atmosphere Jack, Spade, and Ace are giving off while Cherry passes them nervous glances and picks at her cuticles. What a loving wedding party. "Candy. Do you take Malik to be your lawfully wedded husband? To have from this day on, for better or for worse, for richer, for poorer, in sickness and in health, to love and to cherish from this day forward for as long as you both shall live?"

"Mmmhmm," Candy nods, her mouth a tight line and hands

gripping mine too tightly. Pulling her closer, I rest my hands on her hips, making sure I'm all Candy can see.

"You...have to say the words," I implore, my soul surfacing to the plea in my eyes. A shudder runs the length of Candy's spine, indecision clawing at her features.

"Yep, all of the above. I do," she replies in a rush as if the words lingering on her tongue would poison her. On a relieved sigh, she smiles, owning her decision. I, however, am not convinced.

"And do you, Malik, take Candy to be your lawfully wedded wife?" The officiant turns to me, preparing to repeat his speech, when I shake my head. Confusion bleeds from Candy's chocolate brown eyes, and the worry of my next words causing a rift between us almost has me backtracking. Almost.

"I'm sorry beautiful, but no. I do not." Shocked gasps ripple throughout the room but none louder than Candy's. In her reaction, it's clear now I misjudged her willingness to wed me, but it's too late to take it back now. My hands hold fast when she tries to back away as if my touch is scolding her. "Wait, wait, just listen. I want to marry you, Candy, more than anything in this world. But only because you want to, not because you think you have to."

"But...but we do have to," she croaks. Her face crumples, and I can see now what her reservations are really about. Tightening my grip on her waist, I can't bear the distance between us anymore. I pull her into me, our heads lying on each other's shoulders while everyone else in the room watches on.

"No baby, we don't - not like this. We'll work out a plan B, and then when we're all together again, we'll have a civil service for all six of us. It can be in the back of an Applebees with a case of store-branded beer for all I care. As long as you mean the words you say, that's all I want."

"Yeah, we will do that," Candy agrees, nodding into the crook of my neck. I'm sure I feel a trace of wetness there before she shoves me away. "But right now, Jasper's relying on us, and if you won't put your ego aside, there are three other guys here who will." And just like that, a shadow steps in to replace me, and I'm left staring at the back of Spade's ponytail of dreadlocks. Slimy motherfucker.

"What do you say Crazy Girl? Will you do me the honors of being your first husband, and then I'll do everything to make sure Jasper is your second?" Spade winks as I round the pair of them, scowling at the newfound smile that's popped up on Candy's face. "And besides, you owe me for shattering my shoulder blade."

"Erm, this isn't exactly orthodox. The name on the license-" the worried-looking officiant starts, but Ace interrupts him.

"Oh hang on," he shuffles around the papers in his jacket pocket. "Here you are; Spade's all good to go." Handing the document over, Ace beams at my conscience getting the better of me. Jack pats the empty seat beside him, mocking me with a throaty chuckle as I take it. After looking over the paper in his hands, the officiant looks suspiciously between us all until Spade pulls out a stack of bundled cash and places it onto the thick book balanced in his arms.

"Well then, I suppose I'll start from the beginning?" He stutters, unsure of what just happened. But I know I just got cockblocked in the worst way for trying to do right against my future bride. I wanted no doubt in her mind I was the man she'd spend the rest of her life with for no other reason than she loves me.

"No need, I'll do my own vows," Spade announces. Clicking his fingers at me, I roll my eyes and pull out the double ring box stored in my inner pocket. Flicking it open, I pass him the thin white-gold band with a pink heart sapphire I picked out at the mall. My surprise to her if the box hadn't fallen out of the bag in the car and the rest of the Monarchs snatched it up to see. Taking her right hand, Spade holds the ring over her third finger, his piercing blue eyes fixed on hers.

"Well, I didn't expect to be up here with you today, but I can't deny I'd thought about what I'd say if I was. So here it goes," Spade inhales and exhales deeply, stretching his neck like he's about to run a marathon. For Candy's heart, he probably is.

"Candy, my feisty, insatiable love. I can't pretend things will be easy or guarantee you'll live a life free from suffering. Instead, the promise I give you, on behalf of us all, is that you'll never have to suffer alone. All decisions will be discussed, and all plans require us to play our parts. In every aspect of your psychotic life, we will support and worship you. Love and honor you, respect and understand you. Since day one, I knew you belonged to us; a ring and a piece of paper only confirm the fact. Don't see this as throwing away your life. In fact, it's finally about to begin."

Pushing the ring onto her willing finger, the breath saws out of me. Sitting here, looking at them standing there, I can see now Spade was the right fit for this job. He's able to express what we can't put into words, and still, in a moment where he could have taken the credit all for himself, he included us all. The sun peers through the clouds, magnifying the gorgeous couple in black with a glow of approval. Like the cover of a magazine, they stare into each other's eyes, the image of true love as Candy begins her reply.

"I've searched all my life to find the place where I fit. And when I didn't, I told myself it was because I was the lucky one. I'm too much of a hexagon for a square hole, and I made damn sure the world knew about it," Candy sighs, dropping her head. Jack pulls the ring meant for me from the ring box clenched in my hand, and darts over. Giving the ring to Candy, Jack lifts her chin upwards to face Spade and kisses her on the cheek before taking his seat again. A simple action, but the approval Candy needed to continue.

"But then you guys stole my bat and presented the challenge I'd been missing. Not just to annoy you into letting me stay, but the challenge of proving to myself I wasn't too damaged to love. I've never claimed to be easy to understand, but somehow, I feel like you guys do. You're all I've ever wanted," her eyes drag over the four of us, then flick back towards Cherry. "I'll never be wife of the year, but I'll be authentically me, and I think that's enough. I'm starting to see things clearly now. You guys complete my hexagon, and there's no 'me' in team."

"I mean," Spade starts to argue and then decides it's not worth it as she places my ring on his finger. "Yeah, okay, sure. Fucking kiss me Crazy Girl, and let's get our lives started with a bang." Spade's metaphor isn't lost on me, considering where we go from here, but as he crashes her mouth against his, my heart sinks. I should have been the selfish bastard I am and taken her for myself. It should have been me up there, slipping my tongue into her perfectly glossed mouth.

But instead of drowning in my own envy, Jack's patronizing slap on my back and Ace's whooping cheer remind me we're all in this together. She may have just married Spade, but Candy still belongs to all of us. And as soon as we get Jasper back, I'll be making sure she acknowledges it, for better or for worse.

~~Bitchface~~ Tanya

"Still no sign of the Monarchs," Gabriel grunts, picking dirt out from under his nails. Rolling my eyes at his unhelpful observation, I shove his legs aside from where they were crossed upon the desk and stand to pace. Two days. Two fucking days Candy has kept me waiting since Gabriel not so-slyly let our location slip in front of her mom. The papers she needs to sign have been sitting in the plastic sleeve, patiently waiting - unlike me.

Standing in the office's window, I stare out at the hot shop my men set up after the fishing dock closed down. Stolen cars lifted high on the jacks are unrecognizable as their parts are changed out before a fresh paint job is in order. Every single person beneath this roof has pledged themselves to me, the fair but stern leader that will be the new figurehead of Leicester's gang. The old man was too distracted in his final years to notice the ties I was creating, not that he paid me much attention before then. I was supposed to be his wife, and he treated me like a stranger. Someone he was obliged to keep around thanks to our family's arrangement.

"Relax. She'll be here," Gabriel calls out when the drumming of my fingernails becomes too much. I thought so too. but Candy has never failed to surprise me before. I really thought I had her this time, but perhaps the bargaining chip I bagged myself doesn't hold as much sentimental value as I was led to believe. Tilting my head to the red pickup truck, I look over Jasper with open disdain.

Standing in the metal cage I've sealed him inside, his cocky green gaze flicks my way with a satisfied smirk. I'd thought he'd have crumpled by now or begged for freedom at least, but we had to use the tasers just to stop him from doing pull-ups on the bars. Then came the idea to starve him until he threatened to piss in his own mouth, and that's not an image any of us need to see. Grimacing, I turn away to lock the inheritance waiver agreement in the top drawer, safe for the moment before I put a bullet between Candy's eyes and stride from the office.

"It'll all be worth it once we're filthy rich!" Gabriel's voice chases me out of the closing door, grating on my last nerve.

"Yeah. Once I'm filthy rich," I mutter. I swear, my downfall is nothing but being surrounded by mindless idiots. Even though Gabriel's loyalty hasn't gone unnoticed, he hasn't suffered like I have. To be ignored by your betrothed. To lose a child. To have everything you've patiently waited for taken away by one inconvenience that should have never existed. Is it too much to ask for the money I'm owed so I can buy an island and never need to see anyone beyond my servants again? Maybe a toy boy or two would be required too.

My heels beat against the metal steps, my legs constricted in a tight pencil skirt. The blouse I'm wearing is the last I brought with me, and I can't go much longer without washing my hair. The curls are beginning to deflate, and I'm sick of brushing my teeth in a bucket. Still, always dress for the day you want to have, my mom used to say, right before she'd beat me senseless for spilling milk or speaking before I was spoken to. After my father died in a gang fight when I was four, she was determined I'd be the ideal woman to continue our family's work. Well, here I am mom, hoping you're watching from whatever hellhole you're stuck in.

Making my way across the garage, sparks fly in all directions, and machines whirl. I step over a patch of grease, approaching the two men I've set to guard Jasper's cage. They bow on instinct, stepping aside to let me scowl up at the cage in the back of the pickup. Everything's all set to go the instant Candy shows up if she shows up. Resting my hands on my hips, I sigh as Jasper uses the bars to rub his back along like a trapped bear.

"I have to commend your resilience," he grins down at me. "Anyone else would have given up by now, but you just love being humiliated." Biting down on my tongue, I resist snapping back. That's what he wants, and I can't let my own prisoner get under my skin. Instead, I remember all the times I faked an orgasm for him and let that fuel the smug smirk on my face. All that time, he thought he was stringing me along. That I was *his* side piece, hah, more fool him.

"Isn't it more humiliating that your supposed girlfriend hasn't even bothered to come to get you? I left her enough breadcrumbs to be here days ago. I guess she doesn't care for you after all."

"I'd be disappointed if Candy followed your pointless trail. She carves her own path,"

"Even if it means leaving you behind?"

"That's the beauty of loving her. It's all about enjoying the ride while the motor is still running. Anything beyond that is too conventional," he muses, drawing his finger along the inside of the bar. The genuine smile on his face confuses me, and suddenly, I'm rethinking everything. Is it true Candy can drop her men so easily, or is Jasper just trying to get inside my head? The door to the office bangs opens, and I turn to see Gabriel flying across the warehouse, an excitable grin spread across his face.

"Four motorcycles and a quad bike just crossed the perimeter," he beams, tucking his phone away. I raise an eyebrow at Jasper, noting he's fallen silent all of a sudden. In fact, a look of fury tenses his jaw as if he's disappointed Candy turned up for him after all. Clicking my fingers, the two guards are by my side in a second.

"Get the cage down by the dock," I order them, referring to the plan we've had set up for the past two days. On sharp nods, the pair dive into the cab and rev the engine, taking a side exit while the rest of us rush to get into position. Gabriel runs around, barking at people to be ready while I head for the office. Taking the folder out of the drawer, I place it on the desk and wipe at the itchy patch beneath my eyes. I may be exhausted from waiting, but things are finally happening. I'll have my money back within the hour while Candy lies bleeding out at my feet. No matter what rouse she believes, none of her crew will be leaving alive.

Behind the safety glass, anticipation thrums through my tired limbs. Watching the warehouse door rise, a single quad bike sits out front, presenting the woman I've been eager to ensnare in my trap. The other Monarchs are nowhere to be seen, but no matter. The higher the door slides upwards, the more of Candy is visible striding into the entrance, oblivious to the men ducking behind each vehicle with their weapons raised. Leaning over the microphone, I lick my lips before activating the tannoy system.

"Nice of you to turn up," I start before she steps fully into the artificial light. A black dress swishes around her strong legs, highlighted by the leather boots glued to her ankles. The tight bodice encasing her curves perfectly like an angel of death, completed by the pink curls framing her determined face.

Without pausing her strides, Candy reaches beneath her skirt and pulls out a machine-gun before open firing all around. I flinch behind the safety of the glass, having a birds-eye view of my men falling like dominos. Bullets ricochet around the warehouse, the sparks of metal hitting metal preventing anyone from getting a clear shot. A shudder runs through me at the sheer power Candy exudes, rounding car after car and never pausing her fire until the machine-gun finally rings out with a series of empty clicks. By then, there's barely any of my crew left standing, and as Gabriel creeps up with his pistol raised, my voice echoes through the speakers.

"Hold fire," I warn him. Both heads raise my way, the Monarch lookalike glaring at me with resentment. I shake my head slowly, mentally conveying that I need her damn signature on this document before Candy can finally meet her end. Without it, the money will transfer to Jasper, then Jack, and a whole load of messy relations I can't be bothered to trace. It's cleaner and easier this way if Candy is ever the easiest option. Plastering on a fake smile, I raise the microphone to my lips. "Now, now, dear stepdaughter, there's no need for all this bloodshed. Come up here and let's settle this."

"Mmmm, as if I'd enter a room of your choosing. I have something you want, and you have what's mine. I'll wait right here for when you're ready," she shouts back. To emphasize her point, Candy strolls over to a workstation, uncaring of the gun pointed at the back of her head. Settling down on a metal chair, Candy drops her empty machine-gun onto her lap. Grinding my teeth together, I grip the file in my hand and straighten my spine. The few men left move to stand behind me as I emerge from the office once more, cursing my choice of footwear for the hundredth time. Circling the workbench where Candy is reclining, I take the opposite side and lay the document flat on the scuffed surface.

"Let's make this as painful as possible," I state, done with playing her games. "Sign the document, and I'll let Jasper live." It's a risk presuming Candy rates the life of another over her own, but I won't pretend she's walking out of here alive. Rolling her brown eyes at me, she slowly sits upright, crossing one leg over the other.

"First, show me where he is. I knew even you wouldn't be stupid enough to keep him out in the open." A cruel smile grows across my face, the eagerness to reveal all my cards causing me to shake with giddiness.

"With pleasure." Through the open warehouse door, I spy that Jasper is already in place before I point Candy in his direction. Having hooked the cage up on an old crane at the end of the pier, the red pickup is already speeding back around the curved dock. "He's rigged up to a mechanism that will lower him into the water until you've signed this paper. Only then will I give you the control to halt it. The longer you take, the longer he'll have to freeze to death or drown. Your choice." Settling back, I fold my arms with a satisfied grin twisting at my lips. She's cornered, and I can taste the win. If anything, it's much sweeter this way because I've fully earnt it, and I intend to reward myself immensely.

"Have to say, I'm impressed," Candy praises, her face not revealing much other than admiration. Mentally patting myself on the back, I bark at my closest minion to give her a pen, anticipation filling my limbs. The man holds out the pen with a mock bow, and as Candy takes it, that's when I see the sparkling pink diamond on her finger. To be specific, her marriage finger. "Problem is, it's not my inheritance to give over anymore. It's my husband's, whoever that may be."

A faint smirk lifts her lips as she jams the pen into my henchman's eye. He roars, and quick as a flash, the hand Candy had slipped up her skirt, has exchanged the machine-gun clip. I dive for cover, gripping the back of my head as she pours bullets into the last of my men. Gabriel drops to my side, holding a hole on his shoulder that's spewing out blood. Even in his wounded state, he covers me as we crawl behind the shell of the nearest car. His blood leaks onto my blouse, and for the briefest moment, as Gabriel falls over my body, a flash of true devotion appears in his dark eyes. I don't have time to process the closeness of his lips as the shadow of Candy's boots appears beneath the vehicle.

Following the scrape of her heel with my eyes, she halts the gunfire, her attention focused on the sight across the pier. Regardless of my crew or the money, this is the moment she realizes she fucked up. She's messed with me for the last time, and if nothing else today, she's going to feel the pain of losing someone she loves. That's a miracle in itself, but as Gabriel pushes his pistol into my hand, power thrums through my veins. It's not over yet, not until I say so.

CANDY

The chunky chain holding the final piece of my soul slips, stealing the breath directly from my lungs. Tanya's cackle reverberating around the warehouse tells me my reaction didn't go unnoticed, revealing my hand once and for all. I'm not losing a single member of my Monarchs, and if it weren't for the fact Tanya is a raging cuntmuffin, I'd have simply signed the money over months ago. Unfortunately, letting her win in any way would be an insult of justice. Tossing the machine-gun to the ground and keeping my back to the shell of a Chevrolet behind me, I stand slowly, staring at the cage that's slipping closer to the water level below. Hold on Jasp, I have a plan.

"A shit one, yeah," Angus agrees, but at least it's better than nothing. Most likely. I'm just glad he's talking to me again. Holding my ground until the click of the safety sounds behind me, I smirk. Soooo predictable. Spinning suddenly, Tanya's eyes widen as she crouches through the shell of the car, not foreseeing me grabbing the pistol I knew would be pointed at the back of my head. Tugging it down, her finger slips on the trigger. A bullet rips through her thigh, although the sound of gunfire has nothing on the high-pitched howl that leaves her mouth. Twisting the weapon free, I lean further across the leather driver's seat to shoot Gabriel in the face as he tries to save her. Props of being loyal to someone, I suppose, because fuck knows it wasn't his old employers.

Angus tries to lift a heavy-duty chain from the back seat, so I assist, using her distracted screaming to whip it around Tanya's neck. Yanking her back against the headrest, I make short work of looping down her arms when she attempts to scratch my arms free of its skin. With her bloodcurdling cries filling the warehouse, I twist the key conveniently sitting in the ignition, and flatten the pedal to the floor.

Using a ramp provided by the tilted jacks, the Chevrolet crashes through a window mid-air before crashing back down to the ground. I hold onto the steering wheel for dear life, thanks to the lack of a door on my left, nearly causing me to fall out too. Within seconds, the roar of multiple motorbikes rev as expected, but my focus is fixed on the cage at the end of the pier. Jasper's lower half is fully submerged now as he climbs the bars in an attempt to punch the lid free. No such luck, but with the speed I'm flying around the arc-shaped pier, he won't need to. Fighting against the chain holding her in place, Tanya screams like a banshee. Deciding to put her out of her misery, I slam the but of the gun into her temple.

"The more you struggle, the quicker you'll die, and where's the fun in that?" Her delusional muttering is lost to the roar of the engines chasing right behind. I told the boys I'd handle this, and I am. Skidding the car sideways, we drift around the arched pier with the water lapping at either side of the dock. Jasper's face is faintly visible as he gasps in his last gulps of air, spurring on my determination to save him.

"I swear, if I lose one of my men, I will keep reviving and killing you until your body gives up. Then, I'm going to put you on a ventilator and electrocute you every ten minutes while your mind screams on the inside." My voice is loud enough for Tanya to hear every word, her panicked movements showing she's coming back around. No one, and I mean no one, fucks with those I love. These men are my life, my future, my everything. I'll kill for them a thousand times over, and all I need in return is for them to keep breathing.

"Seems like my time here is up." A gruff voice sounds in the back of my head, the jiggly pink owner sitting in my rear-view mirror. I frown at Angus, more confused by the lack of grumpy eyebrows. In fact…he's smiling, with his arm around Hamish.

"What do you mean?" I ask, struggling to focus on driving. The back tire skids off the dock, just righting itself at the last moment. Yet Angus looks as serene as ever, his words cutting through the fog, claiming my thoughts.

"After all this time, after everything that's been done to you, you've finally learned to love. The Monarchs have carved out a special place in your heart. There's no room for me anymore." My foot automatically slams on the brakes before I can stop myself, remembering too late Jasper needs me. Gunning it back to full speed, I shake my head in the mirror, words failing me. Angus will know what I wanted to say anyway, he'll hear my desperate plea. *Don't go. There's always room for you. Please don't leave me.*

"No need for tears," Angus smiles sadly, and I suddenly feel the wetness drip down my cheeks. "You created me as a coping mechanism, but you don't need to cope anymore. You can finally live." Warmth spreads across my nape as if I'm receiving a gummy bear hug, and then in the reflection, Angus and Hamish share one last kiss before they pop. Burst into thin air with a faint sparkle of pink and yellow glitter, as if they never existed.

"No!" I cry out, halting Tanya's barrage of cursing. A stab of pain splits my being in two as a pained scream of my own is torn from me, the tears in my eyes blurring the road up ahead. A motorcycle veers around the side of the car, a voice yelling for me to stop the car.

"I can't go back now. He's dead!" Swerving, the bike is knocked into the water, and I don't stop to look back. My gut aches like it's been punched, my mind spinning. Lowering my forehead to meet the wheel, I struggle to intake small pants of air. A scream slices through my ears from the bitch chained to the passenger seat. I turn my head slowly, a new level of malice emanating from my eyes. She caused this. My evil stepmother.

Guess I'm not too alternative for my fairy-tale ending after all. Except in my world, I'm going to take this bitch down, watch the life drain from her eyes, and then follow into the afterlife to continue the torture. She fucked with my Monarchs, and threatened their livelihood. Forced me into a predicament where I had to care and in turn, lost me Angus. She has so much to pay for as I veer around the final stretch to my destination.

I spot the exact moment Jasper's face dips beneath the water, my foot stamping on the accelerator even further as my mind is made up. A world without Angus isn't a world I agreed to live in, regardless of who claims to love me. And besides, what kind of Queen would I be if I didn't sacrifice myself for my men? I'd rather they honored me in death than shamed me in life.

With my hand clutched around the pistol, we fly off the end of the pier, the vehicle making an almighty splash. Almost immediately, thanks to the lack of doors, the nose tips downwards, plunging us into the murky depths below.

"Hang tight, I'll be back for you," I tell Tanya and dive out. The frigid water dulls my senses the instant I'm submerged, messing with my orientation. Swimming in the direction I think the cage should be, my limbs shake with the heaviness of my chest. It should be enough to sink me, but instead, I keep bobbing to the surface. Forcing myself downwards once more, something solid brushes my fingers, and I grip onto the chain, using it to drag myself downwards.

I'm blind down here, bubbles leaking from my shivering lips. Feeling out the metal roof of the cage, I pull myself down the bars, hunting for the lock with my fingertips. As soon as I think I've found it, I press the gun against the metal as a light bursts to life behind me. I don't look for the source as the limp figure of Jasper is illuminated. His blond hair shifts in the water, his body bumping limply against the bars. Fuck.

Squeezing the trigger, a rain of bubbles explodes from the pistol, blocking the view. Jack appears at my side, his fancy smartphone providing us with the much needed light. As the bubbles subside, I yank on the cage door. Nothing. It didn't work. Bracing my feet on the frame, I tug and tug until Jack winds his arm around my middle and swims me back to the surface.

"The cage won't open," Jack calls to the three silhouettes on the edge of the pier. In unison, the trio have their hands clasped around the chain as they attempt to pull it back to the surface to no avail. It's been too long. Thrashing out of Jack's hold, I try to dive back down to empty the handgun's clip into the lock, but he refuses to let go.

"This doesn't hurt anyone more than me Candy, but you saw what I did. I can't…don't make me lose you too," Jack crumples. I shake my head, refusing to give up. Shoving free of his slippery grip, I dip beneath the water and kick him in the stomach when he tries to stop me. Using the chain like last time, I start to pull myself down when the roof of the cage meets me much sooner than expected. In fact, as I plant my boots on the metal, my back breaches the water. It's rising, but not by the men who are just as surprised as I am the chain is shifting through their fingers. Before long, my entire body is shivering above the surface, the remains of my black wedding dress stuck to my legs. Hunting for the answer to all of our silent question, I spot a redhead standing at the warehouse entrance, a yellow button in her hand. Cherry.

Jack jumps up to grab the gun from my hand before I rise too far from his reach and shoots the revealed lock repeatedly. It finally breaks free, the door struggling to open against the remaining water lapping at the bottom half of the cage. Hopping onto the pier, I aid the others in pulling the cage safely back onto the wooden slats. Ace is the first to make it inside and drags Jasper out, starting chest compressions without faltering. Spade drops down to breathe into Jasper's mouth, and all I can do is merely watch. Malik tugs me into his soaking wet suit, our shared coldness bleeding into each other.

"Why are you so wet?" I ask absent-mindedly. It's not just the temperature making me numb. In fact, I doubt I'll ever feel anything again.

"You ran me off the pier, remember?" I do vaguely, but with that comes the memory of my gummy bear best friend, who is forever lost to me. A spluttered cough draws me back to the present, and I drop to my knees as Jasper twists to expel the water from his lungs. Jack has pulled himself onto the dock in time to slap his twin's back, and despite Jasper probably needing some space, I throw myself onto him.

"Don't you ever do that to me again," I sob into his neck, ignoring his hoarse coughing. Heaving in great gulps of air, Jasper's body shudders violently.

"Die? I can't promise that love," Jasper croaks out, his hand rounding my back.

"Well, you'd better because I can't lose you. None of you, ever." Craning my neck, I glare down at each of my Monarchs with threat lacing my tone. "You wanted me to love all of you, so here it is. We're in this beyond death do we part. I will chase each of you to the ends of this life and the next, reminding you of all the ways you belong to me."

"No chasing required Crazy Girl. We're not going anywhere," Spade places his hand on my shoulder, probably using the ring on his marriage finger to grate on Malik. Whether he's noticed or not, the final Monarch lowers down to join the huddle that's formed around a shivering Jasper.

"I pledge my love and loyalty to not only you but everyone here," Malik holds Jasper's eye. "We're a family, and no one will ever split us up again."

JASPER

'*Breaking news just in. The dead body of a woman has been found after a man trespassed on a closed dock to fish illegally. At two-fifteen this afternoon, he reported the shell of a stolen Chevrolet had risen to the surface of Rosewater lake, where the woman's body was located. After police arrived at the scene, more bodies were discovered inside a nearby warehouse. Coroners believe times of death were sometime within the last two to three days, and police are yet to find any witnesses. If you have any information-'*

I switch off the TV, tossing the remote control aside. With the news we're in the clear, Jack is finally able to stop pacing and drops onto the sofa beside me in Malik's suite. Turns out, a mafia hot shop is the best place to commit murder since there's no surveillance, and the warehouse was registered to a multitude of fake names. Rolling my head across the back of the cushions, I raise a brow at my twin.

"You gonna calm down now? Your nerves are worse than a dip in the icy depths of Rosewater," I force a smirk, swallowing the memory of darkness closing in. As much as I want to pretend that close call didn't affect me because fuck knows Candy would have bounced back without issue, I prefer to just not think about it instead. There's also the fact Jack would insist I was tucked in with three blankets and a hot water bottle for another day. As I keep telling him, I'm fine, and I'm ready to get back to being with my girl.

"When is Malik going to let me out of suite arrest anyway?" I moan, moving to get up. Jack's hand slams down on my chest, and I groan. That's it, I'm done. The nurse gave me the all-clear, and I didn't almost die for the fun of it. I'm owed some glad-you're-alive sex. Shoving him aside, I stand in one swift movement, dropping the blankets to the floor. Like a prison warden, my brother calls for back up, and his two faithful guards appear in the doorway. "You guys were waiting there the whole time, and no one tried to bring me a nail-file cake or follow me into the shower? I promise to drop the soap," I try to joke with Spade when Ace's scowl doesn't budge.

"You heard what Malik said," Spade states, thoroughly unimpressed. "We need to wait until the police have finished snooping into our past employees. Going on the run or doing anything suspicious would just draw unwanted attention and-"

"Yeah, yeah, I know," I roll my eyes, heading for the kitchen. "And us being around will hype up Candy. We can't order her to lay low, so he's back to bossing us around."

"Only until the heat dies down." Ace follows me, his eyes tracking my every moment while I make a coffee. A sigh heaves from my chest as I resign myself to a life under Malik's rule. Regardless of pipe dreams we can travel as a unit where everyone is equal, there's always going to be something. Some sort of trouble following our trail, some deep secrets waiting to creep out of the dark in our happiest moments.

With that thought, I carry the coffee mug to the dining table and set it down awkwardly on the edge of a coaster. The cup tips over, spilling steaming hot liquid all over Malik's expensive tabletop. Like flies on shit, the three men around me curse and rush to clean it up, all the commotion giving me the perfect chance to slip out. Flying down the stairs three at a time, I head straight for the only place that can entertain Candy for two days while we're not around. The bar.

True enough, through the open hole where the mirror used to be, I find her spread across the bar top on her back. Pink hair splays around her beautiful face, and she's donned my old college sweatshirt with nothing else. One leg arched upwards, I note the lack of slurred words as Candy sings to herself, moving her fingers through the air like her own personal conductor. Hearing the rush of footsteps chasing me downstairs, she props herself up on her elbows, grinning wide.

"Well, hello gorgeous," Candy beams, and my heart sings. Right up until I realize she's talking to Jack, who runs through the connecting door right behind me. I'll take the compliment anyway since we have the same face, minus a scar. When she puts her arms out for him, I push Jack aside and take her in my arms.

"I dare say I've earned a day of you being nice to me," I challenge Candy, raising one brow.

"Ahh, you'll have to die for real to deserve that specialty on the Candy Cums Menu." Spinning her around, I bury my face into her neck and nuzzle her until she drops the bullshit. Wrapping her arms around my neck, Candy nudges my face up to plant her lips on mine. Raspberry softness at its finest. Drawing me into a false sense of comfort, her hands smooth over my chest to dive into my sides and tickle insistently. I squirm while my hysterics urge her on until I've planted her ass back on the bar. Gripping Candy's knees, I squeeze them until she can't take it anymore and begs for mercy. Our playtime is short-lived when I spot Malik in the parking lot beside a black BMW.

"What's going on?" I ask, noticing the guys have stepped into my sides.

"The solicitor brought over the contracts for Malik to sign. The deed is being transferred to the new owner, and we'll be getting our eviction notice any minute," Ace tells me in a grave tone. One that shows he's not as amped up about this shift in lifestyle as we'd all previously been. Leaning the paper on the hood of the BMW, Malik scrawls the paper fluidly before placing it back into his inner jacket pocket. The pale blue suit is one he saves for real business, which the expression on his face says this is. Shaking the solicitor's hand, he makes his way back towards us, chewing his chin in thought.

"So that's it then?" Jack asks the second Malik emerges through the door. Nodding, he approaches our group, bringing a solemn atmosphere with him. No one says anything, our thoughts centered on what tomorrow might bring. As Malik joins us, we're all drawn into a hug around Candy, our heads resting on her sprawled-out limbs until a phone rings from somewhere. Slithering out of our holds, Candy reaches beneath the bar and plucks out the cell she never uses.

"Yep," she answers, followed by a string of 'aha's and 'mmhmm's. Sliding off the other side of the bar with the help of a stool, we watch Candy's hips sway in my baggy sweatshirt, her long legs eating up the distance between us and the door. That's when I notice the solicitor has stuck around, his smile welcoming Candy with too much familiarity as she passes through the revolving door. We watch their interaction as he hands her the papers and dips his head before Candy returns to us.

"Wait, what's happening here?" Spade asks first, our feet shuffling forward to descend on Candy like a pack of wolves. A faint blush coats her cheeks, her chocolate eyes looking anywhere we are not.

"Turns out I don't want a life on the road anymore. Not now I have nothing left to run from." Dipping her hand into Malik's jacket pocket, she pulls out his keys and jingles them in the air. "So I bought the bar. This is our home. There's nothing else out there I need to see, but there's a whole load of life I need to start living right here."

Malik swoops in first, gripping Candy's waist and tossing her into the air with a cheer of celebration. The move is so unlike him, so spontaneous and joyful that I'm rendered frozen for a moment. The deed of sale floats from Candy's hand, and I catch it mid-air. Beneath hers and Malik's signatures, the address of the solicitors sticks out. Shepperton, where she went to get her hair done a few weeks ago. Even before Tanya's plot to kill me supposedly veered Candy into realizing the extent of her love, she bought the bar for us, intending to make it our home.

The little green goblin inside stops gnawing at my insides like he has been since I found out about Candy and Spade's wedding. Forced or not, it stung a little to think I was trapped in a literal cage while she was saying her vows to my brother, but it doesn't seem to matter now. If the piece of paper in my hand isn't a declaration of love to us all, I don't know what is. Tossing it aside, I run into the cheering and manhandling of Candy like a sneaky field mouse on a mission. Lifting her legs around my waist, I twist her away from the others and drop her onto the edge of the sofa. My mouth is on hers as my crotch grinds against her naked center, hotter for this incredibly gorgeous psycho than ever.

"Na ah," Candy pulls back from my kiss. Shoving at my chest, she drops back onto the leather and rolls to stand. Groaning at the stunning view I just had of her pink pussy, I palm my sweatpants roughly. "For my reward, I have one small request," she grins, and I can already tell I'm going to hate it. "Or, more specifically, there's one last situation that needs to be addressed. I know there was some hanky panky going on here long before I turned up; I want to see it."

I blink twice, halting the hand rubbing the length of my shaft into a frenzy. The men behind me are deathly still, their stares burning into the back of my head.

"I don't know what you're talking about," I lift my chin, and Candy strolls over towards me. Spinning me by the shoulders, I see the wall of Ace's tensed muscle behind me, his eyes holding a note of truth. Blood rushes to my cheeks, faint drunken memories resurfacing. Secrets we promised to never speak about were left in the past when Malik denied us our basic needs and the drinks were harsh enough to take over.

"I call bullshit," Candy whispers in my ear. "I want to see it. Just once." She gives me a light shove, and I twist away, hiding my erection. Curiosity licks my subconscious, but I can't. Not that I wouldn't like to…but with so many eyes pointed our way and the surprised hitch to Malik's eyebrows making me cringe, I couldn't. "Okay, don't worry about it. I won't force you guys to cross the line you've obviously tiptoed over before, but no one is getting any of this until you do." Leaning back on the arm of the sofa, Candy spreads her legs wide and drops her fingers to tease her clit. Biting down on my bottom lip, I feel the tension between us five shift from embarrassment to desperation. Sliding my eyes to Ace's, there's a half-shrug in his shoulders when Spade curses.

"Oh, for fuck's sake, stop acting so proud," he groans, twisting to grab the back of Jack's head. Forcing their mouths together, it's my turn to look surprised. Jack doesn't protest, neither does he react. Just stands there as Spade forces his tongue into my twin's mouth, making the kiss look a little too authentic. I figured this was just for show, to entertain Candy enough to let it drop, but the longer Spade mouth fucks Jack, the wider my jaw drops.

Tearing himself away, Spade throws Jack's head back and immediately reaches for his jean button. "Happy now, you freaky minx?" He asks, ascending on Candy and entering her with a sharp thrust. Her pleasured groan is music to my ears, the rush of relief sweeping through me. Ace looks sheepish too at our close call, and Malik avoids my gaze completely. Moving in to push Candy's hair over her shoulder, intent on kissing her neck, she slams her palm against my forehead.

"Spade's earned his," she says, followed by a hitched moan as Spade slams back home inside her. "Either man up or enjoy your blue balls. I'm not the only one here who can share your load." Fuck.

To emphasize her point, Candy snaps her fingers and beckons Jack over. Shoving him onto the sofa, she then pauses Spade long enough to turn around and bend over the sofa's arm. Her perfectly peachy ass with the love heart tattoo tilts upwards for Spade while she bends in half to remove Jack's dick from his pants. I feel my own balls ache when she takes him all the way into the back of her throat, choking slightly when Spade takes her too roughly.

"Fuck this shit," I groan, approaching Ace with intent. The glint in his puppy dog brown eyes is undeniable, a rickety bridge being patched between us. Never mind what's been said or transpired, there's nowhere else we belong than in this bar, together in all senses. Bumping his chest, I hover back just in case I'm mistaking the excitement brimming between us. I can't fuck Candy into next week if Ace castrates me for making a move without his consent.

But instead of rejection, Ace dips his head first, giving me the all-clear to plant my lips on his. Large hands settle on my hips as I dive into Ace's touch, his pure masculinity radiating through me. I clutch at the t-shirt clinging to his firm chest, falling into the spell of his stubbled jaw scraping against mine.

"You've all lost your damn minds," Malik huffs, striding away. He may not be a part of this, and maybe Candy will forgive him for it, but the flutter in my chest at the new possibilities can't be denied. Seems that once again, Candy knew best long before I did. This crazy, incredible girl that no one wanted has proven to be all of our lifelines, and apparently, we'll do anything for her. Our love isn't conventional, but it sure is endless, indestructible, and ours.

CANDY

EPILOGUE

"You made it!" I shout, throwing myself down the porch steps and into Cherry's arms. Her hair tickles my arms, the longer length having returned to its natural chestnut hue. A cute summer dress and matching cardigan swishes around her body, her arms trapped inside my hug, clasping at a bottle of red wine. A boy half our size cowers behind her peering out from beneath his heavy fringe. His eyes run over my pale pink sweater, jeans, and Ugg boots, somewhat surprised. No doubt Cherry gave her son a rundown on everything Candy, but a lot has changed this past year. Thankfully, not our bond since we talk every other day on the phone like the best of friends.

After I transferred Cherry half of the inheritance money she deserved, she and Zak moved upstate for a fresh start. From the pictures she's sent, the white manor house looks like every Stepford wife's dream, and I'm happy for her. Me, however, I'm the Monarch's wife and my dreams are a little more niche.

"Come on in, let me give you a tour," I smile, holding out my hand for Zak. "Spade's making milkshakes with extra cream." This has my nephew latching onto me like we haven't just met for the first time. Together, the three of us push through the revolving door of the newly named 'The Queen's Monarchy.' Or Queen's, for short.

"Oh wow, it's so…different," Cherry comments, lacking the words, and I grin.

"We knocked out the whole lower level to extend the place into a proper club, and were each given our own section to redesign. As you can see, this is Ace's haven." The area in front of the bar has been transformed into any gamer's dream. From wall to wall, air hockey, foosball, and pool tables are evenly spaced. To the right, a false wall has been put in to hide a small food preparation area for nachos and cheesy fries mostly. Via a serving hatch, the new employees rollerblade across the glittery lino to serve the frat boys that tend to frequent this area.

Moving deeper inside, we pass into the next zone seamlessly, without any security door or wall like there used to be here. Instead, the twins worked on a mirror image of the bar created behind the original to create an oblong shape. In the center, a glass shelving unit for the inventory creates a divider between the two atmospheres. The mahogany finish is smooth beneath my fingertips as I run my hand across the surface, tipping my head to the bar's manager.

"Hey mom," I salute. She's busy serving a cute guy half her age who has been flirting with her for a while now but manages to blow me a quick kiss. Yeah, a lot's changed. On the other side of the bar is the poker area Spade took charge of. Six poker tables in total, with one set aside for roulette and an official booth. The chips come in various colors, each set with a Monarch's symbol engraved into them.

The very back of the lower level was all Malik. Classic brown leather armchairs, cigar holders, low tables. A coffee machine and waitress whose sole job is making liquor-enhanced coffees. She doesn't mind though - Savannah is going to be a senate of state one day as she gets paid to complete her coursework among being a barista. Hell, we'll sponsor her since we'll no doubt need someone on our side in the future. The first state to permit polygamous marriages, yes please. Plus, the old rich guys this zone attracts tip marvelously.

"What bit did you design?" Cherry asks, struggling to tear her eyes away from the luxurious wallpaper Malik insisted on. Olive green with a gold lead design and ridiculously expensive, but I like to keep my men happy. They make me come better when I do.

"I was hoping you'd ask that," I grin, opening the door to what used to be the basement. Music blasts out like a foghorn to the face, so I close my hands over Zak's ears as I draw them a few steps down the staircase. Strobe lights flash in all directions, the DJ at the booth getting into dancing just as much as the crowd covering every inch of the dance floor. Doesn't matter that the sun's barely set, it's always party time down here. Cherry gives me a thumbs up, but I tell her to wait for it. On cue, streams of foam spout from the vent and coat the audience in splats of white bubbles. Zak giggles, his head juddering in my hands as I draw us back up the stairs. "That was all me," I beam proudly.

For the next half an hour, I bore Cherry with the renovations upstairs. The second level has become our living area, where Zak hangs back to play on the PlayStation with the twins. Ace is burning himself into a sweat in the gym. Spade is in the kitchen, preparing snacks for tonight's celebrations, while Malik is upstairs, probably arguing with the mirror about which suit to wear.

"So, no more separate bedrooms?" Cherry asks, looking in every open doorway. We bulldozed through the twin's rooms to make the 'living area,' which consists of a screen big enough to pass as a cinema. Besides the recliner chairs with drink holders are where the three boys currently are, there's one rounded cuddle chair, huge enough for us all to lie back on. Spade's old room is the sauna/steam room beside the gym, and Ace's is a music studio. The guys fancy themselves as quite the band, while Malik and I laugh on from a distance and reckon they'll perform in the bar sometime.

"Only one bedroom," I answer my sister, pointing up to the

ceiling. "Malik commissioned a bed big enough to fit us all. We haven't spent a night apart since…well, you know," I dodge, still preferring not to think about how I let an out-of-control Tanya almost ruin my carefully crafted harem.

"I'm proud of you Candy, seriously. Look around," Cherry holds her arms out wide. "You did all of this. You united five guys and built yourself a proper home." Biting the sides of my cheeks, I try to reign in the smile that creeps out anyway.

"Come on, it's almost time. Let's help Spade." Before striding away, I bang my fist on the stairwell leading up to the penthouse suite and yell for Malik to join us. Then I call for the others to come help as we enter the kitchen. Spade looks adorable, with a chef's hat over his dreads and an apron displaying a woman's body in a bikini. He's been preparing all day for tonight, and thank fuck, because I'm starving.

"Everyone grab a tray and head on down," Spade tells us, squeezing a piping bag of orange paste onto some tiny cracks. We all obey, even Zak, who opts for the bread buns. Before I'm able to grab the last tray on the counter, a jacket is draped over my shoulders. Not just any, but my Monarch jacket with the Queen of Hearts playing card embroidered on the back.

"It's getting chilly outside," Malik mutters in my ear. Placing a kiss on my neck, he swoops in to take the last tray and I roll my eyes. At some point, this chivalry bullshit will get old, but today's not that day. In fact, I rather enjoy taking a step back from survival mode to simply enjoy myself. Fuck knows, keeping the guys in check is a full-time job in itself, so I know when to pick my battles.

"You coming, gorgeous?" I ask Spade, distracting him from washing the last few spoons in the basin. Dropping them at once, he ditches the apron and hat, taking my offered arm.

"I just wanted it to be special," he mumbles, and I spin in the waiting elevator to pull him in for a kiss. Words fail me most of the time, but my tongue sweeping the length of his seems to say it all. Large hands grip my waist, and by the time the doors ping open again, Spade needs to force himself to release me. Catching up to the others out back, Cherry's eyes flick towards the bar with a frown.

"Are the punters joining us? Your invite made this afternoon sound like a big event."

"It is a big event - my first family cookout," I beam. When Ace found out the day I shot Spade with an arrow was the closest I'd ever gotten to eat properly barbequed food, he started convoluting with the others. We waited for the exterior of the building to be renovated too, creating a mini celebration for the eight of us and my mom whenever she can get away.

A wide, wooden porch now wraps around to join the front, with lanterns hanging every few feet. Down the few steps, the old delivery area has been transformed into a beer garden, complete with fake grass and a row of privately sheltered booths. Through the center, mini sofas and low tables create an open outdoor space for anyone who wants to use them on regular nights. Tucked away in the corner behind a trellis of ivy, a hot tub big enough for us all is ready and waiting for late-night dips under the stars.

Today's main attraction, though, is the massive double grill, multi-level BBQ Jasper has been dying to get his hands on. Not enough to help Spade with the prep work, but we all have our roles to play.

"Everything's freshly hand-made by me," Spade makes sure everyone knows - despite the fact he's been crashing about since he returned from the butchers this morning. "There's burgers, kebabs, sausages. I've marinated the pork chops, minted the lamb, and glazed the ribs."

"You're never lacking in the meat department, are you Spadey?" I pat him on the shoulder, slinking over to where Jasper is lighting the BBQ.

"There's salad too," Spade blushes, his piercing blue eyes shifting to Zak and back.

"Is it hand-tossed?" Ace pitches in, and we all fall into a fit of laughter at Spade's expense. Poor guy snatches a beer from the ice bucket and drops into one of the private booths. We try to coax him out, but when Zak's not looking, he gives us all the middle finger, so I leave him to mope. Jack switches on the surround sound, filling the garden with some tunes from the 90s. Holding out his hand, he pulls me into his fully-healed body and without awaiting permission, captures my mouth with his. Gone are the hesitant days. Jack is back, and he wants everyone to know it as often as possible. Gripping the lapels of my jacket, Jack crushes me close, invading my personal space with his coconut scent.

"You really need to stop using my shower gel," I joke, nibbling at his lip.

"Then you should stop showering with me and massaging it into my-"

"BBQ's ready!" Jasper calls, drawing us over. Looking over my shoulder, I click at Spade, and he heels like a good boy, knowing he'd regret it later if he didn't. Blue balls are a nasty condition to have in this house, especially when your wife is being fucked by other men. By the time he's re-joined my side though, Spade's smile is back, and he links his fingers with mine. "Before I get cooking, let's have a toast."

Malik hands out drinks, passing the promised milkshake to Zak and ruffling his hand through my nephew's brown hair. I'm given the Ejaculating Unicorn's finest gin and tonic, complete with a mini rainbow in a cocktail glass. Everyone else is happy with a simple beer as they click together their bottle necks with Cherry's.

"To fresh beginnings and living the lives we were intended," Jack says, nodding his head to Cherry. I smile at the exchange, thankful he's giving me this. In spite of the past, I finally have a family I can call my own.

"And to our darling wife," Malik adds, his palladium ring tapping against the glass bottle in his hand. "We don't need a ceremony to prove what we know in our hearts. You're our entire world. Our motivation to live, our reason to laugh, and our incentive to love. Nothing makes sense without you." A round of cheers sounds, and instead of averting my gaze, I look from each Monarch to the next. My men. My soldiers who would storm any war I were to create without a moment's pause. But I don't want to fight. I'm done with being angry at a world that didn't want me and content with my small patch of it. Angus was right. There's no need to cope anymore. I can finally live.

Conversations break out in smaller groups as Jasper attends to cooking Spade's carefully prepared food. Ace sits with Zak, showing him some game on his phone that my nephew flinches at and then bursts out laughing. I slide my arms around Jasper's waist, laying my cheek on his shoulder blade to watch Jack strike up an easy conversation with Cherry. She ducks her eyes nervously, but there's no need. Considering the matching rings on each of my Monarchs fingers, which they insisted on wearing, I have no worries. Every now and again, Malik, Jack, or Spade will catch my eye and wink, causing my smile to deepen.

"You should take some of the credit, you know," I rest my chin on Jasper's shoulder. "Without you, I'd have run away and never returned."

"I don't think so," he muses, sliding those emerald green eyes to me. "You belong here and would have found your way back. But if you want to give me the credit, you can get on your knees beneath the barbeque." I share a laugh with Jasp, before a shadow looms over us. Malik slides his arm around my waist, his face downward, to see a text on his phone from one of the new security guys.

"You have a visitor, my love," he tells me, pocketing his phone before kissing my forehead.

"I do?" I ask, frowning. I don't know anyone other than the people on this porch. Pressing my lips against the love heart on Jasper's neck, announcing his love of cock to the world, Malik leads me inside the building. I thought he intended to remain at my side, sniffing out any potential threats, but after retrieving his bottle of whiskey, he retreats back outside. I slip behind the bar, my hackles rising with the worry my new beginning is about to go up in smoke. Call me cautious, but the panic button back here was one of the first additions. After establishing my happily ever after, I'm not about to be blown to pieces by some old enemy.

But as I round the glass divider, my shoulder sag in relief. I didn't recognize her at first, with the lack of face paint beneath her wild purple hair, but the instant those pink and blue eyes settle on me, I knew I was in good company.

"Well, look who it is," I smirk, leaning my forearms on the bar. "What you drinking Kelsii with two ii's? This one's on me."

THE END.

ACKNOWLEDGMENTS

Well…I don't know about you, but I can't believe it's over! Candy has been more than just a deranged figment of my imagination, but a whole new mindset I never knew I had! She's been so much fun to write and never fear, she'll pop up again in the future.

Thank you for reading the I Love Candy Series. Just in case you missed it, a prequel is now available for the curious beans who'd like to understand Candy's inner workings. The novella is based on Candy as a thirteen-year-old runaway finding her feet on the streets. Check out the blurb below, and please be aware a feisty FMC like Candy can't exist with a troubled backstory. Please check the trigger warning before diving in.

FINDIN' CANDY
A Prequel Novella in the I Love Candy Series

Blurb:

So awfully bitter, you'll know me by the aftertaste.

I can't tell you where I'm going, and I can't being to understand where I've been, but I'm alive. Alive and alone, until a savior presents himself in tattered clothes and a frayed beanie.

Taking me under his protection, the promise of a tomorrow seems to be within reach after all. He shows me how to navigate the city, how to steal and survive. And just when I think I might have a future running the streets, my world comes to a halt for pair of stunning hazel eyes. The boy attached isn't too bad either.

But when a group of armed men and a mom I didn't know I had throw my world into chaos, I'm forced to choose between my head and my heart.

Spoiler alert – young love never lasts.

BUY IT NOW: https://amzn.to/3bcueOp

ABOUT MADDISON COLE

Maddison is a married mum of two, and a serial daydreamer. As a huge fan of all romance troupes, from RH to Omegaverse, she finally decided to put pen to paper (finger to keyboard doesn't sound as poetic) and write her own.

As a child, life was moving around the UK and a short stint in the Caribbean, before Maddison has found herself back in the south east of England where she is now happily settled. With a double award in applied arts and an A-level in art history, Maddison is an average musical-loving, Disney-obsessed, jive-dancer with a dark passion for steamy fantasy books.

FOLLOW MADDISON COLE

If you're a new reader to me – welcome to the mad house! My list of writes can be found below and for up-to-date info, make sure to follow my socials! The readers group is the best place for reveals, announcements, giveaways and more, and please never hesitate to reach out! I love hearing from readers

Sign up to my newsletter here:

> http://eepurl.com/hx3Zqr

Also, make sure to join my Facebook readers group, Cole's Reading Moles here:

> www.facebook.com/colesreadingmoles

- facebook.com/maddison.cole.314
- instagram.com/maddison_cole_author
- amazon.com/author/B086ZQ6SW4
- bookbub.com/authors/maddison-cole
- tiktok.com/@coles_moles

MORE BOOKS BY MADDISON COLE

ALL MY PRETTY PSYCHOS

Paranormal RH with ghosts and demons

Queen of Crazy

https://amzn.to/3O4biQt

Kings of Madness

https://amzn.to/3HzvBCY

Hoax: The Untold Story (novella)

https://amzn.to/3xAJhcA

Reign of Chaos (pre-order)

https://amzn.to/3b95PcI

·

I LOVE CANDY

Dark Humor RH - Completed

Findin' Candy (novella)

https://amzn.to/3bcueOp

Crushin' Candy

https://amzn.to/3n0TASf

Smashin' Candy

https://amzn.to/3Oniuai

Friggin' Candy
https://amzn.to/3QwlmUb

The Complete Candy Boxset
https://amzn.to/3t2dqiW.

·

THE WAR AT WAVERSEA
Basketball College MFM Menage - Completed

Perfectly Powerless
https://amzn.to/3OqHTQp

Handsomely Heartless
https://amzn.to/3tMoRfu

Beautifully Boundless
https://amzn.to/3MYiiNG

·

MOON BOUND
Vampire/Shifters Fated Mates Standalones

Exiled Heir
https://amzn.to/3OtlqSD

Privileged Heir
https://amzn.to/3mYwQ5g

·

WILLOWMEAD ACADEMY (CO-WRITTEN WITH EMMA LUNA)

Sexy Student - Teacher Taboo Age Gap Standalone

Life Lessons

https://amzn.to/3tL8eAX

·

A WONDERLUST ADVENTURE: A DERANGED DUET

Retelling of Alice - twenty years on

My Tweedle Boys (pre-order)

https://amzn.to/3wRIqVd

Our Malice (TBC)

·

VICES AND HEDONISM SHARED WORLD

A Reverse Harem MMA Romance

A Night of Pleasure and Wrath

https://amzn.to/3Rgg0fC

·

FINDING LOVE AFTER DEATH (CO-WRITTEN WITH EMMALEIGH WYNTERS)

Haunted by Desire

https://amzn.to/3BaTlvI

Printed in Great Britain
by Amazon